The Confidence-Man and Billy Budd, Sailor

HERMAN MELVILLE

PENGUIN ENGLISH
LIBRARY

PENGUIN BOOKS

Published by the Penguin Group
Penguin Books Ltd, 80 Strand, London WC2R ORL, England
Penguin Group (USA) Inc., 375 Hudson Street, New York, New York 10014, USA
Penguin Group (Canada), 90 Eglinton Avenue East, Suite 700, Toronto, Ontario, Canada M4P 2Y3
(a division of Pearson Penguin Canada Inc.)
Penguin Ireland, 25 St Stephen's Green, Dublin 2, Ireland
(a division of Penguin Books Ltd)
Penguin Group (Australia), 250 Camberwell Road, Camberwell, Victoria 3124, Australia
(a division of Pearson Australia Group Pty Ltd)
Penguin Books India Pvt Ltd, 11 Community Centre, Panchsheel Park, New Delhi – 110 017, India
Penguin Group (NZ), 67 Apollo Drive, Rosedale, Auckland 0632, New Zealand
(a division of Pearson New Zealand Ltd)
Penguin Books (South Africa) (Pty) Ltd, Block D, Rosebank Office Park,
181 Jan Smuts Avenue, Parktown North, Gauteng 2193, South Africa

Penguin Books Ltd, Registered Offices: 80 Strand, London WC2R ORL, England

www.penguin.com

The Confidence-Man first published 1857
Published in Penguin Classics edited by Stephen Matterson 1990
Billy Budd, Sailor first published 1924
Published in Penguin Classics edited by Frederick Busch 1986
This combined edition first published in the Penguin English Library 2012

002

Front cover illustration: T. Johnson

Essay © Daniel G. Hoffman (1961)

Set in 11/13 pt Dante MT Std
Typeset by Jouve (UK), Milton Keynes
Printed in England by Clays Ltd, St Ives plc

ISBN: 978-0-141-19930-6

www.greenpenguin.co.uk

PENGUIN ENGLISH LIBRARY

The Confidence-Man and Billy Budd, Sailor

Herman Melville (1819–91) became in his late twenties a highly successful author of exotic novels based on his experiences as a sailor – writing in quick succession *Typee*, *Omoo*, *Redburn* and *White-Jacket*. However, his masterpiece, *Moby-Dick*, was met with incomprehension and the other later works that are now the basis of his reputation, such as *Bartleby, the Scrivener* and *The Confidence-Man*, were failures. Melville stopped writing fiction and the rest of his long life was spent first as a lecturer and then, for nineteen years, as a customs official in New York City. He was also the author of the immensely long poem *Clarel*, which was similarly dismissed in his lifetime. At the end of his life he wrote *Billy Budd, Sailor*, which was published posthumously in 1924.

Moby-Dick is also published in the Penguin English Library.

Contents

Contents

Contents

Contents

THE

CONFIDENCE-MAN:

HIS MASQUERADE.

BY

HERMAN MELVILLE,

AUTHOR OF " PIAZZA TALES," " OMOO," " TYPEE," ETC. ETC.

Authorised Edition.

LONDON:

LONGMAN, BROWN, GREEN, LONGMANS, & ROBERTS.

1857.

Chapter One

A Mute Goes Aboard a Boat on the Mississippi

At sunrise on a first of April, there appeared, suddenly as Manco Capac at the lake Titicaca, a man in cream-colours, at the water-side in the city of St Louis.

His cheek was fair, his chin downy, his hair flaxen, his hat a white fur one, with a long fleecy nap. He had neither trunk, valise, carpet-bag, nor parcel. No porter followed him. He was unaccompanied by friends. From the shrugged shoulders, titters, whispers, wonderings of the crowd, it was plain that he was, in the extremest sense of the word, a stranger.

In the same moment with his advent, he stepped aboard the favourite steamer *Fidèle*, on the point of starting for New Orleans. Stared at, but unsaluted, with the air of one neither courting nor shunning regard, but evenly pursuing the path of duty, lead it through solitudes or cities, he held on his way along the lower deck until he chanced to come to a placard near the captain's office, offering a reward for the capture of a mysterious impostor, supposed to have recently arrived from the East – quite an original genius in his vocation, as would appear, though wherein his originality consisted was not clearly given; but what purported to be a careful description of his person followed.

As if it had been a play-bill, crowds were gathered about the announcement, and among them certain chevaliers, whose eyes, it was plain, were on the capitals, or, at least, earnestly seeking a sight of them from behind intervening coats; but as for their fingers, they were enveloped in some myth; though, during a chance interval, one of these chevaliers somewhat showed his hand in purchasing from another chevalier, ex-officio a peddler of money-belts, one of his popular safe-guards, while another peddler, who was still another versatile chevalier, hawked, in the thick of the throng, the lives of Meason, the bandit of Ohio, Murrel, the pirate of the Mississippi, and the brothers Harpe, the Thugs of the Green River country, in Kentucky – creatures, with others of the sort, one and all exterminated at the time, and for the most part, like the hunted generations of wolves in the same regions, leaving comparatively few successors; which would seem cause for unalloyed gratulation, and is so to all except those who think that in new countries, where the wolves are killed off, the foxes increase.

Pausing at this spot, the stranger so far succeeded in threading his way, as at last to plant himself just beside the placard, when, producing a small slate and tracing some words upon it, he held it up before him on a level with the placard, so that they who read the one might read the other. The words were these:

'Charity thinketh no evil.'

As, in gaining his place, some little perseverance, not to say persistence, of a mildly inoffensive sort, had been unavoidable, it was not with the best relish that the crowd regarded his apparent intrusion; and upon a more attentive survey, perceiving no badge of authority about him, but rather something quite the contrary – he being of an aspect so singularly innocent; an aspect, too, which they took to be somehow inappropriate to the time and place, and inclining to the notion that his writing was of much the same sort: in short, taking him for some strange kind of simpleton, harmless enough, would he keep to himself, but not wholly unobnoxious as an intruder – they made no scruple to jostle him aside; while one, less kind than the rest, or more of a wag, by an unobserved stroke, dexterously flattened down his fleecy hat upon his head. Without readjusting it, the stranger quietly turned, and writing anew upon the slate, again held it up:

'Charity suffereth long, and is kind.'

Ill pleased with his pertinacity, as they thought it, the crowd a second time thrust him aside, and not without epithets and some buffets, all of which were unresented. But, as if at last despairing of so difficult an adventure, wherein one, apparently a non-resistant, sought to impose his presence upon fighting characters, the stranger now moved slowly away, yet not before altering his writing to this:

'Charity endureth all things.'

Shield-like bearing his slate before him, amid stares and jeers he moved slowly up and down, at his turning points again changing his inscription to –

'Charity believeth all things.'

and then –

'Charity never faileth.'

The word charity, as originally traced, remained throughout uneffaced, not unlike the left-hand numeral of a printed date, otherwise left for convenience in blank.

To some observers, the singularity, if not lunacy, of the stranger was heightened by his muteness, and, perhaps also, by the contrast to his proceedings afforded in the actions – quite in the wonted and sensible order of things – of the barber of the boat, whose quarters, under a smoking-saloon, and over against a bar-room, were next door but two to the captain's office. As if the long, wide, covered deck, hereabouts built up on both sides with shop-like windowed spaces, were some Constantinople arcade or bazaar, where more than one trade is plied, this river barber, aproned and slippered, but rather crusty-looking for the moment, it may be from being newly out of bed, was throwing open his premises for the day, and suitably arranging the exterior. With business-like dispatch, having rattled down his shutters, and at a palm-tree angle set out in the iron fixture his little ornamental pole, and this without overmuch tenderness for the elbows and toes of the crowd, he concluded his operations by bidding people stand still more aside, when, jumping on a stool, he hung over his door, on the customary nail, a gaudy sort of illuminated pasteboard sign, skilfully executed by himself, gilt with the likeness of a razor elbowed in readiness to shave, and also, for the public benefit, with two words not unfrequently seen ashore gracing other shops besides barbers':

'NO TRUST' –

an inscription which, though in a sense not less intrusive than the contrasted ones of the stranger, did not, as it seemed, provoke any corresponding derision or surprise, much less indignation; and still less, to all appearances, did it gain for the inscriber the repute of being a simpleton.

Meanwhile, he with the slate continued moving slowly up and down, not without causing some stares to change into jeers, and some jeers into pushes, and some pushes into punches; when suddenly, in one of his turns, he was hailed from behind by two porters carrying a large trunk; but as the summons, though loud, was without effect, they accidentally or otherwise swung their burden against him, nearly overthrowing him; when, by a quick start, a peculiar inarticulate moan, and a pathetic telegraphing of his fingers, he involuntarily betrayed that he was not only dumb but also deaf.

Presently, as if not wholly unaffected by his reception thus far, he went forward, seating himself in a retired spot on the forecastle, near the foot of a ladder there leading to a deck above, up and down which ladder some of the boatmen, in discharge of their duties, were occasionally going.

From his betaking himself to this humble quarter, it was evident that, as a deck-passenger, the stranger, simple though he seemed, was not entirely ignorant of his place, though his taking a deck-passage might have been partly for convenience; as, from his having no luggage, it was probable that his destination was one of the small wayside landings within a few hours' sail. But, though he might not have a long way to go, yet he seemed already to have come from a very long distance.

Though neither soiled nor slovenly, his cream-coloured suit had a tossed look, almost linty, as if, travelling night and day from some far country beyond the prairies, he had long been without the solace of a bed. His aspect was at once gentle and jaded, and, from the moment of seating himself, increasing in tired abstraction and dreaminess. Gradually overtaken by slumber, his flaxen head drooped, his whole lamb-like figure relaxed, and, half reclining against the ladder's foot, lay motionless, as some sugar-snow in March, which, softly stealing down over night, with its white placidity startles the brown farmer peering out from his threshold at daybreak.

Chapter Two

Showing That Many Men Have Many Minds

'Odd fish!'
  'Poor fellow!'
  'Who can he be?'
  'Casper Hauser.'
  'Bless my soul!'
  'Uncommon countenance.'
  'Green prophet from Utah.'
  'Humbug!'
  'Singular innocence.'
  'Means something.'
  'Spirit-rapper.'
  'Moon-calf.'
  'Piteous.'
  'Trying to enlist interest.'
  'Beware of him.'
  'Fast asleep here, and, doubtless, pick-pockets on board.'
  'Kind of daylight Endymion.'
  'Escaped convict, worn out with dodging.'
  'Jacob dreaming at Luz.'
Such the epitaphic comments, conflictingly spoken or thought, of a miscellaneous company, who, assembled on the overlooking, cross-wise balcony at the forward end of the upper deck hard by, had not witnessed preceding occurrences.

Meantime, like some enchanted man in his grave, happily oblivious of all gossip, whether chiselled or chatted, the deaf and dumb stranger still tranquilly slept, while now the boat started on her voyage.

6

The great ship-canal of Ving-King-Ching, in the Flowery Kingdom, seems the Mississippi in parts, where, amply flowing between low, vine-tangled banks, flat as tow-paths, it bears the huge toppling steamers, bedizened and lacquered within like imperial junks.

Pierced along its great white bulk with two tiers of small embrasure-like windows, well above the water-line, the *Fidèle*, though, might at distance have been taken by strangers for some whitewashed fort on a floating isle.

Merchants on 'change seem the passengers that buzz on her decks, while, from quarters unseen, comes a murmur as of bees in the comb. Fine promenades, domed saloons, long galleries, sunny balconies, confidential passages, bridal chambers, state-rooms plenty as pigeon-holes, and out-of-the-way retreats like secret drawers in an escritoire, present like facilities for publicity or privacy. Auctioneer or coiner, with equal ease, might somewhere here drive his trade.

Though her voyage of twelve hundred miles extends from apple to orange, from clime to clime, yet, like any small ferry-boat, to right and left, at every landing, the huge *Fidèle* still receives additional passengers in exchange for those that disembark; so that, though always full of strangers, she continually, in some degree, adds to, or replaces them with strangers still more strange; like the Rio Janeiro fountain, fed from the Corcovado mountains, which is ever overflowing with strange waters, but never with the same strange particles in every part.

Though hitherto, as has been seen, the man in cream-colours had by no means passed unobserved, yet by stealing into retirement, and there going asleep and continuing so, he seemed to have courted oblivion, a boon not often withheld from so humble an applicant as he. Those staring crowds on the shore were now left far behind, seen dimly clustering like swallows on eaves; while the passengers' attention was soon drawn away to the rapidly shooting high bluffs and shot-towers on the Missouri shore, or the bluff-looking Missourians and towering Kentuckians among the throngs on the decks.

By-and-by – two or three random stoppages having been made, and the last transient memory of the slumberer vanished, and he himself, not unlikely, waked up and landed ere now – the crowd, as is usual, began in all parts to break up from a concourse into various clusters or squads, which in some cases disintegrated again into quartettes, trios, and couples, and even solitaires; involuntarily submitting to that natural law which ordains dissolution equally to the mass, as in time to the member.

As among Chaucer's Canterbury pilgrims, or those oriental ones crossing the Red Sea towards Mecca in the festival month, there was no lack of variety. Natives of all sorts, and foreigners; men of business and men of pleasure; parlour men and backwoodsmen; farm-hunters and fame-hunters; heiress-hunters, gold-hunters, buffalo-hunters, bee-hunters, happiness-hunters, truth-hunters, and still keener hunters after all these hunters. Fine ladies in slippers, and moccasined squaws; Northern speculators and Eastern philosophers; English, Irish, German, Scotch, Danes; Santa Fé traders in striped blankets, and Broadway bucks in cravats of cloth of gold; fine-looking Kentucky boatmen, and Japanese-looking Mississippi cotton-planters; Quakers in full drab, and United States soldiers in full regimentals; slaves, black, mulatto, quadroon; modish young Spanish Creoles, and old-fashioned French Jews; Mormons and Papists; Dives and Lazarus; jesters and mourners, teetotalers and convivialists, deacons and blacklegs; hard-shell Baptists and clay-eaters; grinning negroes, and Sioux chiefs solemn as high-priests. In short, a piebald parliament, an Anacharsis Cloots congress of all kinds of that multiform pilgrim species, man.

As pine, beech, birch, ash, hackmatack, hemlock, spruce, basswood, maple, interweave their foliage in the natural wood, so these varieties of mortals blended their varieties of visage and garb. A Tartar-like picturesqueness; a sort of pagan abandonment and assurance. Here reigned the dashing and all-fusing spirit of the West, whose type is the Mississippi itself, which, uniting the streams of the most distant and opposite zones, pours them along, helter-skelter, in one cosmopolitan and confident tide.

Chapter Three

In Which a Variety of Characters Appear

In the forward part of the boat, not the least attractive object, for a time, was a grotesque negro cripple, in tow-cloth attire and an old coal-sifter of a tambourine in his hand, who, owing to something wrong about his legs, was, in effect, cut down to the stature of a Newfoundland dog; his knotted black fleece and good-natured, honest black face rubbing against the upper part of people's thighs as he made shift to shuffle about, making music, such as it was, and raising a smile even from the gravest. It was curious to see him, out of his very deformity, indigence, and houselessness, so cheerily endured, raising mirth in some of that crowd, whose own purses, hearths, hearts, all their possessions, sound limbs included, could not make gay.

'What is your name, old boy?' said a purple-faced drover, putting his large purple hand on the cripple's bushy wool, as if it were the curled forehead of a black steer.

'Der Black Guinea dey calls me, sar.'

'And who is your master, Guinea?'

'Oh sar, I am der dog widout massa.'

'A free dog, eh? Well, on your account, I'm sorry for that, Guinea. Dogs without masters fare hard.'

'So dey do, sar; so dey do. But you see, sar, dese here legs? What ge'mman want to own dese here legs?'

'But where do you live?'

'All 'long shore, sar; dough now I'se going to see brodder at der landing; but chiefly I libs in der city.'

'St Louis, ah? Where do you sleep there of nights?'

'On der floor of der good baker's oven, sar.'

'In an oven? whose, pray? What baker, I should like to know, bakes such black bread in his oven, alongside of his nice white roll, too. Who is that too charitable baker, pray?'

'Dar he be,' with a broad grin, lifting his tambourine high over his head.

'The sun is the baker, eh?'

'Yes sar, in der city dat good baker warms der stones for dis ole darkie when he sleeps out on der pabements o' nights.'

'But that must be in the summer only, old boy. How about winter, when the cold Cossacks come clattering and jingling? How about winter, old boy?'

'Den dis poor old darkie shakes werry bad, I tell you, sar. Oh sar, oh! don't speak ob der winter,' he added, with a reminiscent shiver, shuffling off into the thickest of the crowd, like a half-frozen black sheep nudging itself a cozy berth in the heart of the white flock.

Thus far not very many pennies had been given him, and, used at last to his strange looks, the less polite passengers of those in that part of the boat began to get their fill of him as a curious object; when suddenly the negro more than revived their first interest by an expedient which, whether by chance or design, was a singular temptation at once to *diversion* and charity, though, even more than his crippled limbs, it put him on a canine footing. In short, as in appearance he seemed a dog, so now, in a merry way, like a dog he began to be treated. Still shuffling among the crowd, now and then he would pause, throwing back his head and opening his mouth like an elephant for tossed apples at a menagerie; when, making a space before him, people would have a bout at a strange sort of pitch-penny game, the cripple's mouth being at once target and purse, and he hailing each expertly-caught copper with a cracked bravura from his tambourine. To be the subject of almsgiving is trying, and to feel in duty bound to appear cheerfully grateful under the trial, must be still more so; but whatever his secret emotions, he swallowed them, while still retaining each copper this side the oesophagus. And nearly always he grinned, and only once or twice did he wince, which was when certain coins, tossed by more playful almoners, came inconveniently near his teeth, an accident whose unwelcomeness was not unedged by the circumstance that the pennies thus thrown proved buttons.

While this game of charity was yet at its height, a limping, gimlet-eyed, sour-faced person – it may be some discharged custom-house officer, who, suddenly stripped of convenient means of support, had resolved to be avenged on government and humanity by making himself miserable for life, either by hating or suspecting everything and everybody – this shallow unfortunate, after sundry sorry observations of the negro, began to croak out something about his deformity being a sham, got up for financial purposes, which immediately threw a damp upon the frolic benignities of the pitch-penny players.

But that these suspicions came from one who himself on a wooden leg went halt, this did not appear to strike anybody present. That cripples, above all men, should be companionable, or, at least, refrain from picking a fellow-limper to pieces, in short, should have a little sympathy in common misfortune, seemed not to occur to the company.

Meantime, the negro's countenance, before marked with even more than patient good-nature, drooped into a heavy-hearted expression, full of the most painful distress. So far abased beneath its proper physical level, that Newfoundland-dog face turned in passively hopeless appeal, as if instinct told it that the right or the wrong might not have overmuch to do with whatever wayward mood superior intelligences might yield to.

But instinct, though knowing, is yet a teacher set below reason, which itself says, in the grave words of Lysander in the comedy, after Puck has made a sage of him with his spell:

The will of man is by his reason swayed.

So that, suddenly change as people may, in their dispositions, it is not always waywardness, but improved judgment, which, as in Lysander's case, or the present, operates with them.

Yes, they began to scrutinize the negro curiously enough; when, emboldened by this evidence of the efficacy of his words, the wooden-legged man hobbled up to the negro, and, with the air of a beadle, would, to prove his alleged imposture on the spot, have stripped him and then driven him away, but was prevented by the crowd's clamour, now taking part with the poor fellow, against one who had just before turned nearly all minds the other way. So he with the wooden leg was forced to retire; when the rest, finding themselves left sole judges in the case, could not resist the opportunity of acting the part: not because it is a human weakness to take pleasure in sitting in judgment upon one in a box, as surely this unfortunate negro now was, but that it strangely sharpens human perceptions, when, instead of standing by and having their fellow-feelings touched by the sight of an alleged culprit severely handled by some one justiciary, a crowd suddenly come to be all justiciaries in the same case themselves; as in Arkansas once, a man was found guilty, by law, of murder, but his condemnation being deemed unjust by the people, they rescued him to try him themselves; whereupon, they, as it turned out, found him even guiltier than the court had done, and forthwith proceeded to execution; so that the gallows presented the truly warning spectacle of a man hanged by his friends.

But not to such extremities, or anything like them, did the present crowd come; they, for the time, being content with putting the negro fairly and discreetly to the question; among other things, asking him, had he any documentary proof, any plain paper about him, attesting that his case was not a spurious one.

'No, no, dis poor ole darkie haint none o' dem waloable papers,' he wailed.

'But is there not some one who can speak a good word for you here?' said a person newly arrived from another part of the boat, a young Episcopal clergyman, in a long, straight-bodied black coat; small in stature, but manly; with a clear face and blue eye; innocence, tenderness, and good sense triumvirate in his air.

'Oh yes, oh yes, ge'mmen,' he eagerly answered, as if his memory, before suddenly frozen up by cold charity, as suddenly thawed back into fluidity at the first kindly word. 'Oh yes, oh yes, dar is aboard here a werry nice, good ge'mman wid a weed, and a ge'mman in a gray coat and white tie, what knows all about me; and a ge'mman wid a big book, too; and a yarb-doctor; and a ge'mman in a yaller west; and a ge'mman wid a brass plate; and a ge'mman in a wiolet robe; and a ge'mman as is a sodjer; and ever so many good, kind, honest ge'mmen more aboard what knows me and will speak for me, God bress 'em; yes, and what knows me as well as dis poor ole darkie knows hisself, God bress him! Oh, find 'em, find 'em,' he earnestly added, 'and let 'em come quick, and show you all, ge'mmen, dat dis poor ole darkie is werry well wordy of all you kind ge'mmen's kind confidence.'

'But how are we to find all these people in this great crowd?' was the question of a bystander, umbrella in hand; a middle-aged person, a country merchant apparently, whose natural good-feeling had been made at least cautious by the unnatural ill-feeling of the discharged custom-house officer.

'Where are we to find them?' half-rebukefully echoed the young Episcopal clergyman. 'I will go find one to begin with,' he quickly added, and, with kind haste suiting the action to the word, away he went.

'Wild-goose-chase!' croaked he with the wooden leg, now again drawing near. 'Don't believe there's a soul of them aboard. Did ever beggar have such heaps of fine friends? He can walk fast enough when he tries, a good deal faster than I; but he can lie yet faster. He's some white operator, betwisted and painted up for a decoy. He and his friends are all humbugs.'

'Have you no charity, friend?' here in self-subdued tones, singularly contrasted with his unsubdued person, said a Methodist minister, advancing; a tall, muscular, martial-looking man, a Tennessean by birth, who in the Mexican war had been volunteer chaplain to a volunteer rifle-regiment.

'Charity is one thing, and truth is another,' rejoined he with the wooden leg: 'he's a rascal, I say.'

'But why not, friend, put as charitable a construction as one can upon the poor fellow?' said the soldier-like Methodist, with increased difficulty maintaining a pacific demeanour towards one whose own asperity seemed so little to entitle him to it: 'he looks honest, don't he?'

'Looks are one thing, and facts are another,' snapped out the other perversely; 'and as to your constructions, what construction can you put upon a rascal, but that a rascal he is?'

'Be not such a Canada thistle,' urged the Methodist, with something less of patience than before. 'Charity, man, charity.'

'To where it belongs with your charity! to heaven with it!' again snapped out the other, diabolically; 'here on earth true charity dotes, and false charity plots. Who betrays a fool with a kiss, the charitable fool has the charity to believe is in love with him, and the charitable knave on the stand gives charitable testimony for his comrade in the box.'

'Surely, friend,' returned the noble Methodist, with much ado restraining his still waxing indignation – 'surely, to say the least, you forget yourself. Apply it home,' he continued, with exterior calmness tremulous with inward emotion. 'Suppose, now, I should exercise no charity in judging your own character by the words which have fallen from you; what sort of vile, pitiless man do you think I would take you for?'

'No doubt' – with a grin – 'some such pitiless man as has lost his piety in much the same way that the jockey loses his honesty.'

'And how is that, friend?' still conscientiously holding back the old Adam in him, as if it were a mastiff he had by the neck.

'Never you mind how it is' – with a sneer; 'but all horses aint virtuous, no more than all men kind; and come close to, and much dealt with, some things are catching. When you find me a virtuous jockey, I will find you a benevolent wise man.'

'Some insinuation there.'

'More fool you that are puzzled by it.'

'Reprobate!' cried the other, his indignation now at last almost boiling over; 'godless reprobate! if charity did not restrain me, I could call you by names you deserve.'

'Could you, indeed?' with an insolent sneer.

'Yea, and teach you charity on the spot,' cried the goaded Methodist, suddenly catching this exasperating opponent by his shabby coat-collar, and shaking him till his timber-toe clattered on the deck like a nine-pin. 'You took me for a non-combatant did you? – thought, seedy coward that you are, that you could abuse a Christian with impunity. You find your mistake' – with another hearty shake.

'Well said and better done, church militant!' cried a voice.

'The white cravat against the world!' cried another.

'Bravo, bravo!' chorused many voices, with like enthusiasm taking sides with the resolute champion.

'You fools!' cried he with the wooden leg, writhing himself loose and inflamedly turning upon the throng; 'you flock of fools, under this captain of fools, in this ship of fools!'

With which exclamations, followed by idle threats against his admonisher, this condign victim to justice hobbled away, as disdaining to hold further argument with such a rabble. But his scorn was more than repaid by the hisses that chased him, in which the brave Methodist, satisfied with the rebuke already administered, was, to omit still better reasons, too magnanimous to join. All he said was, pointing towards the departing recusant, 'There he shambles off on his one lone leg, emblematic of his one-sided view of humanity.'

'But trust your painted decoy,' retorted the other from a distance, pointing back to the black cripple, 'and I have my revenge.'

'But we aint agoing to trust him!' shouted back a voice.

'So much the better,' he jeered back. 'Look you,' he added, coming to a dead halt where he was; 'look you, I have been called a Canada thistle. Very good. And a seedy one: still better. And the seedy Canada thistle has been pretty well shaken among ye; best of all. Dare say some seed has been shaken out; and won't it spring though? And when it does spring, do you cut down the young thistles, and won't they spring the more? It's encouraging and coaxing 'em. Now, when with my thistles your farms shall be well stocked, why then – you may abandon 'em!'

'What does all that mean, now?' asked the country merchant, staring.

'Nothing; the foiled wolf's parting howl,' said the Methodist. 'Spleen, much spleen, which is the rickety child of his evil heart of unbelief: it has made him mad. I suspect him for one naturally reprobate. Oh, friends,' raising his arms as in the pulpit, 'oh beloved, how are we admonished by the melancholy spectacle of this raver. Let us profit by the lesson; and is it not this: that if, next to mistrusting Providence, there be aught that man should pray against, it is against mistrusting his fellow-man. I have been in mad-houses full of tragic mopers, and seen there the end of suspicion: the cynic, in the moody madness, muttering in the corner; for years a barren fixture there; head lopped over, gnawing his own lip, vulture of himself; while, by fits and starts, from the corner opposite came the grimace of the idiot at him.'

'What an example,' whispered one.

'Might deter Timon,' was the response.

'Oh, oh, good ge'mmen, have you no confidence in dis poor ole darkie?' now wailed the returning negro, who, during the late scene, had stumped apart in alarm.

'Confidence in you?' echoed he who had whispered, with abruptly changed air turning short round; 'that remains to be seen.'

'I tell you what it is, Ebony,' in similarly changed tones said he who had responded to the whisperer, 'yonder churl,' pointing toward the wooden leg in the distance, 'is, no doubt, a churlish fellow enough, and I would not wish to be like him; but that is no reason why you may not be some sort of black Jeremy Diddler.'

'No confidence in dis poor ole darkie, den?'

'Before giving you our confidence,' said a third, 'we will wait the report of the kind gentleman who went in search of one of your friends who was to speak for you.'

'Very likely, in that case,' said a fourth, 'we shall wait here till Christmas. Shouldn't wonder, did we not see that kind gentleman again. After seeking awhile in vain, he will conclude he has been made a fool of, and so not return to us for pure shame. Fact is, I begin to feel a little qualmish about the darkie myself. Something queer about this darkie, depend upon it.'

Once more the negro wailed, and turning in despair from the last speaker, imploringly caught the Methodist by the skirt of his coat. But a change had come over that before impassioned intercessor. With an irresolute and troubled air, he mutely eyed the suppliant; against whom, somehow, by what seemed instinctive influences, the distrusts first set on foot were now generally reviving, and, if anything, with added severity.

'No confidence in dis poor ole darkie,' yet again wailed the negro, letting go the coat-skirts and turning appealingly all round him.

'Yes, my poor fellow, *I* have confidence in you,' now exclaimed the country merchant before named, whom the negro's appeal, coming so piteously on the heel of pitilessness, seemed at last humanely to have decided in his favour. 'And here, here is some proof of my trust,' with which, tucking his umbrella under his arm, and diving down his hand into his pocket, he fished forth a purse, and, accidentally, along with it, his business card, which, unobserved, dropped to the deck. 'Here, here, my poor fellow,' he continued, extending a half dollar.

Not more grateful for the coin than the kindness, the cripple's face glowed like a polished copper saucepan, and shuffling a pace nearer, with one upstretched hand he received the alms, while, as unconsciously, his one advanced leather stump covered the card.

Done in despite of the general sentiment, the good deed of the merchant was not, perhaps, without its unwelcome return from the crowd, since that good deed seemed somehow to convey to them a sort of reproach. Still again, and more pertinaciously than ever, the cry arose against the negro, and still again he wailed forth his lament and appeal; among other things, repeating that the friends, of whom already he had partially run off the list, would freely speak for him, would anybody go find them.

'Why don't you go find 'em yourself?' demanded a gruff boatman.

'How can I go find 'em myself? Dis poor ole game-legged darkie's friends must come to him. Oh, whar, whar is dat good friend of dis darkie's, dat good man wid de weed?'

At this point, a steward ringing a bell came along, summoning all persons who had not got their tickets to step to the captain's office; an announcement which speedily thinned the throng about the black cripple, who himself soon forlornly stumped out of sight, probably on much the same errand as the rest.

Chapter Four

Renewal of Old Acquaintance

'How do you do, Mr Roberts?'

'Eh?'

'Don't you know me?'

'No, certainly.'

The crowd about the captain's office having in good time melted away, the above encounter took place in one of the side balconies astern, between a man in mourning clean and respectable, but none of the glossiest, a long weed on his hat, and the country merchant before-mentioned, whom, with the familiarity of an old acquaintance, the former had accosted.

'Is it possible, my dear sir,' resumed he with the weed, 'that you do not recall my countenance? why yours I recall distinctly as if but half an hour, instead of half an age, had passed since I saw you. Don't you recall me, now? Look harder.'

'In my conscience – truly – I protest,' honestly bewildered, 'bless my soul, sir, I don't know you – really, really. But stay, stay,' he hurriedly added, not without gratification, glancing up at the crape on the stranger's hat, 'stay – yes – seems to me, though I have not the pleasure of personally knowing you, yet I am pretty sure I have at least *heard* of you, and recently too, quite recently. A poor negro aboard here referred to you, among others, for a character, I think.'

'Oh, the cripple. Poor fellow, I know him well. They found me. I have said all I could for him. I think I abated their distrust. Would I could have been of more substantial service. And apropos, sir,' he added, 'now that it strikes me, allow me to ask, whether the circumstance of one man, however humble, referring for a character to another man, however afflicted, does not argue more or less of moral worth in the latter?'

The good merchant looked puzzled.

'Still you don't recall my countenance?'

'Still does truth compel me to say that I cannot, despite my best efforts,' was the reluctantly candid reply.

'Can I be so changed? Look at me. Or is it I who am mistaken? – Are you not, sir, Henry Roberts, forwarding merchant, of Wheeling, Virginia? Pray, now, if you use the advertisement of business cards, and happen to have one with you, just look at it, and see whether you are not the man I take you for.'

'Why,' a bit chafed, perhaps, 'I hope I know myself.'

'And yet self-knowledge is thought by some not so easy. Who knows, my dear sir, but for a time you may have taken yourself for somebody else? Stranger things have happened.'

The good merchant stared.

'To come to particulars, my dear sir, I met you, now some six years back, at Brade Brothers & Co.'s office, I think. I was travelling for a Philadelphia house. The senior Brade introduced us, you remember; some business-chat followed, then you forced me home with you to a family tea, and a family time we had. Have you forgotten about the urn, and what I said about Werther's Charlotte, and the bread and butter, and that capital story you told of the large loaf? A hundred times since, I have laughed over it. At least you must recall my name – Ringman, John Ringman.'

'Large loaf? Invited you to tea? Ringman? Ringman? Ring? Ring?'

'Ah sir,' sadly smiling, 'don't ring the changes that way. I see you have a faithless memory, Mr Roberts. But trust in the faithfulness of mine.'

'Well, to tell the truth, in some things my memory aint of the very best,' was the honest rejoinder. 'But still,' he perplexedly added, 'still I –'

'Oh sir, suffice it that it is as I say. Doubt not that we are all well acquainted.'

'But – but I don't like this going dead against my own memory; I –'

'But didn't you admit, my dear sir, that in some things this memory of yours is a little faithless? Now, those who have faithless memories, should they not have some little confidence in the less faithless memories of others?'

'But, of this friendly chat and tea, I have not the slightest –'

'I see, I see; quite erased from the tablet. Pray, sir,' with a sudden illumination, 'about six years back, did it happen to you to receive any injury on the head? Surprising effects have arisen from such a cause. Not alone unconsciousness as to events for a greater or less time immediately subsequent to the injury, but likewise – strange to add – oblivion, entire and incurable, as to events embracing a longer or shorter period immediately preceding it; that is, when the mind at the time was perfectly sensible of them, and fully competent also to register them in the memory, and did in fact so do; but all in vain, for all was afterwards bruised out by the injury.'

After the first start, the merchant listened with what appeared more than ordinary interest. The other proceeded:

'In my boyhood I was kicked by a horse, and lay insensible for a long time. Upon recovering, what a blank! No faintest trace in regard to how I had come near the horse, or what horse it was, or where it was, or that it was a horse at all that had brought me to that pass. For the knowledge of those particulars I am indebted solely to my friends, in whose statements, I need not say, I place implicit reliance, since particulars of some sort there must have been, and why should they deceive me? You see, sir, the mind is ductile, very much so: but images, ductilely received into it, need a certain time to harden and bake in their impressions, otherwise such a casualty as I speak of will in an instant obliterate them, as though they had never been. We are but clay, sir, potter's clay, as the good book says, clay, feeble, and too-yielding clay. But I will not philosophize. Tell me, was it your misfortune to receive any concussion upon the brain about the period I speak of? If so, I will with pleasure supply the void in your memory by more minutely rehearsing the circumstances of our acquaintance.'

The growing interest betrayed by the merchant had not relaxed as the other proceeded. After some hesitation, indeed, something more than hesitation, he confessed that, though he had never received any injury of the sort named, yet, about the time in question, he had in fact been taken with a brain fever, losing his mind completely for a considerable interval. He was continuing, when the stranger with much animation exclaimed:

'There now, you see, I was not wholly mistaken. That brain fever accounts for it all.'

'Nay; but –'

'Pardon me, Mr Roberts,' respectfully interrupting him, 'but time is short, and I have something private and particular to say to you. Allow me.'

Mr Roberts, good man, could but acquiesce, and the two having silently walked to a less public spot, the manner of the man with the weed suddenly assumed a seriousness almost painful. What might be called a writhing expression stole over him. He seemed struggling with some disastrous necessity inkept. He made one or two attempts to speak, but words seemed to choke him. His companion stood in humane surprise, wondering what was to come. At length, with an effort mastering his feelings, in a tolerably composed tone he spoke:

'If I remember, you are a mason, Mr Roberts?'

'Yes, yes.'

Averting himself a moment, as to recover from a return of agitation, the stranger grasped the other's hand; 'and would you not loan a brother a shilling if he needed it?'

The merchant started, apparently, almost as if to retreat.

'Ah, Mr Roberts, I trust you are not one of those business men, who make a business of never having to do with unfortunates. For God's sake don't leave me. I have something on my heart – on my heart. Under deplorable circumstances thrown among strangers, utter strangers. I want a friend in whom I may confide. Yours, Mr Roberts, is almost the first known face I've seen for many weeks.'

It was so sudden an outburst; the interview offered such a contrast to the scene around, that the merchant, though not used to be very indiscreet, yet being not entirely inhumane, remained not entirely unmoved.

The other, still tremulous, resumed:

'I need not say, sir, how it cuts me to the soul, to follow up a social salutation with such words as have just been mine. I know that I jeopardize your good opinion. But I can't help it: necessity knows no law, and heeds no risk. Sir, we are masons, one more step aside; I will tell you my story.'

In a low, half-suppressed tone, he began it. Judging from his auditor's expression, it seemed to be a tale of singular interest, involving calamities against which no integrity, no forethought, no energy, no genius, no piety, could guard.

At every disclosure, the hearer's commiseration increased. No sentimental pity. As the story went on, he drew from his wallet a bank note, but after a while, at some still more unhappy revelation, changed it for another, probably of a somewhat larger amount; which, when the story was concluded, with an air studiously disclamatory of alms-giving, he put into the stranger's hands; who, on his side, with an air studiously disclamatory of alms-taking, put it into his pocket.

Assistance being received, the stranger's manner assumed a kind and degree of decorum which, under the circumstances, seemed almost coldness. After some words, not over ardent, and yet not exactly inappropriate, he took leave, making a bow which had one knows not what of a certain chastened independence about it; as if misery, however burdensome, could not break down self-respect, nor gratitude, however deep, humiliate a gentleman.

He was hardly yet out of sight, when he paused as if thinking; then with hastened steps returning to the merchant, 'I am just reminded that the president, who is also transfer-agent, of the Black Rapids Coal Company, happens to be on board here, and, having been subpoenaed as witness in a stock case on the docket in Kentucky, has his transfer-book with him. A month since, in a panic contrived by artful alarmists, some credulous stock-holders sold out; but, to frustrate the aim of the alarmists, the Company, previously advised of their scheme, so managed it as to get into its own hands those sacrificed shares, resolved that, since a spurious panic must be, the panic-makers should be no gainers by it. The Company, I hear, is now ready, but not anxious, to redispose of those shares; and having obtained them at their depressed value, will now sell them at par, though, prior to the panic, they were held at a handsome figure above. That the readiness of the Company to do this is not generally known, is shown by the fact that the stock still stands on the transfer-book in the Company's name offering to one in funds a rare chance for investment. For, the panic subsiding more and more every day, it will daily be seen how it originated; confidence will be more than restored; there will be a reaction; from the stock's descent its rise will be higher than from no fall, the holders trusting themselves to fear no second fate.'

Having listened at first with curiosity, at last with interest, the merchant replied to the effect, that some time since, through friends concerned with it, he had heard of the Company, and heard well of it, but was ignorant that there had latterly been fluctuations. He added that he was no speculator; that hitherto he had avoided having to do with stocks of any sort, but in the present case he really felt something like being tempted. 'Pray,' in conclusion, 'do you think that upon a pinch anything could be transacted on board here with the transfer-agent? Are you acquainted with him?'

'Not personally. I but happened to hear that he was a passenger.

For the rest, though it might be somewhat informal, the gentleman might not object to doing a little business on board. Along the Mississippi, you know, business is not so ceremonious as at the East.'

'True,' returned the merchant, and looked down a moment in thought, then, raising his head quickly, said, in a tone not so benign as his wonted one, 'This would seem a rare chance, indeed; why, upon first hearing it, did you not snatch at it? I mean for yourself!'

'I? – would it had been possible!'

Not without some emotion was this said, and not without some embarrassment was the reply. 'Ah, yes, I had forgotten.'

Upon this, the stranger regarded him with mild gravity, not a little disconcerting; the more so, as there was in it what seemed the aspect not alone of the superior, but, as it were, the rebuker; which sort of bearing, in a beneficiary towards his benefactor, looked strangely enough; none the less, that, somehow, it sat not altogether unbecomingly upon the beneficiary, being free from anything like the appearance of assumption, and mixed with a kind of painful conscientiousness, as though nothing but a proper sense of what he owed to himself swayed him. At length he spoke:

'To reproach a penniless man with remissness in not availing himself of an opportunity for pecuniary investment – but, no, no; it was forgetfulness; and this, charity will impute to some lingering effect of that unfortunate brain-fever, which, as to occurrences dating yet further back, disturbed Mr Roberts's memory still more seriously.'

'As to that,' said the merchant, rallying, 'I am not –'

'Pardon me, but you must admit, that just now, an unpleasant distrust, however vague, was yours. Ah, shallow as it is, yet, how subtle a thing is suspicion, which at times can invade the humanest of hearts and wisest of heads. But, enough. My object, sir, in calling your attention to this stock, is by way of acknowledgment of your goodness. I but seek to be grateful; if my information leads to nothing, you must remember the motive.'

He bowed, and finally retired, leaving Mr Roberts not wholly without self-reproach, for having momentarily indulged injurious thoughts against one who, it was evident, was possessed of a self-respect which forbade his indulging them himself.

Chapter Five

The Man With the Weed Makes it an Even Question Whether
He Be a Great Sage or a Great Simpleton

'Well, there is sorrow in the world, but goodness too; and goodness that is not greenness, either, no more than sorrow is. Dear
good man. Poor beating heart!'

It was the man with the weed, not very long after quitting the
merchant, murmuring to himself with his hand to his side like
one with the heart-disease.

Meditation over kindness received seemed to have softened
him somewhat, too, it may be, beyond what might, perhaps, have
been looked for from one whose unwonted self-respect in the
hour of need, and in the act of being aided, might have appeared
to some not wholly unlike pride out of place; and pride, in any
place, is seldom very feeling. But the truth, perhaps, is, that those
who are least touched with that vice, besides being not unsuscep-
tible to goodness, are sometimes the ones whom a ruling sense
of propriety makes appear cold, if not thankless, under a favour.
For, at such a time, to be full of warm, earnest words, and heart-
felt protestations, is to create a scene; and well-bred people dislike
few things more than that; which would seem to look as if the
world did not relish earnestness; but, not so; because the world,
being earnest itself, likes an earnest scene, and an earnest man,
very well, but only in their place – the stage. See what sad work
they make of it, who, ignorant of this, flame out in Irish enthusiasm and with Irish sincerity, to a benefactor, who, if a man of
sense and respectability, as well as kindliness, can but be more or
less annoyed by it; and, if of a nervously fastidious nature, as
some are, may be led to think almost as much less favourably of
the beneficiary paining him by his gratitude, as if he had been

guilty of its contrary, instead only of an indiscretion. But, benefi-
ciaries who know better, though they may feel as much, if not
more, neither inflict such pain, nor are inclined to run any risk of
so doing. And these, being wise, are the majority. By which one
sees how inconsiderate those persons are, who, from the absence
of its officious manifestations in the world, complain that there is
not much gratitude extant; when the truth is, that there is as
much of it as there is of modesty; but, both being for the most
part votaries of the shade, for the most part keep out of sight.

What started this was, to account, if necessary, for the changed
air of the man with the weed, who, throwing off in private the
cold garb of decorum and so giving warmly loose to his genuine
heart, seemed almost transformed into another being. This sub-
dued air of softness, too, was toned with melancholy, melancholy
unreserved; a thing which, however at variance with propriety,
still the more attested his earnestness; for one knows not how it
is, but it sometimes happens that, where earnestness is, there,
also, is melancholy.

At the time, he was leaning over the rail at the boat's side, in
his pensiveness, unmindful of another pensive figure near – a
young gentleman with a swan-neck, wearing a lady-like open
shirt collar thrown back, and tied with a black ribbon. From a
square, tableted broach, curiously engraved with Greek characters, he seemed a collegian – not improbably, a sophomore – on
his travels; possibly, his first. A small book bound in Roman vel-
lum was in his hand.

Overhearing his murmuring neighbour, the youth regarded
him with some surprise, not to say interest. But, singularly for a
collegian, being apparently of a retiring nature, he did not speak;
when the other still more increased his diffidence by changing
from soliloquy to colloquy, in a manner strangely mixed of familiarity and pathos.

'Ah, who is this? You did not hear me, my young friend, did
you? Why, you, too, look sad. My melancholy is not catching!'

'Sir, sir,' stammered the other.

'Pray, now,' with a sort of sociable sorrowfulness, slowly sliding along the rail, 'Pray, now, my young friend, what volume have you there? Give me leave,' gently drawing it from him. 'Tacitus!' Then opening it at random, read: 'In general a black and shameful period lies before me.' 'Dear young sir,' touching his arm alarmedly, 'don't read this book. It is poison, moral poison. Even were there truth in Tacitus, such truth would have the operation of falsity, and so still be poison, moral poison. Too well I know this Tacitus. In my college-days he came near souring me into cynicism. Yes, I began to turn down my collar, and go about with a disdainfully joyless expression.'

'Sir, sir, I – I –'

'Trust me. Now, young friend, perhaps you think that Tacitus, like me, is only melancholy; but he's more – he's ugly. A vast difference, young sir, between the melancholy view and the ugly. The one may show the world still beautiful, not so the other. The one may be compatible with benevolence, the other not. The one may deepen insight, the other shallows it. Drop Tacitus. Phrenologically, my young friend, you would seem to have a well-developed head, and large; but cribbed within the ugly view, the Tacitus view, your large brain, like your large ox in the contracted field, will but starve the more. And don't dream, as some of you students may, that, by taking this same ugly view, the deeper meanings of the deeper books will so alone become revealed to you. Drop Tacitus. His subtlety is falsity. To him, in his double-refined anatomy of human nature, is well applied the Scripture saying – "there is a subtle man, and the same is deceived." Drop Tacitus. Come, now, let me throw the book overboard.'

'Sir, I – I –'

'Not a word; I know just what is in your mind, and that is just what I am speaking to. Yes, learn from me that, though the sorrows of the world are great, its wickedness – that is, its ugliness – is small. Much cause to pity man, little to distrust him. I myself have known adversity, and know it still. But for that, do I turn cynic? No, no: it is small beer that sours. To my fellow-creatures I owe alleviations. So, whatever I may have undergone, it but deepens my confidence in my kind. Now, then' (winningly), 'this book – will you let me drown it for you?'

'Really, sir – I –'

'I see, I see. But of course you read Tacitus in order to aid you in understanding human nature – as if truth was ever got at by libel. My young friend, if to know human nature is your object, drop Tacitus and go north to the cemeteries of Auburn and Greenwood.'

'Upon my word, I – I –'

'Nay, I foresee all that. But you carry Tacitus, that shallow Tacitus. What do *I* carry? See' – producing a pocket-volume – 'Akenside – his "Pleasures of Imagination". One of these days you will know it. Whatever our lot, we should read serene and cheery books, fitted to inspire love and trust. But Tacitus! I have long been of opinion that these classics are the bane of colleges; for – not to hint of the immorality of Ovid, Horace, Anacreon, and the rest, and the dangerous theology of Eschylus and others – where will one find views so injurious to human nature as in Thucydides, Juvenal, Lucian, but more particularly Tacitus? When I consider that, ever since the revival of learning, these classics have been the favourites of successive generations of students and studious men, I tremble to think of that mass of unsuspected heresy on every vital topic which for centuries must have simmered unsurmised in the heart of Christendom. But Tacitus – he is the most extraordinary example of a heretic; not one iota of confidence in his kind. What a mockery that such an one should be reputed wise, and Thucydides be esteemed the statesman's manual! But Tacitus – I hate Tacitus; not, though, I trust, with the hate that sins, but a righteous hate. Without confidence himself, Tacitus destroys it in all his readers. Destroys confidence, fraternal confidence, of which God knows that there is in this world none to spare. For, comparatively inexperienced as you are, my dear young friend, did you never observe how little, very little, confidence, there is? I mean between man and man – more particularly between stranger and stranger. In a sad world it is the saddest fact. Confidence! I have sometimes almost thought that confidence is fled; that confidence is the New Astrea – emigrated – vanished – gone.' Then softly sliding nearer, with the softest air, quivering down and looking up, 'could you now, my dear young sir, under such circumstances, by way of experiment, simply have confidence in *me?*'

From the outset, the sophomore, as has been seen, had struggled with an ever-increasing embarrassment, arising, perhaps, from such strange remarks coming from a stranger – such persistent and prolonged remarks, too. In vain had he more than once sought to break the spell by venturing a deprecatory or leave-taking word. In vain. Somehow, the stranger fascinated him. Little wonder, then, that, when the appeal came, he could hardly speak, but, as before intimated, being apparently of a retiring nature, abruptly retired from the spot, leaving the chagrined stranger to wander away in the opposite direction.

Chapter Six

At the Outset of Which Certain Passengers Prove Deaf to the Call of Charity

– 'You – pish! Why will the captain suffer these begging fellows on board?'

These pettish words were breathed by a well-to-do gentleman in a ruby-coloured velvet vest, and with a ruby-coloured cheek, a ruby-headed cane in his hand, to a man in a gray coat and white tie, who, shortly after the interview last described, had accosted him for contributions to a Widow and Orphan Asylum recently founded among the Seminoles. Upon a cursory view, this last person might have seemed, like the man with the weed, one of the less unrefined children of misfortune; but, on a closer observation, his countenance revealed little of sorrow, though much of sanctity.

With added words of touchy disgust, the well-to-do gentleman hurried away. But, though repulsed, and rudely, the man in gray did not reproach, for a time patiently remaining in the chilly loneliness to which he had been left, his countenance, however, not without token of latent though chastened reliance.

At length an old gentleman, somewhat bulky, drew near, and from him also a contribution was sought.

'Look, you,' coming to a dead halt, and scowling upon him. 'Look, you,' swelling his bulk out before him like a swaying balloon, 'look, you, you on others' behalf ask for money; you, a fellow with a face as long as my arm. Hark ye, now: there is such a thing as gravity, and in condemned felons it may be genuine; but of long faces there are three sorts; that of grief's drudge, that of the lantern-jawed man, and that of the impostor. You know best which yours is.'

'Heaven give you more charity, sir.'

'And you less hypocrisy, sir.'

With which words, the hard-hearted old gentleman marched off.

While the other still stood forlorn, the young clergyman, before introduced, passing that way, catching a chance sight of him, seemed suddenly struck by some recollection; and, after a moment's pause, hurried up with: 'Your pardon, but shortly since I was all over looking for you.'

'For me?' as marvelling that one of so little account should be sought for.

'Yes, for you; do you know anything about the negro, apparently a cripple, aboard here? Is he, or is he not, what he seems to be?'

'Ah, poor Guinea! have you, too, been distrusted? you, upon whom nature has placarded the evidence of your claims?'

'Then you do really know him, and he is quite worthy? It relieves me to hear it – much relieves me. Come, let us go find him, and see what can be done.'

'Another instance that confidence may come too late. I am sorry to say that at the last landing I myself – just happening to catch sight of him on the gangway-plank – assisted the cripple ashore. No time to talk, only to help. He may not have told you, but he has a brother in that vicinity.'

'Really, I regret his going without my seeing him again; regret it, more, perhaps, than you can readily think. You see, shortly after leaving St Louis, he was on the forecastle, and there, with many others, I saw him, and put trust in him; so much so, that to convince those who did not, I, at his entreaty, went in search of you, you being one of several individuals he mentioned, and whose personal appearance he more or less described, individuals who he said would willingly speak for him. But, after diligent search, not finding you, and catching no glimpse of any of the others he had enumerated, doubts were at last suggested; but doubts indirectly originating, as I can but think, from prior distrust unfeelingly proclaimed by another. Still, certain it is, I began to suspect.'

'Ha, ha, ha!'

A sort of laugh more like a groan than a laugh; and yet, somehow, it seemed intended for a laugh.

Both turned, and the young clergyman started at seeing the wooden-legged man close behind him, morosely grave as a criminal judge with a mustard-plaster on his back. In the present case the mustard-plaster might have been the memory of certain recent biting rebuffs and mortifications.

'Wouldn't think it was I who laughed, would you?'

'But who was it you laughed at? or rather, tried to laugh at?' demanded the young clergyman, flushing, 'me?'

'Neither you nor any one within a thousand miles of you. But perhaps you don't believe it.'

'If he were of a suspicious temper, he might not,' interposed the man in gray calmly, 'it is one of the imbecilities of the suspicious person to fancy that every stranger, however absent-minded, he sees so much as smiling or gesturing to himself in any odd sort of way, is secretly making him his butt. In some moods, the movements of an entire street, as the suspicious man walks down it, will seem an express pantomimic jeer at him. In short, the suspicious man kicks himself with his own foot.'

'Whoever can do that, ten to one he saves other folks' sole-leather,' said the wooden-legged man with a crusty attempt at humour. But with augmented grin and squirm, turning directly upon the young clergyman, 'you still think it was *you* I was laughing at, just now. To prove your mistake, I will tell you what I *was* laughing at; a story I happened to call to mind just then.'

Whereupon, in his porcupine way, and with sarcastic details, unpleasant to repeat, he related a story, which might, perhaps, in a good-natured version, be rendered as follows:

A certain Frenchman of New Orleans, an old man, less slender in purse than limb, happening to attend the theatre one evening, was so charmed with the character of a faithful wife, as there represented to the life, that nothing would do but he must marry upon it. So marry he did, a beautiful girl from Tennessee, who had first attracted his attention by her liberal mould, and was subsequently recommended to him through her kin, for her equally liberal education and disposition. Though large, the praise proved not too much. For, ere long, rumour more than corroborated it, by whispering that the lady was liberal to a fault. But though various circumstances, which by most Benedicts would have been deemed all but conclusive, were duly recited to the old Frenchman by his friends, yet such was his confidence that not a syllable would he credit, till, chancing one night to return unexpectedly from a journey, upon entering his apartment, a stranger burst from the alcove: 'Begar!' cried he, 'now I *begin* to suspec.'

His story told, the wooden-legged man threw back his head, and gave vent to a long, gasping, rasping sort of taunting cry, intolerable as that of a high-pressure engine jeering off steam; and that done, with apparent satisfaction hobbled away.

'Who is that scoffer?' said the man in gray, not without warmth. 'Who is he, who even were truth on his tongue, his way of speaking it would make truth almost as offensive as falsehood? Who is he?'

'He whom I mentioned to you as having boasted his suspicion of the negro,' replied the young clergyman, recovering from disturbance, 'in short, the person to whom I ascribe the origin of my own distrust; he maintained that Guinea was some white scoundrel, betwisted and painted up for a decoy. Yes, these were his very words, I think.'

'Impossible! he could not be so wrong-headed. Pray, will you call him back, and let me ask him if he were really in earnest?'

The other complied; and, at length, after no few surly objections, prevailed upon the one-legged individual to return for a moment. Upon which, the man in gray thus addressed him: 'This reverend gentleman tells me, sir, that a certain cripple, a poor negro, is by you considered an ingenious impostor. Now, I am not unaware that there are some persons in this world, who, unable to give better proof of being wise, take a strange delight in showing what they think they have sagaciously read in mankind by uncharitable suspicions of them. I hope you are not one of these. In short, would you tell me now, whether you were not merely joking in the notion you threw out about the negro? Would you be so kind?'

'No, I won't be so kind, I'll be so cruel.'

'As you please about that.'

'Well, he's just what I said he was.'

'A white masquerading as a black?'

'Exactly.'

The man in gray glanced at the young clergyman a moment, then quietly whispered to him, 'I thought you represented your friend here as a very distrustful sort of person, but he appears endued with a singular credulity. – Tell me, sir, do you really think that a white could look the negro so? For one, I should call it pretty good acting.'

'Not much better than any other man acts.'

'How? Does all the world act? Am *I*, for instance, an actor? Is my reverend friend here, too, a performer?'

'Yes, don't you both perform acts? To do is to act; so all doers are actors.'

'You trifle. – I ask again, if a white, how could he look the negro so?'

'Never saw the negro-minstrels, I suppose?'

'Yes, but they are apt to overdo the ebony; exemplifying the old saying, not more just than charitable, that "the devil is never so black as he is painted". But his limbs, if not a cripple, how could he twist his limbs so?'

'How do other hypocritical beggars twist theirs? Easy enough to see how they are hoisted up.'

'The sham is evident, then?'

'To the discerning eye,' with a horrible screw of his gimlet one.

'Well, where is Guinea?' said the man in gray; 'where is he? Let us at once find him, and refute beyond cavil this injurious hypothesis.'

'Do so,' cried the one-legged man, 'I'm just in the humour now for having him found, and leaving the streaks of these fingers on his paint, as the lion leaves the streaks of his nails on a Caffre. They wouldn't let me touch him before. Yes, find him, I'll make wool fly, and him after.'

'You forget,' here said the young clergyman to the man in gray, 'that yourself helped poor Guinea ashore.'

'So I did, so I did; how unfortunate. But look now,' to the other, 'I think that without personal proof I can convince you of your mistake. For I put it to you, is it reasonable to suppose that a man with brains, sufficient to act such a part as you say, would take all that trouble, and run all that hazard, for the mere sake of those few paltry coppers, which, I hear, was all that he got for his pains, if pains they were?'

'That puts the case irrefutably,' said the young clergyman, with a challenging glance towards the one-legged man.

'You two green-horns! Money, you think, is the sole motive to pains and hazard, deception and devilry, in this world. How much money did the devil make by gulling Eve?'

Whereupon he hobbled off again with a repetition of his intolerable jeer.

The man in gray stood silently eyeing his retreat a while, and then, turning to his companion, said: 'A bad man, a dangerous man; a man to be put down in any Christian community. – And this was he who was the means of begetting your distrust? Ah, we should shut our ears to distrust, and keep them open only for its opposite.'

'You advance a principle, which, if I had acted upon it this morning, I should have spared myself what I now feel. – That but one man, and he with one leg, should have such ill power given him; his one sour word leavening into congenial sourness (as, to my knowledge, it did) the dispositions, before sweet enough, of a numerous company. But, as I hinted, with me at the time his ill words went for nothing; the same as now; only afterwards they had effect; and I confess, this puzzles me.'

'It should not. With humane minds, the spirit of distrust works something as certain potions do; it is a spirit which may enter such minds, and yet, for a time, longer or shorter, lie in them quiescent; but only the more deplorable its ultimate activity.'

'An uncomfortable solution; for, since that baneful man did but just now anew drop on me his bane, how shall I be sure that my present exemption from its effects will be lasting?'

'You cannot be sure, but you can strive against it.'

'How?'

'By strangling the least symptom of distrust, of any sort, which hereafter, upon whatever provocation, may arise in you.'

'I will do so.' Then added as in soliloquy, 'Indeed, indeed, I was to blame in standing passive under such influences as that one-legged man's. My conscience upbraids me. – The poor negro: you see him occasionally, perhaps?'

'No, not often; though in a few days, as it happens, my engagements will call me to the neighbourhood of his present retreat; and, no doubt, honest Guinea, who is a grateful soul, will come to see me there.'

'Then you have been his benefactor?'

'His benefactor? I did not say that. I have known him.'

'Take this mite. Hand it to Guinea when you see him; say it comes from one who has full belief in his honesty, and is sincerely sorry for having indulged, however transiently, in a contrary thought.'

'I accept the trust. And, by-the-way, since you are of this truly charitable nature, you will not turn away an appeal in behalf of the Seminole Widow and Orphan Asylum?'

'I have not heard of that charity.'

'But recently founded.'

After a pause, the clergyman was irresolutely putting his hand in his pocket, when, caught by something in his companion's expression, he eyed him inquisitively, almost uneasily.

'Ah, well,' smiled the other wanly, 'if that subtle bane, we were speaking of but just now, is so soon beginning to work, in vain my appeal to you. Good-bye.'

'Nay,' not untouched, 'you do me injustice; instead of indulging present suspicions, I had rather make amends for previous ones. Here is something for your asylum. Not much; but every drop helps. Of course you have papers?'

'Of course,' producing a memorandum book and pencil. 'Let me take down name and amount. We publish these names. And now let me give you a little history of our asylum, and the providential way in which it was started.'

Chapter Seven

A Gentleman With Gold Sleeve-buttons

At an interesting point of the narration, and at the moment when, with much curiosity, indeed, urgency, the narrator was being particularly questioned upon that point, he was, as it happened, altogether diverted both from it and his story, by just then catching sight of a gentleman who had been standing in sight from the beginning, but, until now, as it seemed, without being observed by him.

'Pardon me,' said he, rising, 'but yonder is one who I know will contribute, and largely. Don't take it amiss if I quit you.'

'Go: duty before all things,' was the conscientious reply.

The stranger was a man of more than winning aspect. There he stood apart and in repose, and yet, by his mere look, lured the man in gray from his story, much as by its graciousness of bearing, some full-leaved elm, alone in a meadow, lures the noon sickleman to throw down his sheaves, and come and apply for the alms of its shade.

But, considering that goodness is no such rare thing among men – the world familiarly know the noun; a common one in every language – it was curious that what so signalized the stranger, and made him look like a kind of foreigner, among the crowd (as to some it may make him appear more or less unreal in this portraiture), was but the expression of so prevalent a quality. Such goodness seemed his, allied with such fortune, that, so far as his own personal experience could have gone, scarcely could he have known ill, physical or moral; and as for knowing or suspecting the latter in any serious degree (supposing such degree of it to be), by observation or philosophy; for that, probably, his nature, by its opposition, imperfectly qualified, or from it wholly exempted him. For the rest, he might have been five and fifty, perhaps sixty, but tall, rosy, between plump and portly, with a primy, palmy air, and for the time and place, not to hint of his years, dressed with a strangely festive finish and elegance. The inner side of his coat skirts was of white satin, which might have looked especially inappropriate, had it not seemed less a bit of mere tailoring than something of an emblem, as it were; an involuntary emblem, let us say, that what seemed so good about him was not all outside; no, the fine covering had a still finer lining. Upon one hand he wore a white kid glove, but the other hand, which was ungloved, looked hardly less white. Now, as the Fidèle, like most steamboats, was upon deck a little soot-streaked here and there, especially about the railings, it was a marvel how, under such circumstances, these hands retained their spotlessness. But, if you watched them a while, you noticed that they avoided touching anything; you noticed, in short, that a certain negro body-servant, whose hands nature had dyed black, perhaps with the same purpose that millers wear white, this negro servant's hands did most of his master's handling for him; having to do with dirt on his account, but not to his prejudices. But if, with the same undefiledness of consequences to himself, a gentleman could also sin by deputy, how shocking would that be! But it is not permitted to be; and even if it were, no judicious moralist would make proclamation of it.

This gentleman, therefore, there is reason to affirm, was one who, like the Hebrew governor, knew how to keep his hands clean, and who never in his life happened to be run suddenly against by hurrying house-painter, or sweep; in a word, one whose very good luck it was to be a very good man.

Not that he looked as if he were a kind of Wilberforce at all, that superior merit, probably, was not his; nothing in his manner bespoke him righteous, but only good; and though to be good is much below being righteous, and though there is a difference between the two, yet not, it is to be hoped, so incompatible as that a righteous man cannot be a good man; though, conversely, in the pulpit it has been with much cogency urged, that a merely good man, that is, one good merely by his nature, is so far from thereby being righteous, that nothing short of a total change and conversion can make him so; which is something which no honest mind, well read in the history of righteousness, will care to deny; nevertheless, since St Paul himself, agreeing in a sense with the pulpit distinction, though not altogether in the pulpit deduction, and also pretty plainly intimating which of the two qualities in question enjoys his apostolic preference; I say, since St Paul has so meaningly said, that, 'scarcely for a righteous man will one die, yet peradventure for a good man some would even dare to die'; therefore, when we repeat of this gentleman, that he was only a good man, whatever else by severe censors may be objected to him, it is still to be hoped that his goodness will not at least be considered criminal in him. At all events, no man, not even a righteous man, would think it quite right to commit this gentleman to prison for the crime, extraordinary as he might deem it; more especially, as, until everything could be known, there would be some chance that the gentleman might after all be quite as innocent of it as he himself.

It was pleasant to mark the good man's reception of the salute of the righteous man, that is, the man in gray; his inferior, apparently, not more in the social scale than in stature. Like the benign elm again, the good man seemed to wave the canopy of his goodness over that suitor, not in conceited condescension, but with that even amenity of true majesty, which can be kind to any one without stooping to it.

To the plea in behalf of the Seminole widows and orphans, the gentleman, after a question or two duly answered, responded by producing an ample pocket-book in the good old capacious style, of fine green French morocco and workmanship, bound with silk of the same colour, not to omit bills crisp with newness, fresh from the bank, no muckworms' grime upon them. Lucre those bills might be, but as yet having been kept unspotted from the world, not of the filthy sort. Placing now three of those virgin bills in the applicant's hands, he hoped that the smallness of the contribution would be pardoned; to tell the truth, and this at last accounted for his toilet, he was bound but a short run down the river, to attend, in a festive grove, the afternoon wedding of his niece; so did not carry much money with him.

The other was about expressing his thanks when the gentleman in his pleasant way checked him: the gratitude was on the other side. To him, he said, charity was in one sense not an effort, but a luxury; against too great indulgence in which his steward, a humourist, had sometimes admonished him.

In some general talk which followed, relative to organized modes of doing good, the gentleman expressed his regrets that so many benevolent societies as there were, here and there isolated in the land, should not act in concert by coming together, in the way that already in each society the individuals composing it had done, which would result, he thought, in like advantages upon a larger scale. Indeed, such a confederation might, perhaps, be attended with as happy results as politically attended that of the states.

Upon his hitherto moderate enough companion, this suggestion had an effect illustrative in a sort of that notion of Socrates, that the soul is a harmony; for as the sound of a flute, in any particular key, will, it is said, audibly affect the corresponding chord of any harp in good tune within hearing, just so now did some string in him respond, and with animation.

Which animation, by the way, might seem more or less out of character in the man in gray, considering his unsprightly manner when first introduced, had he not already, in certain after colloquies, given proof, in some degree, of the fact that, with certain natures, a soberly continent air at times, so far from arguing emptiness of stuff, is good proof it is there, and plenty of it, because unwasted, and may be used the more effectively, too, when opportunity offers. What now follows on the part of the man in gray will still further exemplify, perhaps somewhat strikingly, the truth, or what appears to be such, of this remark.

'Sir,' said he eagerly, 'I am before you. A project, not dissimilar to yours, was by me thrown out at the World's Fair in London.'

'World's Fair? You there? Pray how was that?'

'First, let me –'

'Nay, but first tell me what took you to the Fair?'

'I went to exhibit an invalid's easy-chair I had invented.'

'Then you have not always been in the charity business?'

'Is it not charity to ease human suffering? I am, and always have been, as I always will be, I trust, in the charity business, as you call it; but charity is not like a pin, one to make the head, and the other the point; charity is a work to which a good workman may be competent in all its branches. I invented my Protean easy-chair in odd intervals stolen from meals and sleep.'

'You call it the Protean easy-chair; pray describe it.'

'My Protean easy-chair is a chair so all over bejointed, behinged, and bepadded, everyway so elastic, springy, and docile to the airiest touch, that in some one of its endlessly-changeable accommodations of back, seat, footboard, and arms, the most restless body, the body most racked, nay, I had almost added the most tormented conscience must, somehow and somewhere, find rest. Believing that I owed it to suffering humanity to make known such a chair to the utmost, I scraped together my little means and off to the World's Fair with it.'

'You did right. But your scheme; how did you come to hit upon that?'

'I was going to tell you. After seeing my invention duly catalogued and placed, I gave myself up to pondering the scene about me. As I dwelt upon that shining pageant of arts, and moving concourse of nations, and reflected that here was the pride of the world glorying in a glass house, a sense of the fragility of worldly grandeur profoundly impressed me. And I said to myself, I will see if this occasion of vanity cannot supply a hint toward a better profit than was designed. Let some world-wide good to the world-wide cause be now done. In short, inspired by the scene, on the fourth day I issued at the World's Fair my prospectus of the World's Charity.'

'Quite a thought. But, pray explain it.'

'The World's Charity is to be a society whose members shall comprise deputies from every charity and mission extant; the one object of the society to be the methodization of the world's benevolence; to which end, the present system of voluntary and promiscuous contribution to be done away, and the Society to be empowered by the various governments to levy, annually, one grand benevolence tax upon all mankind; as in Augustus Caesar's time, the whole world to come up to be taxed; a tax which, for the scheme of it, should be something like the income-tax in England, a tax, also, as before hinted, to be a consolidation-tax of all possible benevolence taxes; as in America here, the state-tax, and the county-tax, and the town-tax, and the poll-tax, are by the assessors rolled into one. This tax, according to my tables, calculated with care, would result in the yearly raising of a fund little short of eight hundred millions; this fund to be annually applied to such objects, and in such modes, as the various charities and missions, in general congress represented, might decree; whereby, in fourteen years, as I estimate, there would have been devoted to good works the sum of eleven thousand two hundred millions; which would warrant the dissolution of the society, as that fund judiciously expended, not a pauper or heathen could remain the round world over.'

'Eleven thousand two hundred millions! And all by passing round a *hat*, as it were.'

'Yes, I am no Fourier, the projector of an impossible scheme, but a philanthropist and a financier, setting forth a philanthropy and a finance which are practicable.'

'Practicable?'

'Yes. Eleven thousand two hundred millions; it will frighten none but a retail philanthropist. What is it but eight hundred millions for each of fourteen years? Now eight hundred millions – what is that, to average it, but one little dollar a head for the population of the planet? And who will refuse, what Turk or Dyak even, his own little dollar for sweet charity's sake? Eight hundred millions! More than that sum is yearly expended by mankind, not only in vanities, but miseries. Consider that bloody spendthrift, War. And are mankind so stupid, so wicked, that, upon the demonstration of these things they will not, amending their ways, devote their superfluities to blessing the world instead of cursing it? Eight hundred millions! They have not to make it, it is theirs already; they have but to direct it from ill to good. And to this, scarce a self-denial is demanded. Actually, they would not in the mass be one farthing the poorer for it; as certainly would they be all the better and happier. Don't you see? But admit, as you must, that mankind is not mad, and my project is practicable. For what creature, but a madman, would not rather do good than ill, when it is plain that, good or ill, it must return upon himself?'

'Your sort of reasoning,' said the good gentleman, adjusting his gold sleeve-buttons, 'seems all reasonable enough, but with mankind it won't do.'

'Then mankind are not reasoning beings, if reason won't do with them.'

'That is not to the purpose. By the way, from the manner in which you alluded to the world's census, it would appear that, according to your world-wide scheme, the pauper not less than the nabob is to contribute to the relief of pauperism, and the heathen not less than the Christian to the conversion of heathenism. How is that?'

'Why, that – pardon me – is quibbling. Now, no philanthropist likes to be opposed with quibbling.'

'Well, I won't quibble any more. But, after all, if I understand your project, there is little specially new in it, further than the magnifying of means now in operation.'

'Magnifying and energizing. For one thing, missions I would thoroughly reform. Missions I would quicken with the Wall street spirit.'

'The Wall street spirit?'

'Yes; for if, confessedly, certain spiritual ends are to be gained but through the auxiliary agency of worldly means, then, to the surer gaining of such spiritual ends, the example of worldly policy in worldly projects should not by spiritual projectors be slighted. In brief, the conversion of the heathen, so far, at least, as depending on human effort, would, by the World's Charity, be let out on contract. So much by bid for converting India, so much for Borneo, so much for Africa. Competition allowed, stimulus would be given. There would be no lethargy of monopoly. We should have no mission-house or tract-house of which slanderers could, with any plausibility, say that it had degenerated in its clerkships into a sort of custom-house. But the main point is the Archimedean money-power that would be brought to bear.'

'You mean the eight hundred million power?'

'Yes. You see, this doing good to the world by driblets amounts to just nothing. I am for doing good to the world with a will. I am for doing good to the world once for all and having done with it. Do but think, my dear sir, of the eddies and maëlstroms of pagans in China. People here have no conception of it. Of a frosty morning in Hong Kong, pauper pagans are found dead in the streets like so many nipped peas in a bin of peas. To be an immortal being in China is no more distinction than to be a snow-flake in a snow-squall. What are a score or two of missionaries to such a people? A pinch of snuff to the kraken. I am for sending ten thousand missionaries in a body and converting the Chinese *en masse* within six months of the debarkation. The thing is then done, and turn to something else.'

'I fear you are too enthusiastic.'

'A philanthropist is necessarily an enthusiast; for without enthusiasm what was ever achieved but commonplace? But again: consider the poor in London. To that mob of misery, what is a joint here and a loaf there? I am for voting to them twenty thousand bullocks and one hundred thousand barrels of flour to begin with. They are then comforted, and no more hunger for one while among the poor of London. And so all round.'

'Sharing the character of your general project, these things, I take it, are rather examples of wonders that were to be wished, than wonders that will happen.'

'And is the age of wonders past? Is the world too old? Is it barren? Think of Sarah.'

'Then I am Abraham reviling the angel (with a smile). But still, as to your design at large, there seems a certain audacity.'

'But if to the audacity of the design there be brought a commensurate circumspectness of execution, how then?'

'Why, do you really believe that your World's Charity will ever go into operation?'

'I have confidence that it will.'

'But may you not be over-confident?'

'For a Christian to talk so!'

'But think of the obstacles!'

'Obstacles? I have confidence to remove obstacles, though mountains. Yes, confidence in the World's Charity to that degree, that, as no better person offers to supply the place, I have nominated myself provisional treasurer, and will be happy to receive subscriptions, for the present to be devoted to striking off a million more of my prospectuses.'

The talk went on; the man in gray revealed a spirit of benevolence which, mindful of the millennial promise, had gone abroad over all the countries of the globe, much as the diligent spirit of the husbandman, stirred by forethought of the coming seed-time, leads him, in March reveries at his fire-side, over every field of his farm. The master chord of the man in gray had been touched, and it seemed as if it would never cease vibrating. A not unsilvery tongue, too, was his, with gestures that were a Pentecost of added ones, and persuasiveness before which granite hearts might crumble into gravel.

Strange, therefore, how his auditor, so singularly good-hearted as he seemed, remained proof to such eloquence; though not, as it turned out, to such pleadings. For, after listening a little longer with pleasant incredulity, presently, as the boat touched his place of destination, the gentleman, with a look of half humour, half pity, put another bank-note into his hands; charitable to the last, if only to the dreams of enthusiasm.

Chapter Eight

A Charitable Lady

If a drunkard in a sober fit is the dullest of mortals, an enthusiast in a reason-fit is not the most lively. And this, without prejudice to his greatly improved understanding: for, if his elation was the height of his madness, his despondency is but the extreme of his sanity. Something thus now, to all appearance, with the man in gray. Society his stimulus, loneliness was his lethargy. Loneliness, like the sea-breeze, blowing off from a thousand leagues of blankness, he did not find, as veteran solitaires do, if anything, too bracing. In short, left to himself, with none to charm forth his latent lymphatic, he insensibly resumes his original air, a quiescent one blended of sad humility and demureness.

Ere long he goes laggingly into the ladies' saloon, as in spiritless quest of somebody; but, after some disappointed glances about him, seats himself upon a sofa with an air of melancholy exhaustion and depression.

At the sofa's further end sits a plump and pleasant person, whose aspect seems to hint that, if she have any weak point, it must be anything rather than her excellent heart. From her twilight dress, neither dawn nor dark, apparently she is a widow just breaking the chrysalis of her mourning. A small gilt testament is in her hand, which she has just been reading. Half-relinquished, she holds the book in reverie, her finger inserted at the thirteenth of 1st Corinthians, to which chapter possibly her attention might have recently been turned, by witnessing the scene of the monitory mute and his slate.

The sacred page no longer meets her eye; but, as at evening, when for a time the western hills shine on though the sun be set, her thoughtful face retains its tenderness though the teacher is forgotten.

Meantime, the expression of the stranger is such as ere long to attract her glance. But no responsive one. Presently, in her somewhat inquisitive survey, her volume drops. It is restored. No encroaching politeness in the act, but kindness, unadorned. The eyes of the lady sparkle. Evidently, she is not now unprepossessed. Soon, bending over, in a low, sad tone, full of deference, the stranger breathes, 'Madam, pardon my freedom, but there is something in that face which strangely draws me. May I ask, are you a sister of the Church?'

'Why – really – you –'

In concern for her embarrassment, he hastens to relieve it, but without seeming so to do. 'It is very solitary for a brother here,' eyeing the showy ladies brocaded in the background. 'I find none to mingle souls with. It may be wrong – I *know* it is – but I cannot force myself to be easy with the people of the world. I prefer the company, however silent, of a brother or sister in good standing. By the way, madam, may I ask if you have confidence?'

'Really, sir – why, sir – really – I –'

'Could you put confidence in *me*, for instance?'

'Really, sir – as much – I mean, as one may wisely put in a – a – stranger – an entire stranger, I had almost said,' rejoined the lady, hardly yet at ease in her affability, drawing aside a little in body, while at the same time her heart might have been drawn as far the other way. A natural struggle between charity and prudence.

'Entire stranger!' with a sigh. 'Ah, who would be a stranger? In vain, I wander; no one will have confidence in me.'

'You interest me,' said the good lady, in mild surprise. 'Can I any way befriend you?'

'No one can befriend me who has not confidence.'

'But I – I have – at least to that degree – I mean that –'

'Nay, nay, you have none – none at all. Pardon, I see it. No confidence. Fool, fond fool that I am to seek it!'

'You are unjust, sir,' rejoins the good lady with heightened interest; 'but it may be that something untoward in your experiences has unduly biassed you. Not that I would cast reflections. Believe me, I – yes, yes – I may say that – that –'

'That you have confidence? Prove it. Let me have twenty dollars.'

'Twenty dollars!'

'There, I told you, madam, you had no confidence.'

The lady was, in an extraordinary way, touched. She sat in a sort of restless torment, knowing not which way to turn. She began twenty different sentences, and left off at the first syllable of each. At last, in desperation, she hurried out, 'Tell me, sir, for what you want the twenty dollars?'

'And did I not?' – then glancing at her half-mourning, – 'for the widow and the fatherless. I am travelling agent of the Widow and Orphan Asylum, recently founded among the Seminoles.'

'And why did you not tell me your object before?' as not a little relieved. 'Poor souls – Indians, too – those cruelly-used Indians. Here, here; how could I hesitate? I am so sorry it is no more.'

'Grieve not for that, madam,' rising and folding up the bank-notes. 'This is an inconsiderable sum, I admit, but,' taking out his pencil and book, 'though I here but register the amount, there is another register, where is set down the motive. Good-bye; you have confidence. Yea, you can say to me as the apostle said to the Corinthians, "I rejoice that I have confidence in you in all things."'

Chapter Nine

Two Business Men Transact a Little Business

– 'Pray, sir, have you seen a gentleman with a weed hereabouts, rather a saddish gentleman? Strange where he can have gone to. I was talking with him not twenty minutes since.'

By a brisk, ruddy-cheeked man in a tasseled travelling-cap, carrying under his arm a ledger-like volume, the above words were addressed to the collegian before introduced, suddenly accosted by the rail to which, not long after his retreat, as in a previous chapter recounted, he had returned, and there remained.

'Have you seen him, sir?'

Rallied from his apparent diffidence by the genial jauntiness of the stranger, the youth answered with unwonted promptitude: 'Yes, a person with a weed was here not very long ago.'

'Saddish?'

'Yes, and a little cracked, too, I should say.'

'It was he. Misfortune, I fear, has disturbed his brain. Now quick, which way did he go?'

'Why just in the direction from which you came, the gangway yonder.'

'Did he? Then the man in the gray coat, whom I just met, said right: he must have gone ashore. How unlucky!'

He stood vexedly twitching at his cap-tassel, which fell over by his whisker, and continued: 'Well, I am very sorry. In fact, I had something for him here.' – Then drawing nearer, 'You see, he applied to me for relief – no, I do him injustice, not that, but he began to intimate, you understand. Well, being very busy just then, I declined; quite rudely, too, in a cold, morose, unfeeling way, I fear. At all events, not three minutes afterwards I felt self-reproach, with a kind of prompting, very peremptory, to deliver

54

over into that unfortunate man's hands a ten dollar bill. You smile. Yes, it may be superstition, but I can't help it; I have my weak side, thank God. Then again,' he rapidly went on, 'we have been so very prosperous lately in our affairs – by we, I mean the Black Rapids Coal Company – that, really, out of my abundance, associative and individual, it is but fair that a charitable investment or two should be made, don't you think so?'

'Sir,' said the collegian without the least embarrassment, 'do I understand that you are officially connected with the Black Rapids Coal Company?'

'Yes, I happen to be president and transfer-agent.'

'You are?'

'Yes, but what is it to you? You don't want to invest?'

'Why, do you sell the stock?'

'Some might be bought, perhaps; but why do you ask? you don't want to invest?'

'But supposing I did,' with cool self-collectedness, 'could you do up the thing for me, and here?'

'Bless my soul,' gazing at him in amaze, 'really, you are quite a businessman. Positively, I feel afraid of you.'

'Oh, no need of that. – You could sell me some of that stock, then?'

'I don't know, I don't know. To be sure, there are a few shares under peculiar circumstances bought in by the Company; but it would hardly be the thing to convert this boat into the Company's office. I think you had better defer investing. So,' with an indifferent air, 'you have seen the unfortunate man I spoke of?'

'Let the unfortunate man go his ways. – What is that large book you have with you?'

'My transfer-book. I am subpoenaed with it to court.'

'Black Rapids Coal Company,' obliquely reading the gilt inscription on the back; 'I have heard much of it. Pray do you happen to have with you any statement of the condition of your company?'

'A statement has lately been printed.'

'Pardon me, but I am naturally inquisitive. Have you a copy with you?'

'I tell you again, I do not think that it would be suitable to convert this boat into the Company's office. – That unfortunate man, did you relieve him at all?'

'Let the unfortunate man relieve himself. – Hand me the statement.'

'Well, you are such a business-man, I can hardly deny you. Here,' handing a small printed pamphlet.

The youth turned it over sagely.

'I hate a suspicious man,' said the other, observing him; 'but I must say I like to see a cautious one.'

'I can gratify you there,' languidly returning the pamphlet; 'for, as I said before, I am naturally inquisitive; I am also circumspect. No appearances can deceive me. Your statement,' he added, 'tells a very fine story; but pray, was not your stock a little heavy a while ago? downward tendency? Sort of low spirits among holders on the subject of that stock?'

'Yes, there was a depression. But how came it? who devised it? The "bears", sir. The depression of our stock was solely owing to the growling, the hypocritical growling, of the bears.'

'How hypocritical?'

'Why, the most monstrous of all hypocrites are these bears: hypocrites by inversion; hypocrites in the simulation of things dark instead of bright; souls that thrive, less upon depression, than the fiction of depression; professors of the wicked art of manufacturing depressions; spurious Jeremiahs; sham Heraclituses, who, the lugubrious day done, return, like sham Lazaruses among the beggars, to make merry over the gains got by their pretended sore heads – scoundrelly bears!'

'You are warm against these bears?'

'If I am, it is less from the remembrance of their stratagems as to our stock, than from the persuasion that these same destroyers of confidence, and gloomy philosophers of the stock-market, though false in themselves, are yet true types of most destroyers of confidence and gloomy philosophers, the world over. Fellows who, whether in stocks, politics, bread-stuffs, morals, metaphysics, religion – be it what it may – trump up their black panics in the naturally quiet brightness, solely with a view to some sort of covert advantage. That corpse of calamity which the gloomy philosopher parades, is but his Good-Enough-Morgan.'

'I rather like that,' knowingly drawled the youth. 'I fancy these gloomy souls as little as the next one. Sitting on my sofa after a champagne dinner, smoking my plantation cigar, if a gloomy fellow come to me – what a bore!'

'You tell him it's all stuff, don't you?'

'I tell him it ain't natural. I say to him, you are happy enough, and you know it; and everybody else is as happy as you, and you know that, too; and we shall all be happy after we are no more, and you know that, too; but no, still you must have your sulk.'

'And do you know whence this sort of fellow gets his sulk? not from life; for he's often too much of a recluse, or else too young to have seen anything of it. No, he gets it from some of those old plays he sees on the stage, or some of those old books he finds up in garrets. Ten to one, he has lugged home from auction a musty old Seneca, and sets about stuffing himself with that stale old hay; and, thereupon, thinks it looks wise and antique to be a croaker, thinks it's taking a stand 'way above his kind.'

'Just so,' assented the youth, 'I've lived some, and seen a good many such ravens at second hand. By the way, strange how that man with the weed, you were inquiring for, seemed to take me for some soft sentimentalist, only because I kept quiet, and thought, because I had a copy of Tacitus with me, that I was reading him for his gloom, instead of his gossip. But I let him talk. And, indeed, by my manner humoured him.'

'You shouldn't have done that, now. Unfortunate man, you must have made quite a fool of him.'

'His own fault if I did. But I like prosperous fellows, comfortable fellows; fellows that talk comfortably and prosperously, like you. Such fellows are generally honest. And, I say now, I happen to have a superfluity in my pocket, and I'll just –'

'– Act the part of a brother to that unfortunate man?'

'Let the unfortunate man be his own brother. What are you dragging him in for all the time? One would think you didn't care to register any transfers, or dispose of any stock – mind running on something else. I say I will invest.'

'Stay, stay, here come some uproarious fellows – this way, this way.'

And with off-handed politeness, the man with the book escorted his companion into a private little haven removed from the brawling swells without.

Business transacted, the two came forth, and walked the deck.

'Now tell me, sir,' said he with the book, 'how comes it that a young gentleman like you, a sedate student at the first appearance, should dabble in stocks and that sort of thing?'

'There are certain sophomorean errors in the world,' drawled the sophomore, deliberately adjusting his shirt-collar, 'not the least of which is the popular notion touching the nature of the modern scholar, and the nature of the modern scholastic sedateness.'

'So it seems, so it seems. Really, this is quite a new leaf in my experience.'

'Experience, sir,' originally observed the sophomore, 'is the only teacher.'

'Hence am I your pupil; for it's only when experience speaks, that I can endure to listen to speculation.'

'My speculations, sir,' dryly drawing himself up, 'have been chiefly governed by the maxim of Lord Bacon; I speculate in those philosophies which come home to my business and bosom – pray, do you know of any other good stocks?'

'You wouldn't like to be concerned in the New Jerusalem, would you?'

'New Jerusalem?'

'Yes, the new and thriving city, so called in northern Minne-sota. It was originally founded by certain fugitive Mormons. Hence the name. It stands on the Mississippi. Here, here is the map,' producing a roll. 'There – there, you see are the public buildings – here the landing – there the park – yonder the botanic gardens – and this, this little dot here, is a perpetual fountain, you understand. You observe there are twenty asterisks. Those are for the lyceums. They have lignum-vitae rostrums.'

'And are all these buildings now standing?'

'All standing – *bona fide*.'

'These marginal squares here, are they the water-lots?'

'Water-lots in the city of New Jerusalem? All terra firma – you don't seem to care about investing, though?'

'Hardly think I should read my title clear, as the law students say,' yawned the collegian.

'Prudent – you are prudent. Don't know that you are wholly out, either. At any rate, I would rather have one of your shares of coal stock than two of this other. Still, considering that the first settlement was by two fugitives, who had swum over naked from the opposite shore – it's a surprising place. It is *bona fide*. – But dear me, I must go. Oh, if by possibility you should come across that unfortunate man –'

'– In that case,' with drawling impatience, 'I will send for the steward, and have him and his misfortunes consigned overboard.'

'Ha, ha! – Now were some gloomy philosopher here, some theological bear, for ever taking occasion to growl down the stock of human nature (with ulterior views, d'ye see, to a fat bene-fice in the gift of the worshippers of Arimanius), he would pronounce that the sign of a hardening heart and a softening brain. Yes, that would be his sinister construction. But it's noth-ing more than the oddity of a genial humour – genial but dry. Confess it. Good-bye.'

Chapter Ten

In the Cabin

Stools, settees, sofas, divans, ottomans; occupying them are clusters of men, old and young, wise and simple; in their hands are cards spotted with diamonds, spades, clubs, hearts; the favourite games are whist, cribbage, and brag. Lounging in arm-chairs or sauntering among the marble-topped tables, amused with the scene, are the comparatively few, who, instead of having hands in the games, for the most part keep their hands in their pockets. These may be the *philosophes*. But here and there, with a curious expression, one is reading a small sort of handbill of anonymous poetry, rather wordily entitled:

ODE

ON THE INTIMATIONS

OF

DISTRUST IN MAN,

UNWILLINGLY INFERRED FROM REPEATED REPULSES,

IN DISINTERESTED ENDEAVOURS

TO PROCURE HIS

CONFIDENCE.

On the floor are many copies, looking as if fluttered down from a balloon. The way they came there was this: A somewhat elderly person, in the quaker dress, had quietly passed through the cabin, and, much in the manner of those railway book-peddlers who precede their proffers of sale by a distribution of puffs, direct or indirect, of the volumes to follow, had, without speaking, handed about the odes, which, for the most part, after a cursory glance, had been disrespectfully tossed aside, as no

doubt the moon-struck production of some wandering rhapsod-
ist.

In due time, book under arm, in trips the ruddy man with the
travelling-cap, who, lightly moving to and fro, looks animatedly
about him, with a yearning sort of gratulatory affinity and longing, expressive of the very soul of sociality; as much as to say,
'Oh, boys, would that I were personally acquainted with each
mother's son of you, since what a sweet world, to make sweet
acquaintance in, is ours, my brothers; yea, and what dear, happy
dogs are we all!'

And just as if he had really warbled it forth, he makes frater-
nally up to one lounging stranger or another, exchanging with
him some pleasant remark.

'Pray, what have you there?' he asked of one newly accosted, a
little, dried-up man, who looked as if he never dined.

'A little ode, – rather queer, too,' was the reply, 'of the same
sort you see strewn on the floor here.'

'I did not observe them. Let me see;' picking one up and looking it over. 'Well now, this is pretty; plaintive, especially the
opening –

> Alas for man, he hath small sense
> Of genial trust and confidence.

– If it be so, alas for him, indeed. Runs off very smoothly, sir.
Beautiful pathos. But do you think the sentiment just?'

'As to that,' said the little dried-up man, 'I think it a kind of
queer thing altogether, and yet I am almost ashamed to add, it
really has set me to thinking; yes and to feeling. Just now, somehow, I feel as it were trustful and genial. I don't know that ever
I felt so much so before. I am naturally numb in my sensibilities;
but this ode, in its way, works on my numbness not unlike a ser-
mon, which, by lamenting over my lying dead in trespasses and
sins, thereby stirs me up to be all alive in well-doing.'

'Glad to hear it, and hope you will do well, as the doctors say. But who snowed the odes about here?'

'I cannot say; I have not been here long.'

'Wasn't an angel, was it? Come, you say you feel genial, let us do as the rest, and have cards.'

'Thank you, I never play cards.'

'A bottle of wine?'

'Thank you, I never drink wine.'

'Cigars?'

'Thank you, I never smoke cigars.'

'Tell stories?'

'To speak truly, I hardly think I know one worth telling.'

'Seems to me, then, this geniality you say you feel waked in you is as water-power in a land without mills. Come, you had better take a genial hand at the cards. To begin, we will play for as small a sum as you please; just enough to make it interesting.'

'Indeed, you must excuse me. Somehow I distrust cards.'

'What, distrust cards? Genial cards? Then for once I join with our sad Philomel here:

> Alas for man, he hath small sense
> Of genial trust and confidence.

Good-bye!'

Sauntering and chatting here and there, again, he with the book at length seems fatigued, looks round for a seat, and spying a partly-vacant settee drawn up against the side, drops down there; soon, like his chance neighbour, who happens to be the good merchant, becoming not a little interested in the scene more immediately before him; a party at whist; two cream-faced, giddy, unpolished youths, the one in a red cravat, the other in a green, opposed to two bland, grave, handsome, self-possessed men of middle age, decorously dressed in a sort of professional black, and apparently doctors of some eminence in the civil law.

By-and-by, after a preliminary scanning of the new-comer next him, the good merchant, sideways leaning over, whispers behind a crumpled copy of the Ode which he holds: 'Sir, I don't like the looks of those two, do you?'

'Hardly,' was the whispered reply; 'those coloured cravats are not in the best taste, at least not to mine; but my taste is no rule for all.'

'You mistake; I mean the other two, and I don't refer to dress, but countenance. I confess I am not familiar with such gentry any further than reading about them in the papers – but those two are – are sharpers, ain't they?'

'Far be from us the captious and fault-finding spirit, my dear sir.'

'Indeed, sir, I would not find fault; I am little given that way; but certainly, to say the least, these two youths can hardly be adepts, while the opposed couple may be even more.'

'You would not hint that the coloured cravats would be so bungling as to lose, and the dark cravats so dextrous as to cheat? – Sour imaginations, my dear sir. Dismiss them. To little purpose have you read the Ode you have there. Years and experience, I trust, have not sophisticated you. A fresh and liberal construction would teach us to regard those four players – indeed, this whole cabin-full of players – as playing at games in which every player plays fair, and not a player but shall win.'

'Now, you hardly mean that; because games in which all may win, such games remain as yet in this world uninvented, I think.'

'Come, come,' luxuriously laying himself back, and casting a free glance upon the players, 'fares all paid; digestion sound; care, toil, penury, grief, unknown; lounging on this sofa, with waistband relaxed, why not be cheerfully resigned to one's fate, nor peevishly pick holes in the blessed fate of the world?'

Upon this, the good merchant, after staring long and hard, and then rubbing his forehead, fell into meditation, at first uneasy, but at last composed, and in the end, once more addressed his companion: 'Well, I see it's good to out with one's private thoughts now and then. Somehow, I don't know why, a certain misty suspiciousness seems inseparable from most of one's private notions about some men and some things; but once out with these misty notions, and their mere contact with other men's soon dissipates, or, at least, modifies them.'

'You think I have done you good, then? may be, I have. But don't thank me, don't thank me. If by words, casually delivered in the social hour, I do any good to right or left, it is but involuntary influence – locust-tree sweetening the herbage under it; no merit at all; mere wholesome accident, of a wholesome nature. – Don't you see?'

Another stare from the good merchant, and both were silent again.

Finding his book, hitherto resting on his lap, rather irksome there, the owner now places it edgewise on the settee, between himself and neighbour; in so doing, chancing to expose the lettering on the back – *Black Rapids Coal Company* – which the good merchant, scrupulously honourable, had much ado to avoid reading, so directly would it have fallen under his eye, had he not conscientiously averted it. On a sudden, as if just reminded of something, the stranger starts up, and moves away, in his haste leaving his book; which the merchant observing, without delay takes it up, and, hurrying after, civilly returns it; in which act he could not avoid catching sight by an involuntary glance of part of the lettering.

'Thank you, thank you, my good sir,' said the other, receiving the volume, and was resuming his retreat, when the merchant spoke: 'Excuse me, but are you not in some way connected with the – the Coal Company I have heard of?'

'There is more than one Coal Company that may be heard of, my good sir,' smiled the other, pausing with an expression of painful impatience, disinterestedly mastered.

'But you are connected with one in particular. – The "Black Rapids", are you not?'

'How did you find that out?'

'Well, sir, I have heard rather tempting information of your Company.'

'Who is your informant, pray?' somewhat coldly.

'A – a person by the name of Ringman.'

'Don't know him. But, doubtless, there are plenty who know our Company, whom our Company does not know; in the same way that one may know an individual, yet be unknown to him. – Known this Ringman long? Old friend, I suppose. – But pardon, I must leave you.'

'Stay, sir, that – that stock.'

'Stock?'

'Yes, it's a little irregular, perhaps, but –'

'Dear me, you don't think of doing any business with me, do you? In my official capacity I have not been authenticated to you. This transfer-book, now,' holding it up so as to bring the lettering in sight, 'how do you know that it may not be a bogus one? And I, being personally a stranger to you, how can you have confidence in me?'

'Because,' knowingly smiled the good merchant, 'if you were other than I have confidence that you are, hardly would you challenge distrust that way.'

'But you have not examined my book.'

'What need to, if already I believe that it is what it is lettered to be?'

'But you had better. It might suggest doubts.'

'Doubts, may be, it might suggest, but not knowledge; for how, by examining the book, should I think I knew any more than I now think I do; since, if it be the true book, I think it so already; and since if it be otherwise, then I have never seen the true one, and don't know what that ought to look like.'

'Your logic I will not criticize, but your confidence I admire, and earnestly, too, jocose as was the method I took to draw it out. Enough, we will go to yonder table, and if there be any business which, either in my private or official capacity, I can help you do, pray command me.'

Chapter Eleven

Only a Page or So

The transaction concluded, the two still remained seated, falling into familiar conversation, by degrees verging into that confidential sort of sympathetic silence, the last refinement and luxury of unaffected good feeling. It is a kind of social superstition to suppose that to be truly friendly one must be saying friendly words all the time, any more than be doing friendly deeds continually; – true friendliness, like true religion, being in a sort independent of works.

At length, the good merchant, whose eyes were pensively resting upon the gay tables in the distance, broke the spell by saying that, from the spectacle before them, one would little divine what other quarters of the boat might reveal. He cited the case, accidentally encountered but an hour or two previous, of a shrunken old miser, clad in shrunken old moleskin, stretched out, an invalid, on a bare plank in the emigrants' quarters, eagerly clinging to life and lucre, though the one was gasping for outlet, and about the other he was in torment lest death, or some other unprincipled cut-purse, should be the means of his losing it; by like feeble tenure holding lungs and pouch, and yet knowing and desiring nothing beyond them; for his mind, never raised above mould, was now all but mouldered away; – to such a degree, indeed, that he had no trust in anything, not even in his parchment bonds, which, the better to preserve from the tooth of time, he had packed down and sealed up, like brandy peaches, in a tin case of spirits.

The worthy man proceeded at some length with these dispiriting particulars. Nor would his cheery companion wholly deny that there might be a point of view from which such a case of extreme want of confidence might, to the humane mind, present features not altogether welcome as wine and olives after dinner. Still, he was not without compensatory considerations, and, upon the whole, took his companion to task for evincing what, in a good-natured, round-about way, he hinted to be a somewhat jaundiced sentimentality. Nature, he added, in Shakespeare's words, had meal and bran; and, rightly regarded, the bran in its way was not to be condemned.

The other was not disposed to question the justice of Shakespeare's thought, but would hardly admit the propriety of the application in this instance, much less of the comment. So, after some further temperate discussion of the pitiable miser, finding that they could not entirely harmonize, the merchant cited another case, that of the negro cripple. But his companion suggested whether the alleged hardships of that alleged unfortunate might not exist more in the pity of the observer than the experience of the observed. He knew nothing about the cripple, nor had seen him, but ventured to surmise that, could one but get at the real state of his heart, he would be found about as happy as most men, if not, in fact, full as happy as the speaker himself. He added that negroes were by nature a singularly cheerful race; no one ever heard of a native-born African Zimmermann or Torquemada; that even from religion they dismissed all gloom; in their hilarious rituals they danced, so to speak, and, as it were, cut pigeon-wings. It was improbable, therefore, that a negro, however reduced to his stumps by fortune, could be ever thrown off the legs of a laughing philosophy.

Foiled again, the good merchant would not desist, but ventured still a third case, that of the man with the weed, whose story, as narrated by himself, and confirmed and filled out by the testimony of a certain man in a gray coat, whom the merchant had afterwards met, he now proceeded to give; and that without holding back those particulars disclosed by the second informant, but which delicacy had prevented the unfortunate man himself from touching upon.

But as the good merchant could, perhaps, do better justice to the man than the story, we shall venture to tell it in other words than his, though not to any other effect.

Chapter Twelve

*Story of the Unfortunate Man, From Which May Be Gathered
Whether or No He Has Been Justly so Entitled*

It appeared that the unfortunate man had had for a wife one of
those natures, anomalously vicious, which would almost tempt a
metaphysical lover of our species to doubt whether the human
form be, in all cases, conclusive evidence of humanity, whether,
sometimes, it may not be a kind of unpledged and indifferent
tabernacle, and whether, once for all to crush the saying of Thra-
sea (an unaccountable one, considering that he himself was so
good a man), that 'he who hates vice, hates humanity', it should
not, in self-defence, be held for a reasonable maxim, that none
but the good are human.

Goneril was young, in person lithe and straight, too straight,
indeed, for a woman, a complexion naturally rosy, and which
would have been charmingly so, but for a certain hardness and
bakedness, like that of the glazed colours on stone-ware. Her
hair was of a deep, rich chestnut, but worn in close, short curls all
round her head. Her Indian figure was not without its impairing
effect on her bust, while her mouth would have been pretty but
for a trace of moustache. Upon the whole, aided by the resources
of the toilet, her appearance at a distance was such, that some
might have thought her, if anything, rather beautiful, though of
a style of beauty rather peculiar and cactus-like.

It was happy for Goneril that her more striking peculiarities
were less of the person than of temper and taste. One hardly
knows how to reveal, that, while having a natural antipathy to
such things as the breast of chicken, or custard, or peach, or
grape, Goneril could yet in private make a satisfactory lunch on
hard crackers and brawn of ham. She liked lemons, and the only

70

kind of candy she loved were little dried sticks of blue clay, secretly carried in her pocket. Withal she had hard, steady health like a squaw's, with as firm a spirit and resolution. Some other points about her were likewise such as pertain to the women of savage life. Lithe though she was, she loved supineness, but upon occasion could endure like a stoic. She was taciturn, too. From early morning till about three o'clock in the afternoon she would seldom speak – it taking that time to thaw her, by all accounts, into but talking terms with humanity. During the interval she did little but look, and keep looking out of her large metallic eyes, which her enemies called cold as a cuttle-fish's, but which by her were esteemed gazelle-like; for Goneril was not without vanity. Those who thought they best knew her, often wondered what happiness such a being could take in life, considering the happiness which is to be had by some natures in the very easy way of simply causing pain to those around them. Those who suffered from Goneril's strange nature might, with one of those hyperboles to which the resentful incline, have pronounced her some kind of toad; but her worst slanderers could never, with any show of justice, have accused her of being a toady. In a large sense she possessed the virtue of independence of mind. Goneril held it flattery to hint praise even of the absent, and even if merited; but honesty, to fling people's imputed faults into their faces. This was thought malice, but it certainly was not passion. Passion is human. Like an icicle-dagger, Goneril at once stabbed and froze; so at least they said; and when she saw frankness and innocence tyrannized into sad nervousness under her spell, according to the same authority, inly she chewed her blue clay, and you could mark that she chuckled. These peculiarities were strange and unpleasing; but another was alleged, one really incomprehensible. In company she had a strange way of touching, as by accident, the hand or arm of comely young men, and seemed to reap a secret delight from it, but whether from the humane satisfaction of having given the evil-touch, as it is called, or whether it was something else in her, not equally wonderful, but quite as deplorable, remained an enigma.

Needless to say what distress was the unfortunate man's, when, engaged in conversation with company, he would suddenly perceive his Goneril bestowing her mysterious touches, especially in such cases where the strangeness of the thing seemed to strike upon the touched person, notwithstanding good-breeding forbade his proposing the mystery, on the spot, as a subject of discussion for the company. In these cases, too, the unfortunate man could never endure so much as to look upon the touched young gentleman afterwards, fearful of the mortification of meeting in his countenance some kind of more or less quizzingly knowing expression. He would shudderingly shun the young gentleman. So that here, to the husband, Goneril's touch had the dread operation of the heathen taboo. Now Goneril brooked no chiding. So, at favourable times, he, in a wary manner, and not indelicately, would venture in private interviews gently to make distant allusions to this questionable propensity. She divined him. But, in her cold loveless way, said it was witless to be telling one's dreams, especially foolish ones; but if the unfortunate man liked connubially to rejoice his soul with such chimeras, much connubial joy might they give him. All this was sad – a touching case – but all might, perhaps, have been borne by the unfortunate man – conscientiously mindful of his vow – for better or for worse – to love and cherish his dear Goneril so long as kind heaven might spare her to him – but when, after all that had happened, the devil of jealousy entered her, a calm, clayey, cakey devil, for none other could possess her, and the object of that deranged jealousy, her own child, a little girl of seven, her father's consolation and pet; when he saw Goneril artfully torment the little innocent, and then play the maternal hypocrite with it, the unfortunate man's patient long-suffering gave way. Knowing that she would neither confess nor amend, and might, possibly, become even worse than she was, he thought it but duty, as a father, to withdraw the child from her; but, loving it as he did, he could not do so without accompanying it into domestic exile himself. Which, hard though it was, he did. Whereupon the whole female neighbourhood, who till now had little enough admired dame Goneril, broke out in indignation against a husband who, without assigning a cause, could deliberately abandon the wife of his bosom, and sharpen the sting to her, too, by depriving her of the solace of retaining her offspring. To all this, self-respect, with Christian charity towards Goneril, long kept the unfortunate man dumb. And well had it been had he continued so; for when, driven to desperation, he hinted something of the truth of the case, not a soul would credit it; while for Goneril, she pronounced all he said to be a malicious invention.

Ere long, at the suggestion of some woman's-rights women, the injured wife began a suit, and, thanks to able counsel and accommodating testimony, succeeded in such a way, as not only to recover custody of the child, but to get such a settlement awarded upon a separation, as to make penniless the unfortunate man (so he averred), besides, through the legal sympathy she enlisted, effecting a judicial blasting of his private reputation. What made it yet more lamentable was, that the unfortunate man, thinking that, before the court, his wisest plan, as well as the most Christian besides, being, as he deemed, not at variance with the truth of the matter, would be to put forth the plea of the mental derangement of Goneril, which done, he could, with less of mortification to himself, and odium to her, reveal in self-defence those eccentricities which had led to his retirement from the joys of wedlock, had much ado in the end to prevent this charge of derangement from fatally recoiling upon himself – especially, when, among other things, he alleged her mysterious touchings. In vain did his counsel, striving to make out the derangement to be where, in fact, if anywhere, it was, urge that, to hold otherwise, to hold that such a being as Goneril was sane, this was constructively a libel upon womankind. Libel be it. And all ended by the unfortunate man's subsequently getting wind of Goneril's intention to procure him to be permanently committed for a lunatic. Upon which he fled, and was now an innocent outcast, wandering forlorn in the great valley of the Mississippi, with a weed on his hat for the loss of his Goneril; for he had lately seen by the papers that she was dead, and thought it but proper to comply with the prescribed form of mourning in such cases. For some days past he had been trying to get money enough to return to his child, and was but now started with inadequate funds.

Now all of this, from the beginning, the good merchant could not but consider rather hard for the unfortunate man.

Chapter Thirteen

*The Man With the Travelling-cap Evinces Much Humanity,
and in a Way Which Would Seem to Show Him to Be
One of the Most Logical of Optimists*

Years ago, a grave American *savan*, being in London, observed at an evening party there, a certain coxcombical fellow, as he thought, an absurd ribbon in his lapel, and full of smart persiflage, whisking about to the admiration of as many as were disposed to admire. Great was the *savan*'s disdain; but, chancing ere long to find himself in a corner with the jackanapes, got into conversation with him, when he was somewhat ill-prepared for the good sense of the jackanapes, but was altogether thrown aback, upon subsequently being whispered by a friend, that the jackanapes was almost as great a *savan* as himself, being no less a personage than Sir Humphry Davy.

The above anecdote is given just here by way of an anticipative reminder to such readers as, from the kind of jaunty levity, or what may have passed for such, hitherto for the most part appearing in the man with the travelling-cap, may have been tempted into a more or less hasty estimate of him; that such readers, when they find the same person, as they presently will, capable of philosophic and humanitarian discourse – no mere casual sentence or two as heretofore at times, but solidly sustained throughout an almost entire sitting; that they may not, like the American *savan*, be thereupon betrayed into any surprise incompatible with their own good opinion of their previous penetration.

The merchant's narration being ended, the other would not deny but that it did in some degree affect him. He hoped he was not without proper feeling for the unfortunate man. But he begged to know in what spirit he bore his alleged calamities. Did he despond or have confidence?

The merchant did not, perhaps, take the exact import of the last member of the question; but answered, that, if whether the unfortunate man was becomingly resigned under his affliction or no, was the point, he could say for him that resigned he was, and to an exemplary degree: for not only, so far as known, did he refrain from any one-sided reflections upon human goodness and human justice, but there was observable in him an air of chastened reliance, and at times tempered cheerfulness.

Upon which the other observed, that since the unfortunate man's alleged experience could not be deemed very conciliatory towards a view of human nature better than human nature was, it largely redounded to his fair-mindedness, as well as piety, that under the alleged dissuasives, apparently so, from philanthropy, he had not, in a moment of excitement, been warped over to the ranks of the misanthropes. He doubted not, also, that with such a man his experience would, in the end, act by a complete and beneficent inversion, and so far from shaking his confidence in his kind, confirm it, and rivet it. Which would the more surely be the case, did he (the unfortunate man) at last become satisfied (as sooner or later he probably would be) that in the distraction of his mind his Goneril had not in all respects had fair play. At all events, the description of the lady, charity could not but regard as more or less exaggerated, and so far unjust. The truth probably was that she was a wife with some blemishes mixed with some beauties. But when the blemishes were displayed, her husband, no adept in the female nature, had tried to use reason with her, instead of something more persuasive. Hence his failure to convince and convert. The act of withdrawing from her seemed, under the circumstances, abrupt. In brief, there were probably small faults on both sides, more than balanced by large virtues; and one should not be hasty in judging.

When the merchant, strange to say, opposed views so calm

and impartial, and again, with some warmth, deplored the case of the unfortunate man, his companion, not without serious-ness, checked him, saying, that this would never do; that though but in the most exceptional case, to admit the existence of unmer-ited misery, more particularly if alleged to have been brought about by unhindered arts of the wicked, such an admission was, to say the least, not prudent; since, with some, it might unfavourably bias their most important persuasions. Not that those persuasions were legitimately servile to such influences. Because, since the common occurrences of life could never, in the nature of things, steadily look one way and tell one story, as flags in the trade-wind; hence, if the conviction of a Providence, for instance, were in any way made dependent upon such varia-bilities as everyday events, the degree of that conviction would, in thinking minds, be subject to fluctuations akin to those of the stock-exchange during a long and uncertain war. Here he glanced aside at his transfer-book, and after a moment's pause continued. It was of the essence of a right conviction of the divine nature, as with a right conviction of the human, that, based less on experi-ence than intuition, it rose above the zones of weather.

When now the merchant, with all his heart, coincided with this (as being a sensible, as well as religious person, he could not but do), his companion expressed satisfaction, that, in an age of some distrust on such subjects, he could yet meet with one who shared with him, almost to the full, so sound and sublime a con-fidence.

Still, he was far from the illiberality of denying that philosophy duly bounded was not permissible. Only he deemed it at least desirable that when such a case as that alleged of the unfortunate man was made the subject of philosophic discussion, it should be so philosophized upon, as not to afford handles to those unblessed with the true light. For, but to grant that there was so much as a mystery about such a case, might by those persons be held for a tacit surrender of the question. And as for the apparent licence temporarily permitted sometimes, to the bad over the good (as was by implication alleged with regard to Goneril and the unfortunate man), it might be injudicious there to lay too much polemic stress upon the doctrine of future retribution as the vindication of present impunity. For though, indeed, to the right-minded that doctrine was true, and of sufficient solace, yet with the perverse the polemic mention of it might but provoke the shallow, though mischievous conceit, that such a doctrine was but tantamount to the one which should affirm that Providence was not now, but was going to be. In short, will all sorts of cavillers, it was best, both for them and everybody, that whoever had the true light should stick behind the secure Malakoff of confidence, nor be tempted forth to hazardous skirmishes on the open ground of reason. Therefore, he deemed it unadvisable in the good man, even in the privacy of his own mind, or in communion with a congenial one, to indulge in too much latitude of philosophizing, or, indeed, of compassionating, since this might beget an indiscreet habit of thinking and feeling which might unexpectedly betray him upon unsuitable occasions. Indeed, whether in private or public, there was nothing which a good man was more bound to guard himself against than, on some topics, the emotional unreserve of his natural heart; for, that the natural heart in certain points was not what it might be, men had been authoritatively admonished.

But he thought he might be getting dry.

The merchant, in his good-nature, thought otherwise, and said that he would be glad to refresh himself with such fruit all day. It was sitting under a ripe pulpit, and better such a seat than under a ripe peach-tree.

The other was pleased to find that he had not, as he feared, been prosing; but would rather not be considered in the formal light of a preacher; he preferred being still received in that of the equal and genial companion. To which end, throwing still more of sociability into his manner, he again reverted to the unfortunate man. Take the very worst view of that case: admit that his Goneril was, indeed, a Goneril; how fortunate to be at last rid of this Goneril, both by nature and by law! If he were acquainted with the unfortunate man, instead of condoling with him, he would congratulate him. Great good fortune had this unfortunate man. Lucky dog, he dared say, after all.

To which the merchant replied, that he earnestly hoped it might be so, and at any rate he tried his best to comfort himself with the persuasion that if the unfortunate man was not happy in this world, he would, at least, be so in another.

His companion made no question of the unfortunate man's happiness in both worlds; and presently calling for some champagne, invited the merchant to partake, upon the playful plea that, whatever notions other than felicitous ones he might associate with the unfortunate man, a little champagne would readily bubble away.

At intervals they slowly quaffed several glasses in silence and thoughtfulness. At last the merchant's expressive face flushed, his eye moistly beamed, his lips trembled with an imaginative and feminine sensibility. Without sending a single fume to his head, the wine seemed to shoot to his heart, and begin soothsaying there. 'Ah,' he cried, pushing his glass from him, 'ah, wine is good, and confidence is good; but can wine or confidence percolate down through all the stony strata of hard considerations, and drop warmly and ruddily into the cold cave of truth? Truth will *not* be comforted. Led by dear charity, lured by sweet hope, fond fancy essays this feat; but in vain; mere dreams and ideals, they explode in your hand, leaving nought but the scorching behind!'

'Why, why, why!' in amaze, at the burst; 'bless me, if *In vino veritas* be a true saying, then, for all the fine confidence you professed with me, just now, distrust, deep distrust, underlies it; and ten thousand strong, like the Irish Rebellion, breaks out in you now. That wine, good wine, should do it! Upon my soul,' half seriously, half humorously, securing the bottle, 'you shall drink no more of it. Wine was meant to gladden the heart, not grieve it; to heighten confidence, not depress it.'

Sobered, shamed, all but confounded, by this raillery, the most telling rebuke under such circumstances, the merchant stared about him, and then, with altered mien, stammeringly confessed, that he was almost as much surprised as his companion, at what had escaped him. He did not understand it; was quite at a loss to account for such a rhapsody popping out of him unbidden. It could hardly be the champagne; he felt his brain unaffected; in fact, if anything, the wine had acted upon it something like white of egg in coffee, clarifying and brightening.

'Brightening? brightening it may be, but less like the white of egg in coffee, than like stove-lustre on a stove – black, brightening. Seriously, I repent calling for the champagne. To a temperament like yours, champagne is not to be recommended. Pray, my dear sir, do you feel quite yourself again? Confidence restored?'

'I hope so; I think I may say it is so. But we have had a long talk, and I think I must retire now.'

So saying, the merchant rose, and making his adieus, left the table with the air of one, mortified at having been tempted by his own honest goodness, accidentally stimulated into making mad disclosures – to himself as to another – of the queer, unaccountable caprices of his natural heart.

Chapter Fourteen

Worth the Consideration of Those to Whom it May Prove Worth Considering

As the last chapter was begun with a reminder looking forwards, so the present must consist of one glancing backwards.

To some, it may raise a degree of surprise that one so full of confidence, as the merchant has throughout shown himself, up to the moment of his late sudden impulsiveness, should, in that instance, have betrayed such a depth of discontent. He may be thought inconsistent, and even so he is. But for this is the author to be blamed? True, it may be urged that there is nothing a writer of fiction should more carefully see to, as there is nothing a sensible reader will more carefully look for, than that, in the depicting of any character, its consistency should be preserved. But this, though at first blush, seeming reasonable enough, may, upon a closer view, prove not so much so. For how does it couple with another requirement – equally insisted upon, perhaps – that, while to all fiction is allowed some play of invention, yet, fiction based on fact should never be contradictory to it; and is it not a fact, that, in real life, a consistent character is a *rara avis*? Which being so, the distaste of readers to the contrary sort in books can hardly arise from any sense of their untrueness. It may rather be from perplexity as to understanding them. But if the acutest sage be often at his wits' ends to understand living character, shall those who are not sages expect to run and read character in those mere phantoms which flit along a page like shadows along a wall? That fiction, where every character can, by reason of its consistency, be comprehended at a glance, either exhibits but sections of character, making them appear for wholes, or else is very untrue to reality; while, on the other hand, that author who draws a character, even though to common view incongruous in its parts, as the flying-squirrel, and, at different periods, as much at variance with itself as the caterpillar is with the butterfly into which it changes, may yet, in so doing, be not false but faithful to facts.

If reason be judge, no writer has produced such inconsistent characters as nature herself has. It must call for no small sagacity in a reader unerringly to discriminate in a novel between the inconsistencies of conception and those of life. As elsewhere, experience is the only guide here; but as no one man's experience can be coextensive with *what is*, it may be unwise in every case to rest upon it. When the duck-billed beaver of Australia was first brought stuffed to England, the naturalists, appealing to their classifications, maintained that there was, in reality, no such creature; the bill in the specimen must needs be, in some way, artificially stuck on.

But let nature, to the perplexity of the naturalists, produce her duck-billed beavers as she may, lesser authors, some may hold, have no business to be perplexing readers with duck-billed characters. Always, they should represent human nature not in obscurity, but transparency, which, indeed, is the practice with most novelists, and is, perhaps, in certain cases, someway felt to be a kind of honour rendered by them to their kind. But whether it involve honour or otherwise might be mooted, considering that, if these waters of human nature can be so readily seen through, it may be either that they are very pure or very shallow. Upon the whole, it might rather be thought, that he, who, in view of its inconsistencies, says of human nature the same that, in view of its contrasts, is said of the divine nature, that it is past finding out, thereby evinces a better appreciation of it than he who, by always representing it in a clear light, leaves it to be inferred that he clearly knows all about it.

But though there is a prejudice against inconsistent characters in books, yet the prejudice bears the other way, when what seemed at first their inconsistency, afterwards, by the skill of the writer, turns out to be their good keeping. The great masters excel in nothing so much as in this very particular. They challenge astonishment at the tangled web of some character, and then raise admiration still greater at their satisfactory unravelling of it; in this way throwing open, sometimes to the understanding even of school misses, the last complications of that spirit which is affirmed by its Creator to be fearfully and wonderfully made.

At least something like this is claimed for certain psychological novelists; nor will the claim be here disputed. Yet, as touching this point, it may prove suggestive, that all those sallies of ingenuity, having for their end the revelation of human nature on fixed principles, have, by the best judges, been excluded with contempt from the ranks of the sciences – palmistry, physiognomy, phrenology, psychology. Likewise, the fact, that in all ages such conflicting views have, by the most eminent minds, been taken of mankind, would, as with other topics, seem some presumption of a pretty general and pretty thorough ignorance of it, – which may appear the less improbable if it be considered that, after poring over the best novels professing to portray human nature, the studious youth will still run risk of being too often at fault upon actually entering the world; whereas, had he been furnished with a true delineation, it ought to fare with him somewhat as with a stranger entering, map in hand, Boston town; the streets may be very crooked, he may often pause; but, thanks to his true map, he does not hopelessly lose his way. Nor, to this comparison, can it be an adequate objection, that the twistings of the town are always the same, and those of human nature subject to variation. The grand points of human nature are the same to-day they were a thousand years ago. The only variability in them is in expression, not in feature.

But as, in spite of seeming discouragement, some mathematicians are yet in hopes of hitting upon an exact method of determining the longitude, the more earnest psychologists may, in the face of previous failures, still cherish expectations with regard to some mode of infallibly discovering the heart of man.

But enough has been said by way of apology for whatever may have seemed amiss or obscure in the character of the merchant; so nothing remains but to turn to our comedy, or, rather, to pass from the comedy of thought to that of action.

Chapter Fifteen

An Old Miser, Upon Suitable Representations, is Prevailed Upon to Venture an Investment

The merchant having withdrawn, the other remained seated alone for a time, with the air of one who, after having conversed with some excellent man, carefully ponders what fell from him, however intellectually inferior it may be, that none of the profit may be lost; happy if from any honest word he has heard he can derive some hint, which, besides confirming him in the theory of virtue, may, likewise, serve for a finger-post to virtuous action.

Ere long his eye brightened, as if some such hint was now caught. He rises, book in hand, quits the cabin, and enters upon a sort of corridor, narrow and dim, a by-way to a retreat less ornate and cheery than the former; in short, the emigrants' quarters; but which, owing to the present trip being a down-river one, will doubtless be found comparatively tenantless. Owing to obstructions against the side windows, the whole place is dim and dusky; very much so, for the most part; yet, by starts, haggardly lit here and there by narrow, capricious skylights in the cornices. But there would seem no special need for light, the place being designed more to pass the night in, than the day; in brief, a pine barrens dormitory, of knotty pine bunks, without bedding. As with the nests in the geometrical towns of the associate penguin and pelican, these bunks were disposed with Philadelphian regularity, but, like the cradle of the oriole, they were pendulous, and moreover, were, so to speak, three-story cradles; the description of one of which will suffice for all.

Four ropes, secured to the ceiling, passed downwards through auger-holes bored in the corners of three rough planks, which at equal distances rested on knots vertically tied in the ropes, the lowermost plank but an inch or two from the floor, the whole affair resembling, on a large scale, rope book-shelves; only, instead of hanging firmly against a wall, they swayed to and fro at the least suggestion of motion, but were more especially lively upon the provocation of a green emigrant sprawling into one, and trying to lay himself out there, when the cradling would be such as almost to toss him back whence he came. In consequence, one less inexperienced, essaying repose on the uppermost shelf, was liable to serious disturbance, should a raw beginner select a shelf beneath. Sometimes a throng of poor emigrants, coming at night in a sudden rain to occupy these oriole nests, would – through ignorance of their peculiarity – bring about such a rocking uproar of carpentry, joining to it such an uproar of exclamations, that it seemed as if some luckless ship, with all its crew, was being dashed to pieces among the rocks. They were beds devised by some sardonic foe of poor travellers, to deprive them of that tranquillity which should precede, as well as accompany, slumber. Procrustean beds, on whose hard grain humble worth and honesty writhed, still invoking repose, while but torment responded. Ah, did any one make such a bunk for himself, instead of having it made for him, it might be just, but how cruel, to say, You must lie on it!

But, purgatory as the place would appear, the stranger advances into it; and, like Orpheus in his gay descent to Tartarus, lightly hums to himself an opera snatch.

Suddenly there is a rustling, then a creaking, one of the cradles swings out from a murky nook, a sort of wasted penguin-flipper is supplicatingly put forth, while a wail like that of Dives is heard: 'Water, water!'

It was the miser of whom the merchant had spoken.

Swift as a sister-of-charity, the stranger hovers over him:

'My poor, poor sir, what can I do for you?'

'Ugh, ugh – water!'

Darting out, he procures a glass, returns, and, holding it to the sufferer's lips, supports his head while he drinks: 'And did they let you lie here, my poor sir, racked with this parching thirst?'

The miser, a lean old man, whose flesh seemed salted cod-fish, dry as combustibles; head, like one whittled by an idiot out of a knot; flat, bony mouth, nipped between buzzard nose and chin; expression, flitting between hunks and imbecile – now one, now the other – he made no response. His eyes were closed, his cheek lay upon an old white moleskin coat, rolled under his head like a wizened apple upon a grimy snow-bank.

Revived at last, he inclined towards his ministrant, and, in a voice disastrous with a cough, said: 'I am old and miserable, a poor beggar, not worth a shoe-string – how can I repay you?'

'By giving me your confidence.'

'Confidence!' he squeaked, with changed manner, while the pallet swung, 'little left at my age, but take the stale remains, and welcome.'

'Such as it is, though, you give it. Very good. Now give me a hundred dollars.'

Upon this the miser was all panic. His hands groped towards his waist, then suddenly flew upward beneath his moleskin pillow, and there lay clutching something out of sight. Meantime, to himself he incoherently mumbled: 'Confidence? Cant, gammon! Confidence? hum, bubble! – Confidence? fetch, gouge! – Hundred dollars? – hundred devils!'

Half spent, he lay mute awhile, then feebly raising himself, in a voice for the moment made strong by the sarcasm, said, 'A hundred dollars? rather high price to put upon confidence. But don't you see I am a poor, old rat here, dying in the wainscot? You have served me; but, wretch that I am, I can but cough you my thanks, – ugh, ugh, ugh!'

This time his cough was so violent that its convulsions were imparted to the plank, which swung him about like a stone in a sling preparatory to its being hurled.

'Ugh, ugh, ugh!'

'What a shocking cough. I wish, my friend, the herb-doctor was here now; a box of his Omni-Balsamic Reinvigorator would do you good.'

'Ugh, ugh, ugh!'

'I've a good mind to go find him. He's aboard somewhere. I saw his long, snuff-coloured surtout. Trust me, his medicines are the best in the world.'

'Ugh, ugh, ugh!'

'Oh, how sorry I am.'

'No doubt of it,' squeaked the other again, 'but go, get your charity out on deck. There parade the pursy peacocks; they don't cough down here in desertion and darkness, like poor old me. Look how scaly a pauper I am, clove with this churchyard cough. Ugh, ugh, ugh!'

'Again, how sorry I feel, not only for your cough, but your poverty. Such a rare chance made unavailable. Did you have but the sum named, how I could invest it for you. Treble profits. But confidence – I fear that, even had you the precious cash, you would not have the more precious confidence I speak of.'

'Ugh, ugh, ugh!' flightingly raising himself. 'What's that? How, how? Then you don't want the money for yourself?'

'My dear, *dear* sir, how could you impute to me such preposterous self-seeking? To solicit out of hand, for my private behoof, a hundred dollars from a perfect stranger? I am not mad, my dear sir.'

'How, how?' still more bewildered, 'do you, then, go about the world, gratis, seeking to invest people's money for them?'

'My humble profession, sir. I live not for myself; but the world will not have confidence in me, and yet confidence in me were great gain.'

'But, but,' in a kind of vertigo, 'what do – do you do – do with people's money? Ugh, ugh! How is the gain made?'

'To tell that would ruin me. That known, every one would be going into the business, and it would be overdone. A secret, a mystery – all I have to do with you is to receive your confidence, and all you have to do with me is, in due time, to receive it back, thrice paid in trebling profits.'

'What, what?' imbecility in the ascendant once more; 'but the vouchers, the vouchers,' suddenly hunkish again.

'Honesty's best voucher is honesty's face.'

'Can't see yours, though,' peering through the obscurity.

From this last alternating flicker of rationality, the miser fell back, sputtering, into his previous gibberish, but it took now an arithmetical turn. Eyes closed, he lay muttering to himself –

'One hundred, one hundred – two hundred, two hundred – three hundred, three hundred.'

He opened his eyes, feebly stared, and still more feebly said –

'It's a little dim here, ain't it? Ugh, ugh! But, as well as my poor old eyes can see, you look honest.'

'I am glad to hear that.'

'If – if, now, I should put' – trying to raise himself, but vainly, excitement having all but exhausted him – 'if, if now, I should put, put –'

'No ifs. Downright confidence, or none. So help me heaven, I will have no half-confidences.'

He said it with an indifferent and superior air, and seemed moving to go.

'Don't, don't leave me, friend; bear with me; age can't help some distrust; it can't friend, it can't. Ugh, ugh, ugh! Oh, I am so old and miserable. I ought to have a guard*ee*an. Tell me, if –'

'If? No more!'

'Stay! how soon – ugh, ugh! – would my money be trebled? How soon, friend?'

'You won't confide. Good-bye!'

'Stay, stay,' falling back now like an infant, 'I confide, I confide; help, friend, my distrust!'

From an old buckskin pouch, tremulously dragged forth, ten hoarded eagles, tarnished into the appearance of ten old horn-buttons, were taken, and half-eagerly, half-reluctantly, offered.

'I know not whether I should accept this slack confidence,' said the other coldly, receiving the gold, 'but an eleventh-hour confidence, a sick-bed confidence, a distempered, death-bed confidence, after all. Give me the healthy confidence of healthy men, with their healthy wits about them. But let that pass. All right. Goodbye!'

'Nay, back, back – receipt, my receipt! Ugh, ugh, ugh! Who are you? What have I done? Where go you? My gold, my gold! Ugh, ugh, ugh!'

But, unluckily for this final flicker of reason, the stranger was now beyond ear-shot, nor was any one else within hearing of so feeble a call.

Chapter Sixteen

A Sick Man, After Some Impatience, is Induced
to Become a Patient

The sky slides into blue, the bluffs into bloom, the rapid Mississippi expands; runs sparkling and gurgling all over in eddies; one magnified wake of a seventy-four. The sun comes out, a golden hussar, from his tent, flashing his helm on the world. All things, warmed in the landscape, leap. Speeds the daedal boat as a dream.

But, withdrawn in a corner, wrapped about in a shawl, sits an unparticipating man, visited, but not warmed, by the sun – a plant whose hour seems over while buds are blowing and seeds are astir. On a stool at his left sits a stranger in a snuff-coloured surtout, the collar thrown back, his hand waving in persuasive gesture, his eye beaming with hope. But not easily may hope be awakened in one long tranced into hopelessness by a chronic complaint.

To some remark the sick man, by word or look, seemed to have just made an impatiently querulous answer, when, with a deprecatory air, the other resumed:

'Nay, think not I seek to cry up my treatment by crying down that of others. And yet, when one is confident he has truth on his side, and that it is not on the other, it is no very easy thing to be charitable; not that temper is the bar, but conscience; for charity would beget toleration, you know, which is a kind of implied permitting, and in effect a kind of countenancing; and that which is countenanced is so far furthered. But should untruth be furthered? Still, while for the world's good I refuse to further the cause of these mineral doctors, I would fain regard them, not as wilful wrong-doers, but good Samaritans erring. And is this – I put it to you, sir – is this the view of an arrogant rival and pretender?'

His physical power all dribbled and gone, the sick man replied not by voice or by gesture; but, with feeble dumb-show of his face, seemed to be saying, 'Pray leave me; who was ever cured by talk?'

But the other, as if not unused to make allowances for such despondency, proceeded; and kindly, yet firmly:

'You tell me, that by advice of an eminent physiologist in Louisville, you took tincture of iron. For what? To restore your lost energy. And how? Why, in healthy subjects iron is naturally found in the blood, and iron in the bar is strong; ergo, iron is the source of animal invigoration. But you being deficient in vigour, it follows that the cause is deficiency of iron. Iron, then, must be put into you; and so your tincture. Now as to the theory here, I am mute. But in modesty assuming its truth, and then, as a plain man viewing that theory in practice, I would respectfully question your eminent physiologist: "Sir," I would say, "though by natural processes, lifeless natures taken as nutriment become vitalized, yet is a lifeless nature, under any circumstances, capable of a living transmission, with all its qualities as a lifeless nature unchanged? If, sir, nothing can be incorporated with the living body but by assimilation, and if that implies the conversion of one thing to a different thing (as, in a lamp, oil is assimilated into flame), is it, in this view, likely, that by banquetting on fat, Calvin Edson will fatten? That is, will what is fat on the board prove fat on the bones? If it will, then, sir, what is iron in the vial will prove iron in the vein." Seems that conclusion too confident?'

But the sick man again turned his dumb-show look, as much as to say, 'Pray leave me. Why, with painful words, hint the vanity of that which the pains of this body have too painfully proved?'

But the other, as if unobservant of that querulous look, went on:

'But this notion, that science can play farmer to the flesh, making there what living soil it pleases, seems not so strange as that other conceit – that science is now-a-days so expert, that in consumptive cases, as yours, it can, by prescription of the inhalation of certain vapours, achieve the sublimest act of omnipotence, breathing into all but lifeless dust the breath of life. For did you not tell me, my poor sir, that by order of the great chemist in Baltimore, for three weeks you were never driven out without a respirator, and for a given time of every day sat bolstered up in a sort of gasometer, inspiring vapours generated by the burning of drugs? as if this concocted atmosphere of man were an antidote to the poison of God's natural air. Oh, who can wonder at that old reproach against science, that it is atheistical? And here is my prime reason for opposing these chemical practitioners, who have sought out so many inventions. For what do their inventions indicate, unless it be that kind and degree of pride in human skill, which seems scarce compatible with reverential dependence upon the power above? Try to rid my mind of it as I may, yet still these chemical practitioners with their tinctures, and fumes, and braziers, and occult incantations, seem to me like Pharaoh's vain sorcerers, trying to beat down the will of heaven. Day and night, in all charity, I intercede for them, that heaven may not, in its own language, be provoked to anger with their inventions; may not take vengeance of their inventions. A thousand pities that you should ever have been in the hands of these Egyptians.'

But again came nothing but the dumb-show look, as much as to say, 'Pray leave me; quacks, and indignation against quacks, both are vain.'

But, once more, the other went on: 'How different we herb-doctors! who claim nothing, invent nothing; but staff in hand, in glades, and upon hillsides, go about in nature, humbly seeking her cures. True Indian doctors, though not learned in names we are not unfamiliar with essences – successors of Solomon the Wise, who knew all vegetables, from the cedar of Lebanon, to the hyssop on the wall. Yes, Solomon was the first of herb-doctors. Nor were the virtues of herbs unhonoured by yet older ages. Is it not writ, that on a moonlight night,

"Medea gathered the enchanted herbs
That did renew old Aeson"?

Ah, would you but have confidence, you should be the new
Aeson, and I your Medea. A few vials of my Omni-Balsamic Reinvigorator would, I am certain, give you some strength.'

Upon this, indignation and abhorrence seemed to work by
their excess the effect promised of the balsam. Roused from that
long apathy of impotence, the cadaverous man started, and, in a
voice that was as the sound of obstructed air gurgling through a
maze of broken honey-combs, cried: 'Begone! You are all alike.
The name of doctor, the dream of helper, condemns you. For
years I have been but a gallipot for your experimentizers to rinse
your experiments into, and now, in this livid skin, partake of the
nature of my contents. Begone! I hate ye.'

'I were inhuman, could I take affront at a want of confidence,
born of too bitter an experience of betrayers. Yet, permit one
who is not without feeling –'

'Begone! Just in that voice talked to me, not six months ago,
the German doctor at the water cure, from which I now return,
six months and sixty pangs nigher my grave.'

'The water-cure? Oh, fatal delusion of the well-meaning
Priessnitz! – Sir, trust me –'

'Begone!'

'Nay, an invalid should not always have his own way. Ah, sir,
reflect how untimely this distrust in one like you. How weak you
are; and weakness, is it not the time for confidence? Yes, when
through weakness everything bids despair, then is the time to get
strength by confidence.'

Relenting in his air, the sick man cast upon him a long glance
of beseeching, as if saying, 'With confidence must come hope;
and how can hope be?'

The herb-doctor took a sealed paper box from his surtout
pocket, and holding it towards him, said solemnly, 'Turn not

away. This may be the last time of health's asking. Work upon yourself; invoke confidence, though from ashes; rouse it; for your life, rouse it, and invoke it, I say.'

The other trembled, was silent; and then, a little commanding himself, asked the ingredients of the medicine.

'Herbs.'

'What herbs? And the nature of them? And the reason for giving them?'

'It cannot be made known.'

'Then I will none of you.'

Sedately observant of the juiceless, joyless form before him, the herb-doctor was mute a moment, then said: 'I give up.'

'How?'

'You are sick, and a philosopher.'

'No, no – not the last.'

'But, to demand the ingredient, with the reason for giving, is the mark of a philosopher; just as the consequence is the penalty of a fool. A sick philosopher is incurable.'

'Why?'

'Because he has no confidence.'

'How does that make him incurable?'

'Because either he spurns his powder, or, if he take it, it proves a blank cartridge, though the same given to a rustic in like extremity, would act like a charm. I am no materialist; but the mind so acts upon the body, that if the one have no confidence, neither has the other.'

Again, the sick man appeared not unmoved. He seemed to be thinking what in candid truth could be said to all this. At length, 'You talk of confidence. How comes it that when brought low himself, the herb-doctor, who was most confident to prescribe in other cases, proves least confident to prescribe in his own; having small confidence in himself for himself?'

'But he has confidence in the brother he calls in. And that he does so, is no reproach to him, since he knows that when the body is prostrated, the mind is not erect. Yes, in this hour the herb-doctor does distrust himself, but not his art.'

The sick man's knowledge did not warrant him to gainsay this. But he seemed not grieved at it; glad to be confuted in a way tending towards his wish.

'Then you give me hope?' his sunken eye turned up.

'Hope is proportioned to confidence. How much confidence you give me, so much hope do I give you. For this,' lifting the box, 'if all depended upon this, I should rest. It is nature's own.'

'Nature!'

'Why do you start?'

'I know not,' with a sort of shudder, 'but I have heard of a book entitled "Nature in Disease".'

'A title I cannot approve; it is suspiciously scientific. "Nature in Disease"? As if nature, divine nature, were aught but health; as if through nature disease is decreed! But did I not before hint of the tendency of science, that forbidden tree? Sir, if despondency is yours from recalling that title, dismiss it. Trust me, nature is health; for health is good, and nature cannot work ill. As little can she work error. Get nature, and you get well. Now, I repeat, this medicine is nature's own.'

Again the sick man could not, according to his light, conscientiously disprove what was said. Neither, as before, did he seem over-anxious to do so; the less, as in his sensitiveness it seemed to him, that hardly could he offer so to do without something like the appearance of a kind of implied irreligion; nor in his heart was he ungrateful, that since a spirit opposite to that pervaded all the herb-doctor's hopeful words, therefore, for hopefulness, he (the sick man) had not alone medical warrant, but also doctrinal.

'Then you do really think,' hectically, 'that if I take this medicine,' mechanically reaching out for it, 'I shall regain my health?'

'I will not encourage false hopes,' relinquishing to him the box, 'I will be frank with you. Though frankness is not always the weakness of the mineral practitioner, yet the herb-doctor must be frank, or nothing. Now then, sir, in your case, a radical cure – such a cure, understand, as should make you robust – such a cure, sir, I do not and cannot promise.'

'Oh, you need not! only restore me the power of being something else to others than a burdensome care, and to myself a droning grief. Only cure me of this misery of weakness; only make me so that I can walk about in the sun and not draw the flies to me, as lured by the coming of decay. Only do that – but that.'

'You ask not much; you are wise; not in vain have you suffered. That little you ask, I think, can be granted. But remember, not in a day, nor a week, nor perhaps a month, but sooner or later; I say not exactly when, for I am neither prophet nor charlatan. Still, if, according to the directions in your box there, you take my medicine steadily, without assigning an especial day, near or remote, to discontinue it, then may you calmly look for some eventual result of good. But again I say, you must have confidence.'

Feverishly he replied that he now trusted he had, and hourly should pray for its increase. When suddenly relapsing into one of those strange caprices peculiar to some invalids, he added: 'But to one like me, it is so hard, so hard. The most confident hopes so often have failed me, and as often have I vowed never, no, never, to trust them again. Oh,' feebly wringing his hands, 'you do not know, you do not know.'

'I know this, that never did a right confidence come to nought. But time is short; you hold your cure, to retain or reject?'

'I retain,' with a clinch, 'and now how much?'

'As much as you can evoke from your heart and heaven.'

'How? – the price of this medicine?'

'I thought it was confidence you meant; how much confidence you should have. The medicine, – that is half a dollar a vial. Your box holds six.'

The money was paid.

'Now, sir,' said the herb-doctor, 'my business calls me away, and it may so be that I shall never see you again; if then –'

He paused, for the sick man's countenance fell blank.

'Forgive me,' cried the other, 'forgive that imprudent phrase "never see you again". Though I solely intended it with reference to myself, yet I had forgotten what your sensitiveness might be. I repeat, then, that it may be that we shall not soon have a second interview, so that hereafter, should another of my boxes be needed, you may not be able to replace it except by purchase at the shops; and in so doing, you may run more or less risk of taking some not salutary mixture. For such is the popularity of the Omni-Balsamic Reinvigorator – thriving not by the credulity of the simple, but the trust of the wise – that certain contrivers have not been idle, though I would not, indeed, hastily affirm of them that they are aware of the sad consequences to the public. Homicides and murderers, some call those contrivers; but I do not; for murder (if such a crime be possible) comes from the heart, and these men's motives come from the purse. Were they not in poverty, I think they would hardly do what they do. Still, the public interests forbid that I should let their needy device for a living succeed. In short, I have adopted precautions. Take the wrapper from any of my vials and hold it to the light, you will see watermarked in capitals the word *confidence*, which is the countersign of the medicine, as I wish it was of the world. The wrapper bears that mark or else the medicine is counterfeit. But if still any lurking doubt should remain, pray enclose the wrapper to this address,' handing a card, 'and by return mail I will answer.'

At first the sick man listened, with the air of vivid interest, but gradually, while the other was still talking, another strange caprice came over him, and he presented the aspect of the most calamitous dejection.

'How now?' said the herb-doctor.

'You told me to have confidence, said that confidence was indispensable, and here you preach to me distrust. Ah, truth will out!'

'I told you, you must have confidence, unquestioning confidence; I meant confidence in the genuine medicine, and the genuine *me*.'

'But in your absence, buying vials purporting to be yours, it seems I cannot have unquestioning confidence.'

'Prove all the vials; trust those which are true.'

'But to doubt, to suspect, to prove – to have all this wearing work to be doing continually – how opposed to confidence. It is evil!'

'From evil comes good. Distrust is a stage to confidence. How has it proved in our interview? But your voice is husky; I have let you talk too much. You hold your cure; I leave you. But stay – when I hear that health is yours, I will not, like some I know, vainly make boasts; but, giving glory where all glory is due, say, with the devout herb-doctor, Iapis in Virgil, when, in the unseen but efficacious presence of Venus, he with simples healed the wound of Aeneas:

> "This is no mortal work, no cure of mine,
> Nor art's effect, but done by power divine."'

Chapter Seventeen

Towards the End of Which the Herb-doctor Proves Himself a Forgiver of Injuries

In a kind of ante-cabin, a number of respectable looking people, male and female, way-passengers, recently come on board, are listlessly sitting in a mutually shy sort of silence.

Holding up a small, square bottle, ovally labelled with the engraving of a countenance full of soft pity as that of the Romish-painted Madonna, the herb-doctor passes slowly among them, benignly urbane, turning this way and that, saying:

'Ladies and gentlemen, I hold in my hand here the Samaritan Pain Dissuader, thrice-blessed discovery of that disinterested friend of humanity whose portrait you see. Pure vegetable extract. Warranted to remove the acutest pain within less than ten minutes. Five hundred dollars to be forfeited on failure. Especially efficacious in heart disease and tic-douloureux. Observe the expression of this pledged friend of humanity. – Price only fifty cents.'

In vain. After the first idle stare, his auditors, – in pretty good health, it seemed – instead of encouraging his politeness, appeared, if anything, impatient of it; and, perhaps, only diffidence, or some small regard for his feelings, prevented them from telling him so. But, insensible to their coldness, or charitably overlooking it, he more wooingly than ever resumed: 'May I venture upon a small supposition? Have I your kind leave, ladies and gentlemen?'

To which modest appeal, no one had the kindness to answer a syllable.

'Well,' said he, resignedly, 'silence is at least not denial, and may be consent. My supposition is this: Possibly some lady, here present, has a dear friend at home, a bed-ridden sufferer from spinal complaint. If so, what gift more appropriate to that sufferer than this tasteful little bottle of Pain Dissuader?'

Again he glanced about him, but met much the same reception as before. Those faces, alien alike to sympathy or surprise, seemed patiently to say, 'We are travellers; and, as such, must expect to meet, and quietly put up with, many antic fools, and more antic quacks.'

'Ladies and gentlemen,' (deferentially fixing his eyes upon their now self-complacent faces) 'ladies and gentlemen, might I, by your kind leave, venture upon one other small supposition? It is this: that there is scarce a sufferer, this noonday, writhing on his bed, but in his hour he sat satisfactorily healthy and happy; that the Samaritan Pain Dissuader is the one only balm for that to which each living creature – who knows? – may be a draughted victim, present or prospective. In short: – Oh, Happiness on my right hand, and oh, Security on my left, can ye wisely adore a Providence, and not think it wisdom to provide? – Provide!' (Uplifting the bottle.)

What immediate effect, if any, this appeal might have had, is uncertain. For just then the boat touched at a houseless landing, scooped, as by a land-slide, out of sombre forests; back through which led a road, the sole one, which, from its narrowness, and its being walled up with story on story of dusk, matted foliage, presented the vista of some cavernous old gorge in a city, like haunted Cock Lane in London. Issuing from that road, and crossing that landing, there stooped his shaggy form in the doorway, and entered the ante-cabin, with a step so burdensome that shot seemed in his pockets, a kind of invalid Titan in homespun; his beard blackly pendant, like the Carolina-moss, and dank with cypress dew; his countenance tawny and shadowy as an iron-ore country in a clouded day. In one hand he carried a heavy walking-stick of swamp-oak; with the other, led a puny girl, walking in moccasins, not improbably his child, but evidently of alien maternity, perhaps Creole, or even Camanche. Her eye would have been large for a woman, and was inky as the pools of falls among mountain-pines. An Indian blanket, orange-hued, and fringed with bead tassel-work, appeared that morning to have shielded the child from heavy showers. Her limbs were tremulous; she seemed a little Cassandra, in nervousness.

No sooner was the pair spied by the herb-doctor, than, with a cheerful air, both arms extended like a host's, he advanced, and taking the child's reluctant hand, said, trippingly: 'On your travels, ah, my little May Queen? Glad to see you. What pretty moccasins. Nice to dance in.' Then with a half caper sang –

> 'Hey diddle, diddle, the cat and the fiddle;
> The cow jumped over the moon.

Come, chirrup, chirrup, my little robin!'

Which playful welcome drew no responsive playfulness from the child, nor appeared to gladden or conciliate the father; but rather, if anything, to dash the dead weight of his heavy-hearted expression with a smile hypochondriacally scornful.

Sobering down now, the herb-doctor addressed the stranger in a manly, business-like way – a transition which, though it might seem a little abrupt, did not appear constrained, and, indeed, served to show that his recent levity was less the habit of a frivolous nature, than the frolic condescension of a kindly heart.

'Excuse me,' said he, 'but, if I err not, I was speaking to you the other day; – on a Kentucky boat wasn't it?'

'Never to me,' was the reply; the voice deep and lonesome enough to have come from the bottom of an abandoned coal-shaft.

'Ah! – But am I again mistaken (his eye falling on the swamp-oak stick), or don't you go a little lame, sir?'

'Never was lame in my life.'

'Indeed? I fancied I had perceived not a limp, but a hitch, a slight hitch; – some experience in these things – divined some hidden cause of the hitch – buried bullet, may be – some dragoons in the Mexican war, discharged with such, you know. – Hard fate!' he sighed; 'little pity for it, for who sees it? – have you dropped anything?'

Why, there is no telling, but the stranger was bowed over, and might have seemed bowing for the purpose of picking up something, were it not that, as arrested in the imperfect posture, he for the moment so remained; slanting his tall stature like a mainmast yielding to the gale, or Adam to the thunder.

The little child pulled him. With a kind of a surge he righted himself; for an instant looked toward the herb-doctor; but, either from emotion or aversion, or both together, withdrew his eyes, saying nothing. Presently, still stooping, he seated himself, drawing his child between his knees, his massy hands tremulous, and still averting his face, while up into the compassionate one of the herb-doctor the child turned a fixed, melancholy glance of repugnance.

The herb-doctor stood observant a moment, then said:

'Surely you have pain, strong pain, somewhere; in strong frames pain is strongest. Try, now, my specific' (holding it up). 'Do but look at the expression of this friend of humanity. Trust me, certain cure for any pain in the world. Won't you look?'

'No,' choked the other.

'Very good. Merry time to you, little May Queen.'

And so, as if he would intrude his cure upon no one, moved pleasantly off, again crying his wares, nor now at last without result. A new-comer, not from the shore, but another part of the boat, a sickly young man, after some questions, purchased a bottle. Upon this, others of the company began a little to wake up as it were; the scales of indifference or prejudice fell from their eyes; now, at last, they seemed to have an inkling that here was something not undesirable which might be had for the buying.

But while, ten times more briskly bland than ever, the

herb-doctor was driving his benevolent trade, accompanying each sale with added praises of the thing graded, all at once the dusk giant, seated at some distance, unexpectedly raised his voice with –

'What was that you last said?'

The question was put distinctly, yet resonantly, as when a great clock-bell – stunning admonisher – strikes one; and the stroke, though single, comes bedded in the belfry clamour.

All proceedings were suspended. Hands held forth for the specific were withdrawn, while every eye turned towards the direction whence the question came. But, no way abashed, the herb-doctor, elevating his voice with even more than wonted self-possession, replied –

'I was saying what, since you wish it, I cheerfully repeat, that the Samaritan Pain Dissuader, which I here hold in my hand, will either cure or ease any pain you please, within ten minutes after its application.'

'Does it produce insensibility?'

'By no means. Not the least of its merits is, that it is not an opiate. It kills pain without killing feeling.'

'You lie! Some pains cannot be eased but by producing insensibility, and cannot be cured but by producing death.'

Beyond this the dusk giant said nothing; neither, for impairing the other's market, did there appear much need to. After eyeing the rude speaker a moment with an expression of mingled admiration and consternation, the company silently exchanged glances of mutual sympathy under unwelcome conviction. Those who had purchased looked sheepish or ashamed; and a cynical-looking little man, with a thin flaggy beard, and a countenance ever wearing the rudiments of a grin, seated alone in a corner commanding a good view of the scene, held a rusty hat before his face.

But, again, the herb-doctor, without noticing the retort, overbearing though it was, began his panegyrics anew, and in a tone more assured than before, going so far now as to say that his specific was sometimes almost as effective in cases of mental suffering as in cases of physical; or rather, to be more precise, in cases when, through sympathy, the two sorts of pain cooperated into a climax of both – in such cases, he said, the specific had done very well. He cited an example: Only three bottles, faithfully taken, cured a Louisiana widow (for three weeks sleepless in a darkened chamber) of neuralgic sorrow for the loss of husband and child, swept off in one night by the last epidemic. For the truth of this, a printed voucher was produced, duly signed.

While he was reading it aloud, a sudden side-blow all but felled him.

It was the giant, who, with a countenance lividly epileptic with hypochondriac mania, exclaimed –

'Profane fiddler on heart-strings! Snake!'

More he would have added, but, convulsed, could not; so, without another word, taking up the child, who had followed him, went with a rocking pace out of the cabin.

'Regardless of decency, and lost to humanity!' exclaimed the herb-doctor, with much ado recovering himself. Then, after a pause, during which he examined his bruise, not omitting to apply externally a little of his specific, and with some success, as it would seem, complained to himself:

'No, no, I won't seek redress; innocence is my redress. But,' turning upon them all, 'if that man's wrathful blow provokes me to no wrath, should his evil distrust arouse you to distrust? I do devoutly hope,' proudly raising voice and arm, 'for the honour of humanity – hope that, despite this coward assault, the Samaritan Pain Dissuader stands unshaken in the confidence of all who hear me!'

But, injured as he was, and patient under it, too, somehow his case excited as little compassion as his oratory now did enthusiasm. Still, pathetic to the last, he continued his appeals, notwithstanding the frigid regard of the company, till, suddenly interrupting himself, as if in reply to a quick summons from without, he said hurriedly, 'I come, I come,' and so, with every token of precipitate dispatch, out of the cabin the herb-doctor went.

Chapter Eighteen

Inquest Into the True Character of the Herb-doctor

'Shan't see that fellow again in a hurry,' remarked an auburn-haired gentleman, to his neighbour with a hook-nose. 'Never knew an operator so completely unmasked.'

'But do you think it the fair thing to unmask an operator that way?'

'Fair? It is right.'

'Supposing that at high 'change on the Paris Bourse, Asmodeus should lounge in, distributing hand-bills, revealing the true thoughts and designs of all the operators present – would that be the fair thing in Asmodeus? Or, as Hamlet says, were it "to consider the thing too curiously"?'

'We won't go into that. But since you admit the fellow to be a knave –'

'I don't admit it. Or, if I did, I take it back. Shouldn't wonder if, after all, he is no knave at all, or, but little of one. What can you prove against him?'

'I can prove that he makes dupes.'

'Many held in honour do the same; and many, not wholly knaves, do it too.'

'How about that last?'

'He is not wholly at heart a knave, I fancy, among whose dupes is himself. Did you not see our quack friend apply to himself his own quackery? A fanatic quack; essentially a fool, though effectively a knave.'

Bending over, and looking down between his knees on the floor, the auburn-haired gentleman meditatively scribbled there awhile with his cane, then, glancing up, said:

'I can't conceive how you, in any way, can hold him a fool. How he talked – so glib, so pat, so well.'

'A smart fool always talks well: takes a smart fool to be tonguey.'

In much the same strain the discussion continued – the hook-nosed gentleman talking at large and excellently, with a view of demonstrating that a smart fool always talks just so. Ere long he talked to such purpose as almost to convince.

Presently, back came the person of whom the auburn-haired gentleman had predicted that he would not return. Conspicuous in the doorway he stood saying, in a clear voice, 'Is the agent of the Seminole Widow and Orphan Asylum within here?'

No one replied.

'Is there within here any agent or any member of any charitable institution whatever?'

No one seemed competent to answer, or, no one thought it worth while to.

'If there be within here any such person, I have in my hand two dollars for him.'

Some interest was manifested.

'I was called away so hurriedly, I forgot this part of my duty. With the proprietor of the Samaritan Pain Dissuader it is a rule, to devote, on the spot, to some benevolent purpose, the half of the proceeds of sales. Eight bottles were disposed of among this company. Hence, four half-dollars remain to charity. Who, as steward, takes the money?'

One or two pair of feet moved upon the floor, as with a sort of itching; but nobody rose.

'Does diffidence prevail over duty? If, I say, there be any gentleman, or any lady either, here present, who is in any connection with any charitable institution whatever, let him or her come forward. He or she happening to have at hand no certificate of such connection, makes no difference. Not of a suspicious temper, thank God, I shall have confidence in whoever offers to take the money.'

A demure-looking woman, in a dress rather tawdry and rumpled, here drew her veil well down and rose; but, marking every eye upon her, thought it advisable, upon the whole, to sit down again.

'Is it to be believed that, in this Christian company, there is no one charitable person? I mean, no one connected with any charity? Well then, is there no object of charity here?'

Upon this, an unhappy-looking woman, in a sort of mourning, neat, but sadly worn, hid her face behind a meagre bundle, and was heard to sob. Meantime, as not seeing or hearing her, the herb-doctor again spoke, and this time not unpathetically:

'Are there none here who feel in need of help, and who, in accepting such help, would feel that they, in their time, have given or done more than may ever be given or done to them? Man or woman, is there none such here?'

The sobs of the woman were more audible, though she strove to repress them. While nearly every one's attention was bent upon her, a man of the appearance of a day-labourer, with a white bandage across his face, concealing the side of the nose, and who, for coolness' sake, had been sitting in his red-flannel shirt-sleeves, his coat thrown across one shoulder, the darned cuffs drooping behind – this man shufflingly rose, and, with a pace that seemed the lingering memento of the lock-step of convicts, went up for a duly-qualified claimant.

'Poor wounded hussar!' sighed the herb-doctor, and dropping the money into the man's clam-shell of a hand turned and departed.

The recipient of the alms was about moving after, when the auburn-haired gentleman staid him: 'Don't be frightened, you; but I want to see those coins. Yes, yes; good silver, good silver. There, take them again, and while you are about it, go bandage the rest of yourself behind something. D'ye hear? Consider yourself, wholly, the scar of a nose, and be off with yourself.'

Being of a forgiving nature, or else from emotion not daring to trust his voice, the man silently, but not without some precipitancy, withdrew.

'Strange,' said the auburn-haired gentleman, returning to his friend, 'the money was good money.'

'Aye, and where your fine knavery now? Knavery to devote the half of one's receipts to charity? He's a fool I say again.'

'Others might call him an original genius.'

'Yes, being original in his folly. Genius? His genius is a cracked pate, and, as this age goes, not much originality about that.'

'May he not be knave, fool, and genius all together?'

'I beg pardon,' here said a third person with a gossiping expression who had been listening, 'but you are somewhat puzzled by this man, and well you may be.'

'Do you know anything about him?' asked the hook-nosed gentleman.

'No, but I suspect him for something.'

'Suspicion. We want knowledge.'

'Well, suspect first, and know next. True knowledge comes but by suspicion or revelation. That's my maxim.'

'And yet,' said the auburn-haired gentleman, 'since a wise man will keep even some certainties to himself, much more some suspicions, at least he will at all events so do till they ripen into knowledge.'

'Do you hear that about the wise man?' said the hook-nosed gentleman, turning upon the new-comer. 'Now what is it you suspect of this fellow?'

'I shrewdly suspect him,' was the eager response, 'for one of those Jesuit emissaries prowling all over our country. The better to accomplish their secret designs, they assume, at times, I am told, the most singular masques; sometimes, in appearance, the absurdest.'

This, though indeed for some reason causing a droll smile upon the face of the hook-nosed gentleman, added a third angle to the discussion, which now became a sort of triangular duel, and ended, at last, with but a triangular result.

Chapter Nineteen

A Soldier of Fortune

'Mexico? Molino del Rey? Resaca de la Palma?'

'Resaca de la *Tombs!*'

Leaving his reputation to take care of itself, since, as is not seldom the case, he knew nothing of its being in debate, the herb-doctor, wandering towards the forward part of the boat, had there espied a singular character in a grimy old regimental coat, a countenance at once grim and wizened, interwoven paralysed legs, stiff as icicles, suspended between rude crutches, while the whole rigid body, like a ship's long barometer on gimbals, swung to and fro, mechanically faithful to the motion of the boat. Looking downward while he swung, the cripple seemed in a brown study.

As moved by the sight, and conjecturing that here was some battered hero from the Mexican battle-fields, the herb-doctor had sympathetically accosted him as above, and received the above rather dubious reply. As, with a half moody, half surly sort of air that reply was given, the cripple, by a voluntary jerk, nervously increased his swing (his custom when seized by emotion), so that one would have thought some squall had suddenly rolled the boat and with it the barometer.

'Tombs? my friend,' exclaimed the herb-doctor in mild surprise. 'You have not descended to the dead, have you? I had imagined you a scarred campaigner, one of the noble children of war, for your dear country a glorious sufferer. But you are Lazarus, it seems.'

'Yes, he who had sores.'

'Ah, the *other* Lazarus. But I never knew that either of them was in the army,' glancing at the dilapidated regimentals.

'That will do now. Jokes enough.'

'Friend,' said the other reproachfully, 'you think amiss. On principle, I greet unfortunates with some pleasant remark, the better to call off their thoughts from their troubles. The physician who is at once wise and humane seldom unreservedly sympathizes with his patient. But come, I am a herb-doctor, and also a natural bone-setter. I may be sanguine, but I think I can do something for you. You look up now. Give me your story. Ere I undertake a cure, I require a full account of the case.'

'You can't help me,' returned the cripple gruffly. 'Go away.'

'You seem sadly destitute of –'

'No I ain't destitute; to-day, at least, I can pay my way.'

'The Natural Bone-setter is happy, indeed, to hear that. But you were premature. I was deploring your destitution, not of cash, but of confidence. You think the Natural Bone-setter can't help you. Well, suppose he can't, have you any objection to telling him your story? You, my friend, have, in a signal way, experienced adversity. Tell me, then, for my private good, how, without aid from the noble cripple, Epictetus, you have arrived at his heroic sang-froid in misfortune.'

At these words the cripple fixed upon the speaker the hard ironic eye of one toughened and defiant in misery, and, in the end, grinned upon him with his unshaven face like an ogre.

'Come, come, be sociable – be human, my friend. Don't make that face; it distresses me.'

'I suppose,' with a sneer, 'you are the man I've long heard of – The Happy Man.'

'Happy? my friend. Yes, at least I ought to be. My conscience is peaceful. I have confidence in everybody. I have confidence that, in my humble profession, I do some little good to the world. Yes, I think that, without presumption, I may venture to assent to the proposition that I am the Happy Man – the Happy Bone-setter.'

'Then you shall hear my story. Many a month I have longed to get hold of the Happy Man, drill him, drop the powder, and leave him to explode at his leisure.'

'What a demoniac unfortunate!' exclaimed the herb-doctor, retreating. 'Regular infernal machine!'

'Look ye,' cried the other, stumping after him, and with his horny hand catching him by a horn button, 'my name is Thomas Fry. Until my –'

– 'Any relation of Mrs Fry?' interrupted the other. 'I still correspond with that excellent lady on the subject of prisons. Tell me, are you any way connected with *my* Mrs Fry?'

'Blister Mrs Fry! What do them sentimental souls know of prisons or any other black fact? I'll tell ye a story of prisons. Ha, ha!'

The herb-doctor shrank, and with reason, the laugh being strangely startling.

'Positively, my friend,' said he, 'you must stop that; I can't stand that; no more of that. I hope I have the milk of kindness, but your thunder will soon turn it.'

'Hold, I haven't come to the milk-turning part yet. My name is Thomas Fry. Until my twenty-third year I went by the nickname of Happy Tom – happy – ha, ha! They called me Happy Tom, d'ye see? because I was so good-natured and laughing all the time, just as I am now – ha, ha!'

Upon this the herb-doctor would, perhaps, have run, but once more the hyena clawed him. Presently, sobering down, he continued:

'Well, I was born in New York, and there I lived a steady, hard-working man, a cooper by trade. One evening I went to a political meeting in the Park – for you must know, I was in those days a great patriot. As bad luck would have it, there was trouble near, between a gentleman who had been drinking wine, and a pavior who was sober. The pavior chewed tobacco, and the gentleman said it was beastly in him, and pushed him, wanting to have his place. The pavior chewed on and pushed back. Well, the gentleman carried a sword-cane, and presently the pavior was down – skewered.'

'How was that?'

'Why you see the pavior undertook something above his strength.'

'The other must have been a Samson then. "Strong as a pavior", is a proverb.'

'So it is, and the gentleman was in body a rather weakly man, but for all that, I say again, the pavior undertook something above his strength.'

'What are you talking about? He tried to maintain his rights, didn't he?'

'Yes; but for all that, I say again, he undertook something above his strength.'

'I don't understand you. But go on.'

'Along with the gentleman, I, with other witnesses, was taken to the Tombs. There was an examination, and, to appear at the trial, the gentleman and witnesses all gave bail – I mean all but me.'

'And why didn't you?'

'Couldn't get it.'

'Steady, hard-working cooper like you; what was the reason you couldn't get bail?'

'Steady, hard-working cooper hadn't no friends. Well, souse I went into a wet cell, like a canal-boat splashing into the lock; locked up in pickle, d'ye see? against the time of the trial.'

'But what had you done?'

'Why, I hadn't got any friends, I tell ye. A worse crime than murder, as ye'll see afore long.'

'Murder? Did the wounded man die?'

'Died the third night.'

'Then the gentleman's bail didn't help him. Imprisoned now, wasn't he?'

'Had too many friends. No, it was *I* that was imprisoned. – But I was going on: They let me walk about the corridor by day; but at night I must into lock. There the wet and the damp struck into my bones. They doctored me, but no use. When the trial came, I was boosted up and said my say.'

'And what was that?'

'My say was that I saw the steel go in, and saw it sticking in.'

'And that hung the gentleman.'

'Hung him with a gold chain! His friends called a meeting in the Park, and presented him with a gold watch and chain upon his acquittal.'

'Acquittal?'

'Didn't I say he had friends?'

There was a pause, broken at last by the herb-doctor's saying: 'Well, there is a bright side to everything. If this speak prosaically for justice, it speaks romantically for friendship! But go on, my fine fellow.'

'My say being said, they told me I might go. I said I could not without help. So the constables helped me, asking *where* would I go? I told them back to the Tombs. I knew no other place. "But where are your friends?" said they. "I have none." So they put me into a hand-barrow with an awning to it, and wheeled me down to the dock and on board a boat, and away to Blackwell's Island to the Corporation Hospital. There I got worse – got pretty much as you see me now. Couldn't cure me. After three years, I grew sick of lying in a grated iron bed alongside of groaning thieves and mouldering burglars. They gave me five silver dollars, and these crutches, and I hobbled off. I had an only brother who went to Indiana, years ago. I begged about, to make up a sum to go to him; got to Indiana at last, and they directed me to his grave. It was on a great plain, in a log-church yard with a stump fence, the old gray roots sticking all ways like moose-antlers. The bier, set over the grave, it being the last dug, was of green hickory; bark on, and green twigs sprouting from it. Some one had planted a bunch of violets on the mound, but it was a poor soil (always choose the poorest soils for grave-yards), and they were all dried to tinder. I was going to sit and rest myself on the bier and think about my brother in heaven, but the bier broke down, the legs being only tacked. So, after driving some hogs out of the yard that were rooting there, I came away, and, not to make too long a story of it, here I am, drifting down stream like any other bit of wreck.'

The herb-doctor was silent for a time, buried in thought. At last, raising his head, he said: 'I have considered your whole story, my friend, and strove to consider it in the light of a commentary on what I believe to be the system of things; but it so jars with all, is so incompatible with all, that you must pardon me, if I honestly tell you, I cannot believe it.'

'That don't surprise me.'

'How?'

'Hardly anybody believes my story, and so to most I tell a different one.'

'How, again?'

'Wait here a bit and I'll show ye.'

With that, taking off his rag of a cap, and arranging his tattered regimentals the best he could, off he went stumping among the passengers in an adjoining part of the deck, saying with a jovial kind of air: 'Sir, a shilling for Happy Tom, who fought at Buena Vista. Lady, something for General Scott's soldier, crippled in both pins at glorious Contreras.'

Now, it so chanced that, unbeknown to the cripple, a primlooking stranger had overheard part of his story. Beholding him, then, on his present begging adventure, this person, turning to the herb-doctor, indignantly said: 'Is it not too bad, sir, that yonder rascal should lie so?'

'Charity never faileth, my good sir,' was the reply. 'The vice of this unfortunate is pardonable. Consider, he lies not out of wantonness.'

'Not out of wantonness. I never heard more wanton lies. In one breath to tell you what would appear to be his true story, and, in the next, away and falsify it.'

'For all that, I repeat, he lies not out of wantonness. A ripe philosopher, turned out of the great Sorbonne of hard times, he thinks that woes, when told to strangers for money, are best sugared. Though the inglorious lock-jaw of his knee-pans in a wet dungeon is a far more pitiable ill than to have been crippled at glorious Contreras, yet he is of opinion that this lighter and false ill shall attract, while the heavier and real one might repel.'

'Nonsense; he belongs to the Devil's regiment; and I have a great mind to expose him.'

'Shame upon you. Dare to expose that poor unfortunate, and by heaven – don't you do it, sir.'

Noting something in his manner, the other thought it more prudent to retire than retort. By-and-by, the cripple came back, and with glee, having reaped a pretty good harvest.

'There,' he laughed, 'you know now what sort of soldier I am.'

'Aye, one that fights not the stupid Mexican, but a foe worthy your tactics – Fortune!'

'Hi, hi!' clamoured the cripple, like a fellow in the pit of a six-penny theatre, then said, 'don't know much what you meant, but it went off well.'

This over, his countenance capriciously put on a morose ogreness. To kindly questions he gave no kindly answers. Unhandsome notions were thrown out about 'free Americky', as he sarcastically called his country. These seemed to disturb and pain the herb-doctor, who, after an interval of thoughtfulness, gravely addressed him in these words:

'You, my worthy friend, to my concern, have reflected upon the government under which you live and suffer. Where is your patriotism? Where your gratitude? True, the charitable may find something in your case, as you put it, partly to account for such reflections as coming from you. Still, be the facts how they may, your reflections are none the less unwarrantable. Grant, for the moment, that your experiences are as you give them; in which case I would admit that government might be thought to have more or less to do with what seems undesirable in them. But it is never to be forgotten that human government, being subordinate to the divine, must needs, therefore, in its degree, partake of the characteristics of the divine. That is, while in general efficacious to happiness, the world's law may yet, in some cases, have, to the eye of reason, an unequal operation, just as, in the same imperfect view, some inequalities may appear in the operations of heaven's law; nevertheless, to one who has a right confidence, final benignity is, in every instance, as sure with the one law as the other. I expound the point at some length, because these are the considerations, my poor fellow, which, weighed as they merit, will enable you to sustain with unimpaired trust the apparent calamities which are yours.'

'What do you talk your hog-latin to me for?' cried the cripple, who, throughout the address, betrayed the most illiterate obduracy; and, with an incensed look, anew he swung himself.

Glancing another way till the spasm passed, the other continued:

'Charity marvels not that you should be somewhat hard of conviction, my friend, since you, doubtless, believe yourself hardly dealt by; but forget not that those who are loved are chastened.'

'Mustn't chasten them too much, though, and too long, because their skin and heart get hard, and feel neither pain nor tickle.'

'To mere reason, your case looks something piteous, I grant. But never despond; many things – the choicest – yet remain. You breathe this bounteous air, are warmed by this gracious sun, and, though poor and friendless, indeed, nor so agile as in your youth, yet, how sweet to roam, day by day, through the groves, plucking the bright mosses and flowers, till forlornness itself becomes a hilarity, and, in your innocent independence, you skip for joy.'

'Fine skipping with these 'ere horse-posts – ha, ha!'

'Pardon; I forgot the crutches. My mind, figuring you after

receiving the benefit of my art, overlooked you as you stand before me.'

'Your art? You call yourself a bone-setter – a natural bone-setter, do ye? Go, bone-set the crooked world, and then come bone-set crooked me.'

'Truly, my honest friend, I thank you for again recalling me to my original object. Let me examine you,' bending down; 'ah, I see, I see; much such a case as the negro's. Did you see him? Oh no, you came aboard since. Well, his case was a little something like yours. I prescribed for him, and I shouldn't wonder at all if, in a very short time, he were able to walk almost as well as myself. Now, have you no confidence in my art?'

'Ha, ha!'

The herb-doctor averted himself; but, the wild laugh dying away, resumed:

'I will not force confidence on you. Still, I would fain do the friendly thing by you. Here, take this box; just rub that liniment on the joints night and morning. Take it. Nothing to pay. God bless you. Good-bye.'

'Stay,' pausing in his swing, not untouched by so unexpected an act; 'stay – thank'ee – but will this really do me good? Honour bright, now; will it? Don't deceive a poor fellow,' with changed mien and glistening eye.

'Try it. Good-bye.'

'Stay, stay! *Sure* it will do me good?'

'Possibly, possibly; no harm in trying. Good-bye.'

'Stay, stay; give me three more boxes, and here's the money.'

'My friend,' returning towards him with a sadly pleased sort of air, 'I rejoice in the birth of your confidence and hopefulness. Believe me that, like your crutches, confidence and hopefulness will long support a man when his own legs will not. Stick to confidence and hopefulness, then, since how mad for the cripple to throw his crutches away. You ask for three more boxes of my liniment. Luckily, I have just that number remaining. Here they are. I sell them at half-a-dollar apiece. But I shall take nothing from you. There; God bless you again; good-bye.'

'Stay,' in a convulsed voice, and rocking himself, 'stay, stay! You have made a better man of me. You have borne with me like a good Christian, and talked to me like one, and all that is enough without making me a present of these boxes. Here is the money. I won't take nay. There, there; and may Almighty goodness go with you.'

As the herb-doctor withdrew, the cripple gradually subsided from his hard rocking into a gentle oscillation. It expressed, perhaps, the soothed mood of his reverie.

Chapter Twenty

Reappearance of One Who May Be Remembered

The herb-doctor had not moved far away, when, in advance of him, this spectacle met his eye. A dried-up old man, with the stature of a boy of twelve, was tottering about like one out of his mind, in rumpled clothes of old moleskin, showing recent contact with bedding, his ferret eyes, blinking in the sunlight of the snowy boat, as imbecilely eager, and, at intervals, coughing, he peered hither and thither as if in alarmed search for his nurse. He presented the aspect of one who, bed-rid, has, through overruling excitement, like that of a fire, been stimulated to his feet.

'You seek some one,' said the herb-doctor, accosting him. 'Can I assist you?'

'Do, do; I am so old and miserable,' coughed the old man. 'Where is he? This long time I've been trying to get up and find him. But I haven't any friends, and couldn't get up till now. Where is he?'

'Who do you mean?' drawing closer, to stay the further wanderings of one so weakly.

'Why, why, why,' now marking the other's dress, 'why you, yes you – you, you – ugh, ugh, ugh!'

'I?'

'Ugh, ugh, ugh! – you are the man he spoke of. Who is he?'

'Faith, that is just what I want to know.'

'Mercy, mercy!' coughed the old man, bewildered, 'ever since seeing him, my head spins round so. I ought to have a guardeean. Is this a snuff-coloured surtout of yours, or ain't it? Somehow, can't trust my senses any more, since trusting him – ugh, ugh, ugh!'

'Oh, you have trusted somebody? Glad to hear it. Glad to hear of any instance of that sort. Reflects well upon all men. But you inquire whether this is a snuff-coloured surtout. I answer it is; and will add that a herb-doctor wears it.'

Upon this the old man, in his broken way, replied that then he (the herb-doctor) was the person he sought – the person spoken of by the other person as yet unknown. He then, with flighty eagerness, wanted to know who this last person was, and where he was, and whether he could be trusted with money to treble it.

'Aye, now, I begin to understand; ten to one you mean my worthy friend, who, in pure goodness of heart, makes people's fortunes for them – their everlasting fortunes, as the phrase goes – only charging his one small commission of confidence. Aye, aye; before intrusting funds with my friend, you want to know about him. Very proper – and, I am glad to assure you, you need have no hesitation; none, none, just none in the world; *bona fide*, none. Turned me in a trice a hundred dollars the other day into as many eagles.'

'Did he? did he? But where is he? Take me to him.'

'Pray, take my arm! The boat is large! We may have something of a hunt! Come on! Ah, is that he?'

'Where? where?'

'O, no; I took yonder coat-skirts for his. But no, my honest friend would never turn tail that way. Ah! –'

'Where? where?'

'Another mistake. Surprising resemblance. I took yonder clergyman for him. Come on!'

Having searched that part of the boat without success, they went to another part, and, while exploring that, the boat sided up to a landing, when, as the two were passing by the open guard, the herb-doctor suddenly rushed towards the disembarking throng, crying out: 'Mr Truman, Mr Truman! There he goes – that's he. Mr Truman, Mr Truman! – Confound that steam-pipe. Mr Truman! for God's sake, Mr Truman! – No, no. – There, the plank's in – too late – we're off.'

With that, the huge boat, with a mighty walrus wallow, rolled away from the shore, resuming her course.

'How vexatious!' exclaimed the herb-doctor, returning. 'Had we been but one single moment sooner. There he goes, now, towards yon hotel, his portmanteau following. You see him, don't you?'

'Where? where?'

'Can't see him any more. Wheel-house shot between. I am very sorry. I should have so liked you to have let him have a hundred or so of your money. You would have been pleased with the investment, believe me.'

'Oh, I *have* let him have some of my money,' groaned the old man.

'You have? My dear sir,' seizing both the miser's hands in both his own and heartily shaking them. 'My dear sir, how I congratulate you. You don't know.'

'Ugh, ugh! I fear I don't,' with another groan. 'His name is Truman, is it?'

'John Truman.'

'Where does he live?'

'In St Louis.'

'Where's his office?'

'Let me see. Jones Street, number one hundred and – no, no – anyway, it's somewhere or other upstairs in Jones Street.'

'Can't you remember the number? Try, now.'

'One hundred – two hundred – three hundred –'

'Oh, my hundred dollars! I wonder whether it will be one hundred, two hundred, three hundred, with them! Ugh, ugh! Can't remember the number?'

'Positively, though I once knew, I have forgotten, quite forgotten it. Strange. But never mind. You will easily learn in St Louis. He is well known there.'

'But I have no receipt – ugh, ugh! Nothing to show – don't know where I stand – ought to have a guard*ee*an – ugh, ugh! Don't know anything. Ugh, ugh!'

'Why, you know that you gave him your confidence, don't you?'

'Oh, yes.'

'Well, then?'

'But what, what – how, how – ugh, ugh!'

'Why, didn't he tell you?'

'No.'

'What! Didn't he tell you that it was a secret, a mystery?'

'Oh – yes.'

'Well, then?'

'But I have no bond.'

'Don't need any with Mr Truman. Mr Truman's word is his bond.'

'But how am I to get my profits – ugh, ugh! – and my money back? Don't know anything. Ugh, ugh!'

'Oh, you must have confidence.'

'Don't say that word again. Makes my head spin so. Oh, I'm so old and miserable, nobody caring for me, everybody fleecing me, and my head spins so – ugh, ugh! – and this cough racks me so. I say again, I ought to have a guardeean.'

'So you ought; and Mr Truman is your guardian to the extent you invested with him. Sorry we missed him just now. But you'll hear from him, all right. It's imprudent, though, to expose yourself this way. Let me take you to your berth.'

Forlornly enough the old miser moved slowly away with him. But, while descending a stairway, he was seized with such coughing that he was fain to pause.

'That is a very bad cough.'

'Church-yard – ugh, ugh! – church-yard cough. – Ugh!'

'Have you tried anything for it?'

'Tired of trying. Nothing does me any good – ugh! ugh! Not even the Mammoth Cave. Ugh! ugh! Denned there six months, but coughed so bad the rest of the coughers – ugh! ugh! – blackballed me out. Ugh, ugh! Nothing does me good.'

'But have you tried the Omni-Balsamic Reinvigorator, sir?'

'That's what that Truman – ugh, ugh! – said I ought to take. Yarb-medicine; you are that yarb-doctor, too?'

'The same. Suppose you try one of my boxes now. Trust me, from what I know of Mr Truman, he is not the gentleman to recommend, even in behalf of a friend, anything of whose excellence he is not conscientiously satisfied.'

'Ugh! – how much?'

'Only two dollars a box.'

'Two dollars? Why don't you say two millions? ugh, ugh! Two dollars, that's two hundred cents; that's eight hundred farthings; that's two thousand mills; and all for one little box of yarb-medicine. My head, my head! – oh, I ought to have a guardeean for my head. Ugh, ugh, ugh, ugh!'

'Well, if two dollars a box seems too much, take a dozen boxes at twenty dollars; and that will be getting four boxes for nothing, and you need use none but those four, the rest you can retail out at a premium, and so cure your cough, and make money by it. Come, you had better do it. Cash down. Can fill an order in a day or two. Here now,' producing a box; 'pure herbs.'

At that moment, seized with another spasm, the miser snatched each interval to fix his half-distrustful, half-hopeful eye upon the medicine, held alluringly up. 'Sure – ugh! Sure it's all nat'ral? Nothing but yarbs? If I only thought it was a purely nat'ral medicine now – all yarbs – ugh, ugh! – oh this cough, this cough – ugh, ugh! – shatters my whole body. Ugh, ugh, ugh!'

'For heaven's sake try my medicine, if but a single box. That it is pure nature you may be confident. Refer you to Mr Truman.'

'Don't know his number – ugh, ugh, ugh, ugh! – Oh this cough. He did speak well of this medicine though; said solemnly it would cure me – ugh, ugh, ugh, ugh! – take off a dollar and I'll have a box.'

'Can't sir, can't.'

'Say a dollar-and-half. Ugh!'

'Can't. Am pledged to the one-price system, only honourable one.'

'Take off a shilling – ugh, ugh!'

'Can't.'

'Ugh, ugh, ugh – I'll take it. – There.'

Grudgingly he handed eight silver coins, but while still in his hand, his cough took him, and they were shaken upon the deck.

One by one, the herb-doctor picked them up, and, examining them, said: 'These are not quarters, these are pistareens; and clipped, and sweated, at that.'

'Oh don't be so miserly – ugh, ugh! – better a beast than a miser – ugh, ugh!'

'Well, let it go. Anything rather than the idea of your not being cured of such a cough. And I hope, for the credit of humanity, you have not made it appear worse than it is, merely with a view to working upon the weak point of my pity, and so getting my medicine the cheaper. Now, mind, don't take it till night. Just before retiring is the time. There, you can get along now, can't you? I would attend you further, but I land presently, and must go hunt up my luggage.'

Chapter Twenty-One
A Hard Case

'Yarbs, yarbs; natur, natur; you foolish old file you! He diddled you with that hocus-pocus, did he? Yarbs and natur will cure your incurable cough, you think?'

It was a rather eccentric-looking person who spoke, somewhat ursine in aspect; sporting a shaggy spencer of the cloth called bear's-skin; a high-peaked cap of racoon-skin, the long bushy tail switching over behind; raw-hide leggings; grim stubble chin; and, to end, a double-barrelled gun in hand – a Missouri bachelor, a Hoosier gentleman, of Spartan leisure and fortune, and equally Spartan manners and sentiments; and, as the sequel may show, not less acquainted, in a Spartan way of his own, with philosophy and books, than with woodcraft and rifles.

He must have overheard some of the talk between the miser and the herb-doctor; for, just after the withdrawal of the one, he made up to the other – now at the foot of the stairs leaning against the baluster there – with the 'greeting' above.

'Think it will cure me?' coughed the miser in echo; 'why shouldn't it? The medicine is nat'ral yarbs, pure yarbs; yarbs must cure me.'

'Because a thing is nat'ral, as you call it, you think it must be good. But who gave you that cough? Was it, or was it not, nature?'

'Sure, you don't think that natur, Dame Natur, will hurt a body, do you?'

'Natur is good Queen Bess; but who's responsible for the cholera?'

'But yarbs, yarbs; yarbs are good?'

'What's deadly-nightshade? Yarb, ain't it?'

'Oh, that a Christian man should speak agin natur and

yarbs – ugh, ugh, ugh! – ain't sick men sent out into the country; sent out to natur and grass?'

'Aye, and poets send out the sick spirit to green pastures, like lame horses turned out unshod to the turf to renew their hoofs. A sort of yarb-doctors in their way, poets have it that for sore hearts, as for sore lungs, nature is the grand cure. But who froze to death my teamster on the prairie? And who made an idiot of Peter the Wild Boy?'

'Then you don't believe in these 'ere yarb-doctors?'

'Yarb-doctors? I remember the lank yarb-doctor I saw once on a hospital-cot in Mobile. One of the faculty passing round and seeing who lay there, said with professional triumph, "Ah, Dr Green, your yarbs don't help ye now, Dr Green. Have to come to us and the mercury now, Dr Green." – Natur! Y-a-r-b-s!'

'Did I hear something about herbs and herb-doctors?' here said a flute-like voice, advancing.

It was the herb-doctor in person. Carpet-bag in hand, he happened to be strolling back that way.

'Pardon me,' addressing the Missourian, 'but if I caught your words aright, you would seem to have little confidence in nature; which, really, in my way of thinking, looks like carrying the spirit of distrust pretty far.'

'And who of my sublime species may you be?' turning short round upon him, clicking his rifle-lock, with an air which would have seemed half cynic, half wild-cat, were it not for the grotesque excess of the expression, which made its sincerity appear more or less dubious.

'One who has confidence in nature, and confidence in man, with some little modest confidence in himself.'

'That's your Confession of Faith, is it? Confidence in man, eh? Pray, which do you think are most, knaves or fools?'

'Having met with few or none of either, I hardly think I am competent to answer.'

'I will answer for you. Fools are most.'

'Why do you think so?'

'For the same reason that I think oats are numerically more than horses. Don't knaves munch up fools just as horses do oats?'

'A droll, sir; you are a droll. I can appreciate drollery – ha, ha, ha!'

'But I'm in earnest.'

'That's the drollery, to deliver droll extravagance with an earnest air – knaves munching up fools as horses oats. – Faith, very droll, indeed, ha, ha, ha! Yes, I think I understand you now, sir. How silly I was to have taken you seriously, in your droll conceits, too, about having no confidence in nature. In reality you have just as much as I have.'

'*I* have confidence in nature? *I*? I say again, there is nothing I am more suspicious of. I once lost ten thousand dollars by nature. Nature embezzled that amount from me; absconded with ten thousand dollars' worth of my property; a plantation on this stream, swept clean away by one of those sudden shiftings of the banks in a freshet; ten thousand dollars' worth of alluvion thrown broad off upon the waters.'

'But have you no confidence that by a reverse shifting that soil will come back after many days? – ah, here is my venerable friend,' observing the old miser, – 'not in your berth yet? Pray, if you *will* keep afoot, don't lean against that baluster; take my arm.'

It was taken; and the two stood together; the old miser leaning against the herb-doctor with something of that air of trustful fraternity with which, when standing, the less strong of the Siamese twins habitually leans against the other.

The Missourian eyed them in silence, which was broken by the herb-doctor.

'You look surprised, sir. Is it because I publicly take under my protection a figure like this? But I am never ashamed of honesty, whatever his coat.'

'Look you,' said the Missourian, after a scrutinizing pause, 'you are a queer sort of chap. Don't know exactly what to make of you. Upon the whole though, you somewhat remind me of the last boy I had on my place.'

'Good, trustworthy boy, I hope?'

'Oh, very! I am now started to get me made some kind of machine to do the sort of work which boys are supposed to be fitted for.'

'Then you have passed a veto upon boys?'

'And men, too.'

'But, my dear sir, does not that again imply more or less lack of confidence? – (Stand up a little, just a very little, my venerable friend; you lean rather hard.) – No confidence in boys, no confidence in men, no confidence in nature. Pray, sir, who or what may you have confidence in?'

'I have confidence in distrust; more particularly as applied to you and your herbs.'

'Well,' with a forbearing smile, 'that is frank. But pray, don't forget that when you suspect my herbs you suspect nature.'

'Didn't I say that before?'

'Very good. For the argument's sake I will suppose you are in earnest. Now, can you, who suspect nature, deny that this same nature, not only kindly brought you into being, but has faithfully nursed you to your present vigorous and independent condition? Is it not to nature that you are indebted for that robustness of mind which you so unhandsomely use to her scandal? Pray, is it not to nature that you owe the very eyes by which you criticize her?'

'No! for the privilege of vision I am indebted to an oculist, who in my tenth year operated upon me in Philadelphia. Nature made me blind, and would have kept me so. My oculist counterplotted her.'

'And yet, sir, by your complexion, I judge you live an out-of-door life; without knowing it, you are partial to nature; you fly to nature, the universal mother.'

'Very motherly! Sir, in the passion-fits of nature, I've known birds fly from nature to me, rough as I look; yes, sir, in a tempest, refuge here,' smiting the folds of his bearskin. 'Fact, sir, fact. Come, come, Mr Palaverer, for all your palavering, did you yourself never shut out nature of a cold, wet night? Bar her out? Bolt her out? Lint her out?'

'As to that,' said the herb-doctor calmly, 'much may be said.'

'Say it, then,' ruffling all his hairs. 'You can't, sir, can't.' Then, as in apostrophe: 'Look you, nature! I don't deny but your clover is sweet, and your dandelions don't roar; but whose hailstones smashed my windows?'

'Sir,' with unimpaired affability, producing one of his boxes, 'I am pained to meet with one who holds nature a dangerous character. Though your manner is refined, your voice is rough; in short, you seem to have a sore throat. In the calumniated name of nature, I present you with this box; my venerable friend here has a similar one; but to you, a free gift, sir. Through her regularly authorized agents, of whom I happen to be one, nature delights in benefiting those who most abuse her. Pray, take it.'

'Away with it! Don't hold it so near. Ten to one there is a torpedo in it. Such things have been. Editors been killed that way. Take it further off, I say.'

'Good heavens! my dear sir –'

'I tell you I want none of your boxes,' snapping his rifle.

'Oh, take it – ugh, ugh! do take it,' chimed in the old miser; 'I wish he would give me one for nothing.'

'You find it lonely, eh,' turning short round; 'gulled yourself, you would have a companion.'

'How can he find it lonely,' returned the herb-doctor, 'or how desire a companion, when here I stand by him; I, even I, in whom he has trust? For the gulling, tell me, is it humane to talk so to this poor old man? Granting that his dependence on my medicine is vain, is it kind to deprive him of what, in mere imagination, if nothing more, may help eke out, with hope, his disease? For you, if you have no confidence, and, thanks to your native health, can get along without it, so far, at least, as trusting in my medicine goes; yet, how cruel an argument to use, with this afflicted one here. Is it not for all the world as if some brawny pugilist, aglow in December, should rush in and put out a hospital-fire, because, forsooth, he feeling no need of artificial heat, the shivering patients shall have none? Put it to your conscience, sir, and you will admit, that whatever be the nature of this afflicted one's trust, you, in opposing it, evince either an erring head or a heart amiss. Come, own, are you not pitiless?'

'Yes, poor soul,' said the Missourian, gravely eyeing the old man – 'yes, it *is* pitiless in one like me to speak too honestly to one like you. You are a late sitter-up in this life; past man's usual bed-time; and truth, though with some it makes a wholesome breakfast, proves to all a supper too hearty. Hearty food, taken late, gives bad dreams.'

'What, in wonder's name – ugh, ugh! – is he talking about?' asked the old miser, looking up to the herb-doctor.

'Heaven be praised for that!' cried the Missourian.

'Out of his mind, ain't he?' again appealed the old miser.

'Pray, sir,' said the herb-doctor to the Missourian, 'for what were you giving thanks just now?'

'For this: that, with some minds, truth is, in effect, not so cruel a thing after all, seeing that, like a loaded pistol found by poor devils of savages, it raises more wonder than terror – its peculiar virtue being unguessed, unless, indeed, by indiscreet handling, it should happen to go off of itself.'

'I pretend not to divine your meaning there,' said the herb-doctor, after a pause, during which he eyed the Missourian with a kind of pinched expression, mixed of pain and curiosity, as if he grieved at his state of mind, and, at the same time, wondered what had brought him to it, – 'but this much I know,' he added, 'that the general cast of your thoughts is, to say the least, unfortunate. There is strength in them, but a strength, whose source, being physical, must wither. You will yet recant.'

'Recant?'

'Yes, when, as with this old man, your evil days of decay come on, when a hoary captive in your chamber, then will you, something like the dungeoned Italian we read of, gladly seek the breast of that confidence begot in the tender time of your youth, blessed beyond telling if it return to you in age.'

'Go back to nurse again, eh? Second childhood, indeed. You are soft.'

'Mercy, mercy!' cried the old miser, 'what is all this? – ugh, ugh! Do talk sense, my good friends. Ain't you,' to the Missourian, 'going to buy some of that medicine?'

'Pray, my venerable friend,' said the herb-doctor, now trying to straighten himself, 'don't lean *quite* so hard, my arm grows numb; abate a little, just a very little.'

'Go,' said the Missourian, 'go lay down in your grave, old man, if you can't stand of yourself. It's a hard world for a leaner.'

'As to his grave,' said the herb-doctor, 'that is far enough off, so he but faithfully take my medicine.'

'Ugh, ugh, ugh! – He says true. No, I ain't – ugh! a going to die yet – ugh, ugh, ugh! Many years to live yet, ugh, ugh, ugh!'

'I approve your confidence,' said the herb-doctor; 'but your coughing distresses me, besides being injurious to you. Pray, let me conduct you to your berth. You are best there. Our friend here will wait till my return, I know.'

With which he led the old miser away, and then, coming back, the talk with the Missourian was resumed.

'Sir,' said the herb-doctor, with some dignity and more feeling, 'now that our infirm friend is withdrawn, allow me, to the full, to express my concern at the words you allowed to escape you in his hearing. Some of those words, if I err not, besides being calculated to beget deplorable distrust in the patient, seemed fitted to convey unpleasant imputations against me, his physician.'

'Suppose they did?' with a menacing air.

'Why, then – then, indeed,' respectfully retreating, 'I fall back upon my previous theory of your general facetiousness. I have the fortune to be in company with a humorist – a wag.'

'Fall back you had better, and wag it is,' cried the Missourian, following him up, and wagging his racoon tail almost into the herb-doctor's face, 'look you!'

'At what?'

'At this coon. Can you, the fox, catch him?'

'If you mean,' returned the other, not unselfpossessed, 'whether I flatter myself that I can in any way dupe you, or impose upon you, or pass myself off upon you for what I am not, I, as an honest man, answer that I have neither the inclination nor the power to do aught of the kind.'

'Honest man? Seems to me you talk more like a craven.'

'You in vain seek to pick a quarrel with me, or put any affront upon me. The innocence in me heals me.'

'A healing like your own nostrums. But you are a queer man – a very queer and dubious man; upon the whole, about the most so I ever met.'

The scrutiny accompanying this seemed unwelcome to the diffidence of the herb-doctor. As if at once to attest the absence of resentment, as well as to change the subject, he threw a kind of familiar cordiality into his air, and said: 'So you are going to get some machine made to do your work? Philanthropic scruples, doubtless, forbid your going as far as New Orleans for slaves?'

'Slaves?' morose again in a twinkling, 'won't have 'em! Bad enough to see whites ducking and grinning round for a favour, without having those poor devils of niggers congeeing round for their corn. Though, to me, the niggers are the freer of the two. You are an abolitionist, ain't you?' he added, squaring himself with both hands on his rifle, used for a staff, and gazing in the herb-doctor's face with no more reverence than if it were a target. 'You are an abolitionist, ain't you?'

'As to that, I cannot so readily answer. If by abolitionist you mean a zealot, I am none; but if you mean a man, who, being a man, feels for all men, slaves included, and by any lawful act, opposed to nobody's interest, and therefore rousing nobody's enmity, would willingly abolish suffering (supposing it, in its degree, to exist) from among mankind, irrespective of colour, then am I what you say.'

'Picked and prudent sentiments. You are the moderate man, the invaluable understrapper of the wicked man. You, the moderate man, may be used for wrong, but are useless for right.'

'From all this,' said the herb-doctor, still forgivingly, 'I infer, that you, a Missourian, though living in a slave-state, are without slave sentiments.'

'Aye, but are you? Is not that air of yours, so spiritlessly enduring and yielding, the very air of a slave? Who is your master, pray; or are you owned by a company?'

'*My* master?'

'Aye, for come from Maine or Georgia, you come from a slave-state, and a slave-pen, where the best breeds are to be bought up at any price from a livelihood to the Presidency. Abolitionism, ye gods, but expresses the fellow-feeling of slave for slave.'

'The back-woods would seem to have given you rather eccentric notions,' now with polite superiority smiled the herb-doctor, still with manly intrepidity forbearing each unmanly thrust. 'But to return: since, for your purpose, you will have neither man nor boy, bond nor free, truly, then some sort of machine for you is all there is left. My desires for your success attend you, sir. – Ah!' glancing shoreward, 'here is Cape Girardeau; I must leave you.'

Chapter Twenty-Two

In the Polite Spirit of the Tusculan Disputations

– ' "Philosophical Intelligence Office" – novel idea! But how did you come to dream that I wanted anything in your absurd line, eh?'

About twenty minutes after leaving Cape Girardeau, the above was growled out over his shoulder by the Missourian to a chance stranger who had just accosted him; a round-backed, baker-kneed man, in a mean five-dollar suit, wearing, collar-wise by a chain, a small brass plate, inscribed P.I.O., and who, with a sort of canine deprecation, slunk obliquely behind.

'How did you come to dream that I wanted anything in your line, eh?'

'Oh, respected sir,' whined the other, crouching a pace nearer, and, in his obsequiousness, seeming to wag his very coat-tails behind him, shabby though they were, 'oh, sir, from long experience, one glance tells me the gentleman who is in need of our humble services.'

'But suppose I did want a boy – what they jocosely call a good boy – how could your absurd office help me? – Philosophical Intelligence Office?'

'Yes, respected sir, an office founded on strictly philosophical and physio–'

'Look you – come up here – how, by philosophy or physiology either, make good boys to order? Come up here. Don't give me a crick in the neck. Come up here, come, sir, come,' calling as if to his pointer. 'Tell me, how put the requisite assortment of good qualities into a boy, as the assorted mince into the pie?'

'Respected sir, our office –'

'You talk much of that office. Where is it? On board this boat?'

'Oh no, sir, I just came aboard. Our office –'

'Came aboard at that last landing, eh? Pray, do you know a herb-doctor there? Smooth scamp in a snuff-coloured surtout?'

'Oh, sir, I was but a sojourner at Cape Girardeau. Though, now that you mention a snuff-coloured surtout, I think I met such a man as you speak of stepping ashore as I stepped aboard, and 'pears to me I have seen him somewhere before. Looks like a very mild Christian sort of person, I should say. Do you know him, respected sir?'

'Not much, but better than you seem to. Proceed with your business.'

With a low, shabby bow, as grateful for the permission, the other began: 'Our office –'

'Look you,' broke in the bachelor with ire, 'have you the spinal complaint? What are you ducking and grovelling about? Keep still. Where's your office?'

'The branch one which I represent is at Alton, sir, in the free state we now pass' (pointing somewhat proudly ashore).

'Free, eh? You a freeman, you flatter yourself? With those coat-tails and that spinal complaint of servility? Free? Just cast up in your private mind who is your master, will you?'

'Oh, oh, oh! I don't understand – indeed – indeed. But, re-spected sir, as before said, our office, founded on principles wholly new –'

'To the devil with your principles! Bad sign when a man begins to talk of his principles. Hold, come back, sir; back here, back, sir, back! I tell you no more boys for me. Nay, I'm a Mede and Per-sian. In my old home in the woods I'm pestered enough with squirrels, weasels, chipmunks, skunks. I want no more wild ver-min to spoil my temper and waste my substance. Don't talk of boys; enough of your boys; a plague of your boys; chilblains on your boys! As for Intelligence Offices, I've lived in the East, and know 'em. Swindling concerns kept by low-born cynics, under a fawning exterior wreaking their cynic malice upon mankind. You are a fair specimen of 'em.'

'Oh dear, dear, dear!'

'Dear? Yes, a thrice dear purchase one of your boys would be to me. A rot on your boys!'

'But, respected sir, if you will not have boys, might we not, in our small way, accommodate you with a man?'

'Accommodate? Pray, no doubt you could accommodate me with a bosom-friend too, couldn't you? Accommodate! Obliging word 'accommodate': there's accommodation notes now, where one accommodates another with a loan, and if he don't pay it pretty quickly, accommodates him with a chain to his foot. Accommodate! God forbid that I should ever be accommodated. No, no. Look you, as I told that cousin-german of yours, the herb-doctor, I'm now on the road to get me made some sort of machine to do my work. Machines for me. My cider-mill – does that ever steal my cider? My mowing-machine – does that ever lay a-bed mornings? My corn-husker – does that ever give me insolence? No: cider-mill, mowing-machine, corn-husker – all faithfully attend to their business. Disinterested, too; no board, no wages; yet doing good all their lives long; shining examples that virtue is its own reward – the only practical Christians I know.'

'Oh dear, dear, dear, dear!'

'Yes, sir: – boys? Start my soul-bolts, what a difference, in a moral point of view, between a corn-husker and a boy! Sir, a corn-husker, for its patient continuance in well-doing, might not unfitly go to heaven. Do you suppose a boy will?'

'A corn-husker in heaven! (turning up the whites of his eyes). Respected sir, this way of talking as if heaven were a kind of Washington patent office museum – oh, oh, oh! – as if mere machine-work and puppet-work went to heaven – oh, oh, oh! Things incapable of free agency, to receive the eternal reward of well-doing – oh, oh, oh.'

'You Praise-God-Barebones you, what are you groaning about? Did I say anything of that sort? Seems to me, though you talk so good, you are mighty quick at a hint the other way, or else you want to pick a polemic quarrel with me.'

'It may be so or not, respected sir,' was now the demure reply; 'but if it be, it is only because as a soldier out of honour is quick in taking affront, so a Christian out of religion is quick, sometimes perhaps a little too much so, in spying heresy.'

'Well,' after an astonished pause, 'for an unaccountable pair, you and the herb-doctor ought to yoke together.'

So saying, the bachelor was eyeing him rather sharply, when he with the brass plate recalled him to the discussion by a hint, not unflattering, that he (the man with the brass plate) was all anxiety to hear him further on the subject of servants.

'About that matter,' exclaimed the impulsive bachelor, going off at the hint like a rocket, 'all thinking minds are, now-a-days, coming to the conclusion – one derived from an immense hereditary experience – see what Horace and others of the ancients say of servants – coming to the conclusion, I say, that boy or man, the human animal is, for most work-purposes, a losing animal. Can't be trusted; less trustworthy than oxen; for conscientiousness a turn-spit dog excels him. Hence these thousand new inventions – carding machines, horse-shoe machines, tunnel-boring machines, reaping machines, apple-paring machines, boot-blacking machines, sewing machines, shaving machines, run-of-errand machines, dumb-waiter machines, and the Lord-only-knows-what machines; all of which announce the era when that refractory animal, the working or serving man, shall be a buried by-gone, a superseded fossil. Shortly prior to which glorious time, I doubt not that a price will be put upon their peltries as upon the knavish 'possums, especially the boys. Yes, sir (ringing his rifle down on the deck), I rejoice to think that the day is at hand, when, prompted to it by law, I shall shoulder this gun and go out a boy-shooting.'

'Oh, now! Lord, Lord, Lord! – But *our* office, respected sir, conducted as I ventured to observe –'

'No, sir,' bristlingly settling his stubble chin in his coon-skins. 'Don't try to oil me; the herb-doctor tried that. My experience, carried now through a course – worse than salivation – a course of five and thirty boys, proves to me that boyhood is a natural state of rascality.'

'Save us, save us!'

'Yes, sir, yes. My name is Pitch; I stick to what I say. I speak from fifteen years' experience; five and thirty boys; American, Irish, English, German, African, Mulatto; not to speak of that China boy sent me by one who well knew my perplexities, from California; and that Lascar boy from Bombay. Thug! I found him sucking the embryo life from my spring eggs. All rascals, sir, every soul of them; Caucasian or Mongol. Amazing the endless variety of rascality in human nature of the juvenile sort. I remember that, having discharged, one after another, twenty-nine boys – each, too, for some wholly unforeseen species of viciousness peculiar to that one peculiar boy – I remember saying to myself: Now, then, surely, I have got to the end of the list, wholly exhausted it; I have only now to get me a boy, any boy different from those twenty-nine preceding boys, and he infallibly shall be that virtuous boy I have so long been seeking. But, bless me! this thirtieth boy – by the way, having at the time long forsworn your intelligence offices, I had him sent to me from the Commissioners of Emigration, all the way from New York, culled out carefully, in fine, at my particular request, from a standing army of eight hundred boys, the flowers of all nations, so they wrote me, temporarily in barracks on an East River island – I say, this thirtieth boy was in person not ungraceful; his deceased mother a lady's maid, or something of that sort; and in manner, why, in a plebeian way, a perfect Chesterfield; very intelligent, too – quick as a flash. But, such suavity! "Please sir! Please sir!" always bowing and saying, "Please sir." In the strangest way, too, combining a filial affection with a menial respect. Took such warm, singular interest in my affairs. Wanted to be considered one of the family –

sort of adopted son of mine, I suppose. Of a morning, when I would go out to my stable, with what childlike good nature he would trot out my nag, "Please sir, I think he's getting fatter and fatter." "But, he don't look very clean, does he?" unwilling to be downright harsh with so affectionate a lad; "and he seems a little hollow inside the haunch there, don't he? or no, perhaps I don't see plain this morning." "Oh, please sir, it's just there I think he's gaining so, please." Polite scamp! I soon found he never gave that wretched nag his oats of nights; didn't bed him either. Was above that sort of chambermaid work. No end to his wilful neglects. But the more he abused my service, the more polite he grew.'

'Oh, sir, some way you mistook him.'

'Not a bit of it. Besides, sir, he was a boy who under a Chester-fieldian exterior hid strong destructive propensities. He cut up my horse-blanket for the bits of leather, for hinges to his chest. Denied it point-blank. After he was gone, found the shreds under his mat-tress. Would slyly break his hoe-handle, too, on purpose to get rid of hoeing. Then be so gracefully penitent for his fatal excess of industrious strength. Offer to mend all by taking a nice stroll to the nighest settlement – cherry-trees in full bearing all the way – to get the broken thing cobbled. Very politely stole my pears, odd pennies, shillings, dollars, and nuts; regular squirrel at it. But I could prove nothing. Expressed to him my suspicions. Said I, moderately enough, "A little less politeness, and a little more hon-esty would suit me better." He fired up; threatened to sue for libel. I won't say anything about his afterwards, in Ohio, being found in the act of gracefully putting a bar across a railroad track, for the reason that a stoker called him the rogue that he was. But enough: polite boys or saucy boys, white boys or black boys, smart boys or lazy boys, Caucasian boys or Mongol boys – all are rascals.'

'Shocking, shocking!' nervously tucking his frayed cravat-end out of sight. 'Surely, respected sir, you labour under a deplorable hallucination. Why, pardon again, you seem to have not the slightest confidence in boys. I admit, indeed, that boys, some of them at least, are but too prone to one little foolish foible or other. But, what then, respected sir, when, by natural laws, they finally outgrow such things, and wholly?'

Having until now vented himself mostly in plaintive dissent of canine whines and groans, the man with the brass-plate seemed beginning to summon courage to a less timid encounter. But, upon his maiden essay, was not very encouragingly handled, since the dialogue immediately continued as follows:

'Boys outgrow what is amiss in them? From bad boys spring good men? Sir, "the child is father of the man"; hence, as all boys are rascals, so are all men. But, God bless me, you must know these things better than I; keeping an intelligence office as you do; a business which must furnish peculiar facilities for studying mankind. Come, come up here, sir; confess you know these things pretty well, after all. Do you not know that all men are rascals, and all boys, too?'

'Sir,' replied the other, spite of his shocked feelings seeming to pluck up some spirit, but not to an indiscreet degree, 'Sir, heaven be praised, I am far, very far from knowing what you say. True,' he thoughtfully continued, 'with my associates, I keep an intelligence office, and for ten years, come October, have, one way or other, been concerned in that line; for no small period in the great city of Cincinnati, too; and though, as you hint, within that long interval, I must have had more or less favourable opportunity for studying mankind – in a business way, scanning not only the faces, but ransacking the lives of several thousands of human beings, male and female, of various nations, both employers and employed, genteel and ungenteel, educated and uneducated; yet – of course, I candidly admit, with some random exceptions, I have, so far as my small observation goes, found that mankind thus domestically viewed, confidentially viewed, I may say; they, upon the whole – making some reasonable allowances for human imperfection – present as pure a moral spectacle as the purest angel could wish. I say it, respected sir, with confidence.'

'Gammon! You don't mean what you say. Else you are like a landsman at sea; don't know the ropes, the very things everlastingly pulled before your eyes. Serpent-like, they glide about, travelling blocks too subtle for you. In short, the entire ship is a riddle. Why, you green ones wouldn't know if she were unseaworthy; but still, with thumbs stuck back into your arm-holes, pace the rotten planks, singing, like a fool, words put into your green mouth by the cunning owner, the man who, heavily insuring it, sends his ship to be wrecked –

A wet sheet and a flowing sea!

– and, sir, now that it occurs to me, your talk, the whole of it, is but a wet sheet and a flowing sea, and an idle wind that follows fast, offering a striking contrast to my own discourse.'

'Sir,' exclaimed the man with the brass-plate, his patience now more or less tasked, 'permit me with deference to hint that some of your remarks are injudiciously worded. And thus we say to our patrons, when they enter our office full of abuse of us because of some worthy boy we may have sent them – some boy wholly misjudged for the time. Yes, sir, permit me to remark that you do not sufficiently consider, that, though a small man, I may have my small share of feelings.'

'Well, well, I didn't mean to wound your feelings at all. And that they are small, very small, I take your word for it. Sorry, sorry. But truth is like a thrashing-machine; tender sensibilities must keep out of the way. Hope you understand me. Don't want to hurt you. All I say is, what I said in the first place, only now I swear it, that all boys are rascals.'

'Sir,' lowly replied the other, still forbearing like an old lawyer badgered in court, or else like a good-hearted simpleton, the butt of mischievous wags, 'Sir, since you come back to the point, will you allow me, in my small, quiet way, to submit to you certain small, quiet views of the subject in hand?'

'Oh, yes!' with insulting indifference, rubbing his chin and looking the other way. 'Oh, yes; go on.'

'Well, then, respected sir,' continued the other, now assuming as genteel an attitude as the irritating set of his pinched five-dollar suit would permit; 'Well, then, sir, the peculiar principles, the strictly philosophical principles, I may say,' guardedly rising in dignity, as he guardedly rose on his toes, 'upon which our office is founded, have led me and my associates, in our small, quiet way, to a careful analytical study of man, conducted, too, on a quiet theory, and with an unobtrusive aim wholly our own. That theory I will not now at large set forth. But some of the discoveries resulting from it, I will, by your permission, very briefly mention; such of them, I mean, as refer to the state of boyhood scientifically viewed.'

'Then you have studied the thing? expressly studied boys, eh? Why didn't you out with that before?'

'Sir, in my small business way, I have not conversed with so many masters, gentlemen masters, for nothing. I have been taught that in this world there is a precedence of opinions as well as of persons. You have kindly given me your views, I am now, with modesty, about to give you mine.'

'Stop flunkying – go on.'

'In the first place, sir, our theory teaches us to proceed by analogy from the physical to the moral. Are we right there, sir? Now, sir, take a young boy, a young male infant rather, a man-child in short – what sir, I respectfully ask, do you in the first place remark?'

'A rascal, sir! present and prospective, a rascal!'

'Sir, if passion is to invade, surely science must evacuate. May I proceed? Well, then, what, in the first place, in a general view, do you remark, respected sir, in that male baby or man-child?'

The bachelor privily growled, but this time, upon the whole, better governed himself than before, though not, indeed, to the degree of thinking it prudent to risk an articulate response.

'What do you remark? I respectfully repeat.' But, as no answer came, only the low, half-suppressed growl, as of Brum in a hollow trunk, the questioner continued: 'Well, sir, if you will permit me, in my small way, to speak for you, you remark, respected sir, an incipient creation; loose sort of sketchy thing; a little preliminary rag-paper study, or careless cartoon, so to speak, of a man. The idea, you see, respected sir, is there; but, as yet, wants filling out. In a word, respected sir, the man-child is at present but little, every way; I don't pretend to deny it; but, then, he *promises* well, does he not? Yes, promises very well indeed, I may say. (So, too, we say to our patrons in reference to some noble little youngster objected to for being a *dwarf*.) But, to advance one step further,' extending his thread-bare leg, as he drew a pace nearer, 'we must now drop the figure of the rag-paper cartoon, and borrow one – to use presently, when wanted – from the horticultural kingdom. Some bud, lily-bud, if you please. Now, such points as the new-born man-child has – as yet not all that could be desired, I am free to confess – still, such as they are, there they are, and palpable as those of an adult. But we stop not here,' taking another step. 'The man-child not only possesses these present points, small though they are, but, likewise – now our horticultural image comes into play – like the bud of the lily, he contains concealed rudiments of others; that is, points at present invisible, with beauties at present dormant.'

'Come, come, this talk is getting too horticultural and beautiful altogether. Cut it short, cut it short!'

'Respected sir,' with a rustily martial sort of gesture, like a decayed corporal's, 'when deploying into the field of discourse the vanguard of an important argument, much more in evolving the grand central forces of a new philosophy of boys, as I may say, surely you will kindly allow scope adequate to the movement in hand, small and humble in its way as that movement may be. Is it worth my while to go on, respected sir?'

'Yes, stop flunkying and go on.'

Thus encouraged, again the philosopher with the brass-plate proceeded:

'Supposing, sir, that worthy gentleman (in such terms, to an applicant for service, we allude to some patron we chance to have in our eye), supposing, respected sir, that worthy gentleman, Adam, to have been dropped overnight in Eden, as a calf in the pasture; supposing that, sir – then how could even the learned serpent himself have foreknown that such a downy-chinned little innocent would eventually rival the goat in a beard? Sir, wise as the serpent was, that eventuality would have been entirely hidden from his wisdom.'

'I don't know about that. The devil is very sagacious. To judge by the event, he appears to have understood man better even than the Being who made him.'

'For God's sake, don't say that, sir! To the point. Can it now with fairness be denied that, in his beard, the man-child prospectively possesses an appendix, not less imposing than patriarchal; and for this goodly beard, should we not by generous anticipation give the man-child, even in his cradle, credit? Should we not now, sir? respectfully I put it.'

'Yes, if like pig-weed he mows it down soon as it shoots,' porcinely rubbing his stubble-chin against his coon-skins.

'I have hinted at the analogy,' continued the other, calmly disregardful of the digression; 'now to apply it. Suppose a boy evince no noble quality. Then generously give him credit for his prospective one. Don't you see? So we say to our patrons when they would fain return a boy upon as unworthy: "Madam, or sir (as the case may be), has this boy a beard?" "No." "Has he, we respectfully ask, as yet, evinced any noble quality?" "No, indeed." "Then, madam, or sir, take him back, we humbly beseech; and keep him till that same noble quality sprouts; for, have confidence, it, like the beard, is in him."'

'Very fine theory,' scornfully exclaimed the bachelor, yet in secret, perhaps, not entirely undisturbed by these strange new views of the matter; 'but what trust is to be placed in it?'

'The trust of perfect confidence, sir. To proceed. Once more, if you please, regard the man-child.'

'Hold!' paw-like thrusting out his bear-skin arm, 'don't intrude that man-child upon me too often. He who loves not bread dotes not on dough. As little of your man-child as your logical arrangements will admit.'

'Anew regard the man-child,' with inspired intrepidity repeated he with the brass-plate, 'in the perspective of his developments, I mean. At first the man-child has no teeth, but about the sixth month – am I right, sir?'

'Don't know anything about it.'

'To proceed then: though at first deficient in teeth, about the sixth month the man-child begins to put forth in that particular. And sweet those tender little puttings-forth are.'

'Very, but blown out of his mouth directly, worthless enough.'

'Admitted. And, therefore, we say to our patrons returning with a boy alleged not only to be deficient in goodness, but redundant in ill: "The lad, madam or sir, evinces very corrupt qualities, does he?" "No end to them." "But, have confidence, there will be; for pray, madam, in this lad's early childhood, were not those frail first teeth, then his, followed by his present sound, even, beautiful and permanent set? And the more objectionable those first teeth became, was not that, madam, we respectfully submit, so much the more reason to look for their speedy substitution by the present sound, even, beautiful and permanent ones?" "True, true, can't deny that." "Then, madam, take him back, we respectfully beg, and wait till, in the now swift course of nature, dropping those transient moral blemishes you complain of, he replacingly buds forth in the sound, even, beautiful and permanent virtues."'

'Very philosophical again,' was the contemptuous reply – the outward contempt, perhaps, proportioned to the inward misgiving. 'Vastly philosophical, indeed, but tell me – to continue your analogy – since the second teeth followed – in fact, came from – the first, is there no chance the blemish may be transmitted?'

'Not at all.' Abating in humility as he gained in the argument. 'The second teeth follow, but do not come from, the first; successors, not sons. The first teeth are not like the germ blossom of the apple, at once the father of, and incorporated into, the growth it foreruns; but they are thrust from their place by the independent undergrowth of the succeeding set – an illustration, by the way, which shows more for me than I meant, though not more than I wish.'

'What does it show?' Surly-looking as a thunder-cloud with the inkept unrest of unacknowledged conviction.

'It shows this, respected sir, that in the case of any boy, especially an ill one, to apply unconditionally the saying, that the "child is father of the man", is, besides implying an uncharitable aspersion of the race, affirming a thing very wide of –'

'– Your analogy,' like a snapping turtle.

'Yes, respected sir.'

'But is analogy argument? You are a punster.'

'Punster, respected sir?' with a look of being aggrieved.

'Yes, you pun with ideas as another man may with words.'

'Oh well, sir, whoever talks in that strain, whoever has no confidence in human reason, whoever despises human reason, in vain to reason with him. Still, respected sir,' altering his air, 'permit me to hint that, had not the force of analogy moved you somewhat, you would hardly have offered to contemn it.'

'Talk away,' disdainfully; 'but pray tell me what has that last analogy of yours to do with your intelligence office business?'

'Everything to do with it, respected sir. From that analogy we derive the reply made to such a patron as, shortly after being supplied by us with an adult servant, proposes to return him upon our hands; not that, while with the patron, said adult has given any cause of dissatisfaction, but the patron has just chanced to hear something unfavourable concerning him from some gentleman who employed said adult long before, while a boy. To which too fastidious patron, we, taking said adult by the hand, and graciously reintroducing him to the patron, say: "Far be it from you, madam, or sir, to proceed in your censure against this adult, in anything of the spirit of an ex-post-facto law. Madam, or sir, would you visit upon the butterfly the sins of the caterpillar? In the natural advance of all creatures, do they not bury themselves over and over again in the endless resurrection of better and better? Madam, or sir, take back this adult; he may have been a caterpillar, but is now a butterfly." '

'Pun away; but even accepting your analogical pun, what does it amount to? Was the caterpillar one creature, and is the butterfly another? The butterfly is the caterpillar in a gaudy cloak; stripped of which, there lies the impostor's long spindle of a body, pretty much worm-shaped as before.'

'You reject the analogy. To the facts then. You deny that a youth of one character can be transformed into a man of an opposite character. Now then – yes, I have it. There's the founder of La Trappe, and Ignatius Loyola; in boyhood, and someway into manhood, both devil-may-care bloods, and yet, in the end, the wonders of the world for anchoritish self-command. These two examples, by-the-way, we cite to such patrons as would hastily return rakish young waiters upon us. "Madam, or sir – patience; patience," we say; "good madam, or sir, would you discharge forth your cask of good wine, because, while working, it riles more or less? Then discharge not forth this young waiter; the good in him is working." "But he is a sad rake." "Therein is his promise; the rake being crude material for the saint." '

'Ah, you are a talking man – what I call a wordy man. You talk, talk.'

'And with submission, sir, what is the greatest judge, bishop or prophet, but a talking man? He talks, talks. It is the peculiar vocation of a teacher to talk. What's wisdom itself but table-talk? The best wisdom in this world, and the last spoken by its teacher, did it not literally and truly come in the form of table-talk?'

'You, you, you!' rattling down his rifle.

'To shift the subject, since we cannot agree. Pray, what is your opinion, respected sir, of St Augustine?'

'St Augustine? What should I, or you either, know of him? Seems to me, for one in such a business, to say nothing of such a coat, that though you don't know a great deal, indeed, yet you know a good deal more than you ought to know, or than you have a right to know, or than it is safe or expedient for you to know, or than, in the fair course of life, you could have honestly come to know. I am of opinion you should be served like a Jew in the middle ages with his gold; this knowledge of yours, which you haven't enough knowledge to know how to make a right use of, it should be taken from you. And so I have been thinking all along.'

'You are merry, sir. But you have a little looked into St Augustine I suppose.'

'St Augustine on Original Sin is my text book. But you, I ask again, where do you find time or inclination for these out-of-the-way speculations? In fact, your whole talk, the more I think of it, is altogether unexampled and extraordinary.'

'Respected sir, have I not already informed you that the quite new method, the strictly philosophical one, on which our office is founded, has led me and my associates to an enlarged study of mankind. It was my fault, if I did not, likewise, hint, that these studies directed always to the scientific procuring of good servants of all sorts, boys included, for the kind gentlemen, our patrons – that these studies, I say, have been conducted equally among all books of all libraries, as among all men of all nations. Then, you rather like St Augustine, sir?'

'Excellent genius!'

'In some points he was; yet, how comes it that under his own hand, St Augustine confesses that, until his thirtieth year, he was a very sad dog?'

'A saint a sad dog?'

'Not the saint, but the saint's irresponsible little forerunner – the boy.'

'All boys are rascals, and so are all men,' again flying off at his tangent; 'my name is Pitch; I stick to what I say.'

'Ah, sir, permit me – when I behold you on this mild summer's eve, thus eccentrically clothed in the skins of wild beasts, I cannot but conclude that the equally grim and unsuitable habit of your mind is likewise but an eccentric assumption, having no basis in your genuine soul, no more than in nature herself.'

'Well, really, now – really,' fidgeted the bachelor, not unaffected in his conscience by these benign personalities, 'really, really, now, I don't know but that I may have been a little bit too hard upon those five and thirty boys of mine.'

'Glad to find you a little softening, sir. Who knows now, but that flexile gracefulness, however questionable at the time of that thirtieth boy of yours, might have been the silky husk of the most solid qualities of maturity. It might have been with him as with the ear of the Indian corn.'

'Yes, yes, yes,' excitedly cried the bachelor, as the light of this new illustration broke in, 'yes, yes; and now that I think of it, how often I've sadly watched my Indian corn in May, wondering whether such sickly, half-eaten sprouts, could ever thrive up into the stiff, stately spear of August.'

'A most admirable reflection, sir, and you have only, according to the analogical theory first started by our office, to apply it to that thirtieth boy in question, and see the result. Had you but kept that thirtieth boy – been patient with his sickly virtues, cultivated them, hoed round them, why what a glorious guerdon would have been yours, when at last you should have had a St Augustine for an ostler.'

'Really, really – well, I am glad I didn't send him to jail, as at first I intended.'

'Oh that would have been too bad. Grant he was vicious. The petty vices of boys are like the innocent kicks of colts, as yet imperfectly broken. Some boys know not virtue only for the same reason they know not French; it was never taught them.

Established upon the basis of parental charity, juvenile asylums exist by law for the benefit of lads convicted of acts which, in adults, would have received other requital. Why? Because, do what they will, society, like our office, at bottom has a Christian confidence in boys. And all this we say to our patrons.'

'Your patrons, sir, seem your marines, to whom you may say anything,' said the other, relapsing. 'Why do knowing employers shun youths from asylums, though offered them at the smallest wages? I'll none of your reformado boys.'

'Such a boy, respected sir, I would not get for you, but a boy that never needed reform. Do not smile, for as whooping-cough and measles are juvenile diseases, and yet some juveniles never have them, so are there boys equally free from juvenile vices. True, for the best of boys, measles may be contagious, and evil communications corrupt good manners; but a boy with a sound mind in a sound body – such is the boy I would get you. If hitherto, sir, you have struck upon a peculiarly bad vein of boys, so much the more hope now of your hitting a good one.'

'That sounds a kind of reasonable, as it were – a little so, really. In fact, though you have said a great many foolish things, very foolish and absurd things, yet, upon the whole, your conversation has been such as might almost lead one less distrustful than I to repose a certain conditional confidence in you, I had almost added in your office, also. Now, for the humour of it, supposing that even I, I myself, really had this sort of conditional confidence, though but a grain, what sort of a boy, in sober fact, could you send me? And what would be your fee?'

'Conducted,' replied the other somewhat loftily, rising now in eloquence as his proselyte, for all his pretences, sunk in conviction, 'conducted upon principles involving care, learning, and labour, exceeding what is usual in kindred institutions, the Philosophical Intelligence Office is forced to charges somewhat higher than customary. Briefly, our fee is three dollars in advance. As for the boy, by a lucky chance, I have a very promising little fellow now in my eye – a very likely little fellow, indeed.'

'Honest?'

'As the day is long. Might trust him with untold millions. Such, at least, were the marginal observations on the phrenological chart of his head, submitted to me by the mother.'

'How old?'

'Just fifteen.'

'Tall? Stout?'

'Uncommonly so, for his age, his mother remarked.'

'Industrious?'

'The busy bee.'

The bachelor fell into a troubled reverie. At last, with much hesitancy, he spoke:

'Do you think now, candidly, that – I say candidly – candidly – could I have some small, limited – some faint, conditional degree of confidence in that boy? Candidly, now?'

'Candidly, you could.'

'A sound boy? A good boy?'

'Never knew one more so.'

The bachelor fell into another irresolute reverie; then said: 'Well, now, you have suggested some rather new views of boys, and men, too. Upon those views in the concrete I at present decline to determine. Nevertheless, for the sake purely of a scientific experiment, I will try that boy. I don't think him an angel, mind. No, no. But I'll try him. There are my three dollars, and here is my address. Send him along this day two weeks. Hold, you will be wanting the money for his passage. There,' handing it somewhat reluctantly.

'Ah, thank you. I had forgotten his passage;' then, altering in manner, and gravely holding the bills, continued: 'Respected sir, never willingly do I handle money not with perfect willingness, nay, with a certain alacrity paid. Either tell me that you have a perfect and unquestioning confidence in me (never mind the boy now) or permit me respectfully to return these bills.'

'Put 'em up, put 'em up!'

'Thank you. Confidence is the indispensable basis of all sorts of business transactions. Without it, commerce between man and man, as between country and country, would, like a watch, run down and stop. And now, supposing that against present expectation the lad should, after all, evince some little undesirable trait, do not, respected sir, rashly dismiss him. Have but patience, have but confidence. Those transient vices will, ere long, fall out, and be replaced by the sound, firm, even and permanent virtues. Ah,' glancing shoreward, towards a grotesquely-shaped bluff, 'there's the Devil's Joke, as they call it; the bell for landing will shortly ring. I must go look up the cook I brought for the inn-keeper at Cairo.'

Chapter Twenty-Three

In Which the Powerful Effect of Natural Scenery is Evinced in the Case of the Missourian, Who, in View of the Region Round About Cairo, Has a Return of His Chilly Fit

At Cairo, the old established firm of Fever & Ague is still settling up its unfinished business; that Creole grave-digger, Yellow Jack – his hand at the mattock and spade has not lost its cunning; while Don Saturninus Typhus, taking his constitutional with Death, Calvin Edson and three undertakers, in the morass, snuffs up the mephitic breeze with zest.

In the dank twilight, fanned with mosquitoes, and sparkling with fire-flies, the boat now lies before Cairo. She has landed certain passengers, and tarries for the coming of expected ones. Leaning over the rail on the inshore side, the Missourian eyes through the dubious medium that swampy and squalid domain; and over it audibly mumbles his cynical mind to himself, as Apemantus' dog may have mumbled his bone. He bethinks him that the man with the brass-plate was to land on this villainous bank, and for that cause, if no other, begins to suspect him. Like one beginning to rouse himself from a dose of chloroform treacherously given, he half divines, too, that he, the philosopher, had unwittingly been betrayed into being an unphilosophical dupe. To what vicissitudes of light and shade is man subject! He ponders the mystery of human subjectivity in general. He thinks he perceives with Crossbones, his favourite author, that, as one may wake up well in the morning, very well, indeed, and brisk as a buck, I thank you, but ere bedtime get under the weather, there is no telling how – so one may wake up wise, and slow of assent, very wise and very slow, I assure you, and for all that, before night, by like trick in the atmosphere, be left in the lurch a ninny.

Health and wisdom equally precious, and equally little as unfluctuating possessions to be relied on.

But where was slipped in the entering wedge? Philosophy, knowledge, experience – were those trusty knights of the castle recreant? No, but unknown to them, the enemy stole on the castle's south side, its genial one, where Suspicion, the warder, parleyed. In fine, his too indulgent, too artless and companionable nature betrayed him. Admonished by which, he thinks he must be a little splenetic in his intercourse henceforth.

He revolves the crafty process of sociable chat, by which, as he fancies, the man with the brass-plate wormed into him, and made such a fool of him as insensibly to persuade him to waive, in his exceptional case, that general law of distrust systematically applied to the race. He revolves, but cannot comprehend, the operation, still less the operator. Was the man a trickster, it must be more for the love than the lucre. Two or three dirty dollars the motive to so many nice wiles? And yet how full of mean needs his seeming. Before his mental vision the person of that threadbare Talleyrand, that impoverished Machiavelli, that seedy Rosicrucian – for something of all these he vaguely deems him – passes now in puzzled review. Fain, in his disfavour, would he make out a logical case. The doctrine of analogies recurs. Fallacious enough doctrine when wielded against one's prejudices, but in corroboration of cherished suspicions not without likelihood. Analogically, he couples the slanting cut of the equivocator's coat-tails with the sinister cast in his eye; he weighs slyboot's sleek speech in the light imparted by the oblique import of the smooth slope of his worn boot-heels; the insinuator's undulating flunkyisms dovetail into those of the flunky beast that windeth his way on his belly.

From these uncordial reveries he is roused by a cordial slap on the shoulder, accompanied by a spicy volume of tobacco smoke, out of which came a voice, sweet as a seraph's:

'A penny for your thoughts, my fine fellow.'

Chapter Twenty-Four

*A Philanthropist Undertakes to Convert a Misanthrope, But
Does Not Get Beyond Confuting Him*

'Hands off!' cried the bachelor, involuntarily covering dejection
with moroseness.

'Hands off? that sort of label won't do in our Fair. Whoever in
our Fair has fine feelings loves to feel the nap of fine cloth, especially when a fine fellow wears it.'

'And who of my fine-fellow species may you be? From the Bra-
zils, ain't you? Toucan fowl. Fine feathers on foul meat.'

This ungentle mention of the toucan was not improbably suggested by the parti-hued, and rather plumagy aspect of the
stranger, no bigot it would seem, but a liberalist, in dress, and
whose wardrobe, almost anywhere but on the liberal Mississippi,
used to all sorts of fantastic informalities, might, even to observers less critical than the bachelor, have looked, if anything, a little
out of the common; but not more so perhaps than, considering
the bear and raccoon costume, the bachelor's own appearance.
In short, the stranger sported a vesture barred with various hues,
that of the cochineal predominating, in style participating of a
Highland plaid, Emir's robe, and French blouse; from its plaited
sort of front peeped glimpses of a flowered regatta-shirt, while,
for the rest, white trowsers of ample duck flowed over maroon-
coloured slippers, and a jaunty smoking-cap of regal purple
crowned him off at top; king of travelled good-fellows, evidently.
Grotesque as all was, nothing looked stiff or unused; all showed
signs of easy service, the least wonted thing setting like a wonted
glove. That genial hand, which had just been laid on the ungenial
shoulder, was now carelessly thrust down before him, sailor-
fashion, into a sort of Indian belt, confining the redundant vesture;

the other held, by its long bright cherry-stem, a Nuremberg pipe in blast, its great porcelain bowl painted in miniature with linked crests and arms of interlinked nations – a florid show. As by subtle saturations of its mellowing essence the tobacco had ripened the bowl, so it looked as if something similar of the interior spirit came rosily out on the cheek. But rosy pipe-bowl, or rosy countenance, all was lost on that unrosy man, the bachelor, who, waiting a moment till the commotion, caused by the boat's renewed progress, had a little abated, thus continued:

'Hark ye,' jeeringly eyeing the cap and belt, 'did you ever see Signor Marzetti in the African pantomime?'

'No; – good performer?'

'Excellent; plays the intelligent ape till he seems it. With such naturalness can a being endowed with an immortal spirit enter into that of a monkey. But where's your tail? In the pantomime, Marzetti, no hypocrite in his monkery, prides himself on that.'

The stranger, now at rest, sideways and genially, on one hip, his right leg cavalierly crossed before the other, the toe of his vertical slipper pointed easily down on the deck, whiffed out a long, leisurely sort of indifferent and charitable puff, betokening him more or less of the mature man of the world, a character which, like its opposite, the sincere Christian's, is not always swift to take offence; and then, drawing near, still smoking, again laid his hand, this time with mild impressiveness, on the ursine shoulder, and not unamiably said: 'That in your address there is a sufficiency of the *fortiter in re* few unbiassed observers will question; but that this is duly attempered with the *suaviter in modo* may admit, I think, of an honest doubt. My dear fellow,' beaming his eyes full upon him, 'what injury have I done you, that you should receive my greeting with a curtailed civility?'

'Off hands'; once more shaking the friendly member from him. 'Who in the name of the great chimpanzee, in whose likeness, you, Marzetti, and the other chatterers are made, who in thunder are you?'

'A cosmopolitan, a catholic man; who, being such, ties himself to no narrow tailor or teacher, but federates, in heart as in costume, something of the various gallantries of men under various suns. Oh, one roams not over the gallant globe in vain. Bred by it, is a fraternal and fusing feeling. No man is a stranger. You accost anybody. Warm and confiding, you wait not for measured advances. And though, indeed, mine, in this instance, have met with no very hilarious encouragement, yet the principle of a true citizen of the world is still to return good for ill. – My dear fellow, tell me how I can serve you.'

'By dispatching yourself, Mr Popinjay-of-the-world, into the heart of the Lunar Mountains. You are another of them. Out of my sight!'

'Is the sight of humanity so very disagreeable to you then? Ah, I may be foolish, but for my part, in all its aspects, I love it. Served up à la Pole, or à la Moor, à la Ladrone, or à la Yankee, that good dish, man, still delights me; or rather is man a wine I never weary of comparing and sipping; wherefore am I a pledged cosmopolitan, a sort of London-Dock-Vault connoisseur, going about from Teheran to Natchitoches, a taster of races; in all his vintages, smacking my lips over this racy creature, man, continually. But as there are teetotal palates which have a distaste even for Amontillado, so I suppose there may be teetotal souls which relish not even the very best brands of humanity. Excuse me, but it just occurs to me that you, my dear fellow, possibly lead a solitary life.'

'Solitary?' starting as at a touch of divination.

'Yes: in a solitary life one insensibly contracts oddities, – talking to one's self now.'

'Been eaves-dropping, eh?'

'Why, a soliloquist in a crowd can hardly but be overheard, and without much reproach to the hearer.'

'You are an eaves-dropper.'

'Well. Be it so.'

'Confess yourself an eaves-dropper.'

'I confess that when you were muttering here I, passing by, caught a word or two, and, by like chance, something previous of your chat with the intelligence-office man; – a rather sensible fellow, by the way; much of my style of thinking; would, for his own sake, he were of my style of dress. Grief to good minds, to see a man of superior sense forced to hide his light under the bushel of an inferior coat. – Well, from what little I heard, I said to myself, Here now is one with the unprofitable philosophy of disesteem for man. Which disease, in the main, I have observed – excuse me – to spring from a certain lowness, if not sourness, of spirits inseparable from sequestration. Trust me, one had better mix in, and do like others. Sad business, this holding out against having a good time. Life is a pic-nic *en costume*; one must take a part, assume a character, stand ready in a sensible way to play the fool. To come in plain clothes, with a long face, as a wiseacre, only makes one a discomfort to himself, and a blot upon the scene. Like your jug of cold water among the wine-flasks, it leaves you unelated among the elated ones. No, no. This austerity won't do. Let me tell you too – *en confiance* – that while revelry may not always merge into ebriety, soberness, in too deep potations, may become a sort of sottishness. Which sober sottishness, in my way of thinking, is only to be cured by beginning at the other end of the horn, to tipple a little.'

'Pray, what society of vintners and old topers are you hired to lecture for?'

'I fear I did not give my meaning clearly. A little story may help. The story of the worthy old woman of Goshen, a very moral old woman, who wouldn't let her shoats eat fattening apples in fall, for fear the fruit might ferment upon their brains, and so make them swinish. Now, during a green Christmas, inauspicious to the old, this worthy old woman fell into a moping decline, took to her bed, no appetite, and refused to see her best friends. In much concern her good man sent for the doctor, who, after seeing the patient and putting a question or two, beckoned the husband out, and said: "Deacon, do you want her cured?" "Indeed I do." "Go directly, then, and buy a jug of Santa Cruz." "Santa Cruz? my wife drink Santa Cruz?" "Either that or die." "But how much?" "As much as she can get down." "But she'll get drunk!" "That's the cure." Wise men, like doctors, must be obeyed. Much against the grain, the sober deacon got the unsober medicine, and, equally against her conscience, the poor old woman took it; but, by so doing, ere long recovered health and spirits, famous appetite, and glad again to see her friends; and having by this experience broken the ice of arid abstinence, never afterwards kept herself a cup too low.'

This story had the effect of surprising the bachelor into interest, though hardly into approval.

'If I take your parable right,' said he, sinking no little of his former churlishness, 'the meaning is, that one cannot enjoy life with gusto unless he renounce the too-sober view of life. But since the too-sober view is, doubtless, nearer true than the too-drunken; I, who rate truth, though cold water, above untruth, though Tokay, will stick to my earthen jug.'

'I see,' slowly spirting upward a spiral staircase of lazy smoke, I see; you go in for the lofty.'

'How?'

'Oh, nothing! but if I wasn't afraid of prosing, I might tell another story about an old boot in a pieman's loft, contracting there between sun and oven an unseemly, dry-seasoned curl and warp. You've seen such leathery old garretteers, haven't you? Very high, sober, solitary, philosophic, grand, old boots, indeed; but I, for my part, would rather be the pieman's trodden slipper on the ground. Talking of piemen, humble-pie before proud-cake for me. This notion of being lone and lofty is a sad mistake. Men I hold in this respect to be like roosters; the one that betakes himself to a lone and lofty perch is the hen-pecked one, or the one that has the pip.'

'You are abusive!' cried the bachelor, evidently touched.

'Who is abused? You, or the race? You won't stand by and see the human race abused? Oh then, you have some respect for the human race.'

'I have some respect for *myself*,' with a lip not so firm as before.

'And what race may *you* belong to? now don't you see, my dear fellow, in what inconsistencies one involves himself by affecting disesteem for men? To a charm, my little stratagem succeeded. Come, come, think better of it, and, as a first step to a new mind, give up solitude. I fear, by the way, you have at some time been reading Zimmermann, that old Mr Megrims of a Zimmermann, whose book on Solitude is as vain as Hume's on Suicide, as Bacon's on Knowledge; and, like these, will betray him who seeks to steer soul and body by it, like a false religion. All they, be they what boasted ones you please, who, to the yearning of our kind after a founded rule of content, offer aught not in the spirit of fellowly gladness based on due confidence in what is above, away with them for poor dupes, or still poorer impostors.'

His manner here was so earnest that scarcely any auditor, perhaps, but would have been more or less impressed by it, while, possibly, nervous opponents might have a little quailed under it. Thinking within himself a moment, the bachelor replied; 'Had you experience, you would know that your tippling theory, take it in what sense you will, is poor as any other. And Rabelais's pro-wine Koran no more trustworthy than Mahomet's anti-wine one.'

'Enough,' for a finality knocking the ashes from his pipe, 'we talk and keep talking, and still stand where we did. What do you say for a walk? My arm, and let's a turn. They are to have dancing on the hurricane-deck to-night. I shall fling them off a Scotch jig, while, to save the pieces, you hold my loose change; and following that, I propose that you, my dear fellow, stack your gun, and throw your bearskins in a sailor's hornpipe – I holding your watch. What do you say?'

At this proposition the other was himself again, all racoon.

'Look you,' thumping down his rifle, 'are you Jeremy Diddler No. 3?'

'Jeremy Diddler? I have heard of Jeremy the prophet, and Jeremy Taylor the divine, but your other Jeremy is a gentleman I am unacquainted with.'

'You are his confidential clerk, ain't you?'

'*Whose*, pray? Not that I think myself unworthy of being confided in, but I don't understand.'

'You are another of them. Somehow I meet with the most extraordinary metaphysical scamps to-day. Sort of visitation of them. And yet that herb-doctor Diddler somehow takes off the raw edge of the Diddlers that come after him.'

'Herb-doctor? who is he?'

'Like you – another of them.'

'*Who?*' Then drawing near, as if for a good long explanatory chat, his left hand spread, and his pipe-stem coming crosswise down upon it like a ferule, 'You think amiss of me. Now to undeceive you, I will just enter into a little argument and –'

'No you don't. No more little arguments for me. Had too many little arguments to-day.'

'But put a case. Can you deny – I dare you to deny – that the man leading a solitary life is peculiarly exposed to the sorriest misconceptions touching strangers?'

'Yes, I *do* deny it,' again, in his impulsiveness, snapping at the controversial bait, 'and I will confute you there in a trice. Look, you –'

'Now, now, now, my dear fellow,' thrusting out both vertical palms for double shields, 'you crowd me too hard. You don't give one a chance. Say what you will, to shun a social proposition like mine, to shun society in any way, evinces a churlish nature – cold, loveless; as, to embrace it, shows one warm and friendly, in fact, sunshiny.'

Here the other, all agog again, in his perverse way, launched

forth into the unkindest references to deaf old worldlings keeping in the deafening world; and gouty gluttons limping to their
gouty gourmandizings; and corsetted coquettes clasping their
corsetted cavaliers in the waltz, all for disinterested society's sake;
and thousands, bankrupt through lavishness, ruining themselves
out of pure love of the sweet company of man – no envies, rival-
ries, or other unhandsome motive to it.

'Ah, now,' deprecating with his pipe, 'irony is so unjust; never
could abide irony; something Satanic about irony. God defend
me from Irony, and Satire his bosom friend.'

'A right knave's prayer, and a right fool's, too,' snapping his
rifle-lock.

'Now be frank. Own that was a little gratuitous. But, no, no,
you didn't mean it; any way, I can make allowances. Ah, did you
but know it, how much pleasanter to puff at this philanthropic
pipe, than still to keep fumbling at that misanthropic rifle. As for
your worldling, glutton, and coquette, though, doubtless, being
such, they may have their little foibles – as who has not? – yet not
one of the three can be reproached with that awful sin of shunning society; awful I call it, for not seldom it presupposes a still
darker thing than itself – remorse.'

'Remorse drives man away from man? How came your fellow-
creature, Cain, after the first murder, to go and build the first city?
And why is it that the modern Cain dreads nothing so much as
solitary confinement?'

'My dear fellow, you get excited. Say what you will, I for one
must have my fellow-creatures round me. Thick, too – I must
have them thick.'

'The pick-pocket, too, loves to have his fellow-creatures round
him. Tut, man! no one goes into the crowd but for his end; and
the end of too many is the same as the pick-pocket's – a purse.'

'Now, my dear fellow, how can you have the conscience to say
that, when it is as much according to natural law that men are
social as sheep gregarious. But grant that, in being social, each

man has his end, do you, upon the strength of that, do you yourself, I say, mix with man, now, immediately, and be your end a
more genial philosophy. Come, let's take a turn.'

Again he offered his fraternal arm; but the bachelor once more
flung it off, and, raising his rifle in energetic invocation, cried:
'Now the high-constable catch and confound all knaves in towns
and rats in grain-bins, and if in this boat, which is a human grain-
bin for the time, any sly, smooth, philandering rat be dodging
now, pin him, thou high rat-catcher, against this rail.'

'A noble burst! shows you at heart a trump. And when a card's
that, little matters it whether it be spade or diamond. You are
good wine that, to be still better, only needs a shaking up. Come,
let's agree that we'll to New Orleans, and there embark for
London – I staying with my friends nigh Primrose Hill, and you
putting up at the Piazza, Covent Garden – Piazza, Covent Garden; for tell me – since you will not be a disciple to the full – tell
me, was not that humour of Diogenes, which led him to live, a
merry-andrew, in the flower-market, better than that of the less
wise Athenian, which made him a skulking scare-crow in pine-
barrens? An injudicious gentleman, Lord Timon.'

'Your hand!' seizing it.

'Bless me, how cordial a squeeze. It is agreed we shall be brothers, then?'

'As much so as a brace of misanthropes can be,' with another
and terrific squeeze. 'I had thought that the moderns had degenerated beneath the capacity of misanthropy. Rejoiced, though
but in one instance, and that disguised, to be undeceived.'

The other stared in blank amaze.

'Won't do. You are Diogenes, Diogenes in disguise. I say Diogenes masquerading as a cosmopolitan.' With ruefully altered
mien, the stranger still stood mute awhile. At length, in a pained
tone spoke: 'How hard the lot of that pleader who, in his zeal
conceding too much, is taken to belong to a side which he but
labours, however ineffectually, to convert!' Then, with another

change of air: 'To you, an Ishmael, disguising in sportiveness my intent, I came ambassador from the human race, charged with the assurance that for your mislike they bore no answering grudge, but sought to conciliate accord between you and them. Yet you take me not for the honest envoy, but I know not what sort of unheard-of spy. Sir,' he less lowly added, 'this mistaking of your man should teach you how you may mistake all men. For God's sake,' laying both hands upon him, 'get you confidence. See how distrust has duped you. I, Diogenes? I, he who, going a step beyond misanthropy, was less a man-hater than a man-hooter? Better were I stark and stiff!'

With which the philanthropist moved away less lightsome than he had come, leaving the discomfited misanthrope to the solitude he held so sapient.

Chapter Twenty-Five

The Cosmopolitan Makes an Acquaintance

In the act of retiring, the cosmopolitan was met by a passenger, who, with the bluff *abord* of the West, thus addressed him, though a stranger.

'Queer 'coon, your friend. Had a little skrimmage with him myself. Rather entertaining old 'coon, if he wasn't so deuced analytical. Reminded me somehow of what I've heard about Colonel John Moredock of Illinois, only your friend ain't quite so good a fellow at bottom, I should think.'

It was in the semicircular porch of a cabin, opening a recess from the deck, lit by a zoned lamp swung overhead, and sending its light vertically down, like the sun at noon. Beneath the lamp stood the speaker, affording to any one disposed to it no unfavourable chance for scrutiny; but the glance now resting on him betrayed no such rudeness.

A man neither tall nor stout, neither short nor gaunt; but with a body fitted, as by measure, to the service of his mind. For the rest, one less favoured perhaps in his features than his clothes; and of these the beauty may have been less in the fit than the cut; to say nothing of the fineness of the nap, seeming out of keeping with something the reverse of fine in the skin; and the unsuitableness of a violet vest, sending up sunset hues to a countenance betokening a kind of bilious habit.

But, upon the whole, it could not be fairly said that his appearance was unprepossessing; indeed, to the congenial, it would have been doubtless not uncongenial; while to others, it could not fail to be at least curiously interesting, from the warm air of florid cordiality, contrasting itself with one knows not what kind of aguish sallowness of saving discretion lurking behind it.

Ungracious critics might have thought that the manner flushed the man, something in the same fictitious way that the vest flushed the cheek. And though his teeth were singularly good, those same ungracious ones might have hinted that they were too good to be true; or rather, were not so good as they might be; since the best false teeth are those made with at least two or three blemishes, the more to look like life. But fortunately for better constructions, no such critics had the stranger now in eye; only the cosmopolitan, who, after, in the first place, acknowledging his advances with a mute salute – in which acknowledgment, if there seemed less of spirit than in his way of accosting the Missourian, it was probably because of the saddening sequel of that late interview – thus now replied: 'Colonel John Moredock,' repeating the words abstractedly; 'that surname recalls reminiscences. Pray,' with enlivened air, 'was he any way connected with the Moredocks of Moredock Hall, Northamptonshire, England?'

'I know no more of the Moredocks of Moredock Hall than of the Burdocks of Burdock Hut,' returned the other, with the air somehow of one whose fortunes had been of his own making; 'all I know is, that the late Colonel John Moredock was a famous one in his time; eye like Lochiel's; finger like a trigger; nerve like a catamount's; and with but two little oddities – seldom stirred without his rifle, and hated Indians like snakes.'

'Your Moredock, then, would seem a Moredock of Misanthrope Hall – the Woods. No very sleek creature, the colonel, I fancy.'

'Sleek or not, he was no uncombed one, but silky bearded and curly headed, and to all but Indians juicy as a peach. But Indians – how the late Colonel John Moredock, Indian-hater of Illinois, did hate Indians, to be sure!'

'Never heard of such a thing. Hate Indians? Why should he or anybody else hate Indians? *I* admire Indians. Indians I have always heard to be one of the finest of the primitive races, possessed of many heroic virtues. Some noble women, too. When I think of

Pocahontas, I am ready to love Indians. Then there's Massasoit, and Philip of Mount Hope, and Tecumseh, and Red-Jacket, and Logan – all heroes; and there's the Five Nations, and Araucanians – federations and communities of heroes. God bless me; hate Indians? Surely the late Colonel John Moredock must have wandered in his mind.'

'Wandered in the woods considerably, but never wandered elsewhere, that I ever heard.'

'Are you in earnest? Was there ever one who so made it his particular mission to hate Indians that, to designate him, a special word has been coined – Indian-hater?'

'Even so.'

'Dear me, you take it very calmly. – But really, I would like to know something about this Indian-hating. I can hardly believe such a thing to be. Could you favour me with a little history of the extraordinary man you mentioned?'

'With all my heart,' and immediately stepping from the porch, gestured the cosmopolitan to a settee near by, on deck. 'There, sir, sit you there, and I will sit here beside you – you desire to hear of Colonel John Moredock. Well, a day in my boyhood is marked with a white stone – the day I saw the colonel's rifle, powder-horn attached, hanging in a cabin on the West bank of the Wabash river. I was going westward a long journey through the wilderness with my father. It was high noon, and we had stopped at the cabin to unsaddle and bait. The man at the cabin pointed out the rifle, and told whose it was, adding that the colonel was that moment sleeping on wolf-skins in the corn-loft above, so we must not talk very loud, for the colonel had been out all night hunting (Indians, mind), and it would be cruel to disturb his sleep. Curious to see one so famous, we waited two hours over, in hopes he would come forth; but he did not. So, it being necessary to get to the next cabin before nightfall, we had at last to ride off without the wished-for satisfaction. Though, to tell the truth, I for one, did not go away entirely ungratified, for, while my father was watering the horses, I slipped back into the cabin, and stepping a round or two up the ladder, pushed my head through the trap, and peered about. Not much light in the loft; but off in the further corner, I saw what I took to be the wolf-skins, and on them a bundle of something, like a drift of leaves; and at one end, what seemed a moss-ball; and over it, deer-antlers branched; and close by, a small squirrel sprang out from a maple-bowl of nuts, brushed the moss-ball with his tail, through a hole, and vanished squeaking. That bit of woodland scene was all I saw. No Colonel Moredock there, unless that moss-ball was his curly head, seen in the back view. I would have gone clear up, but the man below had warned me, that though, from his camping habits, the colonel could sleep through thunder, he was for the same cause amazing quick to waken at the sound of footsteps, however soft, and especially if human.'

'Excuse me,' said the other, softly laying his hand on the narrator's wrist, but I fear the colonel was of a distrustful nature – little or no confidence. He *was* a little suspicious-minded, wasn't he?'

'Not a bit. Knew too much. Suspected nobody, but was not ignorant of Indians. Well: though, as you may gather, I never fully saw the man, yet, have I, one way and another, heard about as much of him as any other; in particular, have I heard his history again and again from my father's friend, James Hall, the judge, you know. In every company being called upon to give this history, which none could better do, the judge at last fell into a style so methodic, you would have thought he spoke less to mere auditors than to an invisible amanuensis; seemed talking for the press; very impressive way with him indeed. And I, having an equally impressible memory, think that, upon a pinch, I can render you the judge upon the colonel almost word for word.'

'Do so, by all means,' said the cosmopolitan, well pleased.

'Shall I give you the judge's philosophy, and all?'

'As to that,' rejoined the other gravely, pausing over the pipe-bowl he was filling, 'the desirableness, to a man of a certain mind, of having another man's philosophy given, depends considerably upon what school of philosophy that other man belongs to. Of what school or system was the judge, pray?'

'Why, though he knew how to read and write, the judge never had much schooling. But I should say he belonged, if anything, to the free-school system. Yes, a true patriot, the judge went in strong for free-schools.'

'In philosophy? The man of a certain mind, then, while respecting the judge's patriotism, and not blind to the judge's capacity for narrative, such as he may prove to have, might, perhaps with prudence, waive an opinion of the judge's probable philosophy. But I am no rigorist; proceed, I beg; his philosophy or not, as you please.'

'Well, I would mostly skip that part, only, to begin, some reconnoitring of the ground in a philosophical way the judge always deemed indispensable with strangers. For you must know that Indian-hating was no monopoly of Colonel Moredock's; but a passion, in one form or other, and to a degree, greater or less, largely shared among the class to which he belonged. And Indian-hating still exists; and, no doubt, will continue to exist, so long as Indians do. Indian-hating, then, shall be my first theme, and Colonel Moredock, the Indian-hater, my next and last.'

With which the stranger, settling himself in his seat, commenced – the hearer paying marked regard, slowly smoking, his glance, meanwhile, steadfastly abstracted towards the deck, but his right ear so disposed towards the speaker that each word came through as little atmospheric intervention as possible. To intensify the sense of hearing, he seemed to sink the sense of sight. No complaisance of mere speech could have been so flattering, or expressed such striking politeness as this mute eloquence of thoroughly digesting attention.

Chapter Twenty-Six

Containing the Metaphysics of Indian-hating, According to the Views of One Evidently Not so Prepossessed as Rousseau in Favour of Savages

'The judge always began in these words: "The backwoodsman's hatred of the Indian has been a topic for some remark. In the earlier times of the frontier the passion was thought to be readily accounted for. But Indian rapine having mostly ceased through regions where it once prevailed, the philanthropist is surprised that Indian-hating has not in like degree ceased with it. He wonders why the backwoodsman still regards the red man in much the same spirit that a jury does a murderer, or a trapper a wild cat – a creature, in whose behalf mercy were not wisdom; truce is vain; he must be executed.

' "A curious point," the judge would continue, "which perhaps not everybody, even upon explanation, may fully understand; while, in order for any one to approach to an understanding, it is necessary for him to learn, or if he already know, to bear in mind, what manner of man the backwoodsman is; as for what manner of man the Indian is, many know, either from history or experience.

' "The backwoodsman is a lonely man. He is a thoughtful man. He is a man strong and unsophisticated. Impulsive, he is what some might call unprincipled. At any rate, he is self-willed; being one who less hearkens to what others may say about things, than looks for himself, to see what are things themselves. If in straits, there are few to help; he must depend upon himself; he must continually look to himself. Hence self-reliance, to the degree of standing by his own judgment, though it stand alone. Not that he deems himself infallible; too many mistakes in following trails

prove the contrary; but he thinks that nature destines such sagacity as she has given him, as she destines it to the 'possum. To
these fellow-beings of the wilds their untutored sagacity is their
best dependence. If with either it prove faulty, if the 'possum's
betray it to the trap, or the backwoodsman's mislead him into
ambuscade, there are consequences to be undergone, but no
self-blame. As with the 'possum, instincts prevail with the backwoodsman over precepts. Like the 'possum the backwoodsman
presents the spectacle of a creature dwelling exclusively among
the works of God, yet these, truth must confess, breed little in
him of a godly mind. Small bowing and scraping is his, further
than when with bent knee he points his rifle, or picks its flint.
With few companions, solitude by necessity his lengthened lot,
he stands the trial – no slight one, since, next to dying, solitude,
rightly borne, is perhaps of fortitude the most rigorous test. But
not merely is the backwoodsman content to be alone, but in no
few cases is anxious to be so. The sight of smoke ten miles off is
provocation to one more remove from man, one step deeper into
nature. Is it that he feels that whatever man may be, man is not
the universe? that glory, beauty, kindness, are not all engrossed by
him? that as the presence of man frights birds away, so, many
bird-like thoughts? Be that how it will, the backwoodsman is not
without some fineness to his nature. Hairy Orson as he looks, it
may be with him as with the Shetland seal – beneath the bristles
lurks the fur.

‘ "Though held in a sort a barbarian, the backwoodsman would
seem to America what Alexander was to Asia – captain in the
vanguard of conquering civilization. Whatever the nation's
growing opulence or power, does it not lackey his heels? Path-
finder, provider of security to those who come after him, for
himself he asks nothing but hardship. Worthy to be compared
with Moses in the Exodus, or the Emperor Julian in Gaul, who on
foot, and bare-browed, at the head of covered or mounted
legions, marched so through the elements, day after day. The tide

of emigration, let it roll as it will, never overwhelms the back-woodsman into itself; he rides upon advance, as the Polynesian upon the comb of the surf.

' "Thus, though he keep moving on through life, he maintains with respect to nature much the same unaltered relation through-out; with her creatures, too, including panthers and Indians. Hence, it is not unlikely that, accurate as the theory of the Peace Congress may be with respect to those two varieties of beings, among others, yet the backwoodsman might be qualified to throw out some practical suggestions.

' "As the child born to a backwoodsman must in turn lead his father's life – a life which, as related to humanity, is related mainly to Indians – it is thought best not to mince matters, out of deli-cacy; but to tell the boy pretty plainly what an Indian is, and what he must expect from him. For however charitable it may be to view Indians as members of the Society of Friends, yet to affirm them such to one ignorant of Indians, whose lonely path lies a long way through their lands, this, in the event, might prove not only injudicious but cruel. At least something of this kind would seem the maxim upon which backwoods education is based. Accordingly, if in youth the backwoodsman incline to know-ledge, as is generally the case, he hears little from his schoolmasters, the old chroniclers of the forest, but histories of Indian lying, Indian theft, Indian double-dealing, Indian fraud and perfidy, Indian want of conscience, Indian blood-thirstiness, Indian diab-olism – histories which, though of wild woods, are almost as full of things unangelic as the Newgate Calendar or the Annals of Europe. In these Indian narratives and traditions the lad is thor-oughly grounded. 'As the twig is bent the tree's inclined.' The instinct of antipathy against an Indian grows in the backwoods-man with the sense of good and bad, right and wrong. In one breath he learns that a brother is to be loved, and an Indian to be hated.

' "Such are the facts," the judge would say, "upon which, if one seek to moralize, he must do so with an eye to them. It is terrible that one creature should so regard another, should make it conscience to abhor an entire race. It is terrible; but is it surprising? Surprising, that one should hate a race which he believes to be red from a cause akin to that which makes some tribes of garden insects green? A race whose name is upon the frontier a *memento mori*; painted to him in every evil light; now a horse-thief like those in Moyamensing; now an assassin like a New York rowdy; now a treaty-breaker like an Austrian; now a Palmer with poisoned arrows; now a judicial murderer and Jeffries, after a fierce farce of trial condemning his victim to bloody death; or a Jew with hospitable speeches cozening some fainting stranger into ambuscade, there to burke him, and account it a deed grateful to Manitou, his god.

' "Still, all this is less advanced as truths of the Indians than as examples of the backwoodsman's impression of them – in which the charitable may think he does them some injustice. Certain it is, the Indians themselves think so; quite unanimously, too. The Indians, indeed, protest against the backwoodsman's view of them; and some think that one cause of their returning his antipathy so sincerely as they do, is their moral indignation at being so libelled by him, as they really believe and say. But whether, on this or any point, the Indians should be permitted to testify for themselves, to the exclusion of other testimony, is a question that may be left to the Supreme Court. At any rate, it has been observed that when an Indian becomes a genuine proselyte to Christianity (such cases, however, not being very many; though, indeed, entire tribes are sometimes nominally brought to the true light), he will not in that case conceal his enlightened conviction, that his race's portion by nature is total depravity; and, in that way, as much as admits that the backwoodsman's worst idea of it is not very far from true; while, on the other hand, those red men who are the greatest sticklers for the theory of Indian virtue, and Indian loving-kindness, are sometimes the arrantest horse-thieves and tomahawkers among them. So, at least, avers the backwoodsman. And though, knowing the Indian nature, as he thinks he does, he fancies he is not ignorant that an Indian may in some points deceive himself almost as effectually as in bush-tactics he can another, yet his theory and his practice as above contrasted seem to involve an inconsistency so extreme, that the backwoodsman only accounts for it on the supposition that when a tomahawking red man advances the notion of the benignity of the red race, it is but part and parcel of that subtle strategy which he finds so useful in war, in hunting, and the general conduct of life."

'In further explanation of that deep abhorrence with which the backwoodsman regards the savage, the judge used to think it might perhaps a little help, to consider what kind of stimulus to it is furnished in those forest histories and traditions before spoken of. In which behalf, he would tell the story of the little colony of Wrights and Weavers, originally seven cousins from Virginia, who, after successive removals with their families, at last established themselves near the southern frontier of the Bloody Ground, Kentucky: "They were strong, brave men; but, unlike many of the pioneers in those days, theirs was no love of conflict for conflict's sake. Step by step they had been lured to their lonely resting-place by the ever-beckoning seductions of a fertile and virgin land, with a singular exemption, during the march, from Indian molestation. But clearings made and houses built, the bright shield was soon to turn its other side. After repeated persecutions and eventual hostilities, forced on them by a dwindled tribe in their neighbourhood – persecutions resulting in loss of crops and cattle; hostilities in which they lost two of their number, ill to be spared, besides others getting painful wounds – the five remaining cousins made, with some serious concessions, a kind of treaty with Mocmohoc, the chief – being to this induced by the harryings of the enemy, leaving them no peace. But they were further prompted, indeed, first incited, by the suddenly changed ways of Mocmohoc, who, though hitherto deemed a savage almost perfidious as Caesar Borgia, yet now put on a seeming the reverse of this, engaging to bury the hatchet, smoke the pipe, and be friends for ever; not friends in the mere sense of renouncing enmity, but in the sense of kindliness, active and familiar.

' "But what the chief now seemed, did not wholly blind them to what the chief had been; so that, though in no small degree influenced by his change of bearing, they still distrusted him enough to covenant with him, among other articles on their side, that though friendly visits should be exchanged between the wig-wams and the cabins, yet the five cousins should never, on any account, be expected to enter the chief's lodge together. The intention was, though they reserved it, that if ever, under the guise of amity, the chief should mean them mischief, and effect it, it should be but partially; so that some of the five might survive, not only for their families' sake, but also for retribution's. Nevertheless, Mocmohoc did, upon a time, with such fine art and pleasing carriage win their confidence, that he brought them all together to a feast of bear's meat, and there, by stratagem, ended them. Years after, over their calcined bones and those of all their families, the chief, reproached for his treachery by a proud hunter whom he had made captive, jeered out, 'Treachery? pale face! 'Twas they who broke their covenant first, in coming all together; they that broke it first, in trusting Mocmohoc.' "

'At this point the judge would pause, and lifting his hand, and rolling his eyes, exclaim in a solemn enough voice, "Circling wiles and bloody lusts. The acuteness and genius of the chief but make him the more atrocious."

'After another pause, he would begin an imaginary kind of dialogue between a backwoodsman and a questioner:

' "But are all Indians like Mocmohoc? – Not all have proved such; but in the least harmful may lie his germ. There is an Indian nature. 'Indian blood is in me,' is the half-breed's threat. – But are

177

not some Indians kind? – Yes, but kind Indians are mostly lazy, and reputed simple – at all events, are seldom chiefs; chiefs among the red men being taken from the active, and those accounted wise. Hence, with small promotion, kind Indians have but proportionate influence. And kind Indians may be forced to do unkind biddings. So 'beware the Indian, kind or unkind,' said Daniel Boone, who lost his sons by them. – But, have all you backwoodsmen been some way victimized by Indians? – No. – Well, and in certain cases may not at least some few of you be favoured by them? – Yes, but scarce one among us so self-important, or so selfish-minded, as to hold his personal exemption from Indian outrage such a set-off against the contrary experience of so many others, as that he must needs, in a general way, think well of Indians; or, if he do, an arrow in his flank might suggest a pertinent doubt.

'"In short," according to the judge, "if we at all credit the backwoodsman, his feeling against Indians, to be taken aright, must be considered as being not so much on his own account as on others', or jointly on both accounts. True it is, scarce a family he knows but some member of it, or connection, has been by Indians maimed or scalped. What avails, then, that some one Indian, or some two or three, treat a backwoodsman friendly-like? He fears me, he thinks. Take my rifle from me, give him motive, and what will come? Or if not so, how know I what involuntary preparations may be going on in him for things as unbeknown in present time to him as me – a sort of chemical preparation in the soul for malice, as chemical preparation in the body for malady."

'Not that the backwoodsman ever used those words, you see, but the judge found him expression for his meaning. And this point he would conclude with saying, that, "What is called a 'friendly Indian' is a very rare sort of creature; and well it was so, for no ruthlessness exceeds that of a 'friendly Indian' turned enemy. A coward friend, he makes a valiant foe.

'"But, thus far the passion in question has been viewed in a general way as that of a community. When to his due share of this the backwoodsman adds his private passion, we have then the stock out of which is formed, if formed at all, the Indian-hater *par excellence.*"

'The Indian-hater *par excellence* the judge defined to be one "who, having with his mother's milk drank in small love for red men, in youth or early manhood, ere the sensibilities become osseous, receives at their hand some signal outrage, or, which in effect is much the same, some of his kin have, or some friend. Now, nature all around him by her solitudes wooing or bidding him muse upon this matter, he accordingly does so, till the thought develops such attraction, that much as straggling vapours troop from all sides to a storm-cloud, so straggling thoughts of other outrages troop to the nucleus thought, assimilate with it, and swell it. At last, taking counsel with the elements, he comes to his resolution. An intenser Hannibal, he makes a vow, the hate of which is a vortex from whose suction scarce the remotest chip of the guilty race may reasonably feel secure. Next, he declares himself and settles his temporal affairs. With the solemnity of a Spaniard turned monk, he takes leave of his kin; or rather, these leave-takings have something of the still more impressive finality of death-bed adieus. Last, he commits himself to the forest primeval; there, so long as life shall be his, to act upon a calm, cloistered scheme of strategical, implacable, and lonesome vengeance. Ever on the noiseless trail; cool, collected, patient; less seen than felt; snuffing, smelling – a Leatherstocking Nemesis. In the settlements he will not be seen again; in eyes of old companions tears may start at some chance thing that speaks of him; but they never look for him, nor call; they know he will not come. Suns and seasons fleet; the tiger-lily blows and falls; babes are born and leap in their mothers' arms; but, the Indian-hater is good as gone to his long home, and 'Terror' is his epitaph."

'Here the judge, not unaffected, would pause again, but

presently resume: "How evident that in strict speech there can be no biography of an Indian-hater *par excellence*, any more than one of a sword-fish, or other deep sea denizen; or, which is still less imaginable, one of a dead man. The career of the Indian-hater *par excellence* has the impenetrability of the fate of a lost steamer. Doubtless, events, terrible ones, have happened, must have happened; but the powers that be in nature have taken order that they shall never become news.

' "But, luckily for the curious, there is a species of diluted Indian-hater, one whose heart proves not so steely as his brain. Soft enticements of domestic life too often draw him from the ascetic trail; a monk who apostatizes to the world at times. Like a mariner, too, though much abroad, he may have a wife and family in some green harbour which he does not forget. It is with him as with the Papist converts in Senegal; fasting and mortification prove hard to bear."

'The judge, with his usual judgment, always thought that the intense solitude to which the Indian-hater consigns himself, has, by its overawing influence, no little to do with relaxing his vow. He would relate instances where, after some months' lonely scoutings, the Indian-hater is suddenly seized with a sort of calenture; hurries openly towards the first smoke, though he knows it is an Indian's, announces himself as a lost hunter, gives the savage his rifle, throws himself upon his charity, embraces him with much affection, imploring the privilege of living a while in his sweet companionship. What is too often the sequel of so distempered a procedure may be best known by those who best know the Indian. Upon the whole, the judge, by two and thirty good and sufficient reasons, would maintain that there was no known vocation whose consistent following calls for such self-containings as that of the Indian-hater *par excellence*. In the highest view, he considered such a soul one peeping out but once an age.

'For the diluted Indian-hater, although the vacations he permits himself impair the keeping of the character, yet, it should not be overlooked that this is the man who, by his very infirmity, enables us to form surmises, however inadequate, of what Indian-hating in its perfection is.'

'One moment,' gently interrupted the cosmopolitan here, 'and let me refill my calumet.'

Which being done, the other proceeded: –

Chapter Twenty-Seven

*Some Account of a Man of Questionable Morality, But Who,
Nevertheless, Would Seem Entitled to the Esteem of That
Eminent English Moralist Who Said He Liked a Good Hater*

'Coming to mention the man to whose story all thus far said was
but the introduction, the judge, who, like you, was a great
smoker, would insist upon all the company taking cigars, and
then lighting a fresh one himself, rise in his place, and, with the
solemnest voice, say – "Gentlemen, let us smoke to the memory
of Colonel John Moredock"; when, after several whiffs taken
standing in deep silence and deeper reverie, he would resume his
seat and his discourse, something in these words:

' "Though Colonel John Moredock was not an Indian-hater *par
excellence*, he yet cherished a kind of sentiment towards the red
man, and in that degree, and so acted out his sentiment as sufficiently to merit the tribute just rendered to his memory.

' "John Moredock was the son of a woman married thrice, and
thrice widowed by a tomahawk. The three successive husbands
of this woman had been pioneers, and with them she had wandered from wilderness to wilderness, always on the frontier. With
nine children, she at last found herself at a little clearing, afterwards Vincennes. There she joined a company about to remove
to the new country of Illinois. On the eastern side of Illinois
there were then no settlements; but on the west side, the shore of
the Mississippi, there were, near the mouth of the Kaskaskia,
some old hamlets of French. To the vicinity of those hamlets,
very innocent and pleasant places, a new Arcadia, Mrs Moredock's party was destined; for thereabouts, among the vines, they
meant to settle. They embarked upon the Wabash in boats, proposing to descend that stream into the Ohio, and the Ohio into

the Mississippi, and so, northwards, towards the point to be reached. All went well till they made the rock of the Grand Tower on the Mississippi, where they had to land and drag their boats round a point swept by a strong current. Here a party of Indians, lying in wait, rushed out and murdered nearly all of them. The widow was among the victims with her children, John excepted, who, some fifty miles distant, was following with a second party.

' "He was just entering upon manhood, when thus left in nature sole survivor of his race. Other youngsters might have turned mourners; he turned avenger. His nerves were electric wires – sensitive, but steel. He was one who, from self-possession, could be made neither to flush nor pale. It is said that when the tidings were brought him, he was ashore sitting beneath a hemlock eating his dinner of venison – and as the tidings were told him, after the first start he kept on eating, but slowly and deliberately, chewing the wild news with the wild meat, as if both together, turned to chyle, together should sinew him to his intent. From that meal he rose an Indian-hater. He rose; got his arms, prevailed upon some comrades to join him, and without delay started to discover who were the actual transgressors. They proved to belong to a band of twenty renegades from various tribes, outlaws even among Indians, and who had formed themselves into a marauding crew. No opportunity for action being at the time presented, he dismissed his friends; told them to go on, thanking them, and saying he would ask their aid at some future day. For upwards of a year, alone in the wilds, he watched the crew. Once, what he thought a favourable chance having occurred – it being midwinter, and the savages encamped, apparently to remain so – he anew mustered his friends, and marched against them; but, getting wind of his coming, the enemy fled, and in such panic that everything was left behind but their weapons. During the winter, much the same thing happened upon two subsequent occasions. The next year he sought them at the head of a party pledged to serve him for forty days. At last the hour came. It was on the shore of the Mississippi. From their covert, Moredock and his men dimly descried the gang of Cains in the red dusk of evening, paddling over to a jungled island in mid-stream, there the more securely to lodge; for Moredock's retributive spirit in the wilderness spoke ever to their trepidations now, like the voice calling through the garden. Waiting until dead of night, the whites swam the river, towing after them a raft laden with their arms. On landing, Moredock cut the fastenings of the enemy's canoes, and turned them, with his own raft, adrift; resolved that there should be neither escape for the Indians, nor safety, except in victory, for the whites. Victorious the whites were; but three of the Indians saved themselves by taking to the stream. Moredock's band lost not a man.

' "Three of the murderers survived. He knew their names and persons. In the course of three years each successively fell by his own hand. All were now dead. But this did not suffice. He made no avowal, but to kill Indians had become his passion. As an athlete, he had few equals; as a shot, none; in single combat, not to be beaten. Master of that woodland-cunning enabling the adept to subsist where the tyro would perish, and expert in all those arts by which an enemy is pursued for weeks, perhaps months, without once suspecting it, he kept to the forest. The solitary Indian that met him, died. When a number was descried, he would either secretly pursue their track for some chance to strike at least one blow; or if, while thus engaged, he himself was discovered, he would elude them by superior skill.

' "Many years he spent thus; and though after a time he was, in a degree, restored to the ordinary life of the region and period, yet it is believed that John Moredock never let pass an opportunity of quenching an Indian. Sins of commission in that kind may have been his, but none of omission.

' "It were to err to suppose," the judge would say, "that this gentleman was naturally ferocious, or peculiarly possessed of those qualities which, unhelped by provocation of events, tend to withdraw man from social life. On the contrary, Moredock was an example of something apparently self-contradicting, certainly curious, but, at the same time, undeniable: namely, that nearly all Indian-haters have at bottom loving hearts; at any rate, hearts, if anything, more generous than the average. Certain it is that, to the degree in which he mingled in the life of the settlements, Moredock showed himself not without humane feelings. No cold husband or colder father, he; and, though often and long away from his household, bore its needs in mind, and provided for them. He could be very convivial; told a good story (though never of his more private exploits), and sung a capital song. Hospitable, not backward to help a neighbour; by report, benevolent, as retributive in secret; while, in a general manner, though sometimes grave – as is not unusual with men of his complexion, a sultry and tragical brown – yet with nobody, Indians excepted, otherwise than courteous in a manly fashion; a moccasined gentleman, admired and loved. In fact, no one more popular, as an incident to follow may prove.

' "His bravery, whether in Indian fight or any other, was unquestionable. An officer in the ranging service during the war of 1812, be acquitted himself with more than credit. Of his soldierly character, this anecdote is told: Not long after Hull's dubious surrender at Detroit, Moredock with some of his rangers rode up at night to a log-house, there to rest till morning. The horses being attended to, supper over, and sleeping-places assigned the troop, the host showed the colonel his best bed, not on the ground like the rest, but a bed that stood on legs. But out of delicacy, the guest declined to monopolize it, or, indeed, to occupy it at all; when, to increase the inducement, as the host thought, he was told that a general officer had once slept in that bed. 'Who, pray?' asked the colonel. 'General Hull.' 'Then you must not take offence,' said the colonel, buttoning up his coat, 'but, really, no coward's bed for me, however comfortable.' Accordingly he took up with valour's bed – a cold one on the ground.

' "At one time the colonel was a member of the territorial council of Illinois, and at the formation of the state government, was pressed to become candidate for governor, but begged to be excused. And, though he declined to give his reasons for declining, yet by those who best knew him the cause was not wholly unsurmised. In his official capacity he might be called upon to enter into friendly treaties with Indian tribes, a thing not to be thought of. And even did no such contingency arise, yet he felt there would be an impropriety in the Governor of Illinois stealing out now and then, during a recess of the legislative bodies, for a few days' shooting at human beings, within the limits of his paternal chief-magistracy. If the governorship offered large honours, from Moredock it demanded larger sacrifices. These were incompatibles. In short, he was not unaware that to be a consistent Indian-hater involves the renunciation of ambition, with its objects – the pomps and glories of the world; and since religion, pronouncing such things vanities, accounts it merit to renounce them, therefore, so far as this goes, Indian-hating, whatever may be thought of it in other respects, may be regarded as not wholly without the efficacy of a devout sentiment." '

Here the narrator paused. Then, after his long and irksome sitting, started to his feet, and regulating his disordered shirt-frill, and at the same time adjustingly shaking his legs down in his rumpled pantaloons, concluded: 'There, I have done; having given you, not my story, mind, or my thoughts, but another's. And now, for your friend Coonskins, I doubt not, that, if the judge were here, he would pronounce him a sort of comprehensive Colonel Moredock, who, too much spreading his passion, shallows it.'

Chapter Twenty-Eight

Moot Points Touching the Late Colonel John Moredock

'Charity, charity!' exclaimed the cosmopolitan, 'never a sound judgment without charity. When man judges man, charity is less a bounty from our mercy than just allowance for the insensible lee-way of human fallibility. God forbid that my eccentric friend should be what you hint. You do not know him, or but imperfectly. His outside deceived you; at first it came near deceiving even me. But I seized a chance, when, owing to indignation against some wrong, he laid himself a little open; I seized that lucky chance, I say, to inspect his heart, and found it an inviting oyster in a forbidding shell. His outside is but put on. Ashamed of his own goodness, he treats mankind as those strange old uncles in romances do their nephews – snapping at them all the time and yet loving them as the apple of their eye.'

'Well, my words with him were few. Perhaps he is not what I took him for. Yes, for aught I know, you may be right.'

'Glad to hear it. Charity, like poetry, should be cultivated, if only for its being graceful. And now, since you have renounced your notion, I should be happy would you, so to speak, renounce your story, too. That story strikes me with even more incredulity than wonder. To me some parts don't hang together. If the man of hate, how could John Moredock be also the man of love? Either his lone campaigns are fabulous as Hercules'; or else, those being true, what was thrown in about his geniality is but garnish. In short, if ever there was such a man as Moredock, he, in my way of thinking, was either misanthrope or nothing; and his misanthropy the more intense from being focused on one race of men. Though, like suicide, man-hatred would seem peculiarly a Roman and a Grecian passion – that is, Pagan; yet, the annals of neither Rome nor Greece can produce the equal in man-hatred of Colonel Moredock, as the judge and you have painted him. As for this Indian-hating in general, I can only say of it what Dr Johnson said of the alleged Lisbon earthquake: "Sir, I don't believe it." '

'Didn't believe it? Why not? Clashed with any little prejudice of his?'

'Dr Johnson had no prejudice; but, like a certain other person,' with an ingenuous smile, 'he had sensibilities, and those were pained.'

'Dr Johnson was a good Christian, wasn't he?'

'He was.'

'Suppose he had been something else?'

'Then small incredulity as to the alleged earthquake.'

'Suppose he had been also a misanthrope?'

'Then small incredulity as to the robberies and murders alleged to have been perpetrated under the pall of smoke and ashes. The infidels of the time were quick to credit those reports and worse. So true it is that, while religion, contrary to the common notion, implies, in certain cases, a spirit of slow reserve as to assent, infidelity, which claims to despise credulity, is sometimes swift to it.'

'You rather jumble together misanthropy and infidelity.'

'I do not jumble them; they are coordinates. For misanthropy, springing from the same root with disbelief of religion, is twin with that. It springs from the same root, I say; for, set aside materialism, and what is an atheist, but one who does not, or will not, see in the universe a ruling principle of love; and what a misanthrope, but one who does not, or will not, see in man a ruling principle of kindness? Don't you see? In either case the vice consists in a want of confidence.'

'What sort of a sensation is misanthropy?'

'Might as well ask me what sort of sensation is hydrophobia. Don't know; never had it. But I have often wondered what it can be like. Can a misanthrope feel warm, I ask myself; take ease? be companionable with himself? Can a misanthrope smoke a cigar and muse? How fares he in solitude? Has the misanthrope such a thing as an appetite? Shall a peach refresh him? The effervescence of champagne, with what eye does he behold it? Is summer good to him? Of long winters how much can he sleep? What are his dreams? How feels he, and what does he, when suddenly awakened, alone, at dead of night, by fusilades of thunder?'

'Like you,' said the stranger, 'I can't understand the misanthrope. So far as my experience goes, either mankind is worthy one's best love, or else I have been lucky. Never has it been my lot to have been wronged, though but in the smallest degree. Cheating, back-biting, superciliousness, disdain, hard-heartedness, and all that brood, I know but by report. Cold regards tossed over the sinister shoulder of a former friend, ingratitude in a beneficiary, treachery in a confidant – such things may be; but I must take somebody's word for it. Now the bridge that has carried me so well over, shall I not praise it?'

'Ingratitude to the worthy bridge not to do so. Man is a noble fellow, and in an age of satirists, I am not displeased to find one who has confidence in him, and bravely stands up for him.'

'Yes, I always speak a good word for man; and what is more, am always ready to do a good deed for him.'

'You are a man after my own heart,' responded the cosmopolitan, with a candour which lost nothing by its calmness. 'Indeed,' he added, 'our sentiments agree so, that were they written in a book, whose was whose, few but the nicest critics might determine.'

'Since we are thus joined in mind,' said the stranger, 'why not be joined in hand?'

'My hand is always at the service of virtue,' frankly extending it to him as to virtue personified.

'And now,' said the stranger, cordially retaining his hand, 'you know our fashion here at the West. It may be a little low, but it is kind. Briefly, we being newly-made friends must drink together. What say you?'

'Thank you; but indeed, you must excuse me.'

'Why?'

'Because, to tell the truth, I have to-day met so many old friends, all free-hearted, convivial gentlemen, that really, really, though for the present I succeed in mastering it, I am at bottom almost in the condition of a sailor who, stepping ashore after a long voyage, ere night reels with loving welcomes, his head of less capacity than his heart.'

At the allusion to old friends, the stranger's countenance a little fell, as a jealous lover's might at hearing from his sweetheart of former ones. But rallying, he said: 'No doubt they treated you to something strong; but wine – surely, that gentle creature, wine; come, let us have a little gentle wine at one of these little tables here. Come, come.' Then essaying to roll about like a full pipe in the sea, sang in a voice which had had more of good-fellowship, had there been less of a latent squeak to it:

> 'Let us drink of the wine of the vine benign,
> That sparkles warm in Sansovine.'

The cosmopolitan, with longing eye upon him, stood as sorely tempted and wavering a moment; then, abruptly stepping towards him, with a look of dissolved surrender, said: 'When mermaid songs move figure-heads, then may glory, gold, and women try their blandishments on me. But a good fellow, singing a good song, he woos forth my every spike, so that my whole hull, like a ship's, sailing by a magnetic rock, caves in with acquiescence. Enough: when one has a heart of a certain sort, it is in vain trying to be resolute.'

Chapter Twenty-Nine

The Boon Companions

The wine, port, being called for, and the two seated at the little table, a natural pause of convivial expectancy ensued; the stranger's eye turned towards the bar near by, watching the red-cheeked, white-aproned man there, blithely dusting the bottle, and invitingly arranging the salver and glasses; when, with a sudden impulse turning round his head towards his companion, he said, 'Ours is friendship at first sight, ain't it?'

'It is,' was the placidly pleased reply: 'and the same may be said of friendship at first sight as of love at first sight: it is the only true one, the only noble one. It bespeaks confidence. Who would go sounding his way into love or friendship, like a strange ship by night, into an enemy's harbour?'

'Right. Boldly in before the wind. Agreeable, how we always agree. By-the-way, though but a formality, friends should know each other's names. What is yours, pray?'

'Francis Goodman. But those who love me call me Frank. And yours?'

'Charles Arnold Noble. But do you call me Charlie.'

'I will, Charlie; nothing like preserving in manhood the fraternal familiarities of youth. It proves the heart a rosy boy to the last.'

'My sentiments again. Ah!'

It was a smiling waiter, with the smiling bottle, the cork drawn; a common quart bottle, but for the occasion fitted at bottom into a little bark basket, braided with porcupine quills, gaily tinted in the Indian fashion. This being set before the entertainer, he regarded it with affectionate interest, but seemed not to understand, or else to pretend not to, a handsome red label pasted on the bottle, bearing the capital letters, P.W.

'P.W.,' said he at last, perplexedly eyeing the pleasing poser, 'now what does P.W. mean?'

'Shouldn't wonder,' said the cosmopolitan gravely, 'if it stood for port wine. You called for port wine, didn't you?'

'Why so it is, so it is!'

'I find some little mysteries not very hard to clear up,' said the other, quietly crossing his legs.

This commonplace seemed to escape the stranger's hearing, for, full of his bottle, he now rubbed his somewhat sallow hands over it, and with a strange kind of cackle, meant to be a chirrup, cried: 'Good wine, good wine; is it not the peculiar bond of good feeling?' Then brimming both glasses, pushed one over, saying, with what seemed intended for an air of fine disdain: 'Ill betide those gloomy sceptics who maintain that now-a-days pure wine is unpurchasable; that almost every variety on sale is less the vintage of vineyards than laboratories; that most bar-keepers are but a set of male Brinvillierses, with complaisant arts practising against the lives of their best friends, their customers.'

A shade passed over the cosmopolitan. After a few minutes' down-cast musing, he lifted his eyes and said: 'I have long thought, my dear Charlie, that the spirit in which wine is regarded by too many in these days is one of the most painful examples of want of confidence. Look at these glasses. He who could mistrust poison in this wine would mistrust consumption in Hebe's cheek. While, as for suspicions against the dealers in wine and sellers of it, those who cherish such suspicions can have but limited trust in the human heart. Each human heart they must think to be much like each bottle of port, not such port as this, but such port as they hold to. Strange traducers, who see good faith in nothing, however sacred. Not medicines, not the wine in sacraments, has escaped them. The doctor with his phial, and the priest with his chalice, they deem equally the unconscious dispensers of bogus cordials to the dying.'

'Dreadful!'

'Dreadful indeed,' said the cosmopolitan solemnly. 'These dis-trusters stab at the very soul of confidence. If this wine,' impressively holding up his full glass, 'if this wine with its bright promise be not true, how shall man be, whose promise can be no brighter? But if wine be false, while men are true, whither shall fly convivial geniality? To think of sincerely-genial souls drinking each other's health at unawares in perfidious and murderous drugs!'

'Horrible!'

'Much too much so to be true, Charlie. Let us forget it. Come, you are my entertainer on this occasion, and yet you don't pledge me. I have been waiting for it.'

'Pardon, pardon,' half confusedly and half ostentatiously lift-ing his glass. 'I pledge you, Frank, with my whole heart, believe me,' taking a draught too decorous to be large, but which, small though it was, was followed by a slight involuntary wryness to the mouth.

'And I return you the pledge, Charlie, heart-warm as it came to me, and honest as this wine I drink it in,' reciprocated the cosmo-politan with princely kindliness in his gesture, taking a generous swallow, concluding in a smack, which, though audible, was not so much so as to be unpleasing.

'Talking of alleged spuriousness of wines,' said he, tranquilly setting down his glass, and then sloping back his head and with friendly fixedness eyeing the wine, 'perhaps the strangest part of those allegings is, that there is, as claimed, a kind of man who, while convinced that on this continent most wines are shams, yet still drinks away at them; accounting wine so fine a thing, that even the sham article is better than none at all. And if the temper-ance people urge that, by this course, he will sooner or later be undermined in health, he answers, "And do you think I don't know that? But health without cheer I hold a bore; and cheer, even of the spurious sort, has its price, which I am willing to pay."'

'Such a man, Frank, must have a disposition ungovernably bacchanalian.'

'Yes, if such a man there be, which I don't credit. It is a fable, but a fable from which I once heard a person of less genius than grotesqueness draw a moral even more extravagant than the fable itself. He said that it illustrated, as in a parable, how that a man of a disposition ungovernably good-natured might still familiarly associate with men, though, at the same time, he believed the greater part of men false-hearted – accounting society so sweet a thing that even the spurious sort was better than none at all. And if the Rochefoucaultites urge that, by this course, he will sooner or later be undermined in security, he answers, "And do you think I don't know that? But security without society I hold a bore; and society, even of the spurious sort, has its price, which I am willing to pay." '

'A most singular theory,' said the stranger with a slight fidget, eyeing his companion with some inquisitiveness, 'indeed, Frank, a most slanderous thought,' he exclaimed in sudden heat and with an involuntary look almost of being personally aggrieved.

'In one sense it merits all you say, and more,' rejoined the other with wonted mildness, 'but, for a kind of drollery in it, charity might, perhaps, overlook something of the wickedness. Humour is, in fact, so blessed a thing, that even in the least virtuous product of the human mind, if there can be found but nine good jokes, some philosophers are clement enough to affirm that those nine good jokes should redeem all the wicked thoughts, though plenty as the populace of Sodom. At any rate, this same humour has something, there is no telling what, of beneficence in it, it is such a catholicon and charm – nearly all men agreeing in relishing it, though they may agree in little else – and in its way it undeniably does such a deal of familiar good in the world, that no wonder it is almost a proverb, that a man of humour, a man capable of a good loud laugh – seem how he may in other things – can hardly be a heartless scamp.'

'Ha, ha, ha!' laughed the other, pointing to the figure of a pale pauper-boy on the deck below, whose pitiableness was touched, as it were, with ludicrousness by a pair of monstrous boots, apparently some mason's discarded ones, cracked with drouth, half eaten by lime, and curled up about the toe like a bassoon. 'Look – ha, ha, ha!'

'I see,' said the other, with what seemed quiet appreciation, but of a kind expressing an eye to the grotesque, without blindness to what in this case accompanied it, 'I see; and the way in which it moves you, Charlie, comes in very apropos to point the proverb I was speaking of. Indeed, had you intended this effect, it could not have been more so. For who that heard that laugh, but would as naturally argue from it a sound heart as sound lungs? True, it is said that a man may smile, and smile, and smile, and be a villain; but it is not said that a man may laugh, and laugh, and laugh, and be one, is it, Charlie?'

'Ha, ha, ha! – no no, no no.'

'Why Charlie, your explosions illustrate my remarks almost as aptly as the chemist's imitation volcano did his lectures. But even if experience did not sanction the proverb, that a good laugher cannot be a bad man, I should yet feel bound in confidence to believe it, since it is a saying current among the people, and I doubt not originated among them, and hence *must* be true; for the voice of the people is the voice of truth. Don't you think so?'

'Of course I do. If Truth don't speak through the people, it never speaks at all; so I heard one say.'

'A true saying. But we stray. The popular notion of humour, considered as index to the heart, would seem curiously confirmed by Aristotle – I think, in his "Politics" (a work, by-the-by, which, however it may be viewed upon the whole, yet, from the tenor of certain sections, should not, without precaution, be placed in the hands of youth) – who remarks that the least lovable men in history seem to have had for humour not only a disrelish, but a hatred; and this, in some cases, along with an extraordinary dry taste for practical punning. I remember it is related of Phalaris, the capricious tyrant of Sicily, that he once caused a poor fellow to be beheaded on a horse-block, for no other cause than having a horse-laugh.'

'Funny Phalaris!'

'Cruel Phalaris!'

As after fire-crackers, there was a pause, both looking downward on the table as if mutually struck by the contrast of exclamations, and pondering upon its significance, if any. So, at least, it seemed; but on one side it might have been otherwise; for presently glancing up, the cosmopolitan said: 'In the instance of the moral, drolly cynic, drawn from the queer bacchanalian fellow we were speaking of, who had his reasons for still drinking spurious wine, though knowing it to be such – there, I say, we have an example of what is certainly a wicked thought, but conceived in humour. I will now give you one of a wicked thought conceived in wickedness. You shall compare the two, and answer, whether in the one case the sting is not neutralized by the humour, and whether in the other the absence of humour does not leave the sting free play. I once heard a wit, a mere wit, mind, an irreligious Parisian wit, say, with regard to the temperance movement, that none, to their personal benefit, joined it sooner than niggards and knaves; because, as he affirmed, the one by it saved money and the other made money, as in ship-owners cutting off the spirit ration without giving its equivalent, and gamblers and all sorts of subtle tricksters sticking to cold water, the better to keep a cool head for business.'

'A wicked thought, indeed!' cried the stranger, feelingly.

'Yes,' leaning over the table on his elbow and genially gesturing at him with his forefinger: 'yes, and, as I said, you don't remark the sting of it?'

'I do, indeed. Most calumnious thought, Frank!'

'No humour in it?'

'Not a bit!'

'Well now, Charlie,' eyeing him with moist regard, 'let us drink. It appears to me you don't drink freely.'

'Oh, oh – indeed, indeed – I am not backward there. I protest, a freer drinker than friend Charlie you will find nowhere,' with feverish zeal snatching his glass, but only in the sequel to dally with it. 'By-the-way, Frank,' said he, perhaps, or perhaps not, to draw attention from himself, 'by-the-way, I saw a good thing the other day; capital thing; a panegyric on the press. It pleased me so, I got it by heart at two readings. It is a kind of poetry, but in a form which stands in something the same relation to blank verse which that does to rhyme. A sort of free-and-easy chant with refrains to it. Shall I recite it?'

'Anything in praise of the press I shall be happy to hear,' rejoined the cosmopolitan, 'the more so,' he gravely proceeded, 'as of late I have observed in some quarters a disposition to disparage the press.'

'Disparage the press?'

'Even so; some gloomy souls affirming that it is proving with that great invention as with brandy or eau-de-vie, which, upon its first discovery, was believed by the doctors to be, as its French name implies, a panacea – a notion which experience, it may be thought, has not fully verified.'

'You surprise me, Frank. Are there really those who so decry the press? Tell me more. Their reasons.'

'Reasons they have none, but affirmations they have many; among other things affirming that, while under dynastic despotisms, the press is to the people little but an improvisatore, under popular ones it is too apt to be their Jack Cade. In fine, these sour sages regard the press in the light of a Colt's revolver, pledged to no cause but his in whose chance hands it may be; deeming the one invention an improvement upon the pen, much akin to what the other is upon the pistol; involving along with the multiplication of the barrel, no consecration of the aim. The term "freedom of the press" they consider on a par with *freedom of Colt's revolver*. Hence, for truth and the right, they hold, to indulge hopes from the one is little more sensible than for Kossuth and Mazzini to indulge hopes from the other. Heart-breaking views enough, you think; but their refutation is in every true reformer's contempt. Is it not so?'

'Without doubt. But go on, go on. I like to hear you,' flatteringly brimming up his glass for him.

'For one,' continued the cosmopolitan, grandly swelling his chest, 'I hold the press to be neither the people's improvisatore, nor Jack Cade; neither their paid fool, nor conceited drudge. I think interest never prevails with it over duty. The press still speaks for truth though impaled, in the teeth of lies though intrenched. Disdaining for it the poor name of cheap diffuser of news, I claim for it the independent apostleship of Advancer of Knowledge – the iron Paul! Paul, I say; for not only does the press advance knowledge, but righteousness. In the press, as in the sun, resides, my dear Charlie, a dedicated principle of beneficent force and light. For the Satanic press, by its coappearance with the apostolic, it is no more an aspersion to that, than to the true sun is the coappearance of the mock one. For all the baleful-looking parhelion, god Apollo dispenses the day. In a word, Charlie, what the sovereign of England is titularly, I hold the press to be actually – Defender of the Faith! – defender of the faith in the final triumph of truth over error, metaphysics over superstition, theory over falsehood, machinery over nature, and the good man over the bad. Such are my views, which, if stated at some length, you, Charlie, must pardon, for it is a theme upon which I cannot speak with cold brevity. And now I am impatient for your panegyric, which, I doubt not, will put mine to the blush.'

'It is rather in the blush-giving vein,' smiled the other; 'but such as it is, Frank, you shall have it.'

'Tell me when you are about to begin,' said the cosmopolitan, 'for, when at public dinners the press is toasted, I always drink the toast standing, and shall stand while you pronounce the panegyric.'

'Very good, Frank; you may stand up now.'

He accordingly did so, when the stranger likewise rose, and uplifting the ruby wine-flask began.

Chapter Thirty

*Opening With a Poetical Eulogy of the Press, and Continuing
With Talk Inspired by the Same*

' "Praise be unto the press, not Faust's, but Noah's; let us extol
and magnify the press, the true press of Noah, from which
breaketh the true morning. Praise be unto the press, not the
black press but the red; let us extol and magnify the press, the red
press of Noah, from which cometh inspiration. Ye pressmen of
the Rhineland and the Rhine, join in with all ye who tread out the
glad tidings on isle Madeira or Mitylene. – Who giveth redness of
eyes by making men long to tarry at the fine print? – Praise be
unto the press, the rosy press of Noah, which giveth rosiness of
hearts, by making men long to tarry at the rosy wine. – Who
hath babblings and contentions? Who, without cause, inflicteth
wounds? Praise be unto the press, the kindly press of Noah,
which knitteth friends, which fuseth foes. – Who may be bribed? –
Who may be bound? – Praise be unto the press, the free press of
Noah, which will not lie for tyrants, but make tyrants speak the
truth. – Then praise be unto the press, the frank old press of
Noah; then let us extol and magnify the press, the brave old press
of Noah; then let us with roses garland and enwreath the press,
the grand old press of Noah, from which flow streams of knowledge which give man a bliss no more unreal than his pain." '

'You deceived me,' smiled the cosmopolitan, as both now
resumed their seats; 'you roguishly took advantage of my simplicity; you archly played upon my enthusiasm. But never mind;
the offence, if any, was so charming.' I almost wish you would
offend again. As for certain poetic left-handers in your panegyric,
those I cheerfully concede to the indefinite privileges of the poet.
Upon the whole, it was quite in the lyric style – a style I always

admire on account of that spirit of Sibyllic confidence and assurance which is, perhaps, its prime ingredient. But come,' glancing at his companion's glass, 'for a lyrist, you let the bottle stay with you too long.'

'The lyre and the vine for ever!' cried the other in his rapture, or what seemed such, heedless of the hint, 'the vine, the vine! is it not the most graceful and bounteous of all growths? And, by its being such, is not something meant – divinely meant? As I live, a vine, a Catawba vine, shall be planted on my grave!'

'A genial thought; but your glass there.'

'Oh, oh,' taking a moderate sip, 'but you, why don't you drink?'

'You have forgotten, my dear Charlie, what I told you of my previous convivialities to-day.'

'Oh,' cried the other, now in manner quite abandoned to the lyric mood, not without contrast to the easy sociability of his companion. 'Oh, one can't drink too much of good old wine – the genuine, mellow old port. Pooh, pooh! drink away.'

'Then keep me company.'

'Of course,' with a flourish, taking another sip – 'suppose we have cigars. Never mind your pipe there; a pipe is best when alone. I say, waiter, bring some cigars – your best.'

They were brought in a pretty little bit of western pottery, representing some kind of Indian utensil, mummy-coloured, set down in a mass of tobacco leaves, whose long, green fans, fancifully grouped, formed with peeps of red the sides of the receptacle.

Accompanying it were two accessories, also bits of pottery, but smaller, both globes; one in guise of an apple flushed with red and gold to the life, and, through a cleft at top, you saw it was hollow. This was for the ashes. The other, gray, with wrinkled surface, in the likeness of a wasp's nest, was the match-box.

'There,' said the stranger, pushing over the cigar-stand, 'help yourself, and I will touch you off,' taking a match. 'Nothing like tobacco,' he added, when the fumes of the cigar began to wreathe, glancing from the smoker to the pottery, 'I will have a Virginia tobacco-plant set over my grave beside the Catawba vine.'

'Improvement upon your first idea, which by itself was good – but you don't smoke.'

'Presently, presently – let me fill your glass again. You don't drink.'

'Thank you; but no more just now. Fill *your* glass.'

'Presently, presently; do you drink on. Never mind me. Now that it strikes me, let me say, that he who, out of superfine gentility or fanatic morality, denies himself tobacco, suffers a more serious abatement in the cheap pleasures of life than the dandy in his iron boot, or the celibate on his iron cot. While for him who would fain revel in tobacco, but cannot, it is a thing at which philanthropists must weep, to see such an one, again and again, madly returning to the cigar, which, for his incompetent stomach, he cannot enjoy, while still, after each shameful repulse, the sweet dream of the impossible good goads him on to his fierce misery once more – poor eunuch!'

'I agree with you,' said the cosmopolitan, still gravely social, 'but you don't smoke.'

'Presently, presently, do you smoke on. As I was saying about –'

'But *why* don't you smoke – come. You don't think that tobacco, when in league with wine, too much enhances the latter's vinous quality – in short, with certain constitutions tends to impair self-possession, do you?'

'To think that, were treason to good fellowship,' was the warm disclaimer. 'No, no. But the fact is, there is an unpropitious flavour in my mouth just now. Ate of a diabolical ragout at dinner, so I shan't smoke till I have washed away the lingering memento of it with wine. But smoke away, you, and pray, don't forget to drink. By-the-way, while we sit here so companionably, giving loose to any companionable nothing, your uncompanionable friend, Coonskins, is, by pure contrast, brought to recollection. If he were but here now, he would see how much of real heart-joy he denies himself by not hob-a-nobbing with his kind.'

'Why,' with loitering emphasis, slowly withdrawing his cigar, 'I thought I had undeceived you there. I thought you had come to a better understanding of my eccentric friend.'

'Well, I thought so, too; but first impressions will return, you know. In truth, now that I think of it, I am led to conjecture from chance things, which dropped from Coonskins, during the little interview I had with him, that he is not a Missourian by birth, but years ago came West here, a young misanthrope from the other side of the Alleghenies, less to make his fortune, than to flee man. Now, since they say trifles sometimes effect great results, I shouldn't wonder, if his history were probed, it would be found that what first indirectly gave his sad bias to Coonskins was his disgust at reading in boyhood the advice of Polonius to Laertes – advice which, in the selfishness it inculcates, is almost on a par with a sort of ballad upon the economies of money-making, to be occasionally seen pasted against the desk of small retail traders in New England.'

'I do hope now, my dear fellow,' said the cosmopolitan with an air of bland protest, 'that, in my presence at least, you will throw out nothing to the prejudice of the sons of the Puritans.'

'Hey-day and high times indeed,' exclaimed the other, nettled, 'sons of the Puritans forsooth! And who be Puritans, that I, an Alabamaian, must do them reverence? A set of sourly conceited old Malvolios, whom Shakespeare laughs his fill at in his comedies.'

'Pray, what were you about to suggest with regard to Polonius,' observed the cosmopolitan with quiet forbearance, expressive of the patience of a superior mind at the petulance of an inferior one; 'how do you characterize his advice to Laertes?'

'As false, fatal, and calumnious,' exclaimed the other, with a degree of ardour befitting one resenting a stigma upon the family escutcheon, 'and for a father to give his son – monstrous. The case you see is this: The son is going abroad, and for the first time. What does the father? Invoke God's blessing upon him? Put the blessed Bible in his trunk? No. Crams him with maxims smacking of my lord Chesterfield, with maxims of France, with maxims of Italy.'

'No, no, be charitable, not that. Why, does he not among other things say:

> "The friends thou hast, and their adoption tried.
> Grapple them to thy soul with hooks of steel"?

Is that compatible with maxims of Italy?'

'Yes it is, Frank. Don't you see? Laertes is to take the best of care of his friends – his proved friends, on the same principle that a wine-corker takes the best of care of his proved bottles. When a bottle gets a sharp knock and don't break, he says, "Ah, I'll keep that bottle." Why? Because he loves it? No, he has particular use for it.'

'Dear, dear!' appealingly turning in distress, 'that – that kind of criticism is – is – in fact – it won't do.'

'Won't truth do, Frank? You are so charitable with everybody, do but consider the tone of the speech. Now I put it to you, Frank; is there anything in it hortatory to high, heroic, disinterested effort? Anything like "sell all thou hast and give to the poor"? And, in other points, what desire seems most in the father's mind, that his son should cherish nobleness for himself, or be on his guard against the contrary thing in others? An irreligious warner, Frank – no devout counsellor, is Polonius. I hate him. Nor can I bear to hear your veterans of the world affirm, that he who steers through life by the advice of old Polonius will not steer among the breakers.'

'No, no – I hope nobody affirms that,' rejoined the cosmopolitan, with tranquil abandonment; sideways reposing his arm at full length upon the table. 'I hope nobody affirms that; because, if Polonius' advice be taken in your sense, then the recommendation of it by men of experience would appear to involve more or less of an unhandsome sort of reflection upon human nature. And yet,' with a perplexed air, 'your suggestions have put things in such a strange light to me as in fact a little to disturb my previous notions of Polonius and what he says. To be frank by your ingenuity you have unsettled me there, to that degree that were it not for our coincidence of opinion in general, I should almost think I was now at length beginning to feel the ill effect of an immature mind, too much consorting with a mature one, except on the ground of first principles in common.'

'Really and truly,' cried the other with a kind of tickled modesty and pleased concern, 'mine is an understanding too weak to throw out grapnels and hug another to it. I have indeed heard of some great scholars in these days, whose boast is less that they have made disciples than victims. But for me, had I the power to do such things, I have not the heart to desire.'

'I believe you, my dear Charlie. And yet, I repeat, by your commentaries on Polonius you have, I know not how, unsettled me; so that now I don't exactly see how Shakespeare meant the words he put in Polonius' mouth.'

'Some say that he meant them to open people's eyes; but I don't think so.'

'Open their eyes?' echoed the cosmopolitan, slowly expanding his; 'what is there in this world for one to open his eyes to? I mean in the sort of invidious sense you cite?'

'Well, others say he meant to corrupt people's morals; and still others, that he had no express intention at all, but in effect opens their eyes and corrupts their morals in one operation. All of which I reject.'

'Of course you reject so crude an hypothesis; and yet, to confess, in reading Shakespeare in my closet, struck by some passage, I have laid down the volume, and said: "This Shakespeare is a queer man." At times seeming irresponsible, he does not always seem reliable. There appears to be a certain – what shall I call it? – hidden sun, say, about him, at once enlightening and mystifying. Now, I should be afraid to say what I have sometimes thought that hidden sun might be.'

'Do you think it was the true light?' with clandestine geniality again filling the other's glass.

'I would prefer to decline answering a categorical question there. Shakespeare has got to be a kind of deity. Prudent minds, having certain latent thoughts concerning him, will reserve them in a condition of lasting probation. Still, as touching avowable speculations, we are permitted a tether. Shakespeare himself is to be adored, not arraigned; but, so we do it with humility, we may a little canvass his characters. There's his Autolycus now, a fellow that always puzzled me. How is one to take Autolycus? A rogue so happy, so lucky, so triumphant, of so almost captivatingly vicious a career that a virtuous man reduced to the poor-house (were such a contingency conceivable), might almost long to change sides with him. And yet, see the words put into his mouth: "Oh," cries Autolycus, as he comes galloping, gay as a buck, upon the stage, "oh," he laughs, "oh, what a fool is Honesty, and Trust, his sworn brother, a very simple gentleman". Think of that. Trust, that is, confidence – that is, the thing in this universe the sacredest – is rattlingly pronounced just the simplest. And the scenes in which the rogue figures seem purposely devised for verification of his principles. Mind, Charlie, I do not say it *is* so, far from it; but I *do* say it seems so. Yes, Autolycus would seem a needy varlet acting upon the persuasion that less is to be got by invoking pockets than picking them, more to be made by an expert knave than a bungling beggar; and for this reason, as he thinks, that the soft heads outnumber the soft hearts. The devil's drilled recruit, Autolycus is joyous as if he wore the livery of heaven. When disturbed by the character and career of one thus wicked and thus happy, my sole consolation is in the fact that no such creature ever existed, except in the powerful imagination which evoked him. And yet, a creature, a living creature, he is, though only a poet was his maker. It may be, that in that paper-and-ink investiture of his, Autolycus acts more effectively upon mankind than he would in a flesh-and-blood one. Can his influence be salutary? True, in Autolycus there is humour; but though, according to my principle, humour is in general to be held a saving quality, yet the case of Autolycus is an exception; because it is his humour which, so to speak, oils his mischievousness. The bravadoing mischievousness of Autolycus is slid into the world on humour, as a pirate schooner, with colours flying, is launched into the sea on greased ways.'

'I approve of Autolycus as little as you,' said the stranger, who, during his companion's commonplaces, had seemed less attentive to them than to maturing within his own mind the original conceptions destined to eclipse them. 'But I cannot believe that Autolycus, mischievous as he must prove upon the stage, can be near so much so as such a character as Polonius.'

'I don't know about that,' bluntly, and yet not impolitely, returned the cosmopolitan; 'to be sure, accepting your view of the old courtier, then if between him and Autolycus you raise the question of unprepossessingness, I grant you the latter comes off best. For a moist rogue may tickle the midriff, while a dry worldling may but wrinkle the spleen.'

'But Polonius is not dry,' said the other excitedly; 'he drules. One sees the fly-blown old fop drule and look wise. His vile wisdom is made the viler by his vile rheuminess. The bowing and cringing, time-serving old sinner – is such an one to give manly precepts to youth? The discreet, decorous, old dotard-of-state; senile prudence; fatuous soullessness! The ribanded old dog is paralytic all down one side, and that the side of nobleness. His soul is gone out. Only nature's automatonism keeps him on his legs. As with some old trees, the bark survives the pith, and will still stand stiffly up, though but to rim round punk, so the body of old Polonius has outlived his soul.'

'Come, come,' said the cosmopolitan with serious air, almost displeased; 'though I yield to none in admiration of earnestness, yet, I think, even earnestness may have limits. To humane minds, strong language is always more or less distressing. Besides, Polonius is an old man – as I remember him upon the stage – with snowy locks. Now charity requires that such a figure – think of it how you will – should at least be treated with civility. Moreover old age is ripeness, and I once heard say, "Better ripe than raw."'

'But not better rotten than raw!' bringing down his hand with energy on the table.

'Why, bless me,' in mild surprise contemplating his heated comrade, 'how you fly out against this unfortunate Polonius – a being that never was, nor will be. And yet, viewed in a Christian light,' he added pensively, 'I don't know that anger against this man of straw is a whit less wise than anger against a man of flesh. Madness, to be mad with anything.'

'That may be, or may not be,' returned the other, a little testily perhaps; 'but I stick to what I said, that it is better to be raw than rotten. And what is to be feared on that head, may be known from this: that it is with the best of hearts as with the best of pears – a dangerous experiment to linger too long upon the scene. This did Polonius. Thank fortune, Frank, I am young, every tooth sound in my head, and if good wine can keep me where I am, long shall I remain so.'

'True,' with a smile. 'But wine, to do good, must be drunk. You have talked much and well, Charlie; but drunk little and indifferently – fill up.'

'Presently, presently,' with a hasty and preoccupied air. 'If I remember right, Polonius hints as much as that one should, under no circumstances, commit the indiscretion of aiding in a pecuniary way an unfortunate friend. He drules out some stale stuff about "loan losing both itself and friend", don't he? But our bottle; is it glued fast? Keep it moving, my dear Frank. Good wine, and upon my soul I begin to feel it, and through me old

Polonius – yes, this wine, I fear, is what excites me so against that detestable old dog without a tooth.'

Upon this, the cosmopolitan, cigar in mouth, slowly raised the bottle, and brought it slowly to the light, looking at it steadfastly, as one might at a thermometer in August, to see not how low it was, but how high. Then whiffing out a puff, set it down, and said: 'Well, Charlie, if what wine you have drunk came out of this bottle, in that case I should say that if – supposing a case – that if one fellow had an object in getting another fellow fuddled, and this fellow to be fuddled was of your capacity, the operation would be comparatively inexpensive. What do you think, Charlie?'

'Why, I think I don't much admire the supposition,' said Charlie, with a look of resentment; 'it ain't safe, depend upon it, Frank, to venture upon too jocose suppositions with one's friends.'

'Why, bless you, Charlie, my supposition wasn't personal, but general. You mustn't be so touchy.'

'If I am touchy it is the wine. Sometimes, when I freely drink it, it has a touchy effect on me, I have observed.'

'Freely drink? you haven't drunk the perfect measure of one glass yet. While for me, this must be my fourth or fifth, thanks to your importunity; not to speak of all I drank this morning, for old acquaintance sake. Drink, drink; you must drink.'

'Oh, I drink while you are talking,' laughed the other; 'you have not noticed it, but I have drunk my share. Have a queer way I learned from a sedate old uncle, who used to tip off his glass unperceived. Do you fill up, and my glass too. There! Now away with that stump, and have a new cigar. Good fellowship for ever!' again in the lyric mood. 'Say, Frank, are we not men? I say are we not human? Tell me, were they not human who engendered us, as before heaven I believe they shall be whom we shall engender? Fill up, up, up, my friend. Let the ruby tide aspire, and all ruby aspirations with it! Up, fill up! Be we convivial. And conviviality, what is it? The word, I mean; what expresses it? A living together. But bats live together, and did you ever hear of convivial bats?'

'If I ever did,' observed the cosmopolitan, 'it has quite slipped my recollection.'

'But *why* did you never hear of convivial bats, nor anybody else? Because bats, though they live together, live not together genially. Bats are not genial souls. But men are; and how delightful to think that the word which among men signifies the highest pitch of geniality, implies, as indispensable auxiliary, the cheery benediction of the bottle. Yes, Frank, to live together in the finest sense, we must drink together. And so, what wonder that he who loves not wine, that sober wretch, has a lean heart – a heart like a wrung-out old bluing-bag, and loves not his kind? Out upon him, to the rag-house with him, hang him – the ungenial soul!'

'Oh, now, now, can't you be convivial without being censorious? I like easy, unexcited conviviality. For the sober man, really, though for my part I naturally love a cheerful glass, I will not prescribe my nature as the law to other natures. So don't abuse the sober man. Conviviality is one good thing, and sobriety is another good thing. So don't be one-sided.'

'Well, if I am one-sided, it is the wine. Indeed, indeed, I have indulged too genially. My excitement upon slight provocation shows it. But yours is a stronger head; drink you. By the way, talking of geniality, it is much on the increase in these days, ain't it?'

'It is, and I hail the fact. Nothing better attests the advance of the humanitarian spirit. In former and less humanitarian ages – the ages of amphitheatres and gladiators – geniality was mostly confined to the fireside and table. But in our age – the age of joint-stock companies and free-and-easies – it is with this precious quality as with precious gold in old Peru, which Pizarro found making up the scullion's sauce-pot as the Inca's crown. Yes, we golden boys, the moderns, have geniality everywhere – a bounty broadcast like moonlight.'

'True, true; my sentiments again. Geniality has invaded each department and profession. We have genial senators, genial authors, genial lecturers, genial doctors, genial clergymen, genial surgeons, and the next thing we shall have genial hangmen.'

'As to the last-named sort of person,' said the cosmopolitan, 'I trust that the advancing spirit of geniality will at last enable us to dispense with him. No murderers – no hangmen. And surely, when the whole world shall have been genialized, it will be as out of place to talk of murderers, as in a Christianized world to talk of sinners.'

'To pursue the thought,' said the other, 'every blessing is attended with some evil, and –'

'Stay,' said the cosmopolitan, 'that may be better let pass for a loose saying, than for hopeful doctrine.'

'Well, assuming that saying's truth, it would apply to the future supremacy of the genial spirit, since then it will fare with the hangman as it did with the weaver when the spinning-jenny whizzed into the ascendant. Thrown out of employment, what could Jack Ketch turn his hand to? Butchering?'

'That he could turn his hand to it seems probable; but that, under the circumstances, it would be appropriate, might in some minds admit of a question. For one, I am inclined to think – and I trust it will not be held fastidiousness – that it would hardly be suitable to the dignity of our nature, that an individual, once employed in attending the last hours of human unfortunates, should, that office being extinct, transfer himself to the business of attending the last hours of unfortunate cattle. I would suggest that the individual turn valet – a vocation to which he would, perhaps, appear not wholly inadapted by his familiar dexterity about the person. In particular, for giving a finishing tie to a gentleman's cravat, I know few who would, in all likelihood, be, from previous occupation, better fitted than the professional person in question.'

'Are you in earnest?' regarding the serene speaker with un-affected curiosity; 'are you really in earnest?'

'I trust I am never otherwise,' was the mildly earnest reply; 'but talking of the advance of geniality, I am not without hopes that it will eventually exert its influence even upon so difficult a subject as the misanthrope.'

'A genial misanthrope! I thought I had stretched the rope pretty hard in talking of genial hangmen. A genial misanthrope is no more conceivable than a surly philanthropist.'

'True,' lightly depositing in an unbroken little cylinder the ashes of his cigar, 'true, the two you name are well opposed.'

'Why, you talk as if there *was* such a being as a surly philanthropist.'

'I do. My eccentric friend, whom you call Coonskins, is an example. Does he not, as I explained to you, hide under a surly air a philanthropic heart? Now, the genial misanthrope, when in the process of eras, he shall turn up, will be the converse of this; under an affable air, he will hide a misanthropical heart. In short, the genial misanthrope will be a new kind of monster, but still no small improvement upon the original one, since, instead of making faces and throwing stones at people, like that poor old crazy man, Timon, he will take steps, fiddle in hand, and set the tickled world a'dancing. In a word, as the progress of Christianization mellows those in manner whom it cannot mend in mind, much the same will it prove with the progress of genialization. And so, thanks to geniality, the misanthrope, reclaimed from his boorish address, will take on refinement and softness – to so genial a degree, indeed, that it may possibly fall out that the misanthrope of the coming century will be almost as popular as, I am sincerely sorry to say, some philanthropists of the present time would seem not to be, as witness my eccentric friend named before.'

'Well,' cried the other, a little weary, perhaps, of a speculation so abstract, 'well, however it may be with the century to come, certainly in the century which is, whatever else one may be, he must be genial or he is nothing. So fill up, fill up, and be genial!'

'I am trying my best,' said the cosmopolitan, still calmly companionable. 'A moment since, we talked of Pizarro, gold, and Peru; no doubt, now, you remember that when the Spaniard first entered Atahalpa's treasure-chamber, and saw such profusion of plate stacked up, right and left, with the wantonness of old barrels in a brewer's yard, the needy fellow felt a twinge of misgiving, of want of confidence, as to the genuineness of an opulence so profuse. He went about rapping the shining vases with his knuckles. But it was all gold, pure gold, good gold, sterling gold, which how cheerfully would have been stamped such at Goldsmiths' Hall. And just so those needy minds, which, through their own insincerity, having no confidence in mankind, doubt lest the liberal geniality of this age be spurious. They are small Pizarros in their way – by the very princeliness of men's geniality stunned into distrust of it.'

'Far be such distrust from you and me, my genial friend,' cried the other fervently; 'fill up, fill up!'

'Well, this all along seems a division of labour,' smiled the cosmopolitan. 'I do about all the drinking, and you do about all – the genial. But yours is a nature competent to do that to a large population. And now, my friend,' with a peculiarly grave air, evidently foreshadowing something not unimportant, and very likely of close personal interest; 'wine, you know, opens the heart, and –'

'Opens it!' with exultation, 'it thaws it right out. Every heart is ice-bound till wine melt it, and reveal the tender grass and sweet herbage budding below, with every dear secret, hidden before like a dropped jewel in a snow-bank, lying there unsuspected through winter till spring.'

'And just in that way, my dear Charlie, is one of my little secrets now to be shown forth.'

'Ah!' eagerly moving round his chair, 'what is it?'

'Be not so impetuous, my dear Charlie. Let me explain. You see, naturally, I am a man not over-gifted with assurance; in general, I am, if anything, diffidently reserved; so, if I shall presently seem otherwise, the reason is, that you, by the geniality you have evinced in all your talk, and especially the noble way in which, while affirming your good opinion of men, you intimated that you never could prove false to any man, but most by your indignation at a particularly illiberal passage in Polonius' advice – in short, in short,' with extreme embarrassment, 'how shall I express what I mean, unless I add that by your whole character you impel me to throw myself upon your nobleness; in one word, put confidence in you, a generous confidence?'

'I see, I see,' with heightened interest, 'something of moment you wish to confide. Now, what is it, Frank? Love affair?'

'No, not that.'

'What, then, my *dear* Frank? Speak – depend upon me to the last. Out with it.'

'Out it shall come, then,' said the cosmopolitan, 'I am in want, urgent want, of money.'

Chapter Thirty-One

A Metamorphosis More Surprising Than Any in Ovid

'In want of money!' pushing back his chair as from a suddenly-disclosed man-trap or crater.

'Yes,' naively assented the cosmopolitan, 'and you are going to loan me fifty dollars. I could almost wish I was in need of more, only for your sake. Yes, my dear Charlie, for your sake; that you might the better prove your noble kindliness, my dear Charlie.'

'None of your dear Charlies,' cried the other, springing to his feet, and buttoning up his coat, as if hastily to depart upon a long journey.

'Why, why, why?' painfully looking up.

'None of your why, why, whys!' tossing out a foot, 'go to the devil, sir! Beggar, impostor! – never so deceived in a man in my life.'

Chapter Thirty-Two

Showing That the Age of Magic and Magicians is Not Yet Over

While speaking or rather hissing those words, the boon companion underwent much such a change as one reads of in fairy-books. Out of old materials sprang a new creature. Cadmus glided into the snake.

The cosmopolitan rose, the traces of previous feeling vanished; looked steadfastly at his transformed friend a moment, then, taking ten half-eagles from his pocket, stooped down, and laid them, one by one, in a circle round him; and, retiring a pace, waved his long tasselled pipe with the air of a necromancer, an air heightened by his costume, accompanying each wave with a solemn murmur of cabalistical words.

Meantime, he within the magic-ring stood suddenly rapt, exhibiting every symptom of a successful charm – a turned cheek, a fixed attitude, a frozen eye; spell-bound, not more by the waving wand than by the ten invincible talismans on the floor.

'Reappear, reappear, reappear, oh, my former friend! Replace this hideous apparition with thy blest shape, and be the token of thy return the words, "My dear Frank."'

'My dear Frank,' now cried the restored friend, cordially stepping out of the ring, with regained self-possession regaining lost identity, 'My dear Frank, what a funny man you are; full of fun as an egg of meat. How could you tell me that absurd story of your being in need? But I relish a good joke too well to spoil it by letting on. Of course, I humoured the thing; and, on my side, put on all the cruel airs you would have me. Come, this little episode of fictitious estrangement will but enhance the delightful reality. Let us sit down again, and finish our bottle.'

'With all my heart,' said the cosmopolitan, dropping the necromancer with the same facility with which he had assumed it. 'Yes,' he added, soberly picking up the gold pieces, and returning them with a chink to his pocket, 'yes, I am something of a funny man now and then; while for you, Charlie,' eyeing him in tenderness, 'what you say about your humouring the thing is true enough; never did man second a joke better than you did just now. You played your part better than I did mine; you played it, Charlie, to the life.'

'You see, I once belonged to an amateur play company; that accounts for it. But come, fill up, and let's talk of something else.'

'Well,' acquiesced the cosmopolitan, seating himself, and quietly brimming his glass, 'what shall we talk about?'

'Oh, anything you please,' a sort of nervously accommodating.

'Well, suppose we talk about Charlemont?'

'Charlemont? What's Charlemont? Who's Charlemont?'

'You shall hear, my dear Charlie,' answered the cosmopolitan. 'I will tell you the story of Charlemont, the gentleman-madman.'

Chapter Thirty-Three

Which May Pass for Whatever it May Prove to Be Worth

But ere be given the rather grave story of Charlemont, a reply must in civility be made to a certain voice which methinks I hear, that in view of past chapters, and more particularly the last, where certain antics appear, exclaims: How unreal all this is! Who did ever dress or act like your cosmopolitan? And who, it might be returned, did ever dress or act like harlequin?

Strange, that in a work of amusement, this severe fidelity to real life should be exacted by any one, who, by taking up such a work, sufficiently shows that he is not unwilling to drop real life, and turn, for a time, to something different. Yes, it is, indeed, strange that any one should clamour for the thing he is weary of; that any one, who, for any cause, finds real life dull, should yet demand of him who is to divert his attention from it, that he should be true to that dullness.

There is another class, and with this class we side, who sit down to a work of amusement tolerably as they sit at a play, and with much the same expectations and feelings. They look that fancy shall evoke scenes different from those of the same old crowd round the custom-house counter, and same old dishes on the boarding-house table, with characters unlike those of the same old acquaintances they meet in the same old way every day in the same old street. And as, in real life, the proprieties will not allow people to act out themselves with that unreserve permitted to the stage; so, in books of fiction, they look not only for more entertainment, but, at bottom, even for more reality, than real life itself can show. Thus, though they want novelty, they want nature, too; but nature unfettered, exhilarated, in effect transformed. In this way of thinking, the people in a fiction, like the people in a play, must dress as nobody exactly dresses, talk as nobody exactly talks, act as nobody exactly acts. It is with fiction as with religion: it should present another world, and yet one to which we feel the tie.

If, then, something is to be pardoned to well-meant endeavour, surely a little is to be allowed to that writer who, in all his scenes, does but seek to minister to what, as he understands it, is the implied wish of the more indulgent lovers of entertainment, before whom harlequin can never appear in a coat too particoloured, or cut capers too fantastic.

One word more. Though every one knows how bootless it is to be in all cases vindicating one's self, never mind how convinced one may be that he is never in the wrong; yet, so precious to man is the approbation of his kind, that to rest, though but under an imaginary censure applied to but a work of imagination, is no easy thing. The mention of this weakness will explain why all such readers as may think they perceive something inharmonious between the boisterous hilarity of the cosmopolitan with the bristling cynic, and his restrained good-nature with the booncompanion, are now referred to that chapter where some similar apparent inconsistency in another character is, on general principles, modestly endeavoured to be apologized for.

Chapter Thirty-Four

In Which the Cosmopolitan Tells the Story of the Gentleman-madman

'Charlemont was a young merchant of French descent, living in St Louis – a man not deficient in mind, and possessed of that sterling and captivating kindliness, seldom in perfection seen but in youthful bachelors, united at times to a remarkable sort of gracefully devil-may-care and witty good-humour. Of course, he was admired by everybody, and loved, as only mankind can love, by not a few. But in his twenty-ninth year a change came over him. Like one whose hair turns gray in a night, so in a day Charlemont turned from affable to morose. His acquaintances were passed without greeting; while, as for his confidential friends, them he pointedly, unscrupulously, and with a kind of fierceness, cut dead.

'One, provoked by such conduct, would fain have resented it with words as disdainful; while another, shocked by the change, and, in concern for a friend, magnanimously overlooking affronts, implored to know what sudden, secret grief had distempered him. But from resentment and from tenderness Charlemont alike turned away.

'Ere long, to the general surprise, the merchant Charlemont was gazetted, and the same day it was reported that he had withdrawn from town, but not before placing his entire property in the hands of responsible assignees for the benefit of creditors.

'Whither he had vanished none could guess. At length, nothing being heard, it was surmised that he must have made away with himself – a surmise, doubtless, originating in the remembrance of the change some months previous to his bankruptcy – a change of a sort only to be ascribed to a mind suddenly thrown from its balance.

'Years passed. It was spring-time, and lo, one bright morning, Charlemont lounged into the St Louis coffee-houses – gay, polite, humane, companionable, and dressed in the height of costly elegance. Not only was he alive, but he was himself again. Upon meeting with old acquaintances, he made the first advances, and in such a manner that it was impossible not to meet him half-way. Upon other old friends, whom he did not chance casually to meet, he either personally called, or left his card and compliments for them; and to several, sent presents of game or hampers of wine.

'They say the world is sometimes harshly unforgiving, but it was not so to Charlemont. The world feels a return of love for one who returns to it as he did. Expressive of its renewed interest was a whisper, an inquiring whisper, how now, exactly, so long after his bankruptcy, it fared with Charlemont's purse. Rumour, seldom at a loss for answers, replied that he had spent nine years in Marseilles in France, and there acquiring a second fortune, had returned with it, a man devoted henceforth to genial friendships.

'Added years went by, and the restored wanderer still the same; or, rather, by his noble qualities, grew up like golden maize in the encouraging sun of good opinions. But still the latent wonder was, what had caused that change in him at a period when, pretty much as now, he was, to all appearance, in the possession of the same fortune, the same friends, the same popularity. But nobody thought it would be the thing to question him here.

'At last, at a dinner at his house, when all the guests but one had successively departed; this remaining guest, an old acquaintance, being just enough under the influence of wine to set aside the fear of touching upon a delicate point, ventured, in a way which perhaps spoke more favourably for his heart than his tact, to beg of his host to explain the one enigma of his life. Deep melancholy overspread the before cheery face of Charlemont; he sat for some moments tremulously silent; then pushing a full decanter towards the guest, in a choked voice, said: "No, no!

when by art, and care, and time, flowers are made to bloom over a grave, who would seek to dig all up again only to know the mystery? – The wine." When both glasses were filled, Charlemont took his, and lifting it, added lowly: "If ever, in days to come, you shall see ruin at hand, and, thinking you understand mankind, shall tremble for your friendships, and tremble for your pride; and, partly through love for the one and fear for the other, shall resolve to be beforehand with the world, and save it from a sin by prospectively taking that sin to yourself, then will you do as one I now dream of once did, and like him will you suffer; but how fortunate and how grateful should you be, if like him, after all that had happened, you could be a little happy again."

'When the guest went away, it was with the persuasion, that though outwardly restored in mind as in fortune, yet, some taint of Charlemont's old malady survived, and that it was not well for friends to touch one dangerous string.'

Chapter Thirty-Five

In Which the Cosmopolitan Strikingly Evinces the Artlessness of His Nature

'Well, what do you think of the story of Charlemont?' mildly asked he who had told it.

'A very strange one,' answered the auditor, who had been such not with perfect ease, 'but is it true?'

'Of course not; it is a story which I told with the purpose of every story-teller – to amuse. Hence, if it seem strange to you, that strangeness is the romance; it is what contrasts it with real life; it is the invention, in brief, the fiction as opposed to the fact. For do but ask yourself, my dear Charlie,' lovingly leaning over towards him, 'I rest it with your own heart now, whether such a forereaching motive as Charlemont hinted he had acted on in his change – whether such a motive, I say, were a sort of one at all justified by the nature of human society? Would you, for one, turn the cold shoulder to a friend – a convivial one, say, whose pennilessness should be suddenly revealed to you?'

'How can you ask me, my dear Frank? You know I would scorn such meanness.' But rising somewhat disconcerted – 'really, early as it is, I think I must retire; my head,' putting up his hand to it, 'feels unpleasantly; this confounded elixir of logwood, little as I drank of it, has played the deuce with me.'

'Little as you drank of this elixir of logwood? Why, Charlie, you are losing your mind. To talk so of the genuine, mellow old port. Yes, I think that by all means you had better away, and sleep it off. There – don't apologize – don't explain – go, go – I understand you exactly. I will see you to-morrow.'

Chapter Thirty-Six

*In Which the Cosmopolitan is Accosted by a Mystic, Whereupon
Ensues Pretty Much Such Talk as Might Be Expected*

As, not without some haste, the boon companion withdrew, a stranger advanced, and touching the cosmopolitan, said: 'I think I heard you say you would see that man again. Be warned; don't you do so.'

He turned, surveying the speaker; a blue-eyed man, sandy-haired, and Saxon-looking; perhaps five and forty; tall, and, but for a certain angularity, well made; little touch of the drawing-room about him, but a look of plain propriety of a Puritan sort, with a kind of farmer dignity. His age seemed betokened more by his brow, placidly thoughtful, than by his general aspect, which had that look of youthfulness in maturity, peculiar sometimes to habitual health of body, the original gift of nature, or in part the effect or reward of steady temperance of the passions, kept so, perhaps, by constitution as much as morality. A neat, comely, almost ruddy cheek, coolly fresh, like a red clover-blossom at coolish dawn – the colour of warmth preserved by the virtue of chill. Toning the whole man, was one-knows-not-what of shrewd-ness and mythiness, strangely jumbled; in that way, he seemed a kind of cross between a Yankee peddler and a Tartar priest, though it seemed as if, at a pinch, the first would not in all prob-ability play second fiddle to the last.

'Sir,' said the cosmopolitan, rising and bowing with slow dig-nity, 'if I cannot with unmixed satisfaction hail a hint pointed at one who has just been clinking the social glass with me, on the other hand, I am not disposed to underrate the motive which, in the present case, could alone have prompted such an intimation. My friend, whose seat is still warm, has retired for the night, leaving more or less in his bottle here. Pray, sit down in his seat, and partake with me; and then, if you choose to hint aught further unfavourable to the man, the genial warmth of whose person in part passes into yours, and whose genial hospitality meanders through you – be it so.'

'Quite beautiful conceits,' said the stranger, now scholastically and artistically eyeing the picturesque speaker, as if he were a statue in the Pitti Palace; 'very beautiful,' then with the gravest interest, 'yours, sir, if I mistake not, must be a beautiful soul – one full of all love and truth; for where beauty is, there must those be.'

'A pleasing belief,' rejoined the cosmopolitan, beginning with an even air, 'and to confess, long ago it pleased me. Yes, with you and Schiller, I am pleased to believe that beauty is at bottom incompatible with ill, and therefore am so eccentric as to have confidence in the latent benignity of that beautiful creature, the rattlesnake, whose lithe neck and burnished maze of tawny gold, as he sleekly curls aloft in the sun, who on the prairie can behold without wonder?'

As he breathed these words, he seemed so to enter into their spirit – as some earnest descriptive speakers will – as unconsciously to wreathe his form and side-long crest his head, till he all but seemed the creature described. Meantime, the stranger regarded him with little surprise, apparently, though with much contemplativeness of a mystical sort, and presently said: 'When charmed by the beauty of that viper, did it never occur to you to change personalities with him? to feel what it was to be a snake? to glide unsuspected in grass? to sting, to kill at a touch; your whole beautiful body one iridescent scabbard of death? In short, did the wish never occur to you to feel yourself exempt from knowledge, and conscience, and revel for a while in the care-free, joyous life of a perfectly instinctive, unscrupulous, and irresponsible creature?'

'Such a wish,' replied the other, not perceptibly disturbed, 'I must confess, never consciously was mine. Such a wish, indeed, could hardly occur to ordinary imaginations, and mine I cannot think much above the average.'

'But now that the idea is suggested,' said the stranger, with infantile intellectuality, 'does it not raise the desire?'

'Hardly. For though I do not think I have any uncharitable prejudice against the rattlesnake, still, I should not like to be one. If I were a rattlesnake now, there would be no such thing as being genial with men – men would be afraid of me, and then I should be a very lonesome and miserable rattlesnake.'

'True, men would be afraid of you. And why? Because of your rattle, your hollow rattle – a sound, as I have been told, like the shaking together of small, dry skulls in a tune of the Waltz of Death. And here we have another beautiful truth. When any creature is by its make inimical to other creatures, nature in effect labels that creature, much as an apothecary does a poison. So that whoever is destroyed by a rattlesnake, or other harmful agent, it is his own fault. He should have respected the label. Hence that significant passage in Scripture, "Who will pity the charmer that is bitten with a serpent?"'

'I would pity him,' said the cosmopolitan, a little bluntly, perhaps.

'But don't you think,' rejoined the other, still maintaining his passionless air, 'don't you think, that for a man to pity where nature is pitiless, is a little presuming?'

'Let casuists decide the casuistry, but the compassion the heart decides for itself. But, sir,' deepening in seriousness, 'as I now for the first realize, you but a moment since introduced the word irresponsible in a way I am not used to. Now, sir, though, out of a tolerant spirit, as I hope, I try my best never to be frightened at any speculation, so long as it is pursued in honesty, yet, for once, I must acknowledge that you do really, in the point cited, cause me uneasiness; because a proper view of the universe, that view which is suited to breed a proper confidence, teaches, if I err not, that since all things are justly presided over, not very many living agents but must be some way accountable.'

'Is a rattlesnake accountable?' asked the stranger, with such a preternaturally cold, gemmy glance out of his pellucid blue eye, that he seemed more a metaphysical merman than a feeling man; 'is a rattlesnake accountable?'

'If I will not affirm that it is,' returned the other, with the caution of no inexperienced thinker, 'neither will I deny it. But if we suppose it so, I need not say that such accountability is neither to you, nor me, nor the Court of Common Pleas, but to something superior.'

He was proceeding, when the stranger would have interrupted him; but as reading his argument in his eye, the cosmopolitan, without waiting for it to be put into words, at once spoke to it. 'You object to my supposition, for but such it is, that the rattlesnake's accountability is not by nature manifest; but might not much the same thing be urged against man's? A *reductio ad absurdum*, proving the objection vain. But if now,' he continued, 'you consider what capacity for mischief there is in a rattlesnake (observe, I do not charge it with being mischievous, I but say it has the capacity), could you well avoid admitting that that would be no symmetrical view of the universe which should maintain that, while to man it is forbidden to kill, without judicial cause, his fellow, yet the rattlesnake has an implied permit of unaccountability to murder any creature it takes capricious umbrage at – man included? – But,' with a wearied air, 'this is no genial talk; at least it is not so to me. Zeal at unawares embarked me in it. I regret it. Pray, sit down, and take some of this wine.'

'Your suggestions are new to me,' said the other, with a kind of condescending appreciativeness, as of one who, out of devotion to knowledge, disdains not to appropriate the least crumb of it, even from a pauper's board; 'and, as I am a very Athenian in hailing a new thought, I cannot consent to let it drop so abruptly. Now, the rattlesnake –'

'Nothing more about rattlesnakes, I beseech,' in distress; 'I must positively decline to re-enter upon that subject. Sit down, sir, I beg, and take some of this wine.'

'To invite me to sit down with you is hospitable,' collectedly acquiescing now in the change of topics; 'and hospitality being fabled to be of oriental origin, and forming, as it does, the subject of a pleasing Arabian romance, as well as being a very romantic thing in itself – hence I always hear the expressions of hospitality with pleasure. But, as for the wine, my regard for that beverage is so extreme, and I am so fearful of letting it sate me, that I keep my love for it in the lasting condition of an untried abstraction. Briefly, I quaff immense draughts of wine from the page of Hafiz, but wine from a cup I seldom as much as sip.'

The cosmopolitan turned a mild glance upon the speaker, who, now occupying the chair opposite him, sat there purely and coldly radiant as a prism. It seemed as if one could almost hear him vitreously chime and ring. That moment a waiter passed, whom, arresting with a sign, the cosmopolitan bid go bring a goblet of ice-water. 'Ice it well, waiter,' said he; 'and now,' turning to the stranger, 'will you, if you please, give me your reason for the warning words you first addressed to me?'

'I hope they were not such warnings as most warnings are,' said the stranger; 'warnings which do not forewarn, but in mockery come after the fact. And yet something in you bids me think now, that whatever latent design your impostor friend might have had upon you, it as yet remains unaccomplished. You read his label.'

'And what did it say? "This is a genial soul." So you see you must either give up your doctrine of labels, or else your prejudice against my friend. But tell me,' with renewed earnestness, 'what do you take him for? What is he?'

'What are you? What am I? Nobody knows who anybody is. The data which life furnishes, towards forming a true estimate of any being, are as insufficient to that end as in geometry one side given would be to determine the triangle.'

'But is not this doctrine of triangles someway inconsistent with your doctrine of labels?'

'Yes; but what of that? I seldom care to be consistent. In a philosophical view, consistency is a certain level at all times, maintained in all the thoughts of one's mind. But, since nature is nearly all hill and dale, how can one keep naturally advancing in knowledge without submitting to the natural inequalities in the progress? Advance into knowledge is just like advance upon the Grand Erie Canal, where, from the character of the country, change of level is inevitable; you are locked up and locked down with perpetual inconsistencies, and yet all the time you get on; while the dullest part of the whole route is what the boatmen call the "long level" – a consistently flat surface of sixty miles through stagnant swamps.'

'In one particular,' rejoined the cosmopolitan, 'your simile is, perhaps, unfortunate. For, after all these weary lockings-up and lockings-down, upon how much of a higher plain do you finally stand? Enough to make it an object? Having from youth been taught reverence for knowledge, you must pardon me if, on but this one account, I reject your analogy. But really you someway bewitch me with your tempting discourse, so that I keep straying from my point unawares. You tell me you cannot certainly know who or what my friend is; pray, what do you conjecture him to be?'

'I conjecture him to be what, among the ancient Egyptians, was called a —' using some unknown word.

'A —! And what is that?'

'A — is what Proclus, in a little note to his third book on the theology of Plato, defines as — —' coming out with a sentence of Greek.

Holding up his glass, and steadily looking through its transparency, the cosmopolitan rejoined: 'That, in so defining the thing, Proclus set it to modern understandings in the most crystal light it was susceptible of, I will not rashly deny; still, if you could put the definition in words suited to perceptions like mine, I should take it for a favour.'

'A favour!' slightly lifting his cool eyebrows; 'a bridal favour I understand, a knot of white ribbons, a very beautiful type of the purity of true marriage; but of other favours I am yet to learn; and still, in a vague way, the word, as you employ it, strikes me as unpleasingly significant in general of some poor, unheroic submission to being done good to.'

Here the goblet of iced-water was brought, and, in compliance with a sign from the cosmopolitan, was placed before the stranger, who, not before expressing acknowledgments, took a draught, apparently refreshing – its very coldness, as with some is the case, proving not entirely uncongenial.

At last, setting down the goblet, and gently wiping from his lips the beads of water freshly clinging there as to the valve of a coral-shell upon a reef, he turned upon the cosmopolitan, and, in a manner the most cool, self-possessed, and matter-of-fact possible, said: 'I hold to the metempsychosis; and whoever I may be now, I feel that I was once the stoic Arrian, and have inklings of having been equally puzzled by a word in the current language of that former time, very probably answering to your word *favour*.'

'Would you favour me by explaining?' said the cosmopolitan, blandly.

'Sir,' responded the stranger, with a very slight degree of severity, 'I like lucidity, of all things, and am afraid I shall hardly be able to converse satisfactorily with you, unless you bear it in mind.'

The cosmopolitan ruminatingly eyed him awhile, then said: 'The best way, as I have heard, to get out of a labyrinth, is to retrace one's steps. I will accordingly retrace mine, and beg you will accompany me. In short, once again to return to the point: for what reason did you warn me against my friend?'

'Briefly, then, and clearly, because, as before said, I conjecture him to be what, among the ancient Egyptians –'

'Pray, now,' earnestly deprecated the cosmopolitan, 'pray, now, why disturb the repose of those ancient Egyptians? What to us are their words or their thoughts? Are we pauper Arabs, without a house of our own, that, with the mummies, we must turn squatters among the dust of the Catacombs?'

'Pharaoh's poorest brick-maker lies proudlier in his rags than the Emperor of all the Russias in his hollands,' oracularly said the stranger; 'for death, though in a worm, is majestic; while life, though in a king, is contemptible. So talk not against mummies. It is a part of my mission to teach mankind a due reverence for mummies.'

Fortunately, to arrest these incoherencies, or rather, to vary them, a haggard, inspired-looking man now approached – a crazy beggar, asking alms under the form of peddling a rhapsodical tract, composed by himself, and setting forth his claims to some rhapsodical apostleship. Though ragged and dirty, there was about him no touch of vulgarity; for, by nature, his manner was not unrefined, his frame slender, and appeared the more so from the broad, untanned frontlet of his brow, tangled over with a dishevelled mass of raven curls, throwing a still deeper tinge upon a complexion like that of a shrivelled berry. Nothing could exceed his look of picturesque Italian ruin and dethronement, heightened by what seemed just one glimmering peep of reason, insufficient to do him any lasting good, but enough, perhaps, to suggest a torment of latent doubts at times, whether his addled dream of glory were true.

Accepting the tract offered him, the cosmopolitan glanced over it, and, seeming to see just what it was, closed it, put it in his pocket, eyed the man a moment, then, leaning over and presenting him with a shilling, said to him, in tones kind and considerate: 'I am sorry, my friend, that I happen to be engaged just now; but, having purchased your work, I promise myself much satisfaction in its perusal at my earliest leisure.'

In his tattered, single-breasted frock-coat, buttoned meagerly up to his chin, the shatter-brain made him a bow, which, for courtesy, would not have misbecome a viscount, then turned with silent appeal to the stranger. But the stranger sat more like a cold prism than ever, while an expression of keen Yankee cuteness, now replacing his former mystical one, lent added icicles to his aspect. His whole air said: 'Nothing from me.' The repulsed petitioner threw a look full of resentful pride and cracked disdain upon him, and went his way.

'Come, now,' said the cosmopolitan, a little reproachfully, 'you ought to have sympathized with that man; tell me, did you feel no fellow-feeling? Look at his tract here, quite in the transcendental vein.'

'Excuse me,' said the stranger, declining the tract, 'I never patronize scoundrels.'

'Scoundrels?'

'I detected in him, sir, a damning peep of sense – damning, I say; for sense in a seeming madman is scoundrelism. I take him for a cunning vagabond, who picks up a vagabond living by adroitly playing the madman. Did you not remark how he flinched under my eye?'

'Really,' drawing a long, astonished breath, 'I could hardly have divined in you a temper so subtly distrustful. Flinched? to be sure he did, poor fellow; you received him with so lame a welcome. As for his adroitly playing the madman, invidious critics might object the same to some one or two strolling magi of these days. But that is a matter I know nothing about. But, once more, and for the last time, to return to the point: why sir, did you warn me against my friend? I shall rejoice, if, as I think it will prove, your want of confidence in my friend rests upon a basis equally slender with your distrust of the lunatic. Come, why did you warn me? Put it, I beseech, in few words, and those English.'

'I warned you against him because he is suspected for what on these boats is known – so they tell me – as a Mississippi operator.'

'An operator, ah? he operates, does he? My friend, then, is something like what the Indians call a Great Medicine, is he? He operates, he purges, he drains off the repletions.'

'I perceive, sir,' said the stranger, constitutionally obtuse to the pleasant drollery, 'that your notion, of what is called a Great Medicine, needs correction. The Great Medicine among the Indians is less a bolus than a man in grave esteem for his politic sagacity.'

'And is not my friend politic? Is not my friend sagacious? By your own definition, is not my friend a Great Medicine?'

'No, he is an operator, a Mississippi operator; an equivocal character. That he is such, I little doubt, having had him pointed out to me as such, by one desirous of initiating me into any little novelty of this western region, where I never before travelled. And, sir, if I am not mistaken, you also are a stranger here (but, indeed, where in this strange universe is not one a stranger?) and that is a reason why I felt moved to warn you against a companion who could not be otherwise than perilous to one of a free and trustful disposition. But I repeat the hope, that, thus far at least, he has not succeeded with you, and trust that, for the future, he will not.'

'Thank you for your concern; but hardly can I equally thank you for so steadily maintaining the hypothesis of my friend's objectionableness. True, I but made his acquaintance for the first to-day, and know little of his antecedents; but that would seem no just reason why a nature like his should not of itself inspire confidence. And since your own knowledge of the gentleman is not, by your account, so exact as it might be, you will pardon me if I decline to welcome any further suggestions unflattering to him. Indeed, sir,' with friendly decision, 'let us change the subject.'

Chapter Thirty-Seven

The Mystical Master Introduces the Practical Disciple

'Both, the subject, and the interlocutor,' replied the stranger rising, and waiting the return towards him of a promenader, that moment turning at the further end of his walk.

'Egbert!' said he, calling.

Egbert, a well-dressed, commercial-looking gentleman of about thirty, responded in a way strikingly deferential, and in a moment stood near, in the attitude less of an equal companion apparently than a confidential follower.

'This,' said the stranger, taking Egbert by the hand and leading him to the cosmopolitan, 'this is Egbert, a disciple. I wish you to know Egbert. Egbert was the first among mankind to reduce to practice the principles of Mark Winsome – principles previously accounted as less adapted to life than the closet. Egbert,' turning to the disciple, who, with seeming modesty, a little shrank under these compliments, 'Egbert, this,' with a salute towards the cosmopolitan, 'is, like all of us, a stranger. I wish you, Egbert, to know this brother stranger; be communicative with him. Particularly if, by anything hitherto dropped, his curiosity has been roused as to the precise nature of my philosophy, I trust you will not leave such curiosity ungratified. You, Egbert, by simply setting forth your practice, can do more to enlighten one as to my theory, than I myself can by mere speech. Indeed, it is by you that I myself best understand myself. For to every philosophy are certain rear parts, very important parts, and these, like the rear of one's head, are best seen by reflection. Now, as in a glass, you, Egbert, in your life, reflect to me the more important part of my system, he, who approves you, approves the philosophy of Mark Winsome.'

Though portions of this harangue may, perhaps, in the phraseology seem self-complacent, yet no trace of self-complacency was perceptible in the speaker's manner, which throughout was plain, unassuming, dignified, and manly; the teacher and prophet seemed to lurk more in the idea, so to speak, than in the mere bearing of him who was the vehicle of it.

'Sir,' said the cosmopolitan, who seemed not a little interested in this new aspect of matters, 'you speak of a certain philosophy, and a more or less occult one it may be, and hint of its bearing upon practical life; pray, tell me, if the study of this philosophy tends to the same formation of character with the experiences of the world?'

'It does; and that is the test of its truth; for any philosophy that, being in operation contradictory to the ways of the world, tends to produce a character at odds with it, such a philosophy must necessarily be but a cheat and a dream.'

'You a little surprise me,' answered the cosmopolitan: 'for, from an occasional profundity in you, and also from your allusions to a profound work on the theology of Plato, it would seem but natural to surmise that, if you are the originator of any philosophy, it must needs so partake of the abstruse, as to exalt it above the comparatively vile uses of life.'

'No uncommon mistake with regard to me,' rejoined the other. Then meekly standing like a Raphael: 'If still in golden accents old Memnon murmurs his riddle, none the less does the balance-sheet of every man's ledger unriddle the profit or loss of life. Sir,' with calm energy, 'man came into this world, not to sit down and muse, not to befog himself with vain subtleties, but to gird up his loins and to work. Mystery is in the morning, and mystery in the night, and the beauty of mystery is everywhere; but still the plain truth remains, that mouth and purse must be filled. If, hitherto, you have supposed me a visionary, be undeceived. I am no one-ideaed one, either; no more than the seers before me. Was not Seneca a usurer? Bacon a courtier? and

Swedenborg, though with one eye on the invisible, did he not keep the other on the main chance? Along with whatever else it may be given me to be, I am a man of serviceable knowledge, and a man of the world. Know me for such. And as for my disciple here,' turning towards him, 'if you look to find any soft Utopianisms and last year's sunsets in him, I smile to think how he will set you right. The doctrines I have taught him will, I trust, lead him neither to the mad-house nor the poor-house, as so many other doctrines have served credulous sticklers. Furthermore,' glancing upon him paternally, 'Egbert is both my disciple and my poet. For poetry is not a thing of ink and rhyme, but of thought and act, and, in the latter way, is by any one to be found anywhere, when in useful action sought. In a word, my disciple here is a thriving young merchant, a practical poet in the West India trade. There,' presenting Egbert's hand to the cosmopolitan, 'I join you, and leave you.' With which words, and without bowing, the master withdrew.

Chapter Thirty-Eight

The Disciple Unbends, and Consents to Act a Social Part

In the master's presence the disciple had stood as one not ignorant of his place; modesty was in his expression, with a sort of reverential depression. But the presence of the superior withdrawn, he seemed lithely to shoot up erect from beneath it, like one of those wire men from a toy snuff-box.

He was, as before said, a young man of about thirty. His countenance of that neuter sort, which, in repose, is neither prepossessing nor disagreeable; so that it seemed quite uncertain how he would turn out. His dress was neat, with just enough of the mode to save it from the reproach of originality; in which general respect, though with a readjustment of details, his costume seemed modelled upon his master's. But, upon the whole, he was, to all appearances, the last person in the world that one would take for the disciple of any transcendental philosophy; though, indeed, something about his sharp nose and shaved chin seemed to hint that if mysticism, as a lesson, ever came in his way, he might, with the characteristic knack of a true New-Englander, turn even so profitless a thing to some profitable account.

'Well,' said he, now familiarly seating himself in the vacated chair, 'what do you think of Mark? Sublime fellow, ain't he?'

'That each member of the human guild is worthy respect, my friend,' rejoined the cosmopolitan, 'is a fact which no admirer of that guild will question; but that, in view of higher natures, the word sublime, so frequently applied to them, can, without confusion, be also applied to man, is a point which man will decide for himself; though, indeed, if he decide it in the affirmative, it is not for me to object. But I am curious to know more of that philosophy of which, at present, I have but inklings. You, its first disciple among men, it seems, are peculiarly qualified to expound it. Have you any objections to begin now?'

'None at all,' squaring himself to the table. 'Where shall I begin? At first principles?'

'You remember that it was in a practical way that you were represented as being fitted for the clear exposition. Now, what you call first principles, I have, in some things, found to be more or less vague. Permit me, then, in a plain way, to suppose some common case in real life, and that done, I would like you to tell me how you, the practical disciple of the philosophy I wish to know about, would, in that case, conduct.'

'A business-like view. Propose the case.'

'Not only the case, but the persons. The case is this: There are two friends, friends from childhood, bosom-friends; one of whom, for the first time, being in need, for the first time seeks a loan from the other, who, so far as fortune goes, is more than competent to grant it. And the persons are to be you and I: you, the friend from whom the loan is sought – I, the friend who seeks it; you, the disciple of the philosophy in question – I, a common man, with no more philosophy than to know that when I am comfortably warm I don't feel cold, and when I have the ague I shake. Mind, now, you must work up your imagination, and, as much as possible, talk and behave just as if the case supposed were a fact. For brevity, you shall call me Frank, and I will call you Charlie. Are you agreed?'

'Perfectly. You begin.'

The cosmopolitan paused a moment, then, assuming a serious and care-worn air, suitable to the part to be enacted, addressed his hypothesized friend.

Chapter Thirty-Nine

The Hypothetical Friends

'Charlie, I am going to put confidence in you.'

'You always have, and with reason. What is it, Frank?'

'Charlie, I am in want – urgent want of money.'

'That's not well.'

'But it *will* be well, Charlie, if you loan me a hundred dollars. I would not ask this of you, only my need is sore, and you and I have so long shared hearts and minds together, however unequally on my side, that nothing remains to prove our friendship but, with the same inequality on my side, to share purses. You will do me the favour, won't you?'

'Favour? What do you mean by asking me to do you a favour?'

'Why, Charlie, you never used to talk so.'

'Because, Frank, you on your side, never used to talk so.'

'But won't you loan me the money?'

'No, Frank.'

'Why?'

'Because my rule forbids. I give away money, but never loan it; and of course the man who calls himself my friend is above receiving alms. The negotiation of a loan is a business transaction. And I will transact no business with a friend. What a friend is, he is socially and intellectually; and I rate social and intellectual friendship too high to degrade it on either side into a pecuniary make-shift. To be sure there are, and I have, what is called business friends; that is, commercial acquaintances, very convenient persons. But I draw a red-ink line between them and my friends in the true sense – my friends social and intellectual. In brief, a true friend has nothing to do with loans; he should have a soul above loans. Loans are such unfriendly accommodations as are to be had from the soulless corporation of a bank, by giving the regular security and paying the regular discount.'

'An *unfriendly* accommodation? Do those words go together handsomely?'

'Like the poor farmer's team, of an old man and a cow – not handsomely, but to the purpose. Look, Frank, a loan of money on interest is a sale of money on credit. To sell a thing on credit may be an accommodation, but where is the friendliness? Few men in their senses, except operators, borrow money on interest, except upon a necessity akin to starvation. Well, now, where is the friendliness of my letting a starving man have, say, the money's worth of a barrel of flour upon the condition that, on a given day, he shall let me have the money's worth of a barrel and a half of flour; especially if I add this further proviso, that if he fail so to do, I shall then, to secure to myself the money's worth of my barrel and his half barrel, put his heart up at public auction, and, as it is cruel to part families, throw in his wife's and children's?'

'I understand,' with a pathetic shudder; 'but even did it come to that, such a step on the creditor's part, let us, for the honour of human nature, hope, were less the intention than the contingency.'

'But, Frank, a contingency not unprovided for in the taking beforehand of due securities.'

'Still, Charlie, was not the loan in the first place a friend's act?'

'And the auction in the last place an enemy's act. Don't you see? The enmity lies couched in the friendship, just as the ruin in the relief.'

'I must be very stupid to-day, Charlie, but really, I can't understand this. Excuse me, my dear friend, but it strikes me that in going into the philosophy of the subject, you go somewhat out of your depth.'

'So said the incautious wader-out to the ocean; but the ocean replied: "It is just the other way, my wet friend," and drowned him.'

'That, Charlie, is a fable about as unjust to the ocean, as some of Aesop's are to the animals. The ocean is a magnanimous element, and would scorn to assassinate a poor fellow, let alone taunting him in the act. But I don't understand what you say about enmity couched in friendship, and ruin in relief.'

'I will illustrate, Frank. The needy man is a train slipped off the rail. He who loans him money on interest is the one who, by way of accommodation, helps get the train back where it belongs; but then, by way of making all square, and a little more, telegraphs to an agent, thirty miles a-head by a precipice, to throw just there, on his account, a beam across the track. Your needy man's principal-and-interest friend is, I say again, a friend with an enmity in reserve. No, no, my dear friend, no interest for me. I scorn interest.'

'Well, Charlie, none need you charge. Loan me without interest.'

'That would be alms again.'

'Alms, if the sum borrowed is returned?'

'Yes; an alms, not of the principal, but the interest.'

'Well, I am in sore need, so I will not decline the alms. Seeing that it is you, Charlie, gratefully will I accept the alms of the interest. No humiliation between friends.'

'Now, how in the refined view of friendship can you suffer yourself to talk so, my dear Frank? It pains me. For though I am not of the sour mind of Solomon, that, in the hour of need, a stranger is better than a brother; yet I entirely agree with my sublime master, who, in his Essay on Friendship, says so nobly, that if he want a terrestrial convenience, not to his friend celestial (or friend social and intellectual) would he go; no: for his terrestrial convenience, to his friend terrestrial (or humbler business friend) he goes. Very lucidly he adds the reason: Because, for the superior nature, which on no account can ever descend to do good, to be annoyed with requests to do it, when the inferior one, which by no instruction can ever rise above that capacity, stands always inclined to it – this is unsuitable.'

'Then I will not consider you as my friend celestial, but as the other.'

'It racks me to come to that; but, to oblige you, I'll do it. We are business friends; business is business. You want to negotiate a loan. Very good. On what paper? Will you pay three per cent a month? Where is your security?'

'Surely you will not exact those formalities from your old schoolmate – him with whom you have so often sauntered down the groves of Academe, discoursing of the beauty of virtue, and the grace that is in kindliness – and all for so paltry a sum. Security? Our being fellow-academics, and friends from childhood up, is security.'

'Pardon me, my dear Frank, our being fellow-academics is the worst of securities; while, our having been friends from childhood up is just no security at all. You forget we are now business friends.'

'And you, on your side, forget, Charlie, that as your business friend I can give you no security; my need being so sore that I cannot get an indorser.'

'No indorser, then, no business loan.'

'Since then, Charlie, neither as the one nor the other sort of friend you have defined, can I prevail with you; how if, combining the two, I sue as both?'

'Are you a centaur?'

'When all is said then, what good have I of your friendship, regarded in what light you will?'

'The good which is in the philosophy of Mark Winsome, as reduced to practice by a practical disciple.'

'And why don't you add, much good may the philosophy of Mark Winsome do me? Ah,' turning invokingly, 'what is friendship, if it be not the helping hand and the feeling heart, the good Samaritan pouring out at need the purse as the vial!'

'Now, my dear Frank, don't be childish. Through tears never did man see his way in the dark. I should hold you unworthy that sincere friendship I bear you, could I think that friendship in the ideal is too lofty for you to conceive. And let me tell you, my dear Frank, that you would seriously shake the foundations of our love, if ever again you should repeat the present scene. The philosophy, which is mine in the strongest way, teaches plain-dealing. Let me, then, now, as at the most suitable time, candidly disclose certain circumstances you seem in ignorance of. Though our friendship began in boyhood, think not that, on my side at least, it began injudiciously. Boys are little men, it is said. You, I juvenilely picked out for my friend, for your favourable points at the time; not the least of which were your good manners, handsome dress, and your parents' rank and repute of wealth. In short, like any grown man, boy though I was, I went into the market and chose me my mutton, not for its leanness, but its fatness. In other words, there seemed in you, the schoolboy who always had silver in his pocket, a reasonable probability that you would never stand in lean need of fat succour; and if my early impression has not been verified by the event, it is only because of the caprice of fortune producing a fallibility of human expectations, however discreet.'

'Oh, that I should listen to this cold-blooded disclosure!'

'A little cold blood in your ardent veins, my dear Frank, wouldn't do you any harm, let me tell you. Cold-blooded? You say that, because my disclosure seems to involve a vile prudence on my side. But not so. My reason for choosing you in part for the points I have mentioned, was solely with a view of preserving inviolate the delicacy of the connection. For – do but think of it – what more distressing to delicate friendship, formed early, than your friend's eventually, in manhood, dropping in of a rainy night for his little loan of five dollars or so? Can delicate friendship stand that? And, on the other side, would delicate friendship, so long as it retained its delicacy, do that? Would you not instinctively say of your dripping friend in the entry, "I have been deceived, fraudulently deceived, in this man; he is no true friend that, in platonic love to demand love-rites"?'

'And rites, doubly rights, they are, cruel Charlie!'

'Take it how you will, heed well how, by too importunately claiming those rights, as you call them, you shake those foundations I hinted of. For though, as it turns out, I, in my early friendship, built me a fair house, on a poor site; yet such pains and cost have I lavished on that house, that, after all, it is dear to me. No, I would not lose the sweet boon of your friendship, Frank. But beware.'

'And of what? Of being in need? Oh, Charlie! you talk not to a god, a being who in himself holds his own estate, but to a man who, being a man, is the sport of fate's wind and wave, and who mounts towards heaven or sinks towards hell, as the billows roll him in trough or on crest.'

'Tut! Frank. Man is no such poor devil as that comes to – no poor drifting sea-weed of the universe. Man has a soul; which, if he will, puts him beyond fortune's finger and the future's spite. Don't whine like fortune's whipped dog, Frank, or by the heart of a true friend, I will cut ye.'

'Cut me you have already, cruel Charlie, and to the quick. Call to mind the days we went nutting, the times we walked in the woods, arms wreathed about each other, showing trunks invined like the trees – oh, Charlie!'

'Pish! we were boys.'

'Then lucky the fate of the first-born of Egypt, cold in the grave ere maturity struck them with a sharper frost. – Charlie?'

'Fie! you're a girl.'

'Help, help, Charlie, I want help!'

'Help? to say nothing of the friend, there is something wrong about the man who wants help. There is somewhere a defect, a want, in brief, a need, a crying need, somewhere about that man.'

'So there is, Charlie. – Help, help!'

'How foolish a cry, when to implore help, is itself the proof of undesert of it.'

'Oh, this, all along, is not you, Charlie, but some ventriloquist who usurps your larynx. It is Mark Winsome that speaks, not Charlie.'

'If so, thank heaven, the voice of Mark Winsome is not alien but congenial to my larynx. If the philosophy of that illustrious teacher find little response among mankind at large, it is less that they do not possess teachable tempers, than because they are so unfortunate as not to have natures predisposed to accord with him.'

'Welcome, that compliment to humanity,' exclaimed Frank with energy, 'the truer because unintended. And long in this respect may humanity remain what you affirm it. And long it will; since humanity, inwardly feeling how subject it is to straits, and hence how precious is help, will, for selfishness' sake, if no other, long postpone ratifying a philosophy that banishes help from the world. But Charlie, Charlie! speak as you used to; tell me you will help me. Were the case reversed, not less freely would I loan you the money than you would ask me to loan it.'

'*I* ask? *I* ask a loan? Frank, by this hand, under no circumstances would I accept a loan, though without asking pressed on me. The experience of China Aster might warn me.'

'And what was that?'

'Not very unlike the experience of the man that built himself a palace of moon-beams, and when the moon set was surprised that his palace vanished with it. I will tell you about China Aster. I wish I could do so in my own words, but unhappily the original story-teller here has so tyrannized over me, that it is quite impossible for me to repeat his incidents without sliding into his style. I forewarn you of this, that you may not think me so maudlin as, in some parts, the story would seem to make its narrator. It is too bad that any intellect, especially in so small a matter, should have such power to impose itself upon another, against its best exerted will, too. However, it is satisfaction to know that the main moral, to which all tends, I fully approve. But, to begin.'

Chapter Forty

*In Which the Story of China Aster is, at Second-hand,
Told by One Who, While Not Disapproving the Moral,
Disclaims the Spirit of the Style*

'China Aster was a young candle-maker of Marietta, at the mouth
of the Muskingum – one whose trade would seem a kind of subordinate branch of that parent craft and mystery of the hosts of
heaven, to be the means, effectively or otherwise, of shedding
some light through the darkness of a planet benighted. But he
made little money by the business. Much ado had poor China
Aster and his family to live; he could, if he chose, light up from
his stores a whole street, but not so easily could he light up with
prosperity the hearts of his household.

'Now, China Aster, it so happened, had a friend, Orchis, a shoemaker; one whose calling it is to defend the understandings of
men from naked contact with the substance of things: a very useful vocation, and which, in spite of all the wiseacres may prophesy,
will hardly go out of fashion so long as rocks are hard and flints
will gall. All at once, by a capital prize in a lottery, this useful
shoemaker was raised from a bench to a sofa. A small nabob was
the shoemaker now, and the understandings of men, let them
shift for themselves. Not that Orchis was, by prosperity, elated
into heartlessness. Not at all. Because, in his fine apparel, strolling one morning into the candlery, and gaily switching about at
the candle-boxes with his gold-headed cane – while poor China
Aster, with his greasy paper cap and leather apron, was selling
one candle for one penny to a poor orange-woman, who, with
the patronizing coolness of a liberal customer, required it to be
carefully rolled up and tied in a half sheet of paper – lively Orchis,
the woman being gone, discontinued his gay switchings and said:

"This is poor business for you, friend China Aster; your capital is too small. You must drop this vile tallow and hold up pure spermaceti to the world. I tell you what it is, you shall have one thousand dollars to extend with. In fact, you must make money, China Aster. I don't like to see your little boy paddling about without shoes, as he does."

'"Heaven bless your goodness, friend Orchis," replied the candle-maker, "but don't take it ill if I call to mind the word of my uncle, the blacksmith, who, when a loan was offered him, declined it, saying: 'To ply my own hammer, light though it be, I think best, rather than piece it out heavier by welding to it a bit of a neighbour's hammer, though that may have some weight to spare; otherwise, were the borrowed bit suddenly wanted again, it might not split off at the welding, but too much to one side or the other."' '

'"Nonsense, friend China Aster, don't be so honest; your boy is barefoot. Besides, a rich man lose by a poor man? Or a friend be the worse by a friend? China Aster, I am afraid that, in leaning over into your vats here, this morning, you have spilled out your wisdom. Hush! I won't hear any more. Where's your desk? Oh, here." With that, Orchis dashed off a check on his bank, and offhandedly presenting it, said: "There, friend China Aster, is your one thousand dollars; when you make it ten thousand, as you soon enough will (for experience, the only true knowledge, teaches me that, for every one, good luck is in store), then, China Aster, why, then you can return me the money or not, just as you please. But, in any event, give yourself no concern, for I shall never demand payment."

'Now, as kind heaven will so have it that to a hungry man bread is a great temptation, and, therefore, he is not too harshly to be blamed, if, when freely offered, he take it, even though it be uncertain whether he shall ever be able to reciprocate; so, to a poor man, proffered money is equally enticing, and the worst that can be said of him, if he accept it, is just what can be said in the other case of the hungry man. In short, the poor candle-maker's scrupulous morality succumbed to his unscrupulous necessity, as is now and then apt to be the case. He took the check, and was about carefully putting it away for the present, when Orchis, switching about again with his gold-headed cane, said: "By-the-way, China Aster, it don't mean anything, but suppose you make a little memorandum of this; won't do any harm, you know." So China Aster gave Orchis his note for one thousand dollars on demand. Orchis took it, and looked at it a moment. "Pooh, I·told you, friend China Aster, I wasn't going ever to make any *demand*." Then tearing up the note, and switching away again at the candle-boxes, said, carelessly; "Put it at four years." So China Aster gave Orchis his note for one thousand dollars at four years. "You see I'll never trouble you about this," said Orchis, slipping it in his pocket-book, "give yourself no further thought, friend China Aster, than how best to invest your money. And don't forget my hint about spermaceti. Go into that, and I'll buy all my light of you," with which encouraging words, he, with wonted, rattling kindness, took leave.

'China Aster remained standing just where Orchis had left him; when, suddenly, two elderly friends, having nothing better to do, dropped in for a chat. The chat over, China Aster, in greasy cap and apron, ran after Orchis, and said: "Friend Orchis, heaven will reward you for your good intentions, but here is your check, and now give me my note."

'"Your honesty is a bore, China Aster," said Orchis not without displeasure. "I won't take the check from you."

'"Then you must take it from the pavement, Orchis," said China Aster; and, picking up a stone, he placed the check under it on the walk.

'"China Aster," said Orchis, inquisitively eyeing him, "after my leaving the candlery just now, what asses dropped in there to advise with you, that now you hurry after me, and act so like a fool? Shouldn't wonder if it was those two old asses that the boys nickname Old Plain Talk and Old Prudence."

'"Yes, it was those two, Orchis, but don't call them names."

' "A brace of spavined old croakers. Old Plain Talk had a shrew for a wife, and that's made him shrewish; and Old Prudence, when a boy, broke down in an apple-stall, and that discouraged him for life. No better sport for a knowing spark like me than to hear Old Plain Talk wheeze out his sour old saws, while Old Prudence stands by, leaning on his staff, wagging his frosty old pow, and chiming in at every clause."

' "How can you speak so, friend Orchis, of those who were my father's friends?"

' "Save me from my friends, if those old croakers were Old Honesty's friends. I call your father so, for every one used to. Why did they let him go in his old age on the town? Why, China Aster, I've often heard from my mother, the chronicler, that those two old fellows, with Old Conscience – as the boys called the crabbed old quaker, that's dead now – they three used to go to the poor-house when your father was there, and get round his bed, and talk to him for all the world as Eliphaz, Bildad, and Zophar did to poor old pauper Job. Yes, Job's comforters were Old Plain Talk, and Old Prudence, and Old Conscience, to your poor old father. Friends? I should like to know who you call foes? With their everlasting croaking and reproaching they tormented poor Old Honesty, your father, to death."

'At these words, recalling the sad end of his worthy parent, China Aster could not restrain some tears. Upon which Orchis said: "Why, China Aster, you are the dolefulest creature. Why don't you, China Aster, take a bright view of life? You will never get on in your business or anything else, if you don't take the bright view of life. It's the ruination of a man to take the dismal one." Then, gaily poking at him with his gold-headed cane, "Why don't you, then? Why don't you be bright and hopeful, like me? Why don't you have confidence, China Aster?"

' "I'm sure I don't know, friend Orchis," soberly replied China Aster, "but may be my not having drawn a lottery prize, like you, may make some difference."

' "Nonsense! before I knew anything about the prize I was gay as a lark, just as gay as I am now. In fact, it has always been a principle with me to hold to the bright view."

'Upon this, China Aster looked a little hard at Orchis, because the truth was, that until the lucky prize came to him, Orchis had gone under the nickname of Doleful Dumps, he having been beforetimes of a hypochondriac turn, so much so as to save up and put by a few dollars of his scanty earnings against that rainy day he used to groan so much about.

' "I tell you what it is, now, friend China Aster," said Orchis, pointing down to the check under the stone, and then slapping his pocket, "the check shall lie there if you say so, but your note shan't keep it company. In fact, China Aster, I am too sincerely your friend to take advantage of a passing fit of the blues in you. You *shall* reap the benefit of my friendship." With which, buttoning up his coat in a jiffy, away he ran, leaving the check behind.

'At first, China Aster was going to tear it up, but thinking that this ought not to be done except in the presence of the drawer of the check, he mused a while, and picking it up, trudged back to the candlery, fully resolved to call upon Orchis soon as his day's work was over, and destroy the check before his eyes. But it so happened that when China Aster called, Orchis was out, and, having waited for him a weary time in vain, China Aster went home, still with the check, but still resolved not to keep it another day. Bright and early next morning he would a second time go after Orchis, and would, no doubt, make a sure thing of it, by finding him in his bed; for since the lottery-prize came to him, Orchis, besides becoming more cheery, had also grown a little lazy. But as destiny would have it, that same night China Aster had a dream, in which a being in the guise of a smiling angel, and holding a kind of cornucopia in her hand, hovered over him, pouring down showers of small gold dollars, thick as kernels of corn. "I am Bright Future, friend China Aster," said the angel, "and if you do what friend Orchis would have you do, just see what will come of it." With which Bright Future, with another swing of her cornucopia, poured such another shower of small gold dollars upon him, that it seemed to bank him up all round, and he waded about in it like a maltster in malt.

'Now, dreams are wonderful things, as everybody knows – so wonderful, indeed, that some people stop not short of ascribing them directly to heaven; and China Aster, who was of a proper turn of mind in everything, thought that in consideration of the dream, it would be but well to wait a little, ere seeking Orchis again. During the day, China Aster's mind dwelling continually upon the dream, he was so full of it, that when Old Plain Talk dropped in to see him, just before dinner time, as he often did, out of the interest he took in Old Honesty's son, China Aster told all about his vision, adding that he could not think that so radiant an angel could deceive; and, indeed, talked at such a rate that one would have thought he believed the angel some beautiful human philanthropist. Something in this sort Old Plain Talk understood him, and, accordingly, in his plain way, said: "China Aster, you tell me that an angel appeared to you in a dream. Now what does that amount to but this, that you dreamed an angel appeared to you? Go right away, China Aster, and return the check as I advised you before. If friend Prudence were here, he would say just the same thing." With which words Old Plain Talk went off to find friend Prudence, but not succeeding, was returning to the candlery himself, when, at a distance mistaking him for a dun who had long annoyed him, China Aster in a panic barred all his doors, and ran to the back part of the candlery, where no knock could be heard.

'By this sad mistake, being left with no friend to argue the other side of the question, China Aster was so worked upon at last, by musing over his dream, that nothing would do but he must get the check cashed, and lay out the money the very same day in buying a good lot of spermaceti to make into candles, by which operation he counted upon turning a better penny than he ever had before in his life; in fact, this he believed would prove the foundation of that famous fortune which the angel had promised him.

'Now, in using the money, China Aster was resolved punctually to pay the interest every six months till the principal should be returned, howbeit not a word about such a thing had been breathed by Orchis; though, indeed, according to custom, as well as law, in such matters, interest would legitimately accrue on the loan, nothing to the contrary having been put in the bond. Whether Orchis at the time had this in mind or not, there is no sure telling; but, to all appearance, he never so much as cared to think about the matter, one way or other.

'Though the spermaceti venture rather disappointed China Aster's sanguine expectations, yet he made out to pay the first six months' interest, and though his next venture turned out still less prosperously, yet by pinching his family in the matter of fresh meat, and what pained him still more, his boys' schooling, he contrived to pay the second six months' interest, sincerely grieved that integrity, as well as its opposite, though not in an equal degree, costs something, sometimes.

'Meanwhile, Orchis had gone on a trip to Europe by advice of a physician; it so happening that, since the lottery-prize came to him, it had been discovered to Orchis that his health was not very firm, though he had never complained of anything before but a slight ailing of the spleen, scarce worth talking about at the time. So Orchis, being abroad, could not help China Aster's paying his interest as he did, however much he might have been opposed to it; for China Aster paid it to Orchis's agent, who was of too business-like a turn to decline interest regularly paid in on a loan.

'But overmuch to trouble the agent on that score was not again to be the fate of China Aster; for, not being of that skeptical spirit which refuses to trust customers, his third venture resulted, through bad debts, in almost a total loss – a bad blow for the candle-maker. Neither did Old Plain Talk, and Old Prudence neglect the opportunity to read him an uncheerful enough lesson upon the consequences of his disregarding their advice in the matter of having nothing to do with borrowed money. "It's all just as I predicted," said Old Plain Talk, blowing his old nose with his old bandana. "Yea, indeed is it," chimed in Old Prudence, rapping his staff on the floor, and then leaning upon it, looking with solemn forebodings upon China Aster. Low-spirited enough felt the poor candle-maker; till all at once who should come with a bright face to him but his bright friend, the angel, in another dream. Again the cornucopia poured out its treasure, and promised still more. Revived by the vision, he resolved not to be downhearted, but up and at it once more – contrary to the advice of Old Plain Talk, backed as usual by his crony, which was to the effect, that, under present circumstances, the best thing China Aster could do, would be to wind up his business, settle, if he could, all his liabilities, and then go to work as a journeyman, by which he could earn good wages, and give up, from that time henceforth, all thoughts of rising above being a paid subordinate to men more able than himself, for China Aster's career thus far plainly proved him the legitimate son of Old Honesty, who, as every one knew, had never shown much business-talent, so little, in fact, that many said of him that he had no business to be in business. And just this plain saying Plain Talk now plainly applied to China Aster, and Old Prudence never disagreed with him. But the angel in the dream did, and, maugre Plain Talk, put quite other notions into the candle-maker.

'He considered what he should do towards re-establishing himself. Doubtless, had Orchis been in the country, he would have aided him in this strait. As it was, he applied to others; and as in the world, much as some may hint to the contrary, an honest man in misfortune still can find friends to stay by him and help him, even so it proved with China Aster, who at last succeeded in borrowing from a rich old farmer the sum of six hundred dollars, at the usual interest of money-lenders, upon the security of a secret bond signed by China Aster's wife and himself, to the effect that all such right and title to any property that should be left her by a well-to-do childless uncle, an invalid tanner, such property should, in the event of China Aster's failing to return the borrowed sum on the given day, be the lawful possession of the moneylender. True, it was just as much as China Aster could possibly do to induce his wife, a careful woman, to sign this bond; because she had always regarded her promised share in her uncle's estate as an anchor well to windward of the hard times in which China Aster had always been more or less involved, and from which, in her bosom, she never had seen much chance of his freeing himself. Some notion may be had of China Aster's standing in the heart and head of his wife, by a short sentence commonly used in reply to such persons as happened to sound her on the point. "China Aster," she would say, "is a good husband, but a bad business man!" Indeed, she was a connection on the maternal side of Old Plain Talk's. But had not China Aster taken good care not to let Old Plain Talk and Old Prudence hear of his dealings with the old farmer, ten to one they would, in some way, have interfered with his success in that quarter.

'It has been hinted that the honesty of China Aster was what mainly induced the money-lender to befriend him in his misfortune, and this must be apparent; for, had China Aster been a different man, the money-lender might have dreaded lest, in the event of his failing to meet his note, he might some way prove slippery – more especially as, in the hour of distress, worked upon by remorse for so jeopardizing his wife's money, his heart might prove a traitor to his bond, not to hint that it was more than doubtful how such a secret security and claim, as in the last resort would be the old farmer's, would stand in a court of law. But though one inference from all this may be, that had China Aster been something else than what he was, he would not have been trusted, and, therefore, he would have been effectually shut out from running his own and wife's head into the usurer's noose;

yet those who, when everything at last came out, maintained that, in this view and to this extent, the honesty of the candle-maker was no advantage to him, in so saying, such persons said what every good heart must deplore, and no prudent tongue will admit.

'It may be mentioned, that the old farmer made China Aster take part of his loan in three old dried-up cows and one lame horse, not improved by the glanders. These were thrown in at a pretty high figure, the old money-lender having a singular prejudice in regard to the high value of any sort of stock raised on his farm. With a great deal of difficulty, and at more loss, China Aster disposed of his cattle at public auction, no private purchaser being found who could be prevailed upon to invest. And now, raking and scraping in every way, and working early and late, China Aster at last started afresh, nor without again largely and confidently extending himself. However, he did not try his hand at the spermaceti again, but, admonished by experience, returned to tallow. But, having bought a good lot of it, by the time he got it into candles, tallow fell so low, and candles with it, that his candles per pound barely sold for what he had paid for the tallow. Meantime, a year's unpaid interest had accrued on Orchis' loan, but China Aster gave himself not so much concern about that as about the interest now due to the old farmer. But he was glad that the principal there had yet some time to run. However, the skinny old fellow gave him some trouble by coming after him every day or two on a scraggy old white horse, furnished with a musty old saddle, and goaded into his shambling old paces with a withered old raw hide. All the neighbours said that surely Death himself on the pale horse was after poor China Aster now. And something so it proved; for, ere long, China Aster found himself involved in troubles mortal enough.

'At this juncture Orchis was heard of. Orchis, it seemed, had returned from his travels, and clandestinely married, and, in a kind of queer way, was living in Pennsylvania among his wife's relations, who, among other things, had induced him to join a church, or rather semi-religious school, of Come-Outers; and what was still more, Orchis, without coming to the spot himself, had sent word to his agent to dispose of some of his property in Marietta, and remit him the proceeds. Within a year after, China Aster received a letter from Orchis, commending him for his punctuality in paying the first year's interest, and regretting the necessity that he (Orchis) was now under of using all his dividends; so he relied upon China Aster's paying the next six months' interest, and of course with the back interest. Not more surprised than alarmed, China Aster thought of taking steamboat to go and see Orchis, but he was saved that expense by the unexpected arrival in Marietta of Orchis in person, suddenly called there by that strange kind of capriciousness lately characterizing him. No sooner did China Aster hear of his old friend's arrival than he hurried to call upon him. He found him curiously rusty in dress, sallow in cheek, and decidedly less gay and cordial in manner, which the more surprised China Aster, because, in former days, he had more than once heard Orchis, in his light rattling way, declare that all he (Orchis) wanted to make him a perfectly happy, hilarious, and benignant man, was a voyage to Europe and a wife, with a free development of his inmost nature.

'Upon China Aster's stating his case, his trusted friend was silent for a time; then, in an odd way, said that he would not crowd China Aster, but still his (Orchis') necessities were urgent. Could not China Aster mortgage the candlery? He was honest, and must have moneyed friends; and could he not press his sales of candles? Could not the market be forced a little in that particular? The profits on candles must be very great. Seeing, now, that Orchis had the notion that the candle-making business was a very profitable one, and knowing sorely enough what an error was here, China Aster tried to undeceive him. But he could not drive the truth into Orchis – Orchis being very obtuse here, and, at the same time, strange to say, very melancholy. Finally, Orchis glanced off from so unpleasing a subject into the most unexpected reflections, taken from a religious point of view, upon the unstableness and deceitfulness of the human heart. But having, as he thought, experienced something of that sort of thing, China Aster did not take exception to his friend's observations, but still refrained from so doing, almost as much for the sake of sympathetic sociality as anything else. Presently, Orchis, without much ceremony, rose, and saying he must write a letter to his wife, bade his friend goodbye, but without warmly shaking him by the hand as of old.

'In much concern at the change, China Aster made earnest inquiries in suitable quarters, as to what things, as yet unheard of, had befallen Orchis, to bring about such a revolution; and learned at last that, besides travelling, and getting married, and joining the sect of Come-Outers, Orchis had somehow got a bad dyspepsia, and lost considerable property through a breach of trust on the part of a factor in New York. Telling these things to Old Plain Talk, that man of some knowledge of the world shook his old head, and told China Aster that, though he hoped it might prove otherwise, yet it seemed to him that all he had communicated about Orchis worked together for bad omens as to his future forbearance – especially, he added with a grim sort of smile, in view of his joining the sect of Come-Outers; for, if some men knew what was their inmost natures, instead of coming out with it, they would try their best to keep it in, which, indeed, was the way with the prudent sort. In all which sour notions Old Prudence, as usual, chimed in.

'When interest-day came again, China Aster, by the utmost exertions, could only pay Orchis' agent a small part of what was due, and a part of that was made up by his children's gift money (bright tenpenny pieces and new quarters, kept in their little money-boxes), and pawning his best clothes, with those of his wife and children, so that all were subjected to the hardship of staying away from church. And the old usurer, too, now beginning to be obstreperous, China Aster paid him his interest and some other pressing debts with money got by, at last, mortgaging the candlery.

'When next interest-day came round for Orchis, not a penny could be raised. With much grief of heart, China Aster so informed Orchis' agent. Meantime the note to the old usurer fell due, and nothing from China Aster was ready to meet it; yet, as heaven sends its rain on the just and unjust alike, by a coincidence not unfavourable to the old farmer, the well-to-do uncle, the tanner, having died, the usurer entered upon possession of such part of his property left by will to the wife of China Aster. When still the next interest-day for Orchis came round, it found China Aster worse off than ever; for besides his other troubles, he was now weak with sickness. Feebly dragging himself to Orchis' agent, he met him in the street, told him just how it was; upon which the agent, with a grave enough face, said that he had instructions from his employer not to crowd him about the interest at present, but to say to him that about the time the note would mature, Orchis would have heavy liabilities to meet, and therefore the note must at that time be certainly paid, and, of course, the back interest with it; and not only so, but, as Orchis had had to allow the interest for good part of the time, he hoped that, for the back interest, China Aster would, in reciprocation, have no objections to allowing interest on the interest annually. To be sure, this was not the law; but, between friends who accommodate each other, it was the custom.

'Just then, Old Plain Talk with Old Prudence turned the corner, coming plump upon China Aster as the agent left him; and whether it was a sun-stroke, or whether they accidentally ran against him, or whether it was his being so weak, or whether it was everything together, or how it was exactly, there is no telling, but poor China Aster fell to the earth, and, striking his head sharply, was picked up senseless. It was a day in July; such a light and heat as only the midsummer banks of the inland Ohio know. China Aster was taken home on a door; lingered a few days with a wandering mind, and kept wandering on, till at last, at dead of night, when nobody was aware, his spirit wandered away into the other world.

'Old Plain Talk and Old Prudence, neither of whom ever omitted attending any funeral, which, indeed, was their chief exercise – these two were among the sincerest mourners who followed the remains of the son of their ancient friend to the grave.

'It is needless to tell of the executions that followed; how that the candlery was sold by the mortgagee; how Orchis never got a penny for his loan; and how, in the case of the poor widow, chastisement was tempered with mercy; for though she was left penniless, she was not left childless. Yet, unmindful of the alleviation, a spirit of complaint, at what she impatiently called the bitterness of her lot and the hardness of the world, so preyed upon her, as ere long to hurry her from the obscurity of indigence to the deeper shades of the tomb.

'But though the straits in which China Aster had left his family had, besides apparently dimming the world's regard, likewise seemed to dim its sense of the probity of its deceased head, and though this, as some thought, did not speak well for the world, yet it happened in this case, as in others, that though the world may for a time seem insensible to that merit which lies under a cloud, yet, sooner or later, it always renders honour where honour is due; for, upon the death of the widow, the freemen of Marietta, as a tribute of respect for China Aster, and an expression of their conviction of his high moral worth, passed a resolution, that until they attained maturity, his children should be considered the town's guests. No mere verbal compliment, like those of some public bodies; for on the same day, the orphans were officially installed in that hospitable edifice where their worthy grandfather, the town's guest before them, had breathed his last breath.

'But sometimes honour may be paid to the memory of an honest man, and still his mound remain without a monument. Not so, however, with the candle-maker. At an early day Plain Talk had procured a plain stone, and was digesting in his mind what pithy word or two to place upon it, when there was discovered, in China Aster's otherwise empty wallet, an epitaph, written, probably, in one of those disconsolate hours, attended with more or less mental aberration, perhaps, so frequent with him for some months prior to his end. A memorandum on the back expressed the wish that it might be placed over his grave. Though with the sentiment of the epitaph Plain Talk did not disagree, he himself being at times of a hypochondriac turn – at least, so many said – yet the language struck him as too much drawn out; so after consultation with Old Prudence, he decided upon making use of the epitaph, yet not without verbal retrenchments. And though, when these were made, the thing still appeared wordy to him, nevertheless, thinking that, since a dead man was to be spoken about, it was but just to let him speak for himself, especially when he spoke sincerely, and when, by so doing, the more salutary lesson would be given, he had the retrenched inscription chiselled as follows upon the stone:

HERE LIE

THE REMAINS OF

CHINA ASTER THE CANDLE-MAKER,

WHOSE CAREER

WAS AN EXAMPLE OF THE TRUTH OF

SCRIPTURE, AS FOUND

IN THE

SOBER PHILOSOPHY

OF

SOLOMON THE WISE;

FOR HE WAS RUINED BY ALLOWING HIMSELF
TO BE PERSUADED,
AGAINST HIS BETTER SENSE,
INTO THE FREE INDULGENCE OF CONFIDENCE
AND
AN ARDENTLY BRIGHT VIEW OF LIFE,
TO THE EXCLUSION
OF
THAT COUNSEL WHICH COMES BY HEEDING
THE
OPPOSITE VIEW.

This inscription raised some talk in the town, and was rather severely criticized by the capitalist – one of a very cheerful turn – who had secured his loan to China Aster by the mortgage; and though it also proved obnoxious to the man who, in town-meeting, had first moved for the compliment to China Aster's memory, and, indeed, was deemed by him a sort of slur upon the candle-maker, to that degree that he refused to believe that the candle-maker himself had composed it, charging Old Plain Talk with the authorship, alleging that the internal evidence showed that none but that veteran old croaker could have penned such a jeremiade – yet, for all this, the stone stood. In everything, of course, Old Plain Talk was seconded by Old Prudence; who, one day going to the graveyard, in great-coat and over-shoes – for, though it was a sunshiny morning, he thought that, owing to heavy dews, dampness might lurk in the ground – long stood before the stone, sharply leaning over on his staff, spectacles on nose, spelling out the epitaph word by word; and, afterwards meeting Old Plain Talk in the street, gave a great rap with his stick, and said: "Friend Plain Talk, that epitaph will do very well. Nevertheless, one short sentence is wanting." Upon which, Plain Talk said it was too late, the chiselled words being so arranged, after the usual manner of such inscriptions, that nothing could be interlined. "Then," said Old Prudence, "I will put it in the shape of a postscript." Accordingly, with the approbation of Old Plain Talk, he had the following words chiselled at the left-hand corner of the stone, and pretty low down:

The root of all was a friendly loan.

Chapter Forty-One

Ending With a Rupture of the Hypothesis

'With what heart,' cried Frank, still in character, 'have you told me this story? A story I can no way approve; for its moral, if accepted, would drain me of all reliance upon my last stay, and, therefore, of my last courage in life. For, what was that bright view of China Aster but a cheerful trust that, if he but kept up a brave heart, worked hard, and ever hoped for the best, all at last would go well? If your purpose, Charlie, in telling me this story, was to pain me, and keenly, you have succeeded; but, if it was to destroy my last confidence, I praise God you have not.'

'Confidence?' cried Charlie, who, on his side, seemed with his whole heart to enter into the spirit of the thing, 'what has confidence to do with the matter? That moral of the story, which I am for commending to you, is this: the folly, on both sides, of a friend's helping a friend. For was not that loan of Orchis to China Aster the first step towards their estrangement? And did it not bring about what in effect was the enmity of Orchis? I tell you, Frank, true friendship, like other precious things, is not rashly to be meddled with. And what more meddlesome between friends than a loan? A regular marplot. For how can you help that the helper must turn out a creditor? And creditor and friend, can they ever be one? no, not in the most lenient case; since, out of lenity to forgo one's claim, is less to be a friendly creditor than to cease to be a creditor at all. But it will not do to rely upon this lenity, no, not in the best man; for the best man, as the worst, is subject to all mortal contingencies. He may travel, he may marry, he may join the Come-Outers, or some equally untoward school or sect, not to speak of other things that more or less tend to new-cast the character. And were there nothing else, who shall answer for his digestion, upon which so much depends?'

'But Charlie, dear Charlie –'

'Nay, wait. – You have hearkened to my story in vain, if you do not see that, however indulgent and right-minded I may seem to you now, that is no guarantee for the future. And into the power of that uncertain personality which, through the mutability of my humanity, I may hereafter become, should not common sense dissuade you, my dear Frank, from putting yourself? Consider. Would you, in your present need, be willing to accept a loan from a friend, securing him by a mortgage on your homestead, and do so, knowing that you had no reason to feel satisfied that the mortgage might not eventually be transferred into the hands of a foe? Yet the difference between this man and that man is not so great as the difference between what the same man may be to-day and what he may be in days to come. For there is no bent of heart or turn of thought which any man holds by virtue of an unalterable nature or will. Even those feelings and opinions deemed most identical with eternal right and truth, it is not impossible but that, as personal persuasions, they may in reality be but the result of some chance tip of Fate's elbow in throwing her dice. For, not to go into the first seeds of things, and passing by the accident of parentage predisposing to this or that habit of mind, descend below these, and tell me, if you change this man's experiences or that man's books, will wisdom go surety for his unchanged convictions? As particular food begets particular dreams, so particular experiences or books particular feelings or beliefs. I will hear nothing of that fine babble about development and its laws; there is no development in opinion and feeling but the developments of time and tide. You may deem all this talk idle, Frank; but conscience bids me show you how fundamental the reasons for treating you as I do.'

'But Charlie, dear Charlie, what new notions are these? I thought that man was no poor drifting weed of the universe, as you phrased it; that, if so minded, he could have a will, a way, a thought, and a heart of his own? But now you have turned everything upside down again, with an inconsistency that amazes and shocks me.'

'Inconsistency? Bah!'

'There speaks the ventriloquist again,' sighed Frank, in bitterness.

Ill pleased, it may be, by this repetition of an allusion little flattering to his originality, however much so to his docility, the disciple sought to carry it off by exclaiming: 'Yes, I turn over day and night, with indefatigable pains, the sublime pages of my master, and unfortunately for you, my dear friend, I find nothing *there* that leads me to think otherwise than I do. But enough: in this matter the experience of China Aster teaches a moral more to the point than anything Mark Winsome can offer, or I either.'

'I cannot think so, Charlie; for neither am I China Aster, nor do I stand in his position. The loan to China Aster was to extend his business with; the loan I seek is to relieve my necessities.'

'Your dress, my dear Frank, is respectable; your cheek is not gaunt. Why talk of necessities when nakedness and starvation beget the only real necessities?'

'But I need relief, Charlie; and so sorely, that I now conjure you to forget that I was ever your friend, while I apply to you only as a fellow-being, whom, surely, you will not turn away.'

'That I will not. Take off your hat, bow over to the ground, and supplicate an alms of me in the way of London Streets, and you shall not be a sturdy beggar in vain. But no man drops pennies into the hat of a friend, let me tell you. If you turn beggar, then, for the honour of noble friendship, I turn stranger.'

'Enough,' cried the other, rising, and with a toss of his shoulders seeming disdainfully to throw off the character he had assumed. 'Enough. I have had my fill of the philosophy of Mark Winsome as put into action. And moonshiny as it in theory may be, yet a very practical philosophy it turns out in effect, as he himself engaged I should find. But, miserable for my race should I be, if I thought he spoke truth when he claimed, for proof of the soundness of his system, that the study of it tended to much the same formation of character with the experiences of the world. – Apt disciple! Why wrinkle the brow, and waste the oil both of life and the lamp, only to turn out a head kept cool by the under ice of the heart? What your illustrious magian has taught you, any poor, old, broken-down, heart-shrunken dandy might have lisped. Pray, leave me, and with you take the last dregs of your inhuman philosophy. And here, take this shilling, and at the first wood-landing buy yourself a few chips to warm the frozen natures of you and your philosopher by.'

With these words and a grand scorn the cosmopolitan turned on his heel, leaving his companion at a loss to determine where exactly the fictitious character had been dropped, and the real one, if any, resumed. If any, because, with pointed meaning, there occurred to him, as he gazed after the cosmopolitan, these familiar lines:

> All the world's a stage,
> And all the men and women merely players;
> They have their exits and their entrances,
> And one man in his time plays many parts.

Chapter Forty-Two

*Upon the Heel of the Last Scene, the Cosmopolitan Enters
the Barber's Shop, a Benediction on His Lips*

'Bless you, barber!'

Now, owing to the lateness of the hour, the barber had been all
alone until within the ten minutes last passed; when, finding himself rather dullish company to himself, he thought he would have
a good time with Souter John and Tam O'Shanter, otherwise
called Somnus and Morpheus, two very good fellows, though
one was not very bright, and the other an arrant rattle-brain,
who, though much listened to by some, no wise man would
believe under oath.

In short, with back presented to the glare of his lamps, and so
to the door, the honest barber was taking what are called cat-
naps, and dreaming in his chair; so that, upon suddenly hearing
the benediction above, pronounced in tones not unangelic, starting up, half awake, he stared before him, but saw nothing, for
the stranger stood behind. What with cat-naps, dreams, and
bewilderments, therefore, the voice seemed a sort of spiritual
manifestation to him; so that, for the moment, he stood all agape,
eyes fixed, and one arm in the air.

'Why, barber, are you reaching up to catch birds there with
salt?'

'Ah!' turning round disenchanted, 'it is only a man, then.'

'*Only* a man? As if to be but man were nothing. But don't be
too sure what I am. You call me *man*, just as the townsfolk called
the angels who, in man's form, came to Lot's house; just as the
Jew rustics called the devils who, in man's form, haunted the
tombs. You can conclude nothing absolute from the human
form, barber.'

'But I can conclude something from that sort of talk, with that sort of dress,' shrewdly thought the barber, eyeing him with regained self-possession, and not without some latent touch of apprehension at being alone with him. What was passing in his mind seemed divined by the other, who now, more rationally and gravely, and as if he expected it should be attended to, said: 'Whatever else you may conclude upon, it is my desire that you conclude to give me a good shave,' at the same time loosening his neck-cloth. 'Are you competent to a good shave, barber?'

'No broker more so, sir,' answered the barber, whom the business-like proposition instinctively made confine to business-ends his views of the visitor.

'Broker? What has a broker to do with lather? A broker I have always understood to be a worthy dealer in certain papers and metals.'

'He, he!' taking him now for some dry sort of joker, whose jokes, he being a customer, it might be as well to appreciate, 'he, he! You understand well enough, sir. Take this seat, sir,' laying his hand on a great stuffed chair, high-backed and high-armed, crimson-covered, and raised on a sort of dais, and which seemed but to lack a canopy and quarterings, to make it in aspect quite a throne, 'take this seat, sir.'

'Thank you,' sitting down; 'and now, pray, explain that about the broker. But look, look – what's this?' suddenly rising, and pointing, with his long pipe, towards a gilt notification swinging among coloured fly-papers from the ceiling, like a tavern sign, '*No Trust*? No trust means distrust; distrust means no confidence. Barber,' turning upon him excitedly, 'what fell suspiciousness prompts this scandalous confession? My life!' stamping his foot, 'if but to tell a dog that you have no confidence in him be matter for affront to the dog, what an insult to take that way the whole haughty race of man by the beard! By my heart, sir! but at least you are valiant; backing the spleen of Thersites with the pluck of Agamemnon.'

'Your sort of talk, sir, is not exactly in my line,' said the barber, rather ruefully, being now again hopeless of his customer, and not without return of uneasiness; 'not in my line, sir,' he emphatically repeated.

'But the taking of mankind by the nose is; a habit, barber, which I sadly fear has insensibly bred in you a disrespect for man. For how, indeed, may respectful conceptions of him coexist with the perpetual habit of taking him by the nose? But, tell me, though I, too, clearly see the import of your notification, I do not, as yet, perceive the object. What is it?'

'Now you speak a little in my line, sir,' said the barber, not unrelieved at this return to plain talk; 'that notification I find very useful, sparing me much work which would not pay. Yes, I lost a good deal, off and on, before putting that up,' gratefully glancing towards it.

'But what is its object? Surely, you don't mean to say, in so many words, that you have no confidence? For instance, now,' flinging aside his neck-cloth, throwing back his blouse, and reseating himself on the tonsorial throne, at sight of which proceeding the barber mechanically filled a cup with hot water from a copper vessel over a spirit-lamp, 'for instance, now, suppose I say to you, "Barber, my dear barber, unhappily I have no small change by me to-night, but shave me, and depend upon your money to-morrow" – suppose I should say that now, you would put trust in me, wouldn't you? You would have confidence?'

'Seeing that it is you, sir,' with complaisance replied the barber, now mixing the lather, 'seeing that it is *you*, sir, I won't answer that question. No need to.'

'Of course, of course – in that view. But, as a supposition – you would have confidence in me, wouldn't you?'

'Why – yes, yes.'

'Then why that sign?'

'Ah, sir, all people ain't like you,' was the smooth reply, at the same time, as if smoothly to close the debate, beginning

269

smoothly to apply the lather, which operation, however, was, by a motion, protested against by the subject, but only out of a desire to rejoin, which was done in these words:

'All people ain't like me. Then I must be either better or worse than most people. Worse, you could not mean; no, barber, you could not mean that; hardly that. It remains, then, that you think me better than most people. But that I ain't vain enough to believe; though, from vanity, I confess, I could never yet, by my best wrestlings, entirely free myself; nor, indeed, to be frank, am I at bottom over anxious to – this same vanity, barber, being so harmless, so useful, so comfortable, so pleasingly preposterous a passion.'

'Very true, sir; and upon my honour, sir, you talk very well. But the lather is getting a little cold, sir.'

'Better cold lather, barber, than a cold heart. Why that cold sign? Ah, I don't wonder you try to shirk the confession. You feel in your soul how ungenerous a hint is there. And yet, barber, now that I look into your eyes – which somehow speak to me of the mother that must have so often looked into them before me – I dare say, though you may not think it, that the spirit of that notification is not one with your nature. For look now, setting business views aside, regarding the thing in an abstract light; in short, supposing a case, barber; supposing, I say, you see a stranger, his face accidentally averted, but his visible part very respectable-looking; what now, barber – I put it to your conscience, to your charity – what would be your impression of that man, in a moral point of view? Being in a signal sense a stranger, would you, for that, signally set him down for a knave?'

'Certainly not, sir; by no means,' cried the barber, humanely resentful.

'You would upon the face of him –'

'Hold, sir,' said the barber, 'nothing about the face; you remember, sir, that is out of sight.'

'I forgot that. Well then, you would, upon the *back* of him, conclude him to be, not improbably, some worthy sort of person; in short, an honest man; wouldn't you?'

'Not unlikely I should, sir.'

'Well now – don't be so impatient with your brush, barber – suppose that honest man meet you by night in some dark corner of the boat where his face would still remain unseen, asking you to trust him for a shave – how then?'

'Wouldn't trust him, sir.'

'But is not an honest man to be trusted?'

'Why – why – yes, sir.'

'There! don't you see, now?'

'See what?' asked the disconcerted barber, rather vexedly.

'Why, you stand self-contradicted, barber; don't you?'

'No,' doggedly.

'Barber,' gravely, and after a pause of concern, 'the enemies of our race have a saying that insincerity is the most universal and inveterate vice of man – the lasting bar to real amelioration, whether of individuals or of the world. Don't you now, barber, by your stubbornness on this occasion, give colour to such a calumny?'

'Hity-tity!' cried the barber, losing patience, and with it respect; 'stubbornness?' Then clattering round the brush in the cup, 'Will you be shaved, or won't you?'

'Barber, I will be shaved, and with pleasure; but, pray, don't raise your voice that way. Why, now, if you go through life gritting your teeth in that fashion, what a comfortless time you will have.'

'I take as much comfort in this world as you or any other man,' cried the barber, whom the other's sweetness of temper seemed rather to exasperate than soothe.

'To resent the imputation of anything like unhappiness I have often observed to be peculiar to certain orders of men,' said the other pensively, and half to himself, 'just as to be indifferent to that imputation, from holding happiness but for a secondary good and inferior grace, I have observed to be equally peculiar to other kinds of men. Pray, barber,' innocently looking up, 'which think you is the superior creature?'

'All this sort of talk,' cried the barber, still unmollified, 'is, as I told you once before, not in my line. In a few minutes I shall shut up this shop. Will you be shaved?'

'Shave away, barber. What hinders?' turning up his face like a flower.

The shaving began, and proceeded in silence, till at length it became necessary to prepare to relather a little – affording an opportunity for resuming the subject, which, on one side, was not let slip.

'Barber,' with a kind of cautious kindliness, feeling his way, 'barber, now have a little patience with me; do; trust me, I wish not to offend. I have been thinking over that supposed case of the man with the averted face, and I cannot rid my mind of the impression that, by your opposite replies to my question at the time, you showed yourself much of a piece with a good many other men – that is, you have confidence, and then again, you have none. Now, what I would ask is, do you think it sensible standing for a sensible man, one foot on confidence and the other on suspicion? Don't you think, barber, that you ought to elect? Don't you think consistency requires that you should either say "I have confidence in all men," and take down your notification; or else say "I suspect all men," and keep it up?'

This dispassionate, if not deferential, way of putting the case, did not fail to impress the barber, and proportionately conciliate him. Likewise, from its pointedness, it served to make him thoughtful; for, instead of going to the copper vessel for more water, as he had purposed, he halted half-way towards it, and, after a pause, cup in hand, said: 'Sir, I hope you would not do me injustice. I don't say, and can't say, and wouldn't say, that I suspect all men; but I *do* say that strangers are not to be trusted, and so,' pointing up to the sign, 'no trust.'

'But look, now, I beg, barber,' rejoined the other deprecatingly, not presuming too much upon the barber's changed temper; 'look, now; to say that strangers are not to be trusted, does not that imply something like saying that mankind is not to be trusted; for the mass of mankind, are they not necessarily strangers to each individual man? Come, come, my friend,' winningly, 'you are no Timon to hold the mass of mankind untrustworthy. Take down your notification; it is misanthropical; much the same sign that Timon traced with charcoal on the forehead of a skull stuck over his cave. Take it down, barber; take it down to-night. Trust men. Just try the experiment of trusting men for this one little trip. Come now, I'm a philanthropist, and will insure you against losing a cent.'

The barber shook his head dryly, and answered, 'Sir, you must excuse me. I have a family.'

Chapter Forty-Three

Very Charming

'So you are a philanthropist, sir,' added the barber with an illuminated look; 'that accounts, then, for all. Very odd sort of man the philanthropist. You are the second one, sir, I have seen. Very odd sort of man, indeed, the philanthropist. Ah, sir,' again meditatively stirring in the shaving-cup, 'I sadly fear, lest you philanthropists know better what goodness is, than what men are.' Then, eyeing him as if he were some strange creature behind cage-bars, 'So you are a philanthropist, sir.'

'I am Philanthropos, and love mankind. And, what is more than you do, barber, I trust them.'

Here the barber, casually recalled to his business, would have replenished his shaving-cup, but finding now that on his last visit to the water-vessel he had not replaced it over the lamp, he did so now; and, while waiting for it to heat again, became almost as sociable as if the heating water were meant for whisky-punch; and almost as pleasantly garrulous as the pleasant barbers in romances.

'Sir,' said he, taking a throne beside his customer (for in a row there were three thrones on the dais, as for the three kings of Cologne, those patron saints of the barber), 'sir, you say you trust men. Well, I suppose I might share some of your trust, were it not for this trade, that I follow, too much letting me in behind the scenes.'

'I think I understand,' with a saddened look; 'and much the same thing I have heard from persons in pursuits different from yours – from the lawyer, from the congressman, from the editor, not to mention others, each, with a strange kind of melancholy vanity, claiming for his vocation the distinction of affording the surest inlets to the conviction that man is no better than he should be. All of which testimony, if reliable, would, by mutual corroboration, justify some disturbance in a good man's mind. But no, no; it is a mistake – all a mistake.'

'True, sir, very true,' assented the barber.

'Glad to hear that,' brightening up.

'Not so fast, sir,' said the barber; 'I agree with you in thinking that the lawyer, and the congressman, and the editor, are in error, but only in so far as each claims peculiar facilities for the sort of knowledge in question; because, you see, sir, the truth is, that every trade or pursuit which brings one into contact with the facts, sir, such trade or pursuit is equally an avenue to those facts.'

'*How* exactly is that?'

'Why, sir, in my opinion – and for the last twenty years I have, at odd times, turned the matter over some in my mind – he who comes to know man, will not remain in ignorance of man. I think I am not rash in saying that; am I, sir?'

'Barber, you talk like an oracle – obscurely, barber, obscurely.'

'Well, sir,' with some self-complacency, 'the barber has always been held an oracle, but as for the obscurity, that I don't admit.'

'But pray, now, by your account, what precisely may be this mysterious knowledge gained in your trade? I grant you, indeed, as before hinted, that your trade, imposing on you the necessity of functionally tweaking the noses of mankind, is, in that respect, unfortunate, very much so; nevertheless, a well-regulated imagination should be proof even to such a provocation to improper conceits. But what I want to learn from you, barber, is, how does the mere handling of the outside of men's heads lead you to distrust the inside of their hearts?'

'What, sir, to say nothing more, can one be for ever dealing in macassar oil, hair dyes, cosmetics, false moustaches, wigs, and toupees, and still believe that men are wholly what they look to be? What think you, sir, are a thoughtful barber's reflections, when, behind a careful curtain, he shaves the thin, dead stubble off a head, and then dismisses it to the world, radiant in curling auburn? To contrast the shamefaced air behind the curtain, the fearful looking forward to being possibly discovered there by a prying acquaintance, with the cheerful assurance and challenging pride with which the same man steps forth again, a gay deception, into the street, while some honest, shock-headed fellow humbly gives him the wall. Ah, sir, they may talk of the courage of truth, but my trade teaches me that truth sometimes is sheepish. Lies, lies, sir, brave lies are the lions!'

'You twist the moral, barber; you sadly twist it. Look, now; take it this way: A modest man thrust out naked into the street, would he not be abashed? Take him in and clothe him; would not his confidence be restored? And in either case, is any reproach involved? Now, what is true of the whole, holds proportionably true of the part. The bald head is a nakedness which the wig is a coat to. To feel uneasy at the possibility of the exposure of one's nakedness at top, and to feel comforted by the consciousness of having it clothed – these feelings, instead of being dishonourable to a bald man, do, in fact, but attest a proper respect for himself and his fellows. And as for the deception, you may as well call the fine roof of a fine chateau a deception, since, like a fine wig, it also is an artificial cover to the head, and equally, in the common eye, decorates the wearer. – I have confuted you, my dear barber; I have confounded you.'

'Pardon,' said the barber, 'but I do not see that you have. His coat and his roof no man pretends to palm off as a part of himself, but the bald man palms off hair, not his, for his own.'

'Not *his*, barber? If he have fairly purchased his hair, the law will protect him in its ownership, even against the claims of the head on which it grew. But it cannot be that you believe what you say, barber; you talk merely for the humour. I could not think so of you as to suppose that you would contentedly deal in the impostures you condemn.'

'Ah, sir, I must live.'

'And can't you do that without sinning against your conscience, as you believe? Take up some other calling.'

'Wouldn't mend the matter much, sir.'

'Do you think, then, barber, that, in a certain point, all the trades and callings of men are much on a par? Fatal, indeed,' raising his hand, 'inexpressibly dreadful, the trade of the barber, if to such conclusions it necessarily leads. Barber,' eyeing him not without emotion, 'you appear to me not so much a misbeliever, as a man misled. Now, let me set you on the right track; let me restore you to trust in human nature, and by no other means than the very trade that has brought you to suspect it.'

'You mean, sir, you would have me try the experiment of taking down that notification,' again pointing to it with his brush; 'but, dear me, while I sit chatting here, the water boils over.'

With which words, and such a well-pleased, sly, snug, expression, as they say some men have when they think their little stratagem has succeeded, he hurried to the copper vessel, and soon had his cup foaming up with white bubbles, as if it were a mug of new ale.

Meantime, the other would have fain gone on with the discourse; but the cunning barber lathered him with so generous a brush, so piled up the foam on him, that his face looked like the yeasty crest of a billow, and vain to think of talking under it, as for a drowning priest in the sea to exhort his fellow-sinners on a raft. Nothing would do, but he must keep his mouth shut. Doubtless, the interval was not, in a meditative way, unimproved; for, upon the traces of the operation being at last removed, the cosmopolitan rose, and, for added refreshment, washed his face and hands; and having generally readjusted himself, began, at last, addressing the barber in a manner different, singularly so, from his previous one. Hard to say exactly what the manner was, any more than to hint it was a sort of magical; in a benign way, not wholly unlike the manner, fabled or otherwise, of certain creatures in nature, which have the power of persuasive fascination – the power of holding another creature by the button of the eye, as it were, despite the serious disinclination, and, indeed, earnest protest, of the victim. With this manner the conclusion of the matter was not out of keeping; for, in the end, all argument and expostulation proved vain, the barber being irresistibly persuaded to agree to try, for the remainder of the present trip, the experiment of trusting men, as both phrased it. True, to save his credit as a free agent, he was loud in averring that it was only for the novelty of the thing that he so agreed, and he required the other, as before volunteered, to go security to him against any loss that might ensue; but still the fact remained, that he engaged to trust men, a thing he had before said he would not do, at least not unreservedly. Still the more to save his credit, he now insisted upon it, as a last point, that the agreement should be put in black and white, especially the security part. The other made no demur; pen, ink, and paper were provided, and grave as any notary the cosmopolitan sat down, but, ere taking the pen, glanced up at the notification, and said: 'First down with that sign, barber – Timon's sign, there; down with it.'

This, being in the agreement, was done – though a little reluctantly – with an eye to the future, the sign being carefully put away in a drawer.

'Now, then, for the writing,' said the cosmopolitan, squaring himself. 'Ah,' with a sigh, 'I shall make a poor lawyer, I fear. Ain't used, you see, barber, to a business which, ignoring the principle of honour, holds no nail fast till clinched. Strange, barber,' taking up the blank paper, 'that such flimsy stuff as this should make such strong hawsers; vile hawsers, too. Barber,' starting up, 'I won't put it in black and white. It were a reflection upon our joint honour. I will take your word, and you shall take mine.'

'But your memory may be none of the best, sir. Well for you, on your side, to have it in black and white, just for a memorandum like, you know.'

'That, indeed! Yes, and it would help *your* memory, too,

wouldn't it, barber? Yours, on your side, being a little weak, too, I dare say. Ah, barber! how ingenious we human beings are; and how kindly we reciprocate each other's little delicacies, don't we? What better proof, now, that we are kind, considerate fellows, with responsive fellow-feelings – eh, barber? But to business. Let me see. What's your name, barber?'

'William Cream, sir.'

Pondering a moment, he began to write; and, after some corrections, leaned back, and read aloud the following:

AGREEMENT
Between
FRANK GOODMAN, Philanthropist, and Citizen of the World,
and
WILLIAM CREAM, Barber of the Mississippi steamer, *Fidèle*.

The first hereby agrees to make good to the last any loss that may come from his trusting mankind, in the way of his vocation, for the residue of the present trip; PROVIDED that William Cream keep out of sight for the given term, his notification of 'No TRUST', and by no other mode convey any, the least hint or intimation, tending to discourage men from soliciting trust from him, in the way of his vocation, for the time above specified; but, on the contrary, he do, by all proper and reasonable words, gestures, manners, and looks, evince a perfect confidence in all men, especially strangers; otherwise, this agreement to be void.

Done, in good faith, this 1st day of April, 18—, at a quarter to twelve o'clock, P.M., in the shop of said William Cream, on board the said boat, *Fidèle*.

'There, barber; will that do?'

'That will do,' said the barber, 'only now put down your name.'

Both signatures being affixed, the question was started by the barber, who should have custody of the instrument; which point, however, he settled for himself, by proposing that both should go together to the captain, and give the document into his hands – the barber hinting that this would be a safe proceeding, because the captain was necessarily a party disinterested, and, what was more, could not, from the nature of the present case, make anything by a breach of trust. All of which was listened to with some surprise and concern.

'Why, barber,' said the cosmopolitan, 'this don't show the right spirit; for me, I have confidence in the captain purely because he is a man; but he shall have nothing to do with our affair; for if you have no confidence in me, barber, I have in you. There, keep the paper yourself,' handing it magnanimously.

'Very good,' said the barber, 'and now nothing remains but for me to receive the cash.'

Though the mention of that word, or any of its singularly numerous equivalents, in serious neighbourhood to a requisition upon one's purse, is attended with a more or less noteworthy effect upon the human countenance, producing in many an abrupt fall of it – in others, a writhing and screwing up of the features to a point not undistressing to behold, in some, attended with a blank pallor and fatal consternation – yet no trace of any of these symptoms was visible upon the countenance of the cosmopolitan, notwithstanding nothing could be more sudden and unexpected than the barber's demand.

'You speak of cash, barber; pray in what connection?'

'In a nearer one, sir,' answered the barber, less blandly, 'than I thought the man with the sweet voice stood, who wanted me to trust him once for a shave, on the score of being a sort of thirteenth cousin.'

'Indeed, and what did you say to him?'

'I said, "Thank you, sir, but I don't see the connection."'

'How could you so unsweetly answer one with a sweet voice?'

'Because, I recalled what the son of Sirach says in the True Book: "An enemy speaketh sweetly with his lips"; and so I did what the son of Sirach advises in such cases: "I believed not his many words." '

'What, barber, do you say that such cynical sort of things are in the True Book, by which, of course, you mean the Bible?'

'Yes, and plenty more to the same effect. Read the Book of Proverbs.'

'That's strange, now, barber; for I never happen to have met with those passages you cite. Before I go to bed this night, I'll inspect the Bible I saw on the cabin-table, to-day. But mind, you mustn't quote the True Book that way to people coming in here; it would be impliedly a violation of the contract. But you don't know how glad I feel that you have for one while signed off all that sort of thing.'

'No, sir; not unless you down with the cash.'

'Cash again! What do you mean?'

'Why, in this paper here, you engage, sir, to insure me against a certain loss, and –'

'Certain? Is it so *certain* you are going to lose?'

'Why, that way of taking the word may not be amiss, but I didn't mean it so. I meant a *certain* loss; you understand, a CER-TAIN loss; that is to say, a certain loss. Now then, sir, what use your mere writing and saying you will insure me, unless before-hand you place in my hands a money-pledge, sufficient to that end?'

'I see; the material pledge.'

'Yes, and I will put it low; say fifty dollars.'

'Now what sort of a beginning is this? You, barber, for a given time engage to trust man, to put confidence in men, and, for your first step, make a demand implying no confidence in the very man you engage with. But fifty dollars is nothing, and I would let you have it cheerfully, only I unfortunately happen to have but little change with me just now.'

'But you have money in your trunk, though?'

'To be sure. But you see – in fact, barber, you must be consistent.

No, I won't let you have the money now; I won't let you violate the inmost spirit of our contract, that way. So good-night, and I will see you again.'

'Stay, sir' – humming and hawing – 'you have forgotten something.'

'Handkerchief? – gloves? No, forgotten nothing. Good-night.'

'Stay, sir – the – the shaving.'

'Ah, I *did* forget that. But now that it strikes me, I shan't pay you at present. Look at your agreement; you must trust. Tut! against loss you hold the guarantee. Good-night, my dear barber.'

With which words he sauntered off, leaving the barber in a maze, staring after.

But it holding true in fascination as in natural philosophy, that nothing can act where it is not, so the barber was not long now in being restored to his self-possession and senses; the first evidence of which perhaps was, that, drawing forth his notification from the drawer, he put it back where it belonged; while, as for the agreement, that he tore up; which he felt the more free to do from the impression that in all human probability he would never again see the person who had drawn it. Whether that impression proved well-founded or not, does not appear. But in after days, telling the night's adventure to his friends, the worthy barber always spoke of his queer customer as the man-charmer – as certain East Indians are called snake-charmers – and all his friends united in thinking him QUITE AN ORIGINAL.

Chapter Forty-Four

*In Which the Last Three Words of the Last Chapter
Are Made the Text of Discourse, Which Will Be Sure of
Receiving More or Less Attention From Those Readers
Who Do Not Skip It*

QUITE AN ORIGINAL. A phrase, we fancy, rather oftener used by the young, or the unlearned, or the untravelled, than by the old, or the well-read, or the man who has made the grand tour. Certainly, the sense of originality exists at its highest in an infant, and probably at its lowest in him who has completed the circle of the sciences.

As for original characters in fiction, a grateful reader will, on meeting with one, keep the anniversary of that day. True, we sometimes hear of an author who, at one creation, produces some two or three score such characters; it may be possible. But they can hardly be original in the sense that Hamlet is, or Don Quixote, or Milton's Satan. That is to say, they are not, in a thorough sense, original at all. They are novel, or singular, or striking, or captivating, or all four at once.

More likely, they are what are called odd characters; but for that, are no more original, than what is called an odd genius, in his way, is. But, if original, whence came they? Or where did the novelist pick them up?

Where does any novelist pick up any character? For the most part, in town, to be sure. Every great town is a kind of man-show, where the novelist goes for his stock, just as the agriculturist goes to the cattle-show for his. But in the one fair, new species of quadrupeds are hardly more rare, than in the other are new species of characters – that is, original ones. Their rarity may still the more appear from this, that, while characters, merely singular, imply but singular forms, so to speak, original ones, truly so, imply original instincts.

In short, a due conception of what is to be held for this sort of personage in fiction would make him almost as much of a prodigy there, as in real history is a new law-giver, a revolutionizing philosopher, or the founder of a new religion.

In nearly all the original characters, loosely accounted such in works of invention, there is discernible something prevailingly local, or of the age; which circumstance, of itself, would seem to invalidate the claim, judged by the principles here suggested.

Furthermore, if we consider, what is popularly held to entitle characters in fiction to being deemed original, is but something personal – confined to itself. The character sheds not its characteristic on its surroundings, whereas, the original character, essentially such, is like a revolving Drummond light, raying away from itself all round it – everything is lit by it, everything starts up to it (mark how it is with Hamlet), so that, in certain minds, there follows upon the adequate conception of such a character, an effect, in its way, akin to that which in Genesis attends upon the beginning of things.

For much the same reason that there is but one planet to one orbit, so can there be but one such original character to one work of invention. Two would conflict to chaos. In this view, to say that there are more than one to a book, is good presumption there is none at all. But for new, singular, striking, odd, eccentric, and all sorts of entertaining and instructive characters, a good fiction may be full of them. To produce such characters, an author, beside other things, must have seen much, and seen through much: to produce but one original character, he must have had much luck.

There would seem but one point in common between this sort of phenomenon in fiction and all other sorts; it cannot be born in the author's imagination – it being as true in literature as in zoology, that all life is from the egg.

In the endeavour to show, if possible, the impropriety of the phrase, *Quite an Original*, as applied by the barber's friends, we have, unawares, been led into a dissertation bordering upon the prosy, perhaps upon the smoky. If so, the best use the smoke can be turned to, will be, by retiring under cover of it, in good trim as may be, to the story.

Chapter Forty-Five

The Cosmopolitan Increases in Seriousness

In the middle of the gentlemen's cabin burned a solar lamp, swung from the ceiling, and whose shade of ground glass was all round fancifully variegated, in transparency, with the image of a horned altar, from which flames rose, alternate with the figure of a robed man, his head encircled by a halo. The light of this lamp, after dazzlingly striking on marble, snow-white and round – the slab of a centre-table beneath – on all sides went rippling off with ever-diminishing distinctness, till, like circles from a stone dropped in water, the rays died dimly away in the furthest nook of the place.

Here and there, true to their place, but not to their function, swung other lamps, barren planets, which had either gone out from exhaustion, or been extinguished by such occupants of berths as the light annoyed, or who wanted to sleep, not see.

By a perverse man, in a berth not remote, the remaining lamp would have been extinguished as well, had not a steward forbade, saying that the commands of the captain required it to be kept burning till the natural light of day should come to relieve it. This steward, who, like many in his vocation, was apt to be a little free-spoken at times, had been provoked by the man's pertinacity to remind him, not only of the sad consequences which might, upon occasion, ensue from the cabin being left in darkness, but, also of the circumstance that, in a place full of strangers, to show one's self anxious to produce darkness there, such an anxiety was, to say the least, not becoming. So the lamp – last survivor of many – burned on, inwardly blessed by those in some berths, and inwardly execrated by those in others.

Keeping his lone vigils beneath his lone lamp, which lighted his book on the table, sat a clean, comely, old man, his head snowy as the marble, and a countenance like that which imagination ascribes to good Simeon, when, having at last beheld the Master of Faith, he blessed him and departed in peace. From his hale look of greenness in winter, and his hands ingrained with the tan, less, apparently, of the present summer, than of accumulated ones past, the old man seemed a well-to-do farmer, happily dismissed, after a thrifty life of activity, from the fields to the fireside – one of those who, at three-score-and-ten, are fresh-hearted as at fifteen; to whom seclusion gives a boon more blessed than knowledge, and at last sends them to heaven untainted by the world, because ignorant of it; just as a countryman putting up at a London inn, and never stirring out of it as a sight-seer, will leave London at last without once being lost in its fog, or soiled by its mud.

Redolent from the barber's shop, as any bridegroom tripping to the bridal chamber might come, and by his look of cheeriness seeming to dispense a sort of morning through the night, in came the cosmopolitan; but marking the old man, and how he was occupied, he toned himself down, and trod softly, and took a seat on the other side of the table, and said nothing. Still there was a kind of waiting expression about him.

'Sir,' said the old man, after looking up puzzled at him a moment, 'sir,' said he, 'one would think this was a coffee-house, and it was war-time, and I had a newspaper here with great news, and the only copy to be had, you sit there looking at me so eager.'

'And so you *have* good news there, sir – the very best of good news.'

'Too good to be true,' here came from one of the curtained berths.

'Hark!' said the cosmopolitan. 'Some one talks in his sleep.'

'Yes,' said the old man, 'and you – *you* seem to be talking in a dream. Why speak you, sir, of news, and all that, when you must see this is a book I have here – the Bible, not a newspaper?'

'I know that; and when you are through with it – but not a moment sooner – I will thank you for it. It belongs to the boat, I believe – a present from a society.'

'Oh, take it, take it!'

'Nay, sir, I did not mean to touch you at all. I simply stated the fact in explanation of my waiting here – nothing more. Read on, sir, or you will distress me.'

This courtesy was not without effect. Removing his spectacles, and saying he had about finished his chapter, the old man kindly presented the volume, which was received with thanks equally kind. After reading for some minutes, until his expression merged from attentiveness into seriousness, and from that into a kind of pain, the cosmopolitan slowly laid down the book, and turning to the old man, who thus far had been watching him with benign curiosity, said: 'Can you, my aged friend, resolve me a doubt – a disturbing doubt?'

'There are doubts, sir,' replied the old man, with a changed countenance, 'there are doubts, sir, which, if man have them, it is not man that can solve them.'

'True; but look, now, what my doubt is. I am one who thinks well of man. I love man. I have confidence in man. But what was told me not a half-hour since? I was told that I would find it written – "Believe not his many words – an enemy speaketh sweetly with his lips" – and also I was told that I would find a good deal more to the same effect, and all in this book. I could not think it; and, coming here to look for myself, what do I read? Not only just what was quoted, but also, as was engaged, more to the same purpose, such as this: "With much communication he will tempt thee; he will smile upon thee, and speak thee fair, and say What wantest thou? If thou be for his profit he will use thee; he will make thee bare, and will not be sorry for it. Observe and take good heed. When thou hearest these things, awake in thy sleep."'

'Who's that describing the confidence-man?' here came from the berth again.

'Awake in his sleep, sure enough, ain't he?' said the cosmopolitan, again looking off in surprise. 'Same voice as before, ain't it? Strange sort of dreamy man, that. Which is his berth, pray?'

'Never mind *him*, sir,' said the old man anxiously, 'but tell me, truly, did you, indeed, read from the book just now?'

'I did,' with changed air, 'and gall and wormwood it is to me, a truster in man; to me a philanthropist.'

'Why,' moved, 'you don't mean to say, that what you repeated is really down there? Man and boy, I have read the good book this seventy years, and don't remember seeing anything like that. Let me see it,' rising earnestly, and going round to him.

'There it is; and there – and there' – turning over the leaves, and pointing to the sentences one by one; 'there – all down in the "Wisdom of Jesus, the Son of Sirach."'

'Ah!' cried the old man, brightening up, 'now I know. Look,' turning the leaves forward and back, till all the Old Testament lay flat on one side, and all the New Testament flat on the other, while in his fingers he supported vertically the portion between, 'look, sir, all this to the right is certain truth, and all this to the left is certain truth, but all I hold in my hand here is apocrypha.'

'Apocrypha?'

'Yes; and there's the word in black and white,' pointing to it. 'And what says the word? It says as much as "not warranted"; for what do college men say of anything of that sort? They say it is apocryphal. The word itself, I have heard from the pulpit, implies something of uncertain credit. So if your disturbance be raised from aught in this apocrypha,' again taking up the pages, 'in that case think no more of it, for it's apocrypha.'

'What's that about the Apocalypse?' here a third time came from the berth.

'He's seeing visions now, ain't he?' said the cosmopolitan, once more looking in the direction of the interruption. 'But, sir,' resuming, 'I cannot tell you how thankful I am for your reminding me about the apocrypha here. For the moment its being such escaped me. Fact is, when all is bound up together, it's sometimes confusing. The uncanonical part should be bound distinct. And, now that I think of it, how well did those learned doctors who rejected for us this whole book of Sirach. I never read anything so calculated to destroy man's confidence in man. This son of Sirach even says – I saw it but just now: "Take heed of thy friends"; not, observe, thy seeming friends, thy hypocritical friends, thy false friends, but thy *friends*, thy real friends – that is to say, not the truest friend in the world is to be implicitly trusted. Can Rochefoucault equal that? I should not wonder if his view of human nature, like Machiavelli's, was taken from this Son of Sirach. And to call it wisdom – the Wisdom of the Son of Sirach! Wisdom, indeed? What an ugly thing wisdom must be! Give me the folly that dimples the cheek, say I, rather than the wisdom that curdles the blood. But no, no; it ain't wisdom; it's apocrypha, as you say, sir. For how can that be trustworthy that teaches distrust?'

'I tell you what it is,' here cried the same voice as before, only more in less of mockery, 'if you two don't know enough to sleep, don't be keeping wiser men awake. And if you want to know what wisdom is, go find it under your blankets.'

'Wisdom?' cried another voice with a brogue; 'arrah, and is't wisdom the two geese are gabbling about all this while? To bed with ye, ye divils, and don't be after burning your fingers with the likes of wisdom.'

'We must talk lower,' said the old man; 'I fear we have annoyed these good people.'

'I should be sorry if wisdom annoyed any one,' said the other; 'but we will lower our voices, as you say. To resume: taking the thing as I did, can you be surprised at my uneasiness in reading passages so charged with the spirit of distrust?'

'No, sir, I am not surprised,' said the old man; then added: 'from what you say, I see you are something of my way of thinking – you think that to distrust the creature, is a kind of distrusting of the Creator. Well, my young friend, what is it? This is rather late for you to be about. What do you want of me?'

These questions were put to a boy in the fragment of an old linen coat, bedraggled and yellow, who, coming in from the deck barefooted on the soft carpet, had been unheard. All pointed and fluttering, the rags of the little fellow's red-flannel shirt, mixed with those of his yellow coat, flamed about him like the painted flames in the robes of a victim in *auto-da-fé*. His face, too, wore such a polish of seasoned grime, that his sloe-eyes sparkled from out it like lustrous sparks in fresh coal. He was a juvenile peddler, or *marchand*, as the polite French might have called him, of traveller's conveniences; and, having no allotted sleeping-place, had, in his wanderings about the boat, spied, through glass doors, the two in the cabin; and, late though it was, thought it might never be too much so for turning a penny.

Among other things, he carried a curious affair – a miniature mahogany door, hinged to its frame, and suitably furnished in all respects but one, which will shortly appear. This little door he now meaningly held before the old man, who, after staring at it a while, said: 'Go thy ways with thy toys, child.'

'Now, may I never get so old and wise as that comes to,' laughed the boy through his grime; and, by so doing, disclosing leopard-like teeth, like those of Murillo's wild beggar-boy's.

'The divils are laughing now, are they?' here came the brogue from the berth. 'What do the divils find to laugh about in wisdom, begorrah? To bed with ye, ye divils, and no more of ye.'

'You see, child, you have disturbed that person,' said the old man; 'you mustn't laugh any more.'

'Ah, now,' said the cosmopolitan, 'don't, pray, say that; don't let him think that poor Laughter is persecuted for a fool in this world.'

'Well,' said the old man to the boy, 'you must, at any rate, speak very low.'

'Yes, that wouldn't be amiss, perhaps,' said the cosmopolitan;

'but, my fine fellow, you were about saying something to my aged friend here; what was it?'

'Oh,' with a lowered voice, coolly opening and shutting his little door, 'only this: when I kept a toy-stand at the fair in Cincinnati last month, I sold more than one old man a child's rattle.'

'No doubt of it,' said the old man. 'I myself often buy such things for my little grandchildren.'

'But these old men I talk of were old bachelors.'

The old man stared at him a moment; then, whispering to the cosmopolitan: 'Strange boy, this; sort of simple, ain't he? Don't know much, hey?'

'Not much,' said the boy, 'or I wouldn't be so ragged.'

'Why, child, what sharp ears you have!' exclaimed the old man.

'If they were duller, I would hear less ill of myself,' said the boy.

'You seem pretty wise, my lad,' said the cosmopolitan; 'why don't you sell your wisdom, and buy a coat?'

'Faith,' said the boy, 'that's what I did to-day, and this is the coat that the price of my wisdom bought. But won't you trade? See, now, it is not the door I want to sell; I only carry the door round for a specimen, like. Look now, sir,' standing the thing up on the table, 'supposing this little door is your state-room door; well,' opening it, 'you go in for the night; you close your door behind you – thus. Now, is all safe?'

'I suppose so, child,' said the old man.

'Of course it is, my fine fellow,' said the cosmopolitan.

'All safe. Well. Now, about two o'clock in the morning, say, a soft-handed gentleman comes softly and tries the knob here – thus; in creeps my soft-handed gentleman; and hey, presto! how comes on the soft cash?'

'I see, I see, child,' said the old man; 'your fine gentleman is a fine thief, and there's no lock to your little door to keep him out'; with which words he peered at it more closely than before.

'Well, now,' again showing his white teeth, 'well, now, some of you old folks are knowing 'uns, sure enough; but now comes the great invention,' producing a small steel contrivance, very simple but ingenious, and which, being clapped on the inside of the little door, secured it as with a bolt. 'There now,' admiringly holding it off at arm's length, 'there now, let that soft-handed gentleman come now a' softly trying this little knob here, and let him keep a' trying till he finds his head as soft as his hand. Buy the traveller's patent lock, sir, only twenty-five cents.'

'Dear me,' cried the old man, 'this beats printing. Yes, child, I will have one, and use it this very night.'

With the phlegm of an old banker pouching the change, the boy now turned to the other: 'Sell you one, sir?'

'Excuse me, my fine fellow, but I never use such blacksmiths' things.'

'Those who give the blacksmith most work seldom do,' said the boy, tipping him a wink expressive of a degree of indefinite knowingness, not uninteresting to consider in one of his years. But the wink was not marked by the old man, nor, to all appearances, by him for whom it was intended.

'Now then,' said the boy, again addressing the old man. 'With your traveller's lock on your door to-night, you will think yourself all safe, won't you?'

'I think I will, child.'

'But how about the window?'

'Dear me, the window, child. I never thought of that. I must see to that.'

'Never you mind about the window,' said the boy, 'nor, to be honour bright, about the traveller's lock either (though I ain't sorry for selling one), do you just buy one of these little jokers,' producing a number of suspender-like objects, which he dangled before the old man; 'money-belts, sir; only fifty cents.'

'Money-belt? never heard of such a thing.'

'A sort of pocket-book,' said the boy, 'only a safer sort. Very good for travellers.'

'Oh, a pocket-book. Queer-looking pocket-books though,

seems to me. Ain't they rather long and narrow for pocket-books?'

'They go round the waist, sir, inside,' said the boy. 'Door open or locked, wide awake on your feet or fast asleep in your chair, impossible to be robbed with a money-belt.'

'I see, I see. It *would* be hard to rob one's money-belt. And I was told to-day the Mississippi is a bad river for pick-pockets. How much are they?'

'Only fifty cents, sir.'

'I'll take one. There!'

'Thank-ee. And now there's a present for ye,' with which, drawing from his breast a batch of little papers, he threw one before the old man, who, looking at it, read *Counterfeit Detector*.

'Very good thing,' said the boy, 'I give it to all my customers who trade seventy-five cents' worth; best present can be made them. Sell you a money-belt, sir?' turning to the cosmopolitan.

'Excuse me, my fine fellow, but I never use that sort of thing; my money I carry loose.'

'Loose bait ain't bad,' said the boy, 'look a lie and find the truth; don't care about a Counterfeit Detector, do ye? or is the wind East, d'ye think?'

'Child,' said the old man in some concern, 'you mustn't sit up any longer, it affects your mind; there, go away, go to bed.'

'If I had some people's brains to lie on, I would,' said the boy, 'but planks is hard, you know.'

'Go, child – go, go!'

'Yes, child – yes, yes,' said the boy, with which roguish parody, by way of congé, he scraped back his hard foot on the woven flowers of the carpet, much as a mischievous steer in May scrapes back his horny hoof in the pasture; and then with a flourish of his hat – which, like the rest of his tatters, was, thanks to hard times, a belonging beyond his years, though not beyond his experience, being a grown man's cast-off beaver – turned, and with the air of a young Caffre, quitted the place.

'That's a strange boy,' said the old man, looking after him. 'I wonder who's his mother; and whether she knows what late hours he keeps?'

'The probability is,' observed the other, 'that his mother does not know. But if you remember, sir, you were saying something, when the boy interrupted you with his door.'

'So I was. – Let me see,' unmindful of his purchases for the moment, 'what, now, was it? What was that I was saying? Do *you* remember?'

'Not perfectly, sir; but, if I am not mistaken, it was something like this: you hoped you did not distrust the creature; for that would imply distrust of the Creator.'

'Yes, that was something like it,' mechanically and unintelligently letting his eye fall now on his purchases.

'Pray, will you put your money in your belt to-night?'

'It's best, ain't it?' with a slight start. 'Never too late to be cautious. "Beware of pick-pockets" is all over the boat.'

'Yes, and it must have been the Son of Sirach, or some other morbid cynic, who put them there. But that's not to the purpose. Since you are minded to it, pray, sir, let me help you about the belt. I think that, between us, we can make a secure thing of it.'

'Oh no, no, no!' said the old man, not unperturbed, 'no, no, I wouldn't trouble you for the world,' then, nervously folding up the belt, 'and I won't be so impolite as to do it for myself, before you, either. But, now that I think of it,' after a pause, carefully taking a little wad from a remote corner of his vest pocket, 'here are two bills they gave me at St Louis, yesterday. No doubt they are all right; but just to pass time, I'll compare them with the Detector here. Blessed boy to make me such a present. Public benefactor, that little boy!'

Laying the Detector square before him on the table, he then, with something of the air of an officer bringing by the collar a brace of culprits to the bar, placed the two bills opposite the Detector, upon which, the examination began, lasting some time, prosecuted with no small research and vigilance, the forefinger of the right hand proving of lawyer-like efficacy in tracing out and pointing the evidence, whichever way it might go.

After watching him a while, the cosmopolitan said in a formal voice, 'Well, what say you, Mr Foreman; guilty, or not guilty? – Not guilty, ain't it?'

'I don't know, I don't know,' returned the old man, perplexed, 'there's so many marks of all sorts to go by, it makes it a kind of uncertain. Here, now, is this bill,' touching one, 'it looks to be a three-dollar bill on the Vicksburgh Trust and Insurance Banking Company. Well, the Detector says –'

'But why, in this case, care what it says? Trust and Insurance! What more would you have?'

'No; but the Detector says, among fifty other things, that, if a good bill, it must have, thickened here and there into the substance of the paper, little wavy spots of red; and it says that they must have a kind of silky feel, being made by the lint of a red silk handkerchief stirred up in the paper-maker's vat – the paper being made to order for the company.'

'Well, and is –'

'Stay. But then it adds, that sign is not always to be relied on; for some good bills get so worn, the red marks get rubbed out. And that's the case with my bill here – see how old it is – or else it's a counterfeit, or else – I don't see right – or else – dear, dear me – I don't know what else to think.'

'What a peck of trouble that Detector makes for you now; believe me, the bill is good; don't be so distrustful. Proves what I've always thought, that much of the want of confidence, in these days, is owing to these Counterfeit Detectors you see on every desk and counter. Puts people up to suspecting good bills. Throw it away, I beg, if only because of the trouble it breeds you.'

'No: it's troublesome, but I think I'll keep it. – Stay, now, here's another sign. It says that, if the bill is good, it must have in one corner, mixed in with the vignette, the figure of a goose, very small, indeed, all but microscopic; and, for added precaution, like the figure of Napoleon outlined by the tree, not observable, even if magnified, unless the attention is directed to it. Now, pore over it as I will, I can't see this goose.'

'Can't see the goose? why, I can; and a famous goose it is. There' (reaching over and pointing to a spot in the vignette).

'I don't see it – dear me – I don't see the goose. Is it a real goose?'

'A perfect goose; beautiful goose.'

'Dear, dear, I don't see it.'

'Then throw that Detector away, I say again; it only makes you purblind; don't you see what a wild-goose-chase it has led you? The bill is good. Throw the Detector away.'

'No; it ain't so satisfactory as I thought for, but I must examine this other bill.'

'As you please, but I can't in conscience assist you any more; pray, then, excuse me.'

So, while the old man with much painstakings resumed his work, the cosmopolitan, to allow him every facility, resumed his reading. At length, seeing that he had given up his undertaking as hopeless, and was at leisure again, the cosmopolitan addressed some gravely interesting remarks to him about the book before him, and, presently, becoming more and more grave, said, as he turned the large volume slowly over on the table, and with much difficulty traced the faded remains of the gilt inscription giving the name of the society who had presented it to the boat, 'Ah, sir, though every one must be pleased at the thought of the presence in public places of such a book, yet there is something that abates the satisfaction. Look at this volume; on the outside, battered as any old valise in the baggage-room; and inside, white and virgin as the hearts of lilies in bud.'

'So it is, so it is,' said the old man sadly, his attention for the first directed to the circumstance.

'Nor is this the only time,' continued the other, 'that I have observed these public Bibles in boats and hotels. All much like this – old without, and new within. True, this aptly typifies that internal freshness, the best mark of truth, however ancient; but then, it speaks not so well as could be wished for the good book's esteem in the minds of the travelling public. I may err, but it seems to me that if more confidence was put in it by the travelling public, it would hardly be so.'

With an expression very unlike that with which he had bent over the Detector, the old man sat meditating upon his companion's remarks awhile; and, at last, with a rapt look, said: 'And yet, of all people, the travelling public most need to put trust in that guardianship which is made known in this book.'

'True, true,' thoughtfully assented the other.

'And one would think they would want to, and be glad to,' continued the old man kindling; 'for, in all our wanderings through this vale, how pleasant, not less than obligatory, to feel that we need start at no wild alarms, provide for no wild perils; trusting in that Power which is alike able and willing to protect us when we cannot ourselves.'

His manner produced something answering to it in the cosmopolitan, who, leaning over towards him, said sadly: 'Though this is a theme on which travellers seldom talk to each other, yet, to you, sir, I will say, that I share something of your sense of security. I have much moved about the world, and still keep at it; nevertheless, though in this land, and especially in these parts of it, some stories are told about steamboats and railroads fitted to make one a little apprehensive, yet, I may say that, neither by land nor by water, am I ever seriously disquieted, however, at times, transiently uneasy; since, with you, sir, I believe in a Committee of Safety, holding silent sessions over all, in an invisible patrol, most alert when we soundest sleep, and whose beat lies as much through forests as towns, along rivers as streets. In short, I never forget that passage of Scripture which says, "Jehovah shall be thy confidence." The traveller who has not this trust, what miserable misgiving must be his; or, what vain, short-sighted care must he take of himself.'

'Even so,' said the old man, lowly.

'There is a chapter,' continued the other, again taking the book, 'which, as not amiss, I must read you. But this lamp, solar-lamp as it is, begins to burn dimly.'

'So it does, so it does,' said the old man with changed air, 'dear me, it must be very late. I must to bed, to bed! Let me see,' rising and looking wistfully all round, first on the stools and settees, and then on the carpet, 'let me see, let me see; – is there anything I have forgot, – forgot? Something I a sort of dimly remember. Something, my son – careful man – told me at starting this morning, this very morning. Something about seeing to – something before I got into my berth. What could it be? Something for safety. Oh, my poor old memory?'

'Let me give a little guess, sir. Life-preserver?'

'So it was. He told me not to omit seeing I had a life-preserver in my state-room; said the boat supplied them, too. But where are they? I don't see any. What are they like?'

'They are something like this, sir, I believe,' lifting a brown stool with a curved tin compartment underneath; 'yes, this, I think, is a life-preserver, sir; and a very good one, I should say, though I don't pretend to know much about such things, never using them myself.'

'Why, indeed, now! Who would have thought it? *that* a life-preserver? That's the very stool I was sitting on, ain't it?'

'It is. And that shows that one's life is looked out for, when he ain't looking out for it himself. In fact, any of these stools here will float you, sir, should the boat hit a snag, and go down in the dark. But, since you want one in your room, pray take this one,' handing it to him. 'I think I can recommend this one; the tin part,' rapping it with his knuckles, 'seems so perfect – sounds so very hollow.'

'Sure it's *quite* perfect, though?' Then, anxiously putting on his spectacles, he scrutinized it pretty closely – 'well soldered? quite tight?'

'I should say so, sir; though, indeed, as I said, I never use this sort of thing myself. Still, I think that in case of a wreck, barring sharp-pointed timbers, you could have confidence in that stool for a special providence.'

'Then, good-night, good-night; and Providence have both of us in its good keeping.'

'Be sure it will,' eyeing the old man with sympathy, as for the moment he stood, money-belt in hand, and life-preserver under arm, 'be sure it will, sir, since in Providence, as in man, you and I equally put trust. But, bless me, we are being left in the dark here. Pah! what a smell, too.'

'Ah, my way now,' cried the old man, peering before him, 'where lies my way to my state-room?'

'I have indifferent eyes, and will show you; but, first, for the good of all lungs, let me extinguish this lamp.'

The next moment, the waning light expired, and with it the waning flames of the horned altar, and the waning halo round the robed man's brow; while in the darkness which ensued, the cosmopolitan kindly led the old man away. Something further may follow of this Masquerade.

Billy Budd, Sailor

Dedicated
to
Jack Chase
Englishman

Wherever that great heart may now be
Here on Earth or harbored in Paradise

Captain of the Maintop
in the year 1843 in the U.S. Frigate
United States

Chapter One

In the time before steamships, or then more frequently than now, a stroller along the docks of any considerable seaport would occasionally have his attention arrested by a group of bronzed mariners, man-of-war's men or merchant sailors in holiday attire, ashore on liberty. In certain instances they would flank, or like a bodyguard quite surround, some superior figure of their own class, moving along with them like Aldebaran among the lesser lights of his constellation. That signal object was the 'Handsome Sailor' of the less prosaic time alike of the military and merchant navies. With no perceptible trace of the vainglorious about him, rather with the offhand unaffectedness of natural regality, he seemed to accept the spontaneous homage of his shipmates.

A somewhat remarkable instance recurs to me. In Liverpool, now half a century ago, I saw under the shadow of the great dingy street-wall of Prince's Dock (an obstruction long since removed) a common sailor so intensely black that he must needs have been a native African of the unadulterate blood of Ham – a symmetric figure much above the average height. The two ends of a gay silk handkerchief thrown loose about the neck danced upon the displayed ebony of his chest, in his ears were big hoops of gold, and a Highland bonnet with a tartan band set off his shapely head. It was a hot noon in July; and his face, lustrous with perspiration, beamed with barbaric good humor. In jovial sallies right and left, his white teeth flashing into view, he rollicked along, the center of a company of his shipmates. These were made up of such an assortment of tribes and complexions as would have well fitted them to be marched up by Anacharsis Cloots before the bar of the first French Assembly as Representatives of the Human

Race. At each spontaneous tribute rendered by the wayfarers to this black pagod of a fellow – the tribute of a pause and stare, and less frequently an exclamation – the motley retinue showed that they took that sort of pride in the evoker of it which the Assyrian priests doubtless showed for their grand sculptured Bull when the faithful prostrated themselves.

To return. If in some cases a bit of a nautical Murat in setting forth his person ashore, the Handsome Sailor of the period in question evinced nothing of the dandified Billy-be-Dam, an amusing character all but extinct now, but occasionally to be encountered, and in a form yet more amusing than the original, at the tiller of the boats on the tempestuous Erie Canal or, more likely, vaporing in the groggeries along the towpath. Invariably a proficient in his perilous calling, he was also more or less of a mighty boxer or wrestler. It was strength and beauty. Tales of his prowess were recited. Ashore he was the champion; afloat the spokesman; on every suitable occasion always foremost. Close-reefing topsails in a gale, there he was, astride the weather yardarm-end, foot in the Flemish horse as stirrup, both hands tugging at the earing as at a bridle, in very much the attitude of young Alexander curbing the fiery Bucephalus. A superb figure, tossed up as by the horns of Taurus against the thunderous sky, cheerily hallooing to the strenuous file along the spar.

The moral nature was seldom out of keeping with the physical make. Indeed, except as toned by the former, the comeliness and power, always attractive in masculine conjunction, hardly could have drawn the sort of honest homage the Handsome Sailor in some examples received from his less gifted associates.

Such a cynosure, at least in aspect, and something such too in nature, though with important variations made apparent as the story proceeds, was welkin-eyed Billy Budd – or Baby Budd, as more familiarly, under circumstances hereafter to be given, he at last came to be called – aged twenty-one, a foretopman of the British fleet toward the close of the last decade of the eighteenth century. It was not very long prior to the time of the narration that follows that he had entered the King's service, having been impressed on the Narrow Seas from a homeward-bound English merchantman into a seventy-four outward bound, H.M.S. *Bellipotent*; which ship, as was not unusual in those hurried days, having been obliged to put to sea short of her proper complement of men. Plump upon Billy at first sight in the gangway the boarding officer, Lieutenant Ratcliffe, pounced, even before the merchantman's crew was formally mustered on the quarter-deck for his deliberate inspection. And him only he elected. For whether it was because the other men when ranged before him showed to ill advantage after Billy, or whether he had some scruples in view of the merchantman's being rather short-handed, however it might be, the officer contented himself with his first spontaneous choice. To the surprise of the ship's company, though much to the lieutenant's satisfaction, Billy made no demur. But, indeed, any demur would have been as idle as the protest of a goldfinch popped into a cage.

Noting this uncomplaining acquiescence, all but cheerful, one might say, the shipmaster turned a surprised glance of silent reproach at the sailor. The shipmaster was one of those worthy mortals found in every vocation, even the humbler ones – the sort of person whom everybody agrees in calling 'a respectable man'. And – nor so strange to report as it may appear to be – though a ploughman of the troubled waters, lifelong contending with the intractable elements, there was nothing this honest soul at heart loved better than simple peace and quiet. For the rest, he was fifty or thereabouts, a little inclined to corpulence, a prepossessing face, unwhiskered, and of an agreeable color – a rather full face, humanely intelligent in expression. On a fair day with a fair wind and all going well, a certain musical chime in his voice seemed to be the veritable unobstructed outcome of the innermost man. He had much prudence, much conscientiousness, and there were occasions when these virtues were the cause of overmuch disquietude in him. On a passage, so long as his craft was in any proximity to land, no sleep for Captain Graveling. He took to heart those serious responsibilities not so heavily borne by some shipmasters.

Now while Billy Budd was down in the forecastle getting his kit together, the *Bellipotent*'s lieutenant, burly and bluff, nowise disconcerted by Captain Graveling's omitting to proffer the customary hospitalities on an occasion so unwelcome to him, an omission simply caused by preoccupation of thought, unceremoniously invited himself into the cabin, and also to a flask from the spirit locker, a receptacle which his experienced eye instantly discovered. In fact he was one of those sea dogs in whom all the hardship and peril of naval life in the great prolonged wars of his time never impaired the natural instinct for sensuous enjoyment. His duty he always faithfully did; but duty is sometimes a dry obligation, and he was for irrigating its aridity, whensoever possible, with a fertilizing decoction of strong waters. For the cabin's proprietor there was nothing left but to play the part of the enforced host with whatever grace and alacrity were practicable. As necessary adjuncts to the flask, he silently placed tumbler and water jug before the irrepressible guest. But excusing himself from partaking just then, he dismally watched the unembarrassed officer deliberately diluting his grog a little, then tossing it off in three swallows, pushing the empty tumbler away, yet not so far as to be beyond easy reach, at the same time settling himself in his seat and smacking his lips with high satisfaction, looking straight at the host.

These proceedings over, the master broke the silence; and there lurked a rueful reproach in the tone of his voice: 'Lieutenant, you are going to take my best man from me, the jewel of 'em.'

'Yes, I know,' rejoined the other, immediately drawing back the tumbler preliminary to a replenishing. 'Yes, I know. Sorry.'

'Beg pardon, but you don't understand, Lieutenant. See here, now. Before I shipped that young fellow, my forecastle was a rat-pit of quarrels. It was black times, I tell you, aboard the *Rights* here. I was worried to that degree my pipe had no comfort for me. But Billy came; and it was like a Catholic priest striking peace in an Irish shindy. Not that he preached to them or said or did anything in particular; but a virtue went out of him, sugaring the sour ones. They took to him like hornets to treacle; all but the buffer of the gang, the big shaggy chap with the fire-red whiskers. He indeed, out of envy, perhaps, of the newcomer, and thinking such a 'sweet and pleasant fellow,' as he mockingly designated him to the others, could hardly have the spirit of a gamecock, must needs bestir himself in trying to get up an ugly row with him. Billy forbore with him and reasoned with him in a pleasant way – he is something like myself, Lieutenant, to whom aught like a quarrel is hateful – but nothing served. So, in the second dogwatch one day, the Red Whiskers in presence of the others, under pretense of showing Billy just whence a sirloin steak was cut – for the fellow had once been a butcher – insultingly gave him a dig under the ribs. Quick as lightning Billy let fly his arm. I dare say he never meant to do quite so much as he did, but anyhow he gave the burly fool a terrible drubbing. It took about half a minute, I should think. And lord bless you, the lubber was astonished at the celerity. And will you believe it, Lieutenant, the Red Whiskers now really loves Billy – loves him, or is the biggest hypocrite that ever I heard of. But they all love him. Some of 'em do his washing, darn his old trousers for him; the carpenter is at odd times making a pretty little chest of drawers for him. Anybody will do anything for Billy Budd; and it's the happy family here. But now, Lieutenant, if that young fellow goes – I know how it will be aboard the *Rights*. Not again very soon shall I, coming up from dinner, lean over the capstan smoking a quiet pipe – no, not very soon again, I think. Ay, Lieutenant, you are going to take away the jewel of 'em; you are going to take away my peacemaker!' And with that the good soul had really some ado in checking a rising sob.

'Well,' said the lieutenant, who had listened with amused interest to all this and now was waxing merry with his tipple: 'well, blessed are the peacemakers, especially the fighting peacemakers. And such are the seventy-four beauties some of which you see poking their noses out of the portholes of yonder warship lying to for me,' pointing through the cabin window at the *Bellipotent*. 'But courage! Don't look so downhearted, man. Why, I pledge you in advance the royal approbation. Rest assured that His Majesty will be delighted to know that in a time when his hardtack is not sought for by sailors with such avidity as should be, a time also when some shipmasters privily resent the borrowing from them a tar or two for the service; His Majesty, I say, will be delighted to learn that *one* shipmaster at least cheerfully surrenders to the King the flower of his flock, a sailor who with equal loyalty makes no dissent. – But where's my beauty? Ah,' looking through the cabin's open door, 'here he comes; and, by Jove, lugging along his chest – Apollo with his portmanteau! – My man,' stepping out to him, 'you can't take that big box aboard a warship. The boxes there are mostly shot boxes. Put your duds in a bag, lad. Boot and saddle for the cavalryman, bag and hammock for the man-of-war's man.'

The transfer from chest to bag was made. And, after seeing his man into the cutter and then following him down, the lieutenant pushed off from the *Rights-of-Man*. That was the merchant ship's name, though by her master and crew abbreviated in sailor fashion into the *Rights*. The hardheaded Dundee owner was a staunch admirer of Thomas Paine, whose book in rejoinder to Burke's arraignment of the French Revolution had then been published for some time and had gone everywhere. In christening his vessel after the title of Paine's volume the man of Dundee was something like his contemporary ship-owner, Stephen Girard of Philadelphia, whose sympathies, alike with his native land and its liberal philosophers, he evinced by naming his ships after Voltaire, Diderot, and so forth.

But now, when the boat swept under the merchantman's stern, and officer and oarsmen were noting – some bitterly and others with a grin – the name emblazoned there; just then it was that the new recruit jumped up from the bow where the coxswain had directed him to sit, and waving hat to his silent shipmates sorrowfully looking over at him from the taffrail, bade the lads a genial good-bye. Then, making a salutation as to the ship herself, 'And good-bye to you too, old *Rights-of-Man*.'

'Down, sir!' roared the lieutenant, instantly assuming all the rigor of his rank, though with difficulty repressing a smile.

To be sure, Billy's action was a terrible breach of naval decorum. But in that decorum he had never been instructed; in consideration of which the lieutenant would hardly have been so energetic in reproof but for the concluding farewell to the ship. This he rather took as meant to convey a covert sally on the new recruit's part, a sly slur at impressment in general, and that of himself in especial. And yet, more likely, if satire it was in effect, it was hardly so by intention, for Billy, though happily endowed with the gaiety of high health, youth, and a free heart, was yet by no means of a satirical turn. The will to it and the sinister dexterity were alike wanting. To deal in double meanings and insinuations of any sort was quite foreign to his nature.

As to his enforced enlistment, that he seemed to take pretty much as he was wont to take any vicissitude of weather. Like the animals, though no philosopher, he was, without knowing it, practically a fatalist. And it may be that he rather liked this adventurous turn in his affairs, which promised an opening into novel scenes and martial excitements.

Aboard the *Bellipotent* our merchant sailor was forthwith rated as an able seaman and assigned to the starboard watch of the foretop. He was soon at home in the service, not at all disliked for his unpretentious good looks and a sort of genial happy-go-lucky air. No merrier man in his mess; in marked contrast to certain other individuals included like himself among the impressed portion of the ship's company; for these when not actively employed were sometimes, and more particularly in the last dog-watch when the drawing near of twilight induced revery, apt to fall into a saddish mood which in some partook of sullenness. But they were not so young as our foretopman, and no few of them must have known a hearth of some sort, others may have had wives and children left, too probably, in uncertain circumstances, and hardly any but must have had acknowledged kith and kin, while for Billy, as will shortly be seen, his entire family was practically invested in himself.

Chapter Two

Though our new-made foretopman was well received in the top and on the gun decks, hardly here was he that cynosure he had previously been among those minor ship's companies of the merchant marine, with which companies only had he hitherto consorted.

He was young; and despite his all but fully developed frame, in aspect looked even younger than he really was, owing to a lingering adolescent expression in the as yet smooth face all but feminine in purity of natural complexion but where, thanks to his seagoing, the lily was quite suppressed and the rose had some ado visibly to flush through the tan.

To one essentially such a novice in the complexities of factitious life, the abrupt transition from his former and simpler sphere to the ampler and more knowing world of a great warship; this might well have abashed him had there been any conceit or vanity in his composition. Among her miscellaneous multitude, the *Bellipotent* mustered several individuals who however inferior in grade were of no common natural stamp, sailors more signally susceptive of that air which continuous martial discipline and repeated presence in battle can in some degree impart even to the average man. As the Handsome Sailor, Billy Budd's position aboard the seventy-four was something analogous to that of a rustic beauty transplanted from the provinces and brought into competition with the highborn dames of the court. But this change of circumstances he scarce noted. As little did he observe that something about him provoked an ambiguous smile in one or two harder faces among the bluejackets. Nor less unaware was he of the peculiar favorable effect his person and demeanour had upon the more intelligent gentlemen of the quarter-deck. Nor could this well have been otherwise. Cast in a mold peculiar to the finest physical examples of those Englishmen in whom the Saxon strain would seem not at all to partake of any Norman or other admixture, he showed in face that humane look of reposeful good nature which the Greek sculptor in some instances gave to his heroic strong-man, Hercules. But this again was subtly modified by another and pervasive quality. The ear, small and shapely, the arch of the foot, the curve in mouth and nostril, even the indurated hand dyed to the orange-tawny of the toucan's bill, a hand telling alike of the halyards and tar bucket; but, above all, something in the mobile expression, and every chance attitude and movement, something suggestive of a mother eminently favored by Love and the Graces; all this strangely indicated a lineage in direct contradiction to his lot. The mysteriousness here became less mysterious through a matter of fact elicited when Billy at the capstan was being formally mustered into the service. Asked by the officer, a small, brisk little gentleman as it chanced, among other questions, his place of birth, he replied, 'Please, sir, I don't know.'

'Don't know where you were born? Who was your father?'

'God knows, sir.'

Struck by the straightforward simplicity of these replies, the officer next asked, 'Do you know anything about your beginning?'

'No, sir. But I have heard that I was found in a pretty silk-lined basket hanging one morning from the knocker of a good man's door in Bristol.'

'*Found*, say you? Well,' throwing back his head and looking up and down the new recruit; 'well, it turns out to have been a pretty good find. Hope they'll find some more like you, my man; the fleet sadly needs them.'

Yes, Billy Budd was a foundling, a presumable by-blow, and, evidently, no ignoble one. Noble descent was as evident in him as in a blood horse.

For the rest, with little or no sharpness of faculty or any trace of the wisdom of the serpent, nor yet quite a dove, he possessed that kind and degree of intelligence going along with the unconventional rectitude of a sound human creature, one to whom not yet has been proffered the questionable apple of knowledge. He was illiterate; he could not read, but he could sing, and like the illiterate nightingale was sometimes the composer of his own song.

Of self-consciousness he seemed to have little or none, or about as much as we may reasonably impute to a dog of Saint Bernard's breed.

Habitually living with the elements and knowing little more of the land than as a beach, or, rather, that portion of the terraqueous globe providentially set apart for dance-houses, doxies, and tapsters, in short what sailors call a 'fiddler's green', his simple nature remained unsophisticated by those moral obliquities which are not in every case incompatible with that manufacturable thing known as respectability. But are sailors, frequenters of fiddler's greens, without vices? No; but less often than with landsmen do their vices, so called, partake of crookedness of heart, seeming less to proceed from viciousness than exuberance of vitality after long constraint: frank manifestations in accordance with natural law. By his original constitution aided by the co-operating influences of his lot, Billy in many respects was little more than a sort of upright barbarian, much such perhaps as Adam presumably might have been ere the urbane Serpent wriggled himself into his company.

And here be it submitted that apparently going to corroborate the doctrine of man's Fall, a doctrine now popularly ignored, it is observable that where certain virtues pristine and unadulterate peculiarly characterize anybody in the external uniform of civilization, they will upon scrutiny seem not to be derived from custom or convention, but rather to be out of keeping with these, as if indeed exceptionally transmitted from a period prior to

Cain's city and citified man. The character marked by such qualities has to an unvitiated taste an untampered-with flavor like that of berries, while the man thoroughly civilized, even in a fair specimen of the breed, has to the same moral palate a questionable smack as of a compounded wine. To any stray inheritor of these primitive qualities found, like Caspar Hauser, wandering dazed in any Christian capital of our time, the good-natured poet's famous invocation, near two thousand years ago, of the good rustic out of his latitude in the Rome of the Caesars, still appropriately holds:

> Honest and poor, faithful in word and thought,
> What hath thee, Fabian, to the city brought?

Though our Handsome Sailor had as much of masculine beauty as one can expect anywhere to see; nevertheless, like the beautiful woman in one of Hawthorne's minor tales, there was just one thing amiss in him. No visible blemish indeed, as with the lady; no, but an occasional liability to a vocal defect. Though in the hour of elemental uproar or peril he was everything that a sailor should be, yet under sudden provocation of strong heart-feeling his voice, otherwise singularly musical, as if expressive of the harmony within, was apt to develop an organic hesitancy, in fact more or less of a stutter or even worse. In this particular Billy was a striking instance that the arch interferer, the envious marplot of Eden, still has more or less to do with every human consignment to this planet of Earth. In every case, one way or another he is sure to slip in his little card, as much as to remind us – I too have a hand here.

The avowal of such an imperfection in the Handsome Sailor should be evidence not alone that he is not presented as a conventional hero, but also that the story in which he is the main figure is no romance.

Chapter Three

At the time of Billy Budd's arbitrary enlistment into the *Bellipotent* that ship was on her way to join the Mediterranean fleet. No long time elapsed before the junction was effected. As one of that fleet the seventy-four participated in its movements, though at times on account of her superior sailing qualities, in the absence of frigates, dispatched on separate duty as a scout and at times on less temporary service. But with all this the story has little concernment, restricted as it is to the inner life of one particular ship and the career of an individual sailor.

It was the summer of 1797. In the April of that year had occurred the commotion at Spithead followed in May by a second and yet more serious outbreak in the fleet at the Nore. The latter is known, and without exaggeration in the epithet, as 'the Great Mutiny'. It was indeed a demonstration more menacing to England than the contemporary manifestoes and conquering and proselyting armies of the French Directory. To the British Empire the Nore Mutiny was what a strike in the fire brigade would be to London threatened by general arson. In a crisis when the kingdom might well have anticipated the famous signal that some years later published along the naval line of battle what it was that upon occasion England expected of Englishmen; *that* was the time when at the mastheads of the three-deckers and seventy-fours moored in her own roadstead – a fleet the right arm of a Power then all but the sole free conservative one of the Old World – the bluejackets, to be numbered by thousands, ran up with huzzas the British colors with the union and cross wiped out; by that cancellation transmuting the flag of founded law and freedom defined, into the enemy's red meteor of unbridled and unbounded revolt. Reasonable discontent growing out of practical grievances in the fleet had been ignited into irrational combustion as by live cinders blown across the Channel from France in flames.

The event converted into irony for a time those spirited strains of Dibdin – as a song-writer no mean auxiliary to the English government at that European conjuncture – strains celebrating, among other things, the patriotic devotion of the British tar: 'And as for my life, 'tis the King's!'

Such an episode in the Island's grand naval story her naval historians naturally abridge, one of them (William James) candidly acknowledging that fain would he pass it over did not 'impartiality forbid fastidiousness'. And yet his mention is less a narration than a reference, having to do hardly at all with details. Nor are these readily to be found in the libraries. Like some other events in every age befalling states everywhere, including America, the Great Mutiny was of such character that national pride along with views of policy would fain shade it off into the historical background. Such events cannot be ignored, but there is a considerate way of historically treating them. If a well-constituted individual refrains from blazoning aught amiss or calamitous in his family, a nation in the like circumstance may without reproach be equally discreet.

Though after parleyings between government and the ring-leaders, and concessions by the former as to some glaring abuses, the first uprising – that at Spithead – with difficulty was put down, or matters for the time pacified; yet at the Nore the unforeseen renewal of insurrection on a yet larger scale, and emphasized in the conferences that ensued by demands deemed by the authorities not only inadmissible but aggressively insolent, indicated – if the Red Flag did not sufficiently do so – what was the spirit animating the men. Final suppression, however, there was; but only made possible perhaps by the unswerving loyalty of the marine corps and a voluntary resumption of loyalty among influential sections of the crews.

To some extent the Nore Mutiny may be regarded as analogous to the distempering irruption of contagious fever in a frame constitutionally sound, and which anon throws it off.

At all events, of these thousands of mutineers were some of the tars who not so very long afterwards – whether wholly prompted thereto by patriotism, or pugnacious instinct, or by both – helped to win a coronet for Nelson at the Nile, and the naval crown of crowns for him at Trafalgar. To the mutineers, those battles and especially Trafalgar were a plenary absolution and a grand one. For all that goes to make up scenic naval display and heroic magnificence in arms, those battles, especially Trafalgar, stand unmatched in human annals.

Chapter Four

In this matter of writing, resolve as one may to keep to the main road, some bypaths have an enticement not readily to be withstood. I am going to err into such a bypath. If the reader will keep me company I shall be glad. At the least, we can promise ourselves that pleasure which is wickedly said to be in sinning, for a literary sin the divergence will be.

Very likely it is no new remark that the inventions of our time have at last brought about a change in sea warfare in degree corresponding to the revolution in all warfare effected by the original introduction from China into Europe of gunpowder. The first European firearm, a clumsy contrivance, was, as is well known, scouted by no few of the knights as a base implement, good enough peradventure for weavers too craven to stand up crossing steel with steel in frank fight. But as ashore knightly valor, though shorn of its blazonry, did not cease with the knights, neither on the seas – though nowadays in encounters there a certain kind of displayed gallantry be fallen out of date as hardly applicable under changed circumstances – did the nobler qualities of such naval magnates as Don John of Austria, Doria, Van Tromp, Jean Bart, the long line of British admirals, and the American Decaturs of 1812 become obsolete with their wooden walls.

Nevertheless, to anybody who can hold the Present at its worth without being inappreciative of the Past, it may be forgiven, if to such an one the solitary old hulk at Portsmouth, Nelson's *Victory*, seems to float there, not alone as the decaying monument of a fame incorruptible, but also as a poetic reproach, softened by its picturesqueness, to the *Monitors* and yet mightier hulls of the European ironclads. And this not altogether because such craft are unsightly, unavoidably lacking the symmetry and grand lines of the old battleships, but equally for other reasons.

There are some, perhaps, who while not altogether inaccessible to that poetic reproach just alluded to, may yet on behalf of the new order be disposed to parry it; and this to the extent of iconoclasm, if need be. For example, prompted by the sight of the star inserted in the *Victory's* quarter-deck designating the spot where the Great Sailor fell, these martial utilitarians may suggest considerations implying that Nelson's ornate publication of his person in battle was not only unnecessary, but not military, nay, savored of foolhardiness and vanity. They may add, too, that at Trafalgar it was in effect nothing less than a challenge to death; and death came; and that but for his bravado the victorious admiral might possibly have survived the battle, and so, instead of having his sagacious dying injunctions overruled by his immediate successor in command, he himself when the contest was decided might have brought his shattered fleet to anchor, a proceeding which might have averted the deplorable loss of life by shipwreck in the elemental tempest that followed the martial one.

Well, should we set aside the more than disputable point whether for various reasons it was possible to anchor the fleet, then plausibly enough the Benthamites of war may urge the above. But the *might-have-been* is but boggy ground to build on. And, certainly, in foresight as to the larger issue of an encounter, and anxious preparations for it – buoying the deadly way and mapping it out, as at Copenhagen – few commanders have been so painstakingly circumspect as this same reckless declarer of his person in fight.

Personal prudence, even when dictated by quite other than selfish considerations, surely is no special virtue in a military man; while an excessive love of glory, impassioning a less burning impulse, the honest sense of duty, is the first. If the name *Wellington* is not so much of a trumpet to the blood as the simpler name *Nelson*, the reason for this may perhaps be inferred from the above. Alfred in his funeral ode on the victor of Waterloo ventures not to call him the greatest soldier of all time, though in the same ode he invokes Nelson as 'the greatest sailor since our world began'.

At Trafalgar Nelson on the brink of opening the fight sat down and wrote his last brief will and testament. If under the presentiment of the most magnificent of all victories to be crowned by his own glorious death, a sort of priestly motive led him to dress his person in the jewelled vouchers of his own shining deeds; if thus to have adorned himself for the altar and the sacrifice were indeed vainglory, then affectation and fustian is each more heroic line in the great epics and dramas, since in such lines the poet but embodies in verse those exaltations of sentiment that a nature like Nelson, the opportunity being given, vitalizes into acts.

Chapter Five

Yes, the outbreak at the Nore was put down. But not every grievance was redressed. If the contractors, for example, were no longer permitted to ply some practices peculiar to their tribe everywhere, such as providing shoddy cloth, rations not sound, or false in the measure; not the less impressment, for one thing, went on. By custom sanctioned for centuries, and judicially maintained by a Lord Chancellor as late as Mansfield, that mode of manning the fleet, a mode now fallen into a sort of abeyance but never formally renounced, it was not practicable to give up in those years. Its abrogation would have crippled the indispensable fleet, one wholly under canvas, no steam power, its innumerable sails and thousands of cannon, everything in short, worked by muscle alone; a fleet the more insatiate in demand for men, because then multiplying its ships of all grades against contingencies present and to come of the convulsed Continent.

Discontent foreran the Two Mutinies, and more or less it lurkingly survived them. Hence it was not unreasonable to apprehend some return of trouble sporadic or general. One instance of such apprehensions: In the same year with this story, Nelson, then Rear Admiral Sir Horatio, being with the fleet off the Spanish coast, was directed by the admiral in command to shift his pennant from the *Captain* to the *Theseus*; and for this reason: that the latter ship having newly arrived on the station from home, where it had taken part in the Great Mutiny, danger was apprehended from the temper of the men; and it was thought that an officer like Nelson was the one, not indeed to terrorize the crew into base subjection, but to win them, by force of his mere presence and heroic personality, back to an allegiance if not as enthusiastic as his own yet as true.

So it was that for a time, on more than one quarter-deck, anxiety did exist. At sea, precautionary vigilance was strained against relapse. At short notice an engagement might come on. When it did, the lieutenants assigned to batteries felt it incumbent on them, in some instances, to stand with drawn swords behind the men working the guns.

Chapter Six

But on board the seventy-four in which Billy now swung his hammock, very little in the manner of the men and nothing obvious in the demeanor of the officers would have suggested to an ordinary observer that the Great Mutiny was a recent event. In their general bearing and conduct the commissioned officers of a warship naturally take their tone from the commander, that is if he have that ascendancy of character that ought to be his.

Captain the Honorable Edward Fairfax Vere, to give his full title, was a bachelor of forty or thereabouts, a sailor of distinction even in a time prolific of renowned seamen. Though allied to the higher nobility, his advancement had not been altogether owing to influences connected with that circumstance. He had seen much service, been in various engagements, always acquitting himself as an officer mindful of the welfare of his men, but never tolerating an infraction of discipline; thoroughly versed in the science of his profession, and intrepid to the verge of temerity, though never injudiciously so. For his gallantry in the West Indian waters as flag lieutenant under Rodney in that admiral's crowning victory over De Grasse, he was made a post captain.

Ashore, in the garb of a civilian, scarce anyone would have taken him for a sailor, more especially that he never garnished unprofessional talk with nautical terms, and grave in his bearing, evinced little appreciation of mere humor. It was not out of keeping with these traits that on a passage when nothing demanded his paramount action, he was the most undemonstrative of men. Any landsman observing this gentleman not conspicuous by his stature and wearing no pronounced insignia, emerging from his cabin to the open deck, and noting the silent

325

deference of the officers retiring to leeward, might have taken him for the King's guest, a civilian aboard the King's ship, some highly honorable discreet envoy on his way to an important post. But in fact this unobtrusiveness of demeanor may have proceeded from a certain unaffected modesty of manhood sometimes accompanying a resolute nature, a modesty evinced at all times not calling for pronounced action, which shown in any rank of life suggests a virtue aristocratic in kind. As with some others engaged in various departments of the world's more heroic activities, Captain Vere though practical enough upon occasion would at times betray a certain dreaminess of mood. Standing alone on the weather side of the quarterdeck, one hand holding by the rigging, he would absently gaze off at the blank sea. At the presentation to him then of some minor matter interrupting the current of his thoughts, he would show more or less irascibility; but instantly he would control it.

In the navy he was popularly known by the appellation 'Starry Vere'. How such a designation happened to fall upon one who whatever his sterling qualities was without any brilliant ones, was in this wise: A favorite kinsman, Lord Denton, a freehearted fellow, had been the first to meet and congratulate him upon his return to England from his West Indian cruise; and but the day previous turning over a copy of Andrew Marvell's poems had lighted, not for the first time, however, upon the lines entitled 'Appleton House', the name of one of the seats of their common ancestor, a hero in the German wars of the seventeenth century, in which poem occur the lines:

> This 'tis to have been from the first
> In a domestic heaven nursed,
> Under the discipline severe
> Of Fairfax and the starry Vere.

And so, upon embracing his cousin fresh from Rodney's great victory wherein he had played so gallant a part, brimming over with just family pride in the sailor of their house, he exuberantly exclaimed, 'Give ye joy, Ed; give ye joy, my starry Vere!' This got currency, and the novel prefix serving in familiar parlance readily to distinguish the *Bellipotent*'s captain from another Vere his senior, a distant relative, an officer of like rank in the navy, it remained permanently attached to the surname.

Chapter Seven

In view of the part that the commander of the *Bellipotent* plays in scenes shortly to follow, it may be well to fill out that sketch of him outlined in the previous chapter.

Aside from his qualities as a sea officer Captain Vere was an exceptional character. Unlike no few of England's renowned sailors, long and arduous service with signal devotion to it had not resulted in absorbing and *salting* the entire man. He had a marked leaning toward everything intellectual. He loved books, never going to sea without a newly replenished library, compact but of the best. The isolated leisure, in some cases so wearisome, falling at intervals to commanders even during a war cruise, never was tedious to Captain Vere. With nothing of that literary taste which less heeds the thing conveyed than the vehicle, his bias was toward those books to which every serious mind of superior order occupying any active post of authority in the world naturally inclines: books treating of actual men and events no matter of what era – history, biography, and unconventional writers like Montaigne, who, free from cant and convention, honestly and in the spirit of common sense philosophize upon realities. In this line of reading he found confirmation of his own more reserved thoughts – confirmation which he had vainly sought in social converse, so that as touching most fundamental topics, there had got to be established in him some positive convictions which he forefelt would abide in him essentially unmodified so long as his intelligent part remained unimpaired. In view of the troubled period in which his lot was cast, this was well for him. His settled convictions were as a dike against those invading waters of novel opinion social, political, and otherwise, which carried away as in a torrent no few minds in those days, minds by nature not inferior to his own. While other members of that aristocracy to which by birth he belonged were incensed at the innovators mainly because their theories were inimical to the privileged classes, Captain Vere disinterestedly opposed them not alone because they seemed to him insusceptible of embodiment in lasting institutions, but at war with the peace of the world and the true welfare of mankind.

With minds less stored than his and less earnest, some officers of his rank, with whom at times he would necessarily consort, found him lacking in the companionable quality, a dry and bookish gentleman, as they deemed. Upon any chance withdrawal from their company one would be apt to say to another something like this: 'Vere is a noble fellow, Starry Vere. 'Spite the gazettes, Sir Horatio' (meaning him who became Lord Nelson) 'is at bottom scarce a better seaman or fighter. But between you and me now, don't you think there is a queer streak of the pedantic running through him? Yes, like the King's yarn in a coil of navy rope?'

Some apparent ground there was for this sort of confidential criticism; since not only did the captain's discourse never fall into the jocosely familiar, but in illustrating of any point touching the stirring personages and events of the time he would be as apt to cite some historic character or incident of antiquity as he would be to cite from the moderns. He seemed unmindful of the circumstance that to his bluff company such remote allusions, however pertinent they might really be, were altogether alien to men whose reading was mainly confined to the journals. But considerateness in such matters is not easy to natures constituted like Captain Vere's. Their honesty prescribes to them directness, sometimes far-reaching like that of a migratory fowl that in its flight never heeds when it crosses a frontier.

Chapter Eight

The lieutenants and other commissioned gentlemen forming Captain Vere's staff it is not necessary here to particularize, nor needs it to make any mention of any of the warrant officers. But among the petty officers was one who, having much to do with the story, may as well be forthwith introduced. His portrait I essay, but shall never hit it. This was John Claggart, the master-at-arms. But that sea title may to landsmen seem somewhat equivocal. Originally, doubtless, that petty officer's function was the instruction of the men in the use of arms, sword or cutlass. But very long ago, owing to the advance in gunnery making hand-to-hand encounters less frequent and giving to niter and sulphur the pre-eminence over steel, that function ceased; the master-at-arms of a great warship becoming a sort of chief of police charged among other matters with the duty of preserving order on the populous lower gun decks.

Claggart was a man about five-and-thirty, somewhat spare and tall, yet of no ill figure upon the whole. His hand was too small and shapely to have been accustomed to hard toil. The face was a notable one, the features all except the chin cleanly cut as those on a Greek medallion; yet the chin, beardless as Tecumseh's, had something of strange protuberant broadness in its make that recalled the prints of the Reverend Dr Titus Oates, the historic deponent with the clerical drawl in the time of Charles II and the fraud of the alleged Popish Plot. It served Claggart in his office that his eye could cast a tutoring glance. His brow was of the sort phrenologically associated with more than average intellect; silken jet curls partly clustering over it, making a foil to the pallor below, a pallor tinged with a faint shade of amber akin to the hue

of time-tinted marbles of old. This complexion, singularly contrasting with the red or deeply bronzed visages of the sailors, and
in part the result of his official seclusion from the sunlight,
though it was not exactly displeasing, nevertheless seemed to
hint of something defective or abnormal in the constitution and
blood. But his general aspect and manner were so suggestive of
an education and career incongruous with his naval function that
when not actively engaged in it he looked like a man of high
quality, social and moral, who for reasons of his own was keeping
incog. Nothing was known of his former life. It might be that he
was an Englishman; and yet there lurked a bit of accent in his
speech suggesting that possibly he was not such by birth, but
through naturalization in early childhood. Among certain grizzled sea gossips of the gun decks and forecastle went a rumor
perdue that the master-at-arms was a *chevalier* who had volunteered into the King's navy by way of compounding for some
mysterious swindle whereof he had been arraigned at the King's
Bench. The fact that nobody could substantiate this report was,
of course, nothing against its secret currency. Such a rumor once
started on the gun decks in reference to almost anyone below the
rank of a commissioned officer would, during the period assigned
to this narrative, have seemed not altogether wanting in credibility to the tarry old wiseacres of a man-of-war crew. And indeed a
man of Claggart's accomplishments, without prior nautical
experience entering the navy at mature life, as he did, and necessarily allotted at the start to the lowest grade in it; a man too who
never made allusion to his previous life ashore; these were circumstances which in the dearth of exact knowledge as to his true
antecedents opened to the invidious a vague field for unfavorable
surmise.

But the sailors' dogwatch gossip concerning him derived a
vague plausibility from the fact that now for some period the
British navy could so little afford to be squeamish in the matter
of keeping up the muster rolls, that not only were press gangs

notoriously abroad both afloat and ashore, but there was little or no secret about another matter, namely, that the London police were at liberty to capture any able-bodied suspect, any questionable fellow at large, and summarily ship him to the dockyard or fleet. Furthermore, even among voluntary enlistments there were instances where the motive thereto partook neither of patriotic impulse nor yet of a random desire to experience a bit of sea life and martial adventure. Insolvent debtors of minor grade, together with the promiscuous lame ducks of morality, found in the navy a convenient and secure refuge, secure because, once enlisted aboard a King's ship, they were as much in sanctuary as the transgressor of the Middle Ages harboring himself under the shadow of the altar. Such sanctioned irregularities, which for obvious reasons the government would hardly think to parade at the time and which consequently, and as affecting the least influential class of mankind, have all but dropped into oblivion, lend color to something for the truth whereof I do not vouch, and hence have some scruple in stating; something I remember having seen in print though the book I cannot recall; but the same thing was personally communicated to me now more than forty years ago by an old pensioner in a cocked hat with whom I had a most interesting talk on the terrace at Greenwich, a Baltimore Negro, a Trafalgar man. It was to this effect: In the case of a warship short of hands whose speedy sailing was imperative, the deficient quota, in lack of any other way of making it good, would be eked out by drafts culled direct from the jails. For reasons previously suggested it would not perhaps be easy at the present day directly to prove or disprove the allegation. But allowed as a verity, how significant would it be of England's straits at the time confronted by those wars which like a flight of harpies rose shrieking from the din and dust of the fallen Bastille. That era appears measurably clear to us who look back at it, and but read of it. But to the grandfathers of us graybeards, the more thoughtful of them, the genius of it presented an aspect like that of Camoëns' Spirit of the Cape, an eclipsing menace mysterious and prodigious. Not America was exempt from apprehension. At the height of Napoleon's unexampled conquests, there were Americans who had fought at Bunker Hill who looked forward to the possibility that the Atlantic might prove no barrier against the ultimate schemes of this French portentous upstart from the revolutionary chaos who seemed in act of fulfilling judgment prefigured in the Apocalypse.

But the less credence was to be given to the gun-deck talk touching Claggart, seeing that no man holding his office in a man-of-war can ever hope to be popular with the crew. Besides, in derogatory comments upon anyone against whom they have a grudge, or for any reason or no reason mislike, sailors are much like landsmen: they are apt to exaggerate or romance it.

About as much was really known to the *Bellipotent's* tars of the master-at-arms' career before entering the service as an astronomer knows about a comet's travels prior to its first observable appearance in the sky. The verdict of the sea quidnuncs has been cited only by way of showing what sort of moral impression the man made upon rude uncultivated natures whose conceptions of human wickedness were necessarily of the narrowest, limited to ideas of vulgar rascality – a thief among the swinging hammocks during a night watch, or the man-brokers and land-sharks of the seaports.

It was no gossip, however, but fact that though, as before hinted, Claggart upon his entrance into the navy was, as a novice, assigned to the least honorable section of a man-of-war's crew, embracing the drudgery, he did not long remain there. The superior capacity he immediately evinced, his constitutional sobriety, an ingratiating deference to superiors, together with a peculiar ferreting genius manifested on a singular occasion; all this, capped by a certain austere patriotism, abruptly advanced him to the position of master-at-arms.

Of this maritime chief of police the ship's corporals, so called, were the immediate subordinates, and compliant ones; and this, as is to be noted in some business departments ashore, almost to a degree inconsistent with entire moral volition. His place put various converging wires of underground influence under the chief's control, capable when astutely worked through his understrappers of operating to the mysterious discomfort, if nothing worse, of any of the sea commonalty.

Chapter Nine

Life in the foretop well agreed with Billy Budd. There, when not actually engaged on the yards yet higher aloft, the topmen, who as such had been picked out for youth and activity, constituted an aerial club lounging at ease against the smaller stun'sails rolled up into cushions, spinning yarns like the lazy gods, and frequently amused with what was going on in the busy world of the decks below. No wonder then that a young fellow of Billy's disposition was well content in such society. Giving no cause of offense to anybody, he was always alert at a call. So in the merchant service it had been with him. But now such a punctiliousness in duty was shown that his topmates would sometimes good-naturedly laugh at him for it. This heightened alacrity had its cause, namely, the impression made upon him by the first formal gangway-punishment he had ever witnessed, which befell the day following his impressment. It had been incurred by a little fellow, young, a novice afterguardsman absent from his assigned post when the ship was being put about; a dereliction resulting in a rather serious hitch to that maneuver, one demanding instantaneous promptitude in letting go and making fast. When Billy saw the culprit's naked back under the scourge, gridironed with red welts and worse, when he marked the dire expression in the liberated man's face as with his woolen shirt flung over him by the executioner he rushed forward from the spot to bury himself in the crowd, Billy was horrified. He resolved that never through remissness would he make himself liable to such a visitation or do or omit aught that might merit even verbal reproof. What then was his surprise and concern when ultimately he found himself getting into petty trouble occasionally about such matters as the stowage of his bag or something amiss in his hammock, matters under the police oversight of the ship's corporals of the lower decks, and which brought down on him a vague threat from one of them.

So heedful in all things as he was, how could this be? He could not understand it, and it more than vexed him. When he spoke to his young topmates about it they were either lightly incredulous or found something comical in his unconcealed anxiety. 'Is it your bag, Billy?' said one. 'Well, sew yourself up in it, bully boy, and then you'll be sure to know if anybody meddles with it.'

Now there was a veteran aboard who because his years began to disqualify him for more active work had been recently assigned duty as mainmastman in his watch, looking to the gear belayed at the rail roundabout that great spar near the deck. At off-times the foretopman had picked up some acquaintance with him, and now in his trouble it occurred to him that he might be the sort of person to go to for wise counsel. He was an old Dansker long anglicized in the service, of few words, many wrinkles, and some honorable scars. His wizened face, time-tinted and weather-stained to the complexion of an antique parchment, was here and there peppered blue by the chance explosion of a gun cartridge in action.

He was an *Agamemnon* man, some two years prior to the time of this story having served under Nelson when still captain in that ship immortal in naval memory, which dismantled and in part broken up to her bare ribs is seen a grand skeleton in Haden's etching. As one of a boarding party from the *Agamemnon* he had received a cut slantwise along one temple and cheek leaving a long pale scar like a streak of dawn's light falling athwart the dark visage. It was on account of that scar and the affair in which it was known that he had received it, as well as from his blue-peppered complexion, that the Dansker went among the *Bellipotent's* crew by the name of 'Board-Her-in-the-Smoke'.

Now the first time that his small weasel eyes happened to light on Billy Budd, a certain grim internal merriment set all his ancient wrinkles into antic play. Was it that his eccentric unsentimental old sapience, primitive in its kind, saw or thought it saw something which in contrast with the warship's environment looked oddly incongruous in the Handsome Sailor? But after slyly studying him at intervals, the old Merlin's equivocal merriment was modified; for now when the twain would meet, it would start in his face a quizzing sort of look, but it would be but momentary and sometimes replaced by an expression of speculative query as to what might eventually befall a nature like that, dropped into a world not without some mantraps and against whose subtleties simple courage lacking experience and address, and without any touch of defensive ugliness, is of little avail; and where such innocence as man is capable of does yet in a moral emergency not always sharpen the faculties or enlighten the will.

However it was, the Dansker in his ascetic way rather took to Billy. Nor was this only because of a certain philosophic interest in such a character. There was another cause. While the old man's eccentricities, sometimes bordering on the ursine, repelled the juniors, Billy, undeterred thereby, revering him as a salt hero, would make advances, never passing the old *Agamemnon* man without a salutation marked by that respect which is seldom lost on the aged, however crabbed at times or whatever their station in life.

There was a vein of dry humor, or what not, in the mastman; and, whether in freak of patriarchal irony touching Billy's youth and athletic frame, or for some other and more recondite reason, from the first in addressing him he always substituted *Baby* for Billy, the Dansker in fact being the originator of the name by which the foretopman eventually became known aboard ship.

Well then, in his mysterious little difficulty going in quest of the wrinkled one, Billy found him off duty in a dogwatch ruminating by himself, seated on a shot box of the upper gun deck, now and then surveying with a somewhat cynical regard certain of the more swaggering promenaders there. Billy recounted his trouble, again wondering how it all happened. The salt seer attentively listened, accompanying the foretopman's recital with queer twitchings of his wrinkles and problematical little sparkles of his small ferret eyes. Making an end of his story, the foretopman asked, 'And now, Dansker, do tell me what you think of it.'

The old man, shoving up the front of his tarpaulin and deliberately rubbing the long slant scar at the point where it entered the thin hair, laconically said, 'Baby Budd, *Jemmy Legs*' (meaning the master-at-arms) 'is down on you.'

'*Jemmy Legs!*' ejaculated Billy, his welkin eyes expanding. 'What for? Why, he calls me "the sweet and pleasant young fellow", they tell me.'

'Does he so?' grinned the grizzled one; then said, 'Ay, Baby lad, a sweet voice has Jemmy Legs.'

'No, not always. But to me he has. I seldom pass him but there comes a pleasant word.'

'And that's because he's down upon you, Baby Budd.'

Such reiteration, along with the manner of it, incomprehensible to a novice, disturbed Billy almost as much as the mystery for which he had sought explanation. Something less unpleasingly oracular he tried to extract; but the old sea Chiron, thinking perhaps that for the nonce he had sufficiently instructed his young Achilles, pursed his lips, gathered all his wrinkles together, and would commit himself to nothing further.

Years, and those experiences which befall certain shrewder men subordinated lifelong to the will of superiors, all this had developed in the Dansker the pithy guarded cynicism that was his leading characteristic.

Chapter Ten

The next day an incident served to confirm Billy Budd in his incredulity as to the Dansker's strange summing up of the case submitted. The ship at noon, going large before the wind, was rolling on her course, and he below at dinner and engaged in some sportful talk with the members of his mess, chanced in a sudden lurch to spill the entire contents of his soup pan upon the new-scrubbed deck. Claggart, the master-at-arms, official rattan in hand, happened to be passing along the battery in a bay of which the mess was lodged, and the greasy liquid streamed just across his path. Stepping over it, he was proceeding on his way without comment, since the matter was nothing to take notice of under the circumstances, when he happened to observe who it was that had done the spilling. His countenance changed. Pausing, he was about to ejaculate something hasty at the sailor, but checked himself, and pointing down to the streaming soup, playfully tapped him from behind with his rattan, saying in a low musical voice peculiar to him at times, 'Handsomely done, my lad! And handsome is as handsome did it, too!' And with that passed on. Not noted by Billy as not coming within his view was the involuntary smile, or rather grimace, that accompanied Claggart's equivocal words. Aridly it drew down the thin corners of his shapely mouth. But everybody taking his remark as meant for humorous, and at which therefore as coming from a superior they were bound to laugh 'with counterfeited glee', acted accordingly; and Billy, tickled, it may be, by the allusion to his being the Handsome Sailor, merrily joined in; then addressing his messmates exclaimed, 'There now, who says that Jemmy Legs is down on me!'

'And who said he was, Beauty?' demanded one Donald with some surprise. Whereat the foretopman looked a little foolish, recalling that it was only one person, Board-Her-in-the-Smoke, who had suggested what to him was the smoky idea that this master-at-arms was in any peculiar way hostile to him. Meantime that functionary, resuming his path, must have momentarily worn some expression less guarded than that of the bitter smile, usurping the face from the heart – some distorting expression perhaps, for a drummer-boy heedlessly frolicking along from the opposite direction and chancing to come into light collision with his person was strangely disconcerted by his aspect. Nor was the impression lessened when the official, impetuously giving him a sharp cut with the rattan, vehemently exclaimed, 'Look where you go!'

Chapter Eleven

What was the matter with the master-at-arms? And, be the matter what it might, how could it have direct relation to Billy Budd, with whom prior to the affair of the spilled soup he had never come into any special contact official or otherwise? What indeed could the trouble have to do with one so little inclined to give offense as the merchantship's 'peacemaker,' even him who in Claggart's own phrase was 'the sweet and pleasant young fellow'? Yes, why should Jemmy Legs, to borrow the Dansker's expression, be 'down' on the Handsome Sailor? But, at heart and not for nothing, as the late chance encounter may indicate to the discerning, down on him, secretly down on him, he assuredly was.

Now to invent something touching the more private career of Claggart, something involving Billy Budd, of which something the latter should be wholly ignorant, some romantic incident implying that Claggart's knowledge of the young bluejacket began at some period anterior to catching sight of him on board the seventy-four – all this, not so difficult to do, might avail in a way more or less interesting to account for whatever of enigma may appear to lurk in the case. But in fact there was nothing of the sort. And yet the cause necessarily to be assumed as the sole one assignable is in its very realism as much charged with that prime element of Radcliffian romance, the mysterious, as any that the ingenuity of the author of *The Mysteries of Udolpho* could devise. For what can more partake of the mysterious than an antipathy spontaneous and profound such as is evoked in certain exceptional mortals by the mere aspect of some other mortal, however harmless he may be, if not called forth by this very harmlessness itself?

Now there can exist no irritating juxtaposition of dissimilar personalities comparable to that which is possible aboard a great warship fully manned and at sea. There, every day among all ranks, almost every man comes into more or less of contact with almost every other man. Wholly there to avoid even the sight of an aggravating object one must needs give it Jonah's toss or jump overboard himself. Imagine how all this might eventually operate on some peculiar human creature the direct reverse of a saint!

But for the adequate comprehending of Claggart by a normal nature these hints are insufficient. To pass from a normal nature to him one must cross 'the deadly space between'. And this is best done by indirection.

Long ago an honest scholar, my senior, said to me in reference to one who like himself is now no more, a man so unimpeachably respectable that against him nothing was ever openly said though among the few something was whispered, 'Yes, X—— is a nut not to be cracked by the tap of a lady's fan. You are aware that I am the adherent of no organized religion, much less of any philosophy built into a system. Well, for all that, I think that to try and get into X——, enter his labyrinth and get out again, without a clue derived from some source other than what is known as "knowledge of the world" – that were hardly possible, at least for me.'

'Why,' said I, 'X——, however singular a study to some, is yet human, and knowledge of the world assuredly implies the knowledge of human nature, and in most of its varieties.'

'Yes, but a superficial knowledge of it, serving ordinary purposes. But for anything deeper, I am not certain whether to know the world and to know human nature be not two distinct branches of knowledge, which while they may coexist in the same heart, yet either may exist with little or nothing of the other. Nay, in an average man of the world, his constant rubbing with it blunts that finer spiritual insight indispensable to the understanding of the essential in certain exceptional characters, whether evil ones or good. In a matter of some importance I have seen a girl wind an old lawyer about her little finger. Nor was it the dotage of senile love. Nothing of the sort. But he knew law better than he knew the girl's heart. Coke and Blackstone hardly shed so much light into obscure spiritual places as the Hebrew prophets. And who were they? Mostly recluses.'

At the time, my inexperience was such that I did not quite see the drift of all this. It may be that I see it now. And, indeed, if that lexicon which is based on Holy Writ were any longer popular, one might with less difficulty define and denominate certain phenomenal men. As it is, one must turn to some authority not liable to the charge of being tinctured with the biblical element.

In a list of definitions included in the authentic translation of Plato, a list attributed to him, occurs this: 'Natural Depravity: a depravity according to nature', a definition which, though savoring of Calvinism, by no means involves Calvin's dogma as to total mankind. Evidently its intent makes it applicable but to individuals. Not many are the examples of this depravity which the gallows and jail supply. At any rate, for notable instances, since these have no vulgar alloy of the brute in them, but invariably are dominated by intellectuality, one must go elsewhere. Civilization, especially if of the austerer sort, is auspicious to it. It folds itself in the mantle of respectability. It has certain negative virtues serving as silent auxiliaries. It never allows wine to get within its guard. It is not going too far to say that it is without vices or small sins. There is a phenomenal pride in it that excludes them. It is never mercenary or avaricious. In short, the depravity here meant partakes nothing of the sordid or sensual. It is serious, but free from acerbity. Though no flatterer of mankind it never speaks ill of it.

But the thing which in eminent instances signalizes so exceptional a nature is this: Though the man's even temper and discreet bearing would seem to intimate a mind peculiarly subject to the law of reason, not the less in heart he would seem to riot in complete exemption from that law, having apparently little to do with reason further than to employ it as an ambidexter implement for effecting the irrational. That is to say: Toward the accomplishment of an aim which in wantonness of atrocity would seem to partake of the insane, he will direct a cool judgment sagacious and sound. These men are madmen, and of the most dangerous sort, for their lunacy is not continuous, but occasional, evoked by some special object; it is protectively secretive, which is as much as to say it is self-contained, so that when, moreover, most active it is to the average mind not distinguishable from sanity, and for the reason above suggested: that whatever its aims may be – and the aim is never declared – the method and the outward proceeding are always perfectly rational.

Now something such an one was Claggart, in whom was the mania of an evil nature, not engendered by vicious training or corrupting books or licentious living, but born with him and innate, in short 'a depravity according to nature'.

Dark sayings are these, some will say. But why? Is it because they somewhat savor of Holy Writ in its phrase 'mystery of iniquity'? If they do, such savor was far enough from being intended, for little will it commend these pages to many a reader of today.

The point of the present story turning on the hidden nature of the master-at-arms has necessitated this chapter. With an added hint or two in connection with the incident at the mess, the resumed narrative must be left to vindicate, as it may, its own credibility.

Chapter Twelve

That Claggart's figure was not amiss, and his face, save the chin, well molded, has already been said. Of these favorable points he seemed not insensible, for he was not only neat but careful in his dress. But the form of Billy Budd was heroic; and if his face was without the intellectual look of the pallid Claggart's, not the less was it lit, like his, from within, though from a different source. The bonfire in his heart made luminous the rose-tan in his cheek.

In view of the marked contrast between the persons of the twain, it is more than probable that when the master-at-arms in the scene last given applied to the sailor the proverb 'Handsome is as handsome does', he there let escape an ironic inkling, not caught by the young sailors who heard it, as to what it was that had first moved him against Billy, namely, his significant personal beauty.

Now envy and antipathy, passions irreconcilable in reason, nevertheless in fact may spring conjoined like Chang and Eng in one birth. Is Envy then such a monster? Well, though many an arraigned mortal has in hopes of mitigated penalty pleaded guilty to horrible actions, did ever anybody seriously confess to envy? Something there is in it universally felt to be more shameful than even felonious crime. And not only does everybody disown it, but the better sort are inclined to incredulity when it is in earnest imputed to an intelligent man. But since its lodgment is in the heart not the brain, no degree of intellect supplies a guarantee against it. But Claggart's was no vulgar form of the passion. Nor, as directed toward Billy Budd, did it partake of that streak of apprehensive jealousy that marred Saul's visage perturbedly brooding on the comely young David. Claggart's envy struck deeper. If askance he eyed the good looks, cheery health, and frank enjoyment of young life in Billy Budd, it was because these went along with a nature that, as Claggart magnetically felt, had in its simplicity never willed malice or experienced the reactionary bite of that serpent. To him, the spirit lodged within Billy, and looking out from his welkin eyes as from windows, that ineffability it was which made the dimple in his dyed cheek, suppled his joints, and dancing in his yellow curls made him preeminently the Handsome Sailor. One person excepted, the master-at-arms was perhaps the only man in the ship intellectually capable of adequately appreciating the moral phenomenon presented in Billy Budd. And the insight but intensified his passion, which assuming various secret forms within him, at times assumed that of cynic disdain, disdain of innocence – to be nothing more than innocent! Yet in an aesthetic way he saw the charm of it, the courageous free-and-easy temper of it, and fain would have shared it, but he despaired of it.

With no power to annul the elemental evil in him, though readily enough he could hide it; apprehending the good, but powerless to be it; a nature like Claggart's, surcharged with energy as such natures almost invariably are, what recourse is left to it but to recoil upon itself and, like the scorpion for which the Creator alone is responsible, act out to the end the part allotted it.

Chapter Thirteen

Passion, and passion in its profoundest, is not a thing demanding a palatial stage whereon to play its part. Down among the groundlings, among the beggars and rakers of the garbage, profound passion is enacted. And the circumstances that provoke it, however trivial or mean, are no measure of its power. In the present instance the stage is a scrubbed gun deck, and one of the external provocations a man-of-war's man's spilled soup.

Now when the master-at-arms noticed whence came that greasy fluid streaming before his feet, he must have taken it – to some extent wilfully, perhaps – not for the mere accident it assuredly was, but for the sly escape of a spontaneous feeling on Billy's part more or less answering to the antipathy on his own. In effect a foolish demonstration, he must have thought, and very harmless, like the futile kick of a heifer, which yet were the heifer a shod stallion would not be so harmless. Even so was it that into the gall of Claggart's envy he infused the vitriol of his contempt. But the incident confirmed to him certain telltale reports purveyed to his ear by 'Squeak', one of his more cunning corporals, a grizzled little man, so nicknamed by the sailors on account of his squeaky voice and sharp visage ferreting about the dark corners of the lower decks after interlopers, satirically suggesting to them the idea of a rat in a cellar.

From his chief's employing him as an implicit tool in laying little traps for the worriment of the foretopman – for it was from the master-at-arms that the petty persecutions heretofore adverted to had proceeded – the corporal, having naturally enough concluded that his master could have no love for the sailor, made it his business, faithful understrapper that he was, to foment the ill blood by perverting to his chief certain innocent frolics of the good-natured foretopman, besides inventing for his mouth sundry contumelious epithets he claimed to have overheard him let fall. The master-at-arms never suspected the veracity of these reports, more especially as to the epithets, for he well knew how secretly unpopular may become a master-at-arms, at least a master-at-arms of those days, zealous in his function, and how the blue-jackets shoot at him in private their raillery and wit; the nickname by which he goes among them (Jemmy Legs) implying under the form of merriment their cherished disrespect and dislike. But in view of the greediness of hate for pabulum it hardly needed a purveyor to feed Claggart's passion.

An uncommon prudence is habitual with the subtler depravity, for it has everything to hide. And in case of an injury but suspected, its secretiveness voluntarily cuts it off from enlightenment or disillusion; and, not unreluctantly, action is taken upon surmise as upon certainty. And the retaliation is apt to be in monstrous disproportion to the supposed offense; for when in anybody was revenge in its exactions aught else but an inordinate usurer? But how with Claggart's conscience? For though consciences are unlike as foreheads, every intelligence, not excluding the scriptural devils who 'believe and tremble', has one. But Claggart's conscience being but the lawyer to his will, made ogres of trifles, probably arguing that the motive imputed to Billy in spilling the soup just when he did, together with the epithets alleged, these, if nothing more, made a strong case against him; nay, justified animosity into a sort of retributive righteousness. The Pharisee is the Guy Fawkes prowling in the hid chambers underlying some natures like Claggart's. And they can really form no conception of an unreciprocated malice. Probably the master-at-arms' clandestine persecution of Billy was started to try the temper of the man; but it had not developed any quality in him that enmity could make official use of or even pervert into plausible self-justification; so that the occurrence at the mess, petty if it were, was a welcome one to that peculiar conscience assigned to be the private mentor of Claggart; and, for the rest, not improbably it put him upon new experiments.

Chapter Fourteen

Not many days after the last incident narrated, something befell Billy Budd that more graveled him than aught that had previously occurred.

It was a warm night for the latitude; and the foretopman, whose watch at the time was properly below, was dozing on the uppermost deck whither he had ascended from his hot hammock, one of hundreds suspended so closely wedged together over a lower gun deck that there was little or no swing to them. He lay as in the shadow of a hillside, stretched under the lee of the booms, a piled ridge of spare spars amidships between foremast and mainmast among which the ship's largest boat, the launch, was stowed. Alongside of three other slumberers from below, he lay near that end of the booms which approaches the foremast; his station aloft on duty as a foretopman being just over the deck-station of the forecastlemen, entitling him according to usage to make himself more or less at home in that neighborhood.

Presently he was stirred into semiconsciousness by somebody, who must have previously sounded the sleep of the others, touching his shoulder, and then, as the foretopman raised his head, breathing into his ear in a quick whisper, 'Slip into the lee forechains, Billy; there is something in the wind. Don't speak. Quick, I will meet you there,' and disappearing.

Now Billy, like sundry other essentially good-natured ones, had some of the weaknesses inseparable from essential good nature; and among these was a reluctance, almost an incapacity of plumply saying *no* to an abrupt proposition not obviously absurd on the face of it, nor obviously unfriendly, nor iniquitous.

And being of warm blood, he had not the phlegm tacitly to negative any proposition by unresponsive inaction. Like his sense of
fear, his apprehension as to aught outside of the honest and natural was seldom very quick. Besides, upon the present occasion,
the drowse from his sleep still hung upon him.

However it was, he mechanically rose and, sleepily wondering
what could be in the wind, betook himself to the designated
place, a narrow platform, one of six, outside of the high bulwarks
and screened by the great deadeyes and multiple columned lan-
yards of the shrouds and backstays; and, in a great warship of
that time, of dimensions commensurate to the hull's magnitude;
a tarry balcony in short, overhanging the sea, and so secluded
that one mariner of the *Bellipotent*, a Nonconformist old tar of a
serious turn, made it even in daytime his private oratory.

In this retired nook the stranger soon joined Billy Budd. There
was no moon as yet; a haze obscured the starlight. He could not
distinctly see the stranger's face. Yet from something in the out-
line and carriage, Billy took him, and correctly, for one of the
afterguard.

'Hist! Billy,' said the man, in the same quick cautionary whisper as before. 'You were impressed, weren't you? Well, so was I';
and he paused, as to mark the effect. But Billy, not knowing
exactly what to make of this, said nothing. Then the other: 'We
are not the only impressed ones, Billy. There's a gang of us. –
Couldn't you – help – at a pinch?'

'What do you mean?' demanded Billy, here thoroughly shaking off his drowse.

'Hist, hist!' the hurried whisper now growing husky. 'See here,'
and the man held up two small objects faintly twinkling in the
night-light; 'see, they are yours, Billy, if you'll only –'

But Billy broke in, and in his resentful eagerness to deliver
himself his vocal infirmity somewhat intruded. 'D– d– damme, I
don't know what you are d– d– driving at, or what you mean, but
you had better g– g– go where you belong!' For the moment the

fellow, as confounded, did not stir; and Billy, springing to his feet, said, 'If you d– don't start, I'll t– t– toss you back over the r– rail!' There was no mistaking this, and the mysterious emissary decamped, disappearing in the direction of the mainmast in the shadow of the booms.

'Hallo, what's the matter?' here came growling from a fore-castleman awakened from his deck-doze by Billy's raised voice. And as the foretopman reappeared and was recognized by him: 'Ah, Beauty, is it you? Well, something must have been the matter, for you st– st– stuttered.'

'Oh,' rejoined Billy, now mastering the impediment, 'I found an afterguardsman in our part of the ship here, and I bid him be off where he belongs.'

'And is that all you did about it, Foretopman?' gruffly demanded another, an irascible old fellow of brick-colored visage and hair who was known to his associate forecastlemen as 'Red Pepper'. 'Such sneaks I should like to marry to the gunner's daughter!' – by that expression meaning that he would like to subject them to disciplinary castigation over a gun.

However, Billy's rendering of the matter satisfactorily accounted to these inquirers for the brief commotion, since of all the sections of a ship's company the forecastlemen, veterans for the most part and bigoted in their sea prejudices, are the most jealous in resenting territorial encroachments, especially on the part of any of the afterguard, of whom they have but a sorry opinion – chiefly landsmen, never going aloft except to reef or furl the mainsail, and in no wise competent to handle a marlin-spike or turn in a deadeye, say.

Chapter Fifteen

This incident sorely puzzled Billy Budd. It was an entirely new experience, the first time in his life that he had ever been personally approached in underhand intriguing fashion. Prior to this encounter he had known nothing of the afterguardsman, the two men being stationed wide apart, one forward and aloft during his watch, the other on deck and aft.

What could it mean? And could they really be guineas, those two glittering objects the interloper had held up to his (Billy's) eyes? Where could the fellow get guineas? Why, even spare buttons are not so plentiful at sea. The more he turned the matter over, the more he was nonplussed, and made uneasy and discomfited. In his disgustful recoil from an overture which, though he but ill comprehended, he instinctively knew must involve evil of some sort, Billy Budd was like a young horse fresh from the pasture suddenly inhaling a vile whiff from some chemical factory, and by repeated snortings trying to get it out of his nostrils and lungs. This frame of mind barred all desire of holding farther parley with the fellow, even were it but for the purpose of gaining some enlightenment as to his design in approaching him. And yet he was not without natural curiosity to see how such a visitor in the dark would look in broad day.

He espied him the following afternoon in his first dogwatch below, one of the smokers on that forward part of the upper gun deck allotted to the pipe. He recognized him by his general cut and build more than by his round freckled face and glassy eyes of pale blue, veiled with lashes all but white. And yet Billy was a bit uncertain whether indeed it were he – yonder chap about his own age chatting and laughing in freehearted way, leaning against a gun; a genial young fellow enough to look at, and something of a rattle-brain, to all appearance. Rather chubby too for a sailor, even an afterguardsman. In short, the last man in the world, one would think, to be overburdened with thoughts, especially those perilous thoughts that must needs belong to a conspirator in any serious project, or even to the underling of such a conspirator.

Although Billy was not aware of it, the fellow, with a sidelong watchful glance, had perceived Billy first, and then noting that Billy was looking at him, thereupon nodded a familiar sort of friendly recognition as to an old acquaintance, without interrupting the talk he was engaged in with the group of smokers. A day or two afterwards, chancing in the evening promenade on a gun deck to pass Billy, he offered a flying word of good-fellowship, as it were, which by its unexpectedness, and equivocalness under the circumstances, so embarrassed Billy that he knew not how to respond to it, and let it go unnoticed.

Billy was now left more at a loss than before. The ineffectual speculations into which he was led were so disturbingly alien to him that he did his best to smother them. It never entered his mind that here was a matter which, from its extreme question-ableness, it was his duty as a loyal bluejacket to report in the proper quarter. And, probably, had such a step been suggested to him, he would have been deterred from taking it by the thought, one of novice magnanimity, that it would savor overmuch of the dirty work of a telltale. He kept the thing to himself. Yet upon one occasion he could not forbear a little disburdening himself to the old Dansker, tempted thereto perhaps by the influence of a balmy night when the ship lay becalmed; the twain, silent for the most part, sitting together on deck, their heads propped against the bulwarks. But it was only a partial and anonymous account that Billy gave, the unfounded scruples above referred to prevent-ing full disclosure to anybody. Upon hearing Billy's version, the sage Dansker seemed to divine more than he was told; and after a little meditation, during which his wrinkles were pursed as into a point, quite effacing for the time that quizzing expression his face sometimes wore: 'Didn't I say so, Baby Budd?'

'Say what?' demanded Billy.

'Why, *Jemmy Legs* is *down* on you.'

'And what,' rejoined Billy in amazement, 'has *Jemmy Legs* to do with that cracked afterguardsman?'

'Ho, it was an afterguardsman, then. A cat's-paw, a cat's-paw!' And with that exclamation, whether it had reference to a light puff of air just then coming over the calm sea, or a subtler relation to the afterguardsman, there is no telling, the old Merlin gave a twisting wrench with his black teeth at his plug of tobacco, vouchsafing no reply to Billy's impetuous question, though now repeated, for it was his wont to relapse into grim silence when interrogated in skeptical sort as to any of his sententious oracles, not always very clear ones, rather partaking of that obscurity which invests most Delphic deliverances from any quarter.

Long experience had very likely brought this old man to that bitter prudence which never interferes in aught and never gives advice.

Chapter Sixteen

Yes, despite the Dansker's pithy insistence as to the master-at-arms being at the bottom of these strange experiences of Billy on board the *Bellipotent*, the young sailor was ready to ascribe them to almost anybody but the man who, to use Billy's own expression, 'always had a pleasant word for him'. This is to be wondered at. Yet not so much to be wondered at. In certain matters, some sailors even in mature life remain unsophisticated enough. But a young seafarer of the disposition of our athletic foretopman is much of a child-man. And yet a child's utter innocence is but its blank ignorance, and the innocence more or less wanes as intelligence waxes. But in Billy Budd intelligence, such as it was, had advanced while yet his simple-mindedness remained for the most part unaffected. Experience is a teacher indeed; yet did Billy's years make his experience small. Besides, he had none of that intuitive knowledge of the bad which in natures not good or incompletely so foreruns experience, and therefore may pertain, as in some instances it too clearly does pertain, even to youth.

And what could Billy know of man except of man as a mere sailor? And the old-fashioned sailor, the veritable man before the mast, the sailor from boyhood up, he, though indeed of the same species as a landsman, is in some respects singularly distinct from him. The sailor is frankness, the landsman is finesse. Life is not a game with the sailor, demanding the long head – no intricate games of chess where few moves are made in straightforwardness and ends are attained by indirection, an oblique, tedious, barren game hardly worth that poor candle burnt out in playing it.

Yes, as a class, sailors are in character a juvenile race. Even their deviations are marked by juvenility, this more especially holding true with the sailors of Billy's time. Then too, certain things which apply to all sailors do more pointedly operate here and there upon the junior one. Every sailor, too, is accustomed to obey orders without debating them; his life afloat is externally ruled for him; he is not brought into that promiscuous commerce with mankind where unobstructed free agency on equal terms – equal superficially, at least – soon teaches one that unless upon occasion he exercise a distrust keen in proportion to the fairness of the appearance, some foul turn may be served him. A ruled undemonstrative distrustfulness is so habitual, not with businessmen so much as with men who know their kind in less shallow relations than business, namely, certain men of the world, that they come at last to employ it all but unconsciously; and some of them would very likely feel real surprise at being charged with it as one of their general characteristics.

Chapter Seventeen

But after the little matter at the mess Billy Budd no more found himself in strange trouble at times about his hammock or his clothes bag or what not. As to that smile that occasionally sunned him, and the pleasant passing word, these were, if not more frequent, yet if anything more pronounced than before.

But for all that, there were certain other demonstrations now. When Claggart's unobserved glance happened to light on belted Billy rolling along the upper gun deck in the leisure of the second dogwatch, exchanging passing broadsides of fun with other young promenaders in the crowd, that glance would follow the cheerful sea Hyperion with a settled meditative and melancholy expression, his eyes strangely suffused with incipient feverish tears. Then would Claggart look like the man of sorrows. Yes, and sometimes the melancholy expression would have in it a touch of soft yearning, as if Claggart could even have loved Billy but for fate and ban. But this was an evanescence, and quickly repented of, as it were, by an immitigable look, pinching and shriveling the visage into the momentary semblance of a wrinkled walnut. But sometimes catching sight in advance of the foretopman coming in his direction, he would, upon their nearing, step aside a little to let him pass, dwelling upon Billy for the moment with the glittering dental satire of a Guise. But upon any abrupt unforeseen encounter a red light would flash forth from his eye like a spark from an anvil in a dusk smithy. That quick, fierce light was a strange one, darted from orbs which in repose were of a color nearest approaching a deeper violet, the softest of shades.

Though some of these caprices of the pit could not but be

observed by their object, yet were they beyond the construing of such a nature. And the thews of Billy were hardly compatible with that sort of sensitive spiritual organization which in some cases instinctively conveys to ignorant innocence an admonition of the proximity of the malign. He thought the master-at-arms acted in a manner rather queer at times. That was all. But the occasional frank air and pleasant word went for what they purported to be, the young sailor never having heard as yet of the 'too fair-spoken man'.

Had the foretopman been conscious of having done or said anything to provoke the ill will of the official, it would have been different with him, and his sight might have been purged if not sharpened. As it was, innocence was his blinder.

So was it with him in yet another matter. Two minor officers, the armorer and captain of the hold, with whom he had never exchanged a word, his position in the ship not bringing him into contact with them, these men now for the first began to cast upon Billy, when they chanced to encounter him, that peculiar glance which evidences that the man from whom it comes has been some way tampered with, and to the prejudice of him upon whom the glance lights. Never did it occur to Billy as a thing to be noted or a thing suspicious, though he well knew the fact, that the armorer and captain of the hold, with the ship's yeoman, apothecary, and others of that grade, were by naval usage messmates of the master-at-arms, men with ears convenient to his confidential tongue.

But the general popularity that came from our Handsome Sailor's manly forwardness upon occasion and irresistible good nature, indicating no mental superiority tending to excite an invidious feeling, this good will on the part of most of his shipmates made him the less to concern himself about such mute aspects toward him as those whereto allusion has just been made, aspects he could not so fathom as to infer their whole import.

As to the afterguardsman, though Billy for reasons already

given necessarily saw little of him, yet when the two did happen to meet, invariably came the fellow's offhand cheerful recognition, sometimes accompanied by a passing pleasant word or two. Whatever that equivocal young person's original design may really have been, or the design of which he might have been the deputy, certain it was from his manner upon these occasions that he had wholly dropped it.

It was as if his precocity of crookedness (and every vulgar villain is precocious) had for once deceived him, and the man he had sought to entrap as a simpleton had through his very simplicity ignominiously baffled him.

But shrewd ones may opine that it was hardly possible for Billy to refrain from going up to the afterguardsman and bluntly demanding to know his purpose in the initial interview so abruptly closed in the forechains. Shrewd ones may also think it but natural in Billy to set about sounding some of the other impressed men of the ship in order to discover what basis, if any, there was for the emissary's obscure suggestions as to plotting disaffection aboard. Yes, shrewd ones may so think. But something more, or rather something else than mere shrewdness is perhaps needful for the due understanding of such a character as Billy Budd's.

As to Claggart, the monomania in the man – if that indeed it were – as involuntarily disclosed by starts in the manifestations detailed, yet in general covered over by his self-contained and rational demeanor; this, like a subterranean fire, was eating its way deeper and deeper in him. Something decisive must come of it.

Chapter Eighteen

After the mysterious interview in the forechains, the one so abruptly ended there by Billy, nothing especially germane to the story occurred until the events now about to be narrated.

Elsewhere it has been said that in the lack of frigates (of course better sailers than line-of-battle ships) in the English squadron up the Straits at that period, the *Bellipotent* 74 was occasionally employed not only as an available substitute for a scout, but at times on detached service of more important kind. This was not alone because of her sailing qualities, not common in a ship of her rate, but quite as much, probably, that the character of her commander, it was thought, specially adapted him for any duty where under unforeseen difficulties a prompt initiative might have to be taken in some matter demanding knowledge and ability in addition to those qualities implied in good seamanship. It was on an expedition of the latter sort, a somewhat distant one, and when the *Bellipotent* was almost at her furthest remove from the fleet, that in the latter part of an afternoon watch she unexpectedly came in sight of a ship of the enemy. It proved to be a frigate. The latter, perceiving through the glass that the weight of men and metal would be heavily against her, invoking her light heels crowded sail to get away. After a chase urged almost against hope and lasting until about the middle of the first dogwatch, she signally succeeded in effecting her escape.

Not long after the pursuit had been given up, and ere the excitement incident thereto had altogether waned away, the master-at-arms, ascending from his cavernous sphere, made his appearance cap in hand by the mainmast respectfully waiting the notice of Captain Vere, then solitary walking the weather side of the quarter-deck, doubtless somewhat chafed at the failure of the pursuit. The spot where Claggart stood was the place allotted to men of lesser grades seeking some more particular interview either with the officer of the deck or the captain himself. But from the latter it was not often that a sailor or petty officer of those days would seek a hearing; only some exceptional cause would, according to established custom, have warranted that.

Presently, just as the commander, absorbed in his reflections, was on the point of turning aft in his promenade, he became sensible of Claggart's presence, and saw the doffed cap held in deferential expectancy. Here be it said that Captain Vere's personal knowledge of this petty officer had only begun at the time of the ship's last sailing from home, Claggart then for the first, in transfer from a ship detained for repairs, supplying on board the *Bellipotent* the place of a previous master-at-arms disabled and ashore.

No sooner did the commander observe who it was that now deferentially stood awaiting his notice than a peculiar expression came over him. It was not unlike that which uncontrollably will flit across the countenance of one at unawares encountering a person who, though known to him indeed, has hardly been long enough known for thorough knowledge, but something in whose aspect nevertheless now for the first provokes a vaguely repellent distaste. But coming to a stand and resuming much of his wonted official manner, save that a sort of impatience lurked in the intonation of the opening word, he said, 'Well? What is it, Master-at-arms?'

With the air of a subordinate grieved at the necessity of being a messenger of ill tidings, and while conscientiously determined to be frank yet equally resolved upon shunning overstatement, Claggart at this invitation, or rather summons to disburden, spoke up. What he said, conveyed in the language of no uneducated man, was to the effect following, if not altogether in these words, namely, that during the chase and preparations for the possible encounter he had seen enough to convince him that at least one sailor aboard was a dangerous character in a ship mustering some who not only had taken a guilty part in the late serious troubles, but others also who, like the man in question, had entered His Majesty's service under another form than enlistment.

At this point Captain Vere with some impatience interrupted him: 'Be direct, man; say *impressed men.*'

Claggart made a gesture of subservience, and proceeded. Quite lately he (Claggart) had begun to suspect that on the gun decks some sort of movement prompted by the sailor in question was covertly going on, but he had not thought himself warranted in reporting the suspicion so long as it remained indistinct. But from what he had that afternoon observed in the man referred to, the suspicion of something clandestine going on had advanced to a point less removed from certainty. He deeply felt, he added, the serious responsibility assumed in making a report involving such possible consequences to the individual mainly concerned, besides tending to augment those natural anxieties which every naval commander must feel in view of extraordinary outbreaks so recent as those which, he sorrowfully said it, it needed not to name.

Now at the first broaching of the matter Captain Vere, taken by surprise, could not wholly dissemble his disquietude. But as Claggart went on, the former's aspect changed into restiveness under something in the testifier's manner in giving his testimony. However, he refrained from interrupting him. And Claggart, continuing, concluded with this: 'God forbid, your honor, that the *Bellipotent*'s should be the experience of the –'

'Never mind that!' here peremptorily broke in the superior, his face altering with anger, instinctively divining the ship that the other was about to name, one in which the Nore Mutiny had assumed a singularly tragical character that for a time jeopardized the life of its commander. Under the circumstances he was indignant at the purposed allusion. When the commissioned officers themselves were on all occasions very heedful how they referred to the recent events in the fleet, for a petty officer unnecessarily to allude to them in the presence of his captain, this struck him as a most immodest presumption. Besides, to his quick sense of self-respect it even looked under the circumstances something like an attempt to alarm him. Nor at first was he without some surprise that one who so far as he had hitherto come under his notice had shown considerable tact in his function should in this particular evince such lack of it.

But these thoughts and kindred dubious ones flitting across his mind were suddenly replaced by an intuitional surmise which, though as yet obscure in form, served practically to affect his reception of the ill tidings. Certain it is that, long versed in everything pertaining to the complicated gun-deck life, which like every other form of life has its secret mines and dubious side, the side popularly disclaimed, Captain Vere did not permit himself to be unduly disturbed by the general tenor of his subordinate's report.

Furthermore, if in view of recent events prompt action should be taken at the first palpable sign of recurring insubordination, for all that, not judicious would it be, he thought, to keep the idea of lingering disaffection alive by undue forwardness in crediting an informer, even if his own subordinate and charged among other things with police surveillance of the crew. This feeling would not perhaps have so prevailed with him were it not that upon a prior occasion the patriotic zeal officially evinced by Claggart had somewhat irritated him as appearing rather supersensible and strained. Furthermore, something even in the official's self-possessed and somewhat ostentatious manner in making his specifications strangely reminded him of a bandsman, a perjurous witness in a capital case before a courtmartial ashore of which when a lieutenant he (Captain Vere) had been a member.

Now the peremptory check given to Claggart in the matter of

the arrested allusion was quickly followed up by this: 'You say that there is at least one dangerous man aboard. Name him.'

'William Budd, a foretopman, your honor.'

'William Budd!' repeated Captain Vere with unfeigned astonishment. 'And mean you the man that Lieutenant Ratcliffe took from the merchantman not very long ago, the young fellow who seems to be so popular with the men – Billy the Handsome Sailor, as they call him?'

'The same, your honor; but for all his youth and good looks, a deep one. Not for nothing does he insinuate himself into the good will of his shipmates, since at the least they will at a pinch say – all hands will – a good word for him, and at all hazards. Did Lieutenant Ratcliffe happen to tell your honor of that adroit fling of Budd's, jumping up in the cutter's bow under the merchantman's stern when he was being taken off? It is even masked by that sort of good-humored air that at heart he resents his impressment. You have but noted his fair cheek. A mantrap may be under the ruddy-tipped daisies.'

Now the Handsome Sailor as a signal figure among the crew had naturally enough attracted the captain's attention from the first. Though in general not very demonstrative to his officers, he had congratulated Lieutenant Ratcliffe upon his good fortune in lighting on such a fine specimen of the *genus homo*, who in the nude might have posed for a statue of a young Adam before the Fall. As to Billy's adieu to the ship *Rights-of-Man*, which the boarding lieutenant had indeed reported to him, but, in a deferential way, more as a good story than aught else, Captain Vere, though mistakenly understanding it as a satiric sally, had but thought so much the better of the impressed man for it; as a military sailor, admiring the spirit that could take an arbitrary enlistment so merrily and sensibly. The foretopman's conduct, too, so far as it had fallen under the captain's notice, had confirmed the first happy augury, while the new recruit's qualities as a 'sailorman' seemed to be such that he had thought of recommending him to the executive officer for promotion to a place that would more frequently bring him under his own observation, namely, the captaincy of the mizzentop, replacing there in the starboard watch a man not so young whom partly for that reason he deemed less fitted for the post. Be it parenthesized here that since the mizzentopmen have not to handle such breadths of heavy canvas as the lower sails on the mainmast and foremast, a young man if of the right stuff not only seems best adapted to duty there, but in fact is generally selected for the captaincy of that top, and the company under him are light hands and often but striplings. In sum, Captain Vere had from the beginning deemed Billy Budd to be what in the naval parlance of the time was called a 'King's bargain': that is to say, for His Britannic Majesty's navy a capital investment at small outlay or none at all.

After a brief pause, during which the reminiscences above mentioned passed vividly through his mind and he weighed the import of Claggart's last suggestion conveyed in the phrase 'mantrap under the daisies', and the more he weighed it the less reliance he felt in the informer's good faith, suddenly he turned upon him and in a low voice demanded: 'Do you come to me, Master-at-arms, with so foggy a tale? As to Budd, cite me an act or spoken word of his confirmatory of what you in general charge against him. Stay,' drawing nearer to him; 'heed what you speak. Just now, and in a case like this, there is a yardarm-end for the false witness.'

'Ah, your honor!' sighed Claggart, mildly shaking his shapely head as in sad deprecation of such unmerited severity of tone. Then, bridling – erecting himself as in virtuous self-assertion – he circumstantially alleged certain words and acts which collectively, if credited, led to presumptions mortally inculpating Budd. And for some of these averments, he added, substantiating proof was not far.

With gray eyes impatient and distrustful essaying to fathom to the bottom Claggart's calm violet ones, Captain Vere again heard him out; then for the moment stood ruminating. The mood he evinced, Claggart – himself for the time liberated from the other's scrutiny – steadily regarded with a look difficult to render: a look curious of the operation of his tactics, a look such as might have been that of the spokesman of the envious children of Jacob deceptively imposing upon the troubled patriarch the blood-dyed coat of young Joseph.

Though something exceptional in the moral quality of Captain Vere made him, in earnest encounter with a fellow man, a veritable touchstone of that man's essential nature, yet now as to Claggart and what was really going on in him his feeling partook less of intuitional conviction than of strong suspicion clogged by strange dubieties. The perplexity he evinced proceeded less from aught touching the man informed against – as Claggart doubtless opined – than from considerations how best to act in regard to the informer. At first, indeed, he was naturally for summoning that substantiation of his allegations which Claggart said was at hand. But such a proceeding would result in the matter at once getting abroad, which in the present stage of it, he thought, might undesirably affect the ship's company. If Claggart was a false witness – that closed the affair. And therefore, before trying the accusation, he would first practically test the accuser; and he thought this could be done in a quiet, undemonstrative way.

The measure he determined upon involved a shifting of the scene, a transfer to a place less exposed to observation than the broad quarter-deck. For although the few gun-room officers there at the time had, in due observance of naval etiquette, withdrawn to leeward the moment Captain Vere had begun his promenade on the deck's weather side; and though during the colloquy with Claggart they of course ventured not to diminish the distance; and though throughout the interview Captain Vere's voice was far from him, and Claggart's silvery and low; and the wind in the cordage and the wash of the sea helped the more to put them beyond earshot; nevertheless, the interview's continuance already had attracted observation from some top-men aloft and other sailors in the waist or further forward.

Having determined upon his measures, Captain Vere forth-with took action. Abruptly turning to Claggart, he asked, 'Master-at-arms, is it now Budd's watch aloft?'

'No, your honor.'

Whereupon, 'Mr Wilkes!' summoning the nearest midship-man. 'Tell Albert to come to me.' Albert was the captain's hammock-boy, a sort of sea valet in whose discretion and fidelity his master had much confidence. The lad appeared.

'You know Budd, the foretopman?'

'I do, sir.'

'Go find him. It is his watch off. Manage to tell him out of ear-shot that he is wanted aft. Contrive it that he speaks to nobody. Keep him in talk yourself. And not till you get well aft here, not till then let him know that the place where he is wanted is my cabin. You understand. Go. – Master-at-arms, show yourself on the decks below, and when you think it time for Albert to be com-ing with his man, stand by quietly to follow the sailor in.'

Chapter Nineteen

Now when the foretopman found himself in the cabin, closeted there, as it were, with the captain and Claggart, he was surprised enough. But it was a surprise unaccompanied by apprehension or distrust. To an immature nature essentially honest and humane, forewarning intimations of subtler danger from one's kind come tardily if at all. The only thing that took shape in the young sailor's mind was this: Yes, the captain, I have always thought, looks kindly upon me. Wonder if he's going to make me his coxswain. I should like that. And may be now he is going to ask the master-at-arms about me.

'Shut the door there, sentry,' said the commander; 'stand without, and let nobody come in. – Now, Master-at-arms, tell this man to his face what you told of him to me,' and stood prepared to scrutinize the mutually confronting visages.

With the measured step and calm collected air of an asylum physician approaching in the public hall some patient beginning to show indications of a coming paroxysm, Claggart deliberately advanced within short range of Billy and, mesmerically looking him in the eye, briefly recapitulated the accusation.

Not at first did Billy take it in. When he did, the rose-tan of his cheek looked struck as by white leprosy. He stood like one impaled and gagged. Meanwhile the accuser's eyes, removing not as yet from the blue dilated ones, underwent a phenomenal change, their wonted rich violet color blurring into a muddy purple. Those lights of human intelligence, losing human expression, were gelidly protruding like the alien eyes of certain uncatalogued creatures of the deep. The first mesmeristic glance was one of serpent fascination; the last was the paralyzing lurch of the torpedo fish.

'Speak, man!' said Captain Vere to the transfixed one, struck by his aspect even more than by Claggart's. 'Speak! Defend yourself!' Which appeal caused but a strange dumb gesturing and gurgling in Billy; amazement at such an accusation so suddenly sprung on inexperienced nonage; this, and, it may be, horror of the accuser's eyes, serving to bring out his lurking defect and in this instance for the time intensifying it into a convulsed tongue-tie; while the intent head and entire form straining forward in an agony of ineffectual eagerness to obey the injunction to speak and defend himself, gave an expression to the face like that of a condemned vestal priestess in the moment of being buried alive, and in the first struggle against suffocation.

Though at the time Captain Vere was quite ignorant of Billy's liability to vocal impediment, he now immediately divined it, since vividly Billy's aspect recalled to him that of a bright young schoolmate of his whom he had once seen struck by much the same startling impotence in the act of eagerly rising in the class to be foremost in response to a testing question put to it by the master. Going close up to the young sailor, and laying a soothing hand on his shoulder, he said, 'There is no hurry, my boy. Take your time, take your time.' Contrary to the effect intended, these words so fatherly in tone, doubtless touching Billy's heart to the quick, prompted yet more violent efforts at utterance – efforts soon ending for the time in confirming the paralysis, and bringing to his face an expression which was as a crucifixion to behold. The next instant, quick as the flame from a discharged cannon at night, his right arm shot out, and Claggart dropped to the deck. Whether intentionally or but owing to the young athlete's superior height, the blow had taken effect full upon the forehead, so shapely and intellectual-looking a feature in the master-at-arms; so that the body fell over lengthwise, like a heavy plank tilted from erectness. A gasp or two, and he lay motionless.

'Fated boy,' breathed Captain Vere in tone so low as to be almost a whisper, 'what have you done! But here, help me.'

The twain raised the felled one from the loins up into a sitting position. The spare form flexibly acquiesced, but inertly. It was like handling a dead snake. They lowered it back. Regaining erectness, Captain Vere with one hand covering his face stood to all appearance as impassive as the object at his feet. Was he absorbed in taking in all the bearings of the event and what was best not only now at once to be done, but also in the sequel? Slowly he uncovered his face; and the effect was as if the moon emerging from eclipse should reappear with quite another aspect than that which had gone into hiding. The father in him, manifested towards Billy thus far in the scene, was replaced by the military disciplinarian. In his official tone he bade the foretopman retire to a stateroom aft (pointing it out), and there remain till thence summoned. This order Billy in silence mechanically obeyed. Then going to the cabin door where it opened on the quarter-deck, Captain Vere said to the sentry without, 'Tell somebody to send Albert here.' When the lad appeared, his master so contrived it that he should not catch sight of the prone one. 'Albert,' he said to him, 'tell the surgeon I wish to see him. You need not come back till called.'

When the surgeon entered – a self-poised character of that grave sense and experience that hardly anything could take him aback – Captain Vere advanced to meet him, thus unconsciously intercepting his view of Claggart, and, interrupting the other's wonted ceremonious salutation, said, 'Nay. Tell me how it is with yonder man,' directing his attention to the prostrate one.

The surgeon looked, and for all his self-command somewhat started at the abrupt revelation. On Claggart's always pallid complexion, thick black blood was now oozing from nostril and ear. To the gazer's professional eye it was unmistakably no living man that he saw.

'Is it so, then?' said Captain Vere, intently watching him. 'I thought it. But verify it.' Whereupon the customary tests confirmed the surgeon's first glance, who now, looking up in unfeigned concern, cast a look of intense inquisitiveness upon his superior. But Captain Vere, with one hand to his brow, was standing motionless. Suddenly, catching the surgeon's arm convulsively, he exclaimed, pointing down to the body, 'It is the divine judgment on Ananias! Look!'

Disturbed by the excited manner he had never before observed in the *Bellipotent*'s captain, and as yet wholly ignorant of the affair, the prudent surgeon nevertheless held his peace, only again looking an earnest interrogatory as to what it was that had resulted in such a tragedy.

But Captain Vere was now again motionless, standing absorbed in thought. Again starting, he vehemently exclaimed, 'Struck dead by an angel of God! Yet the angel must hang!'

At these passionate interjections, mere incoherences to the listener as yet unapprised of the antecedents, the surgeon was profoundly discomposed. But now, as recollecting himself, Captain Vere in less passionate tone briefly related the circumstances leading up to the event. 'But come; we must dispatch,' he added. 'Help me to remove him' (meaning the body) 'to yonder compartment,' designating one opposite that where the foretopman remained immured. Anew disturbed by a request that, as implying a desire for secrecy, seemed unaccountably strange to him, there was nothing for the subordinate to do but comply.

'Go now,' said Captain Vere with something of his wonted manner. 'Go now. I presently shall call a drumhead court. Tell the lieutenants what has happened, and tell Mr Mordant' (meaning the captain of marines), 'and charge them to keep the matter to themselves.'

Chapter Twenty

Full of disquietude and misgiving, the surgeon left the cabin. Was Captain Vere suddenly affected in his mind, or was it but a transient excitement, brought about by so strange and extraordinary a tragedy? As to the drumhead court, it struck the surgeon as impolitic, if nothing more. The thing to do, he thought, was to place Billy Budd in confinement, and in a way dictated by usage, and postpone further action in so extraordinary a case to such time as they should rejoin the squadron, and then refer it to the admiral. He recalled the unwonted agitation of Captain Vere and his excited exclamations, so at variance with his normal manner. Was he unhinged?

But assuming that he is, it is not so susceptible of proof. What then can the surgeon do? No more trying situation is conceivable than that of an officer subordinate under a captain whom he suspects to be not mad, indeed, but yet not quite unaffected in his intellects. To argue his order to him would be insolence. To resist him would be mutiny.

In obedience to Captain Vere, he communicated what had happened to the lieutenants and captain of marines, saying nothing as to the captain's state. They fully shared his own surprise and concern. Like him too, they seemed to think that such a matter should be referred to the admiral.

Chapter Twenty-One

Who in the rainbow can draw the line where the violet tint ends and the orange tint begins? Distinctly we see the difference of the colors, but where exactly does the one first blendingly enter into the other? So with sanity and insanity. In pronounced cases there is no question about them. But in some supposed cases, in various degrees supposedly less pronounced, to draw the exact line of demarcation few will undertake, though for a fee becoming considerate some professional experts will. There is nothing nameable but that some men will, or undertake to, do it for pay.

Whether Captain Vere, as the surgeon professionally and privately surmised, was really the sudden victim of any degree of aberration, every one must determine for himself by such light as this narrative may afford.

That the unhappy event which has been narrated could not have happened at a worse juncture was but too true. For it was close on the heel of the suppressed insurrections, an aftertime very critical to naval authority, demanding from every English sea commander two qualities not readily interfusable – prudence and rigor. Moreover, there was something crucial in the case.

In the jugglery of circumstances preceding and attending the event on board the *Bellipotent*, and in the light of that martial code whereby it was formally to be judged, innocence and guilt personified in Claggart and Budd in effect changed places. In a legal view the apparent victim of the tragedy was he who had sought to victimize a man blameless; and the indisputable deed of the latter, navally regarded, constituted the most heinous of military crimes. Yet more. The essential right and wrong involved in the matter, the clearer that might be, so much the worse for the responsibility of a loyal sea commander, inasmuch as he was not authorized to determine the matter on that primitive basis.

Small wonder then that the *Bellipotent*'s captain, though in general a man of rapid decision, felt that circumspectness not less than promptitude was necessary. Until he could decide upon his course, and in each detail; and not only so, but until the concluding measure was upon the point of being enacted, he deemed it advisable, in view of all the circumstances, to guard as much as possible against publicity. Here he may or may not have erred. Certain it is, however, that subsequently in the confidential talk of more than one or two gun rooms and cabins he was not a little criticized by some officers, a fact imputed by his friends and vehemently by his cousin Jack Denton to professional jealousy of Starry Vere. Some imaginative ground for invidious comment there was. The maintenance of secrecy in the matter, the confining all knowledge of it for a time to the place where the homicide occurred, the quarterdeck cabin; in these particulars lurked some resemblance to the policy adopted in those tragedies of the palace which have occurred more than once in the capital founded by Peter the Barbarian.

The case indeed was such that fain would the *Bellipotent*'s captain have deferred taking any action whatever respecting it further than to keep the foretopman a close prisoner till the ship rejoined the squadron and then submitting the matter to the judgment of his admiral.

But a true military officer is in one particular like a true monk. Not with more of self-abnegation will the latter keep his vows of monastic obedience than the former his vows of allegiance to martial duty.

Feeling that unless quick action was taken on it, the deed of the foretopman, so soon as it should be known on the gun decks, would tend to awaken any slumbering embers of the Nore among the crew, a sense of the urgency of the case overruled in Captain Vere every other consideration. But though a conscientious disciplinarian, he was no lover of authority for mere authority's sake. Very far was he from embracing opportunities for monopolizing to himself the perils of moral responsibility, none at least that could properly be referred to an official superior or shared with him by his official equals or even subordinates. So thinking, he was glad it would not be at variance with usage to turn the matter over to a summary court of his own officers, reserving to himself, as the one on whom the ultimate accountability would rest, the right of maintaining a supervision of it, or formally or informally interposing at need. Accordingly a drumhead court was summarily convened, he electing the individuals composing it: the first lieutenant, the captain of marines, and the sailing master.

In associating an officer of marines with the sea lieutenant and the sailing master in a case having to do with a sailor, the commander perhaps deviated from general custom. He was prompted thereto by the circumstance that he took that soldier to be a judicious person, thoughtful, and not altogether incapable of grappling with a difficult case unprecedented in his prior experience. Yet even as to him he was not without some latent misgiving, for withal he was an extremely good-natured man, an enjoyer of his dinner, a sound sleeper, and inclined to obesity – a man who though he would always maintain his manhood in battle might not prove altogether reliable in a moral dilemma involving aught of the tragic. As to the first lieutenant and the sailing master, Captain Vere could not but be aware that though honest natures, of approved gallantry upon occasion, their intelligence was mostly confined to the matter of active seamanship and the fighting demands of their profession.

The court was held in the same cabin where the unfortunate affair had taken place. This cabin, the commander's, embraced the entire area under the poop deck. Aft, and on either side, was a small stateroom, the one now temporarily a jail and the other a dead-house, and a yet smaller compartment, leaving a space between expanding forward into a goodly oblong of length coinciding with the ship's beam. A skylight of moderate dimension was overhead, and at each end of the oblong space were two sashed porthole windows easily convertible back into embrasures for short carronades.

All being quickly in readiness, Billy Budd was arraigned, Captain Vere necessarily appearing as the sole witness in the case, and as such temporarily sinking his rank, though singularly maintaining it in a matter apparently trivial, namely, that he testified from the ship's weather side, with that object having caused the court to sit on the lee side. Concisely he narrated all that had led up to the catastrophe, omitting nothing in Claggart's accusation and deposing as to the manner in which the prisoner had received it. At this testimony the three officers glanced with no little surprise at Billy Budd, the last man they would have suspected either of the mutinous design alleged by Claggart or the undeniable deed he himself had done. The first lieutenant, taking judicial primacy and turning toward the prisoner, said, 'Captain Vere has spoken. Is it or is it not as Captain Vere says?'

In response came syllables not so much impeded in the utterance as might have been anticipated. They were these: 'Captain Vere tells the truth. It is just as Captain Vere says, but it is not as the master-at-arms said. I have eaten the King's bread and I am true to the King.'

'I believe you, my man,' said the witness, his voice indicating a suppressed emotion not otherwise betrayed.

'God will bless you for that, your honor!' not without stammering said Billy, and all but broke down. But immediately he was recalled to self-control by another question, to which with the same emotional difficulty of utterance he said, 'No, there was no malice between us. I never bore malice against the master-at-arms. I am sorry that he is dead. I did not mean to kill him. Could I have used my tongue I would not have struck him. But he foully lied to my face and in presence of my captain, and I had to say something, and I could only say it with a blow, God help me!'

In the impulsive aboveboard manner of the frank one the court saw confirmed all that was implied in words that just previously had perplexed them, coming as they did from the testifier to the tragedy and promptly following Billy's impassioned disclaimer of mutinous intent – Captain Vere's words, 'I believe you, my man.'

Next it was asked of him whether he knew of or suspected aught savoring of incipient trouble (meaning mutiny, though the explicit term was avoided) going on in any section of the ship's company.

The reply lingered. This was naturally imputed by the court to the same vocal embarrassment which had retarded or obstructed previous answers. But in main it was otherwise here, the question immediately recalling to Billy's mind the interview with the afterguardsman in the forechains. But an innate repugnance to playing a part at all approaching that of an informer against one's own shipmates – the same erring sense of uninstructed honor which had stood in the way of his reporting the matter at the time, though as a loyal man-of-war's man it was incumbent on him, and failure so to do, if charged against him and proven, would have subjected him to the heaviest of penalties; this, with the blind feeling now his that nothing really was being hatched, prevailed with him. When the answer came it was a negative.

'One question more,' said the officer of marines, now first speaking and with a troubled earnestness. 'You tell us that what the master-at-arms said against you was a lie. Now why should he have so lied, so maliciously lied, since you declare there was no malice between you?'

At that question, unintentionally touching on a spiritual sphere wholly obscure to Billy's thoughts, he was nonplussed, evincing a confusion indeed that some observers, such as can readily be imagined, would have construed into involuntary evidence of hidden guilt. Nevertheless, he strove some way to answer, but all at once relinquished the vain endeavor, at the same time turning an appealing glance towards Captain Vere as deeming him his best helper and friend. Captain Vere, who had been seated for a time, rose to his feet, addressing the interrogator. 'The question you put to him comes naturally enough. But how can he rightly answer it? – or anybody else, unless indeed it be he who lies within there,' designating the compartment where lay the corpse. 'But the prone one there will not rise to our summons. In effect, though, as it seems to me, the point you make is hardly material. Quite aside from any conceivable motive actuating the master-at-arms, and irrespective of the provocation to the blow, a martial court must needs in the present case confine its attention to the blow's consequence, which consequence justly is to be deemed not otherwise than as the striker's deed.'

This utterance, the full significance of which it was not at all likely that Billy took in, nevertheless caused him to turn a wistful interrogative look toward the speaker, a look in its dumb expressiveness not unlike that which a dog of generous breed might turn upon his master, seeking in his face some elucidation of a previous gesture ambiguous to the canine intelligence. Nor was the same utterance without marked effect upon the three officers, more especially the soldier. Couched in it seemed to them a meaning unanticipated, involving a prejudgment on the speaker's part. It served to augment a mental disturbance previously evident enough.

The soldier once more spoke, in a tone of suggestive dubiety addressing at once his associates and Captain Vere: 'Nobody is present – none of the ship's company, I mean – who might shed lateral light, if any is to be had, upon what remains mysterious in this matter.'

'That is thoughtfully put,' said Captain Vere; 'I see your drift. Ay, there is a mystery; but, to use a scriptural phrase, it is a "mystery of iniquity", a matter for psychologic theologians to discuss. But what has a military court to do with it? Not to add that for us any possible investigation of it is cut off by the lasting tongue-tie of – him – in yonder,' again designating the mortuary stateroom. 'The prisoner's deed – with that alone we have to do.'

To this, and particularly the closing reiteration, the marine soldier, knowing not how aptly to reply, sadly abstained from saying aught. The first lieutenant, who at the outset had not unnaturally assumed primacy in the court, now overrulingly instructed by a glance from Captain Vere, a glance more effective than words, resumed that primacy. Turning to the prisoner, 'Budd,' he said, and scarce in equable tones, 'Budd, if you have aught further to say for yourself, say it now.'

Upon this the young sailor turned another quick glance toward Captain Vere; then, as taking a hint from that aspect, a hint confirming his own instinct that silence was now best, replied to the lieutenant, 'I have said all, sir.'

The marine – the same who had been the sentinel without the cabin door at the time that the foretopman, followed by the master-at-arms, entered it – he, standing by the sailor throughout these judicial proceedings, was now directed to take him back to the after compartment originally assigned to the prisoner and his custodian. As the twain disappeared from view, the three officers, as partially liberated from some inward constraint associated with Billy's mere presence, simultaneously stirred in their seats. They exchanged looks of troubled indecision, yet feeling that decide they must and without long delay. For Captain Vere, he for the time stood – unconsciously with his back toward them, apparently in one of his absent fits – gazing out from a sashed porthole to windward upon the monotonous blank of the twilight sea. But the court's silence continuing, broken only at moments by brief consultations, in low earnest tones, this served to arouse him and energize him. Turning, he to-and-fro paced the cabin athwart; in the returning ascent to windward climbing the slant deck in the ship's lee roll, without knowing it symbolizing thus in his action a mind resolute to surmount difficulties even if against primitive instincts strong as the wind and the sea. Presently he came to a stand before the three. After scanning their faces he stood less as mustering his thoughts for expression than as one inly deliberating how best to put them to well-meaning men not intellectually mature, men with whom it was necessary to demonstrate certain principles that were axioms to himself. Similar impatience as to talking is perhaps one reason that deters some minds from addressing any popular assemblies.

When speak he did, something, both in the substance of what he said and his manner of saying it, showed the influence of unshared studies modifying and tempering the practical training of an active career. This, along with his phraseology, now and then was suggestive of the grounds whereon rested that imputation of a certain pedantry socially alleged against him by certain naval men of wholly practical cast, captains who nevertheless would frankly concede that His Majesty's navy mustered no more efficient officer of their grade than Starry Vere.

What he said was to this effect: 'Hitherto I have been but the witness, little more; and I should hardly think now to take another tone, that of your coadjutor for the time, did I not perceive in you – at the crisis too – a troubled hesitancy, proceeding, I doubt not, from the clash of military duty with moral scruple – scruple vitalized by compassion. For the compassion, how can I otherwise than share it? But, mindful of paramount obligations, I strive against scruples that may tend to enervate decision. Not, gentlemen, that I hide from myself that the case is an exceptional one. Speculatively regarded, it well might be referred to a jury of casuists. But for us here, acting not as casuists or moralists, it is a case practical, and under martial law practically to be dealt with.

'But your scruples: do they move as in a dusk? Challenge them. Make them advance and declare themselves. Come now; do they import something like this: If, mindless of palliating circumstances, we are bound to regard the death of the master-at-arms as the prisoner's deed, then does that deed constitute a capital crime whereof the penalty is a mortal one? But in natural justice is nothing but the prisoner's overt act to be considered? How can we adjudge to summary and shameful death a fellow creature innocent before God, and whom we feel to be so? – Does that state it aright? You sign sad assent. Well, I too feel that, the full force of that. It is Nature. But do these buttons that we wear attest that our allegiance is to Nature? No, to the King. Though the ocean, which is inviolate Nature primeval, though this be the element where we move and have our being as sailors, yet as the King's officers lies our duty in a sphere correspondingly natural? So little is that true, that in receiving our commissions we in the most important regards ceased to be natural free agents. When war is declared are we the commissioned fighters previously consulted? We fight at command. If our judgments approve the war, that is but coincidence. So in other particulars. So now. For suppose condemnation to follow these present proceedings. Would it be so much we ourselves that would condemn as it would be martial law operating through us? For that law and the rigor of it, we are not responsible. Our vowed responsibility is in this: That however pitilessly that law may operate in any instances, we nevertheless adhere to it and administer it.

'But the exceptional in the matter moves the hearts within you. Even so too is mine moved. But let not warm hearts betray heads that should be cool. Ashore in a criminal case, will an upright judge allow himself off the bench to be waylaid by some tender kinswoman of the accused seeking to touch him with her tearful plea? Well, the heart here, sometimes the feminine in man, is as that piteous woman, and hard though it be, she must here be ruled out.'

He paused, earnestly studying them for a moment; then resumed.

'But something in your aspect seems to urge that it is not solely the heart that moves in you, but also the conscience, the private conscience. But tell me whether or not, occupying the position we do, private conscience should not yield to that imperial one formulated in the code under which alone we officially proceed?'

Here the three men moved in their seats, less convinced than agitated by the course of an argument troubling but the more the spontaneous conflict within.

Perceiving which, the speaker paused for a moment; then abruptly changing his tone, went on.

'To steady us a bit, let us recur to the facts. – In wartime at sea a man-of-war's man strikes his superior in grade, and the blow kills. Apart from its effect the blow itself is, according to the Articles of War, a capital crime. Furthermore –'

'Ay, sir,' emotionally broke in the officer of marines, 'in one sense it was. But surely Budd proposed neither mutiny nor homicide.'

'Surely not, my good man. And before a court less arbitrary and more merciful than a martial one, that plea would largely extenuate. At the Last Assizes it shall acquit. But how here? We proceed under the law of the Mutiny Act. In feature no child can resemble his father more than that Act resembles in spirit the thing from which it derives – War. In His Majesty's service – in this ship, indeed – there are Englishmen forced to fight for the King against their will. Against their conscience, for aught we know. Though as their fellow creatures some of us may appreciate their position, yet as navy officers what reck we of it? Still less recks the enemy. Our impressed men he would fain cut down in the same swath with our volunteers. As regards the enemy's naval conscripts, some of whom may even share our own abhorrence of the regicidal French Directory, it is the same on our side. War looks but to the frontage, the appearance. And the Mutiny Act, War's child, takes after the father. Budd's intent or non-intent is nothing to the purpose.

'But while, put to it by those anxieties in you which I cannot but respect, I only repeat myself – while thus strangely we prolong proceedings that should be summary – the enemy may be sighted and an engagement result. We must do; and one of two things must we do – condemn or let go.'

'Can we not convict and yet mitigate the penalty?' asked the sailing master, here speaking, and falteringly, for the first.

'Gentlemen, were that clearly lawful for us under the circumstances, consider the consequences of such clemency. The people' (meaning the ship's company) 'have native sense; most of them are familiar with our naval usage and tradition; and how would they take it? Even could you explain to them – which our official position forbids – they, long molded by arbitrary discipline, have not that kind of intelligent responsiveness that might qualify them to comprehend and discriminate. No, to the people the foretopman's deed, however it be worded in the announcement, will be plain homicide committed in a flagrant act of mutiny. What penalty for that should follow, they know. But it does not follow. *Why?* they will ruminate. You know what sailors are. Will they not revert to the recent outbreak at the Nore? Ay. They know the well-founded alarm – the panic it struck throughout England. Your clement sentence they would account pusillanimous. They would think that we flinch, that we are afraid of them – afraid of practicing a lawful rigor singularly demanded at this juncture, lest it should provoke new troubles. What shame to us such a conjecture on their part, and how deadly to discipline. You see then, whither, prompted by duty and the law, I steadfastly drive. But I beseech you, my friends, do not take me amiss. I feel as you do for this unfortunate boy. But did he know our hearts, I take him to be of that generous nature that he would feel even for us on whom in this military necessity so heavy a compulsion is laid.'

With that, crossing the deck he resumed his place by the sashed porthole, tacitly leaving the three to come to a decision. On the cabin's opposite side the troubled court sat silent. Loyal lieges, plain and practical, though at bottom they dissented from some points Captain Vere had put to them, they were without the faculty, hardly had the inclination, to gainsay one whom they felt to be an earnest man, one too not less their superior in mind than in naval rank. But it is not improbable that even such of his words as were not without influence over them, less came home to them than his closing appeal to their instinct as sea officers: in the forethought he threw out as to the practical consequences to discipline, considering the unconfirmed tone of the fleet at the time, should a man-of-war's man's violent killing at sea of a superior in grade be allowed to pass for aught else than a capital crime demanding prompt infliction of the penalty.

Not unlikely they were brought to something more or less akin to that harassed frame of mind which in the year 1842 actuated the commander of the U.S. brig-of-war *Somers* to resolve, under the so-called Articles of War, Articles modeled upon the English Mutiny Act, to resolve upon the execution at sea of a midshipman and two sailors as mutineers designing the seizure of the brig. Which resolution was carried out though in a time of peace and within not many days' sail of home. An act vindicated by a naval court of inquiry subsequently convened ashore. History, and here cited without comment. True, the circumstances on board the *Somers* were different from those on board the *Bellipotent*. But the urgency felt, well-warranted or otherwise, was much the same.

Says a writer whom few know, 'Forty years after a battle it is easy for a noncombatant to reason about how it ought to have been fought. It is another thing personally and under fire to have to direct the fighting while involved in the obscuring smoke of it. Much so with respect to other emergencies involving considerations both practical and moral, and when it is imperative promptly to act. The greater the fog the more it imperils the steamer, and speed is put on though at the hazard of running somebody down. Little ween the snug card players in the cabin of the responsibilities of the sleepless man on the bridge.'

In brief, Billy Budd was formally convicted and sentenced to be hung at the yardarm in the early morning watch, it being now night. Otherwise, as is customary in such cases, the sentence would forthwith have been carried out. In wartime on the field or in the fleet, a mortal punishment decreed by a drumhead court – on the field sometimes decreed by but a nod from the general – follows without delay on the heel of conviction, without appeal.

Chapter Twenty-Two

It was Captain Vere himself who of his own motion communicated the finding of the court to the prisoner, for that purpose going to the compartment where he was in custody and bidding the marine there to withdraw for the time.

Beyond the communication of the sentence, what took place at this interview was never known. But in view of the character of the twain briefly closeted in that stateroom, each radically sharing in the rarer qualities of our nature – so rare indeed as to be all but incredible to average minds however much cultivated – some conjectures may be ventured.

It would have been in consonance with the spirit of Captain Vere should he on this occasion have concealed nothing from the condemned one – should he indeed have frankly disclosed to him the part he himself had played in bringing about the decision, at the same time revealing his actuating motives. On Billy's side it is not improbable that such a confession would have been received in much the same spirit that prompted it. Not without a sort of joy, indeed, he might have appreciated the brave opinion of him implied in his captain's making such a confidant of him. Nor, as to the sentence itself, could he have been insensible that it was imparted to him as to one not afraid to die. Even more may have been. Captain Vere in end may have developed the passion sometimes latent under an exterior stoical or indifferent. He was old enough to have been Billy's father. The austere devotee of military duty, letting himself melt back into what remains primeval in our formalized humanity, may in end have caught Billy to his heart, even as Abraham may have caught young Isaac on the brink of resolutely offering him up in obedience to the exacting behest. But there is no telling the sacrament, seldom if in any case revealed to the gadding world, wherever under circumstances at all akin to those here attempted to be set forth two of great Nature's nobler order embrace. There is privacy at the time, inviolable to the survivor; and holy oblivion, the sequel to each diviner magnanimity, providentially covers all at last.

The first to encounter Captain Vere in act of leaving the compartment was the senior lieutenant. The face he beheld, for the moment one expressive of the agony of the strong, was to that officer, though a man of fifty, a startling revelation. That the condemned one suffered less than he who mainly had effected the condemnation was apparently indicated by the former's exclamation in the scene soon perforce to be touched upon.

Chapter Twenty-Three

Of a series of incidents with a brief term rapidly following each other, the adequate narration may take up a term less brief, especially if explanation or comment here and there seem requisite to the better understanding of such incidents. Between the entrance into the cabin of him who never left it alive, and him who when he did leave it left it as one condemned to die; between this and the closeted interview just given, less than an hour and a half had elapsed. It was an interval long enough, however, to awaken speculations among no few of the ship's company as to what it was that could be detaining in the cabin the master-at-arms and the sailor; for a rumor that both of them had been seen to enter it and neither of them had been seen to emerge, this rumor had got abroad upon the gun decks and in the tops, the people of a great warship being in one respect like villagers, taking microscopic note of every outward movement or non-movement going on. When therefore, in weather not at all tempestuous, all hands were called in the second dogwatch, a summons under such circumstances not usual in those hours, the crew were not wholly unprepared for some announcement extraordinary, one having connection too with the continued absence of the two men from their wonted haunts.

There was a moderate sea at the time; and the moon, newly risen and near to being at its full, silvered the white spar deck wherever not blotted by the clear-cut shadows horizontally thrown of fixtures and moving men. On either side the quarterdeck the marine guard under arms was drawn up; and Captain Vere, standing in his place surrounded by all the wardroom officers, addressed his men. In so doing, his manner showed neither more nor less than that properly pertaining to his supreme position aboard his own ship. In clear terms and concise he told them what had taken place in the cabin: that the master-at-arms was dead, that he who had killed him had been already tried by a summary court and condemned to death, and that the execution would take place in the early morning watch. The word *mutiny* was not named in what he said. He refrained too from making the occasion an opportunity for any preachment as to the maintenance of discipline, thinking perhaps that under existing circumstances in the navy the consequence of violating discipline should be made to speak for itself.

Their captain's announcement was listened to by the throng of standing sailors in a dumbness like that of a seated congregation of believers in hell listening to the clergyman's announcement of his Calvinistic text.

At the close, however, a confused murmur went up. It began to wax. All but instantly, then, at a sign, it was pierced and suppressed by shrill whistles of the boatswain and his mates. The word was given to about ship.

To be prepared for burial Claggart's body was delivered to certain petty officers of his mess. And here, not to clog the sequel with lateral matters, it may be added that at a suitable hour, the master-at-arms was committed to the sea with every funeral honor properly belonging to his naval grade.

In this proceeding as in every public one growing out of the tragedy strict adherence to usage was observed. Nor in any point could it have been at all deviated from, either with respect to Claggart or Billy Budd, without begetting undesirable speculations in the ship's company, sailors, and more particularly men-of-war's men, being of all men the greatest sticklers for usage. For similar cause, all communication between Captain Vere and the condemned one ended with the closeted interview already given, the latter being now surrendered to the ordinary routine preliminary to the end. His transfer under guard from

the captain's quarters was effected without unusual precautions –
at least no visible ones. If possible, not to let the men so much as
surmise that their officers anticipate aught amiss from them is
the tacit rule in a military ship. And the more that some sort of
trouble should really be apprehended, the more do the officers
keep that apprehension to themselves, though not the less unos-
tentatious vigilance may be augmented. In the present instance,
the sentry placed over the prisoner had strict orders to let no one
have communication with him but the chaplain. And certain
unobtrusive measures were taken absolutely to insure this point.

Chapter Twenty-Four

In a seventy-four of the old order the deck known as the upper gun deck was the one covered over by the spar deck, which last, though not without its armament, was for the most part exposed to the weather. In general it was at all hours free from hammocks; those of the crew swinging on the lower gun deck and berth deck, the latter being not only a dormitory but also the place for the stowing of the sailors' bags, and on both sides lined with the large chests or movable pantries of the many messes of the men.

On the starboard side of the *Bellipotent*'s upper gun deck, behold Billy Budd under sentry lying prone in irons in one of the bays formed by the regular spacing of the guns comprising the batteries on either side. All these pieces were of the heavier caliber of that period. Mounted on lumbering wooden carriages, they were hampered with cumbersome harness of breeching and strong side-tackles for running them out. Guns and carriages, together with the long rammers and shorter linstocks lodged in loops overhead – all these, as customary, were painted black; and the heavy hempen breechings, tarred to the same tint, wore the like livery of the undertakers. In contrast with the funereal hue of these surroundings, the prone sailor's exterior apparel, white jumper and white duck trousers, each more or less soiled, dimly glimmered in the obscure light of the bay like a patch of discolored snow in early April lingering at some upland cave's black mouth. In effect he is already in his shroud, or the garments that shall serve him in lieu of one. Over him but scarce illuminating him, two battle lanterns swing from two massive beams of the deck above. Fed with the oil supplied by the war contractors (whose gains, honest or otherwise, are in every land an anticipated portion of the harvest of death), with flickering splashes of dirty yellow light they pollute the pale moonshine all but ineffectually struggling in obstructed flecks through the open ports from which the tampioned cannon protrude. Other lanterns at intervals serve but to bring out somewhat the obscurer bays which, like small confessionals or side-chapels in a cathedral, branch from the long dim-vistaed broad aisle between the two batteries of that covered tier.

Such was the deck where now lay the Handsome Sailor. Through the rose-tan of his complexion no pallor could have shown. It would have taken days of sequestration from the winds and the sun to have brought about the effacement of that. But the skeleton in the cheekbone at the point of its angle was just beginning delicately to be defined under the warm-tinted skin. In fervid hearts self-contained, some brief experiences devour our human tissue as secret fire in a ship's hold consumes cotton in the bale.

But now lying between the two guns, as nipped in the vice of fate, Billy's agony, mainly proceeding from a generous young heart's virgin experience of the diabolical incarnate and effective in some men – the tension of that agony was over now. It survived not the something healing in the closeted interview with Captain Vere. Without movement, he lay as in a trance, that adolescent expression previously noted as his taking on something akin to the look of a slumbering child in the cradle when the warm hearth-glow of the still chamber at night plays on the dimples that at whiles mysteriously form in the cheek, silently coming and going there. For now and then in the gyved one's trance a serene happy light born of some wandering reminiscence or dream would diffuse itself over his face, and then wane away only anew to return.

The chaplain, coming to see him and finding him thus, and perceiving no sign that he was conscious of his presence, attentively regarded him for a space, then slipping aside, withdrew for the time, peradventure feeling that even he, the minister of Christ though receiving his stipend from Mars, had no consolation to proffer which could result in a peace transcending that which he beheld. But in the small hours he came again. And the prisoner, now awake to his surroundings, noticed his approach, and civilly, all but cheerfully, welcomed him. But it was to little purpose that in the interview following, the good man sought to bring Billy Budd to some godly understanding that he must die, and at dawn. True, Billy himself freely referred to his death as a thing close at hand; but it was something in the way that children will refer to death in general, who yet among their other sports will play a funeral with hearse and mourners.

Not that like children Billy was incapable of conceiving what death really is. No, but he was wholly without irrational fear of it, a fear more prevalent in highly civilized communities than those so-called barbarous ones which in all respects stand nearer to unadulterate Nature. And, as elsewhere said, a barbarian Billy radically was – as much so, for all the costume, as his countrymen the British captives, living trophies, made to march in the Roman triumph of Germanicus. Quite as much so as those later barbarians, young men probably, and picked specimens among the earlier British converts to Christianity, at least nominally such, taken to Rome (as today converts from lesser isles of the sea may be taken to London), of whom the Pope at that time, admiring the strangeness of their personal beauty so unlike the Italian stamp, their clear ruddy complexion and curled flaxen locks, exclaimed, 'Angles' (meaning *English*, the modern derivative), 'Angles, do you call them? And is it because they look so like angels?' Had it been later in time, one would think that the Pope had in mind Fra Angelico's seraphs, some of whom, plucking apples in gardens of the Hesperides, have the faint rosebud complexion of the more beautiful English girls.

If in vain the good chaplain sought to impress the young barbarian with ideas of death akin to those conveyed in the skull, dial and crossbones on old tombstones, equally futile to all appearance were his efforts to bring home to him the thought of salvation and a Savior. Billy listened, but less out of awe or reverence, perhaps, than from a certain natural politeness, doubtless at bottom regarding all that in much the same way that most mariners of his class take any discourse abstract or out of the common tone of the workaday world. And this sailor way of taking clerical discourse is not wholly unlike the way in which the primer of Christianity, full of transcendent miracles, was received long ago on tropic isles by any superior *savage*, so called – a Tahitian, say, of Captain Cook's time or shortly after that time. Out of natural courtesy he received, but did not appropriate. It was like a gift placed in the palm of an outreached hand upon which the fingers do not close.

But the *Bellipotent*'s chaplain was a discreet man possessing the good sense of a good heart. So he insisted not in his vocation here. At the instance of Captain Vere, a lieutenant had apprised him of pretty much everything as to Billy; and since he felt that innocence was even a better thing than religion wherewith to go to Judgment, he reluctantly withdrew; but in his emotion not without first performing an act strange enough in an Englishman, and under the circumstances yet more so in any regular priest. Stooping over, he kissed on the fair cheek his fellow man, a felon in martial law, one whom though on the confines of death he felt he could never convert to a dogma; nor for all that did he fear for his future.

Marvel not that having been made acquainted with the young sailor's essential innocence the worthy man lifted not a finger to avert the doom of such a martyr to martial discipline. So to do would not only have been as idle as invoking the desert, but would also have been an audacious transgression of the bounds of his function, one as exactly prescribed to him by military law as that of the boatswain or any other naval officer. Bluntly put, a chaplain is the minister of the Prince of Peace serving in the host of the God of War – Mars. As such, he is as incongruous as a musket would be on the altar at Christmas. Why, then, is he there? Because he indirectly subserves the purpose attested by the cannon; because too he lends the sanction of the religion of the meek to that which practically is the abrogation of everything but brute Force.

Chapter Twenty-Five

The night so luminous on the spar deck, but otherwise on the cavernous ones below, levels so like the tiered galleries in a coal mine – the luminous night passed away. But like the prophet in the chariot disappearing in heaven and dropping his mantle to Elisha, the withdrawing night transferred its pale robe to the breaking day. A meek, shy light appeared in the East, where stretched a diaphanous fleece of white furrowed vapor. That light slowly waxed. Suddenly *eight bells* was struck aft, responded to by one louder metallic stroke from forward. It was four o'clock in the morning. Instantly the silver whistles were heard summoning all hands to witness punishment. Up through the great hatchways rimmed with racks of heavy shot the watch below came pouring, overspreading with the watch already on deck the space between the mainmast and foremast including that occupied by the capacious launch and the black booms tiered on either side of it, boat and booms making a summit of observation for the powder-boys and younger tars. A different group comprising one watch of topmen leaned over the rail of that sea balcony, no small one in a seventy-four, looking down on the crowd below. Man or boy, none spake but in whisper, and few spake at all. Captain Vere – as before, the central figure among the assembled commissioned officers – stood nigh the break of the poop deck facing forward. Just below him on the quarter-deck the marines in full equipment were drawn up much as at the scene of the promulgated sentence.

At sea in the old time, the execution by halter of a military sailor was generally from the foreyard. In the present instance, for special reasons the mainyard was assigned. Under an arm of that yard the prisoner was presently brought up, the chaplain attending him. It was noted at the time, and remarked upon afterwards, that in this final scene the good man evinced little or nothing of the perfunctory. Brief speech indeed he had with the condemned one, but the genuine Gospel was less on his tongue than in his aspect and manner towards him. The final preparations personal to the latter being speedily brought to an end by two boatswain's mates, the consummation impended. Billy stood facing aft. At the penultimate moment, his words, his only ones, words wholly unobstructed in the utterance, were these: 'God bless Captain Vere!' Syllables so unanticipated coming from one with the ignominious hemp about his neck – a conventional felon's benediction directed aft towards the quarters of honor; syllables too delivered in the clear melody of a singing bird on the point of launching from the twig – had a phenomenal effect, not unenhanced by the rare personal beauty of the young sailor, spiritualized now through late experiences so poignantly profound.

Without volition, as it were, as if indeed the ship's populace were but the vehicles of some vocal current electric, with one voice from alow and aloft came a resonant sympathetic echo: 'God bless Captain Vere!' And yet at that instant Billy alone must have been in their hearts, even as in their eyes.

At the pronounced words and the spontaneous echo that voluminously rebounded them, Captain Vere, either through stoic self-control or a sort of momentary paralysis induced by emotional shock, stood erectly rigid as a musket in the ship-armorer's rack.

The hull, deliberately recovering from the periodic roll to leeward, was just regaining an even keel when the last signal, a preconcerted dumb one, was given. At the same moment it chanced that the vapory fleece hanging low in the East was shot through with a soft glory as of the fleece of the Lamb of God seen in mystical vision, and simultaneously therewith, watched by the wedged mass of upturned faces, Billy ascended; and, ascending, took the full rose of the dawn.

In the pinioned figure arrived at the yard-end, to the wonder of all no motion was apparent, none save that created by the slow roll of the hull in moderate weather, so majestic in a great ship ponderously cannoned.

Chapter Twenty-Six

When some days afterwards, in reference to the singularity just mentioned, the purser, a rather ruddy, rotund person more accurate as an accountant than profound as a philosopher, said at mess to the surgeon, 'What testimony to the force lodged in will power,' the latter, saturnine, spare, and tall, one in whom a discreet causticity went along with a manner less genial than polite, replied, 'Your pardon, Mr Purser. In a hanging scientifically conducted – and under special orders I myself directed how Budd's was to be effected – any movement following the completed suspension and originating in the body suspended, such movement indicates mechanical spasm in the muscular system. Hence the absence of that is no more attributable to will power, as you call it, than to horsepower – begging your pardon.'

'But this muscular spasm you speak of, is not that in a degree more or less invariable in these cases?'

'Assuredly so, Mr Purser.'

'How then, my good sir, do you account for its absence in this instance?'

'Mr Purser, it is clear that your sense of the singularity in this matter equals not mine. You account for it by what you call will power – a term not yet included in the lexicon of science. For me, I do not, with my present knowledge, pretend to account for it at all. Even should we assume the hypothesis that at the first touch of the halyards the action of Budd's heart, intensified by extraordinary emotion at its climax, abruptly stopped – much like a watch when in carelessly winding it up you strain at the finish, thus snapping the chain – even under that hypothesis how account for the phenomenon that followed?'

'You admit, then, that the absence of spasmodic movement was phenomenal.'

'It was phenomenal, Mr Purser, in the sense that it was an appearance the cause of which is not immediately to be assigned.'

'But tell me, my dear sir,' pertinaciously continued the other, 'was the man's death effected by the halter, or was it a species of euthanasia?'

'*Euthanasia*, Mr Purser, is something like your *will power*: I doubt its authenticity as a scientific term – begging your pardon again. It is at once imaginative and metaphysical – in short, Greek. – But,' abruptly changing his tone, 'there is a case in the sick bay that I do not care to leave to my assistants. Beg your pardon, but excuse me.' And rising from the mess he formally withdrew.

Chapter Twenty-Seven

The silence at the moment of execution and for a moment or two continuing thereafter, a silence but emphasized by the regular wash of the sea against the hull or the flutter of a sail caused by the helmsman's eyes being tempted astray, this emphasized silence was gradually disturbed by a sound not easily to be verbally rendered. Whoever has heard the freshet-wave of a torrent suddenly swelled by pouring showers in tropical mountains, showers not shared by the plain; whoever has heard the first muffled murmur of its sloping advance through precipitous woods may form some conception of the sound now heard. The seeming remoteness of its source was because of its murmurous indistinctness, since it came from close by, even from the men passed on the ship's open deck. Being inarticulate, it was dubious in significance further than it seemed to indicate some capricious revulsion of thought or feeling such as mobs ashore are liable to, in the present instance possibly implying a sullen revocation on the men's part of their involuntary echoing of Billy's benediction. But ere the murmur had time to wax into clamor it was met by a strategic command, the more telling that it came with abrupt unexpectedness: 'Pipe down the starboard watch, Boatswain, and see that they go.'

Shrill as the shriek of the sea hawk, the silver whistles of the boatswain and his mates pierced that ominous low sound, dissipating it; and yielding to the mechanism of discipline the throng was thinned by one-half. For the remainder, most of them were set to temporary employments connected with trimming the yards and so forth, business readily to be got up to serve occasion by any officer of the deck.

Now each proceeding that follows a mortal sentence

pronounced at sea by a drumhead court is characterized by promptitude not perceptibly merging into hurry, though bordering that. The hammock, the one which had been Billy's bed when alive, having already been ballasted with shot and otherwise prepared to serve for his canvas coffin, the last offices of the sea undertakers, the sailmaker's mates, were now speedily completed. When everything was in readiness a second call for all hands, made necessary by the strategic movement before mentioned, was sounded, now to witness burial.

The details of this closing formality it needs not to give. But when the tilted plank let slide its freight into the sea, a second strange human murmur was heard, blended now with another inarticulate sound proceeding from certain larger seafowl who, their attention having been attracted by the peculiar commotion in the water resulting from the heavy sloped dive of the shotted hammock into the sea, flew screaming to the spot. So near the hull did they come, that the stridor or bony creak of their gaunt double-jointed pinions was audible. As the ship under light airs passed on, leaving the burial spot astern, they still kept circling it low down with the moving shadow of their outstretched wings and the croaked requiem of their cries.

Upon sailors as superstitious as those of the age preceding ours, men-of-war's men too who had just beheld the prodigy of repose in the form suspended in air, and now foundering in the deeps; to such mariners the action of the seafowl, though dictated by mere animal greed for prey, was big with no prosaic significance. An uncertain movement began among them, in which some encroachment was made. It was tolerated but for a moment. For suddenly the drum beat to quarters, which familiar sound happening at least twice every day, had upon the present occasion a signal peremptoriness in it. True martial discipline long continued superinduces in average man a sort of impulse whose operation at the official word of command much resembles in its promptitude the effect of an instinct.

The drumbeat dissolved the multitude, distributing most of them along the batteries of the two covered gun decks. There, as wonted, the guns' crews stood by their respective cannon erect and silent. In due course the first officer, sword under arm and standing in his place on the quarter-deck, formally received the successive reports of the sworded lieutenants commanding the sections of batteries below; the last of which reports being made, the summed report he delivered with the customary salute to the commander. All this occupied time, which in the present case was the object in beating to quarters at an hour prior to the customary one. That such variance from usage was authorized by an officer like Captain Vere, a martinet as some deemed him, was evidence of the necessity for unusual action implied in what he deemed to be temporarily the mood of his men: 'With mankind,' he would say, 'forms, measured forms, are everything; and this is the import couched in the story of Orpheus with his lyre spellbinding the wild denizens of the wood.' And this he once applied to the disruption of forms going on across the Channel and the consequences thereof.

At this unwonted muster at quarters, all proceeded as at the regular hour. The band on the quarter-deck played a sacred air, after which the chaplain went through the customary morning service. That done, the drum beat the retreat; and toned by music and religious rites subserving the discipline and purposes of war, the men in their wonted orderly manner dispersed to the places allotted them when not at the guns.

And now it was full day. The fleece of low-hanging vapor had vanished, licked up by the sun that late had so glorified it. And the circumambient air in the clearness of its serenity was like smooth white marble in the polished block not yet removed from the marble-dealer's yard.

Chapter Twenty-Eight

The symmetry of form attainable in pure fiction cannot so readily be achieved in a narration essentially having less to do with fable than with fact. Truth uncompromisingly told will always have its ragged edges; hence the conclusion of such a narration is apt to be less finished than an architectural finial.

How it fared with the Handsome Sailor during the year of the Great Mutiny has been faithfully given. But though properly the story ends with his life, something in way of sequel will not be amiss. Three brief chapters will suffice.

In the general rechristening under the Directory of the craft originally forming the navy of the French monarchy, the *St Louis* line-of-battle ship was named the *Athée* (the *Atheist*). Such a name, like some other substituted ones in the Revolutionary fleet, while proclaiming the infidel audacity of the ruling power, was yet, though not so intended to be, the aptest name, if one consider it, ever given to a warship; far more so indeed than the *Devastation*, the *Erebus* (the *Hell*), and similar names bestowed upon fighting ships.

On the return passage to the English fleet from the detached cruise during which occurred the events already recorded, the *Bellipotent* fell in with the *Athée*. An engagement ensued, during which Captain Vere, in the act of putting his ship alongside the enemy with a view of throwing his boarders across her bulwarks, was hit by a musket ball from a porthole of the enemy's main cabin. More than disabled, he dropped to the deck and was carried below to the same cockpit where some of his men already lay. The senior lieutenant took command. Under him the enemy was finally captured, and though much crippled was by rare good fortune successfully taken into Gibraltar, an English port not very distant from the scene of the fight. There, Captain Vere with the rest of the wounded was put ashore. He lingered for some days, but the end came. Unhappily he was cut off too early for the Nile and Trafalgar. The spirit that 'spite its philosophic austerity may yet have indulged in the most secret of all passions, ambition, never attained to the fulness of fame.

Not long before death, while lying under the influence of that magical drug which, soothing the physical frame, mysteriously operates on the subtler element in man, he was heard to murmur words inexplicable to his attendant: 'Billy Budd, Billy Budd.' That these were not the accents of remorse would seem clear from what the attendant said to the *Bellipotent*'s senior officer of marines, who, as the most reluctant to condemn of the members of the drumhead court, too well knew, though here he kept the knowledge to himself, who Billy Budd was.

Chapter Twenty-Nine

Some few weeks after the execution, among other matters under the head of 'News from the Mediterranean', there appeared in a naval chronicle of the time, an authorized weekly publication, an account of the affair. It was doubtless for the most part written in good faith, though the medium, partly rumor, through which the facts must have reached the writer served to deflect and in part falsify them. The account was as follows:

'On the tenth of the last month a deplorable occurrence took place on board H.M.S. *Bellipotent*. John Claggart, the ship's master-at-arms, discovering that some sort of plot was incipient among an inferior section of the ship's company, and that the ringleader was one William Budd; he, Claggart, in the act of arraigning the man before the captain, was vindictively stabbed to the heart by the suddenly drawn sheath knife of Budd.

'The deed and the implement employed sufficiently suggest that though mustered into the service under an English name the assassin was no Englishman, but one of those aliens adopting English cognomens whom the present extraordinary necessities of the service have caused to be admitted into it in considerable numbers.

'The enormity of the crime and the extreme depravity of the criminal appear the greater in view of the character of the victim, a middle-aged man respectable and discreet, belonging to that minor official grade, the petty officers, upon whom, as none know better than the commissioned gentlemen, the efficiency of His Majesty's navy so largely depends. His function was a responsible one, at once onerous and thankless; and his fidelity in it the greater because of his strong patriotic impulse. In this instance as in so many other instances in these days, the character of this unfortunate man signally refutes, if refutation were needed, that peevish saying attributed to the late Dr Johnson, that patriotism is the last refuge of a scoundrel.

'The criminal paid the penalty of his crime. The promptitude of the punishment has proved salutary. Nothing amiss is now apprehended aboard H.M.S. *Bellipotent*.'

The above, appearing in a publication now long ago super-annuated and forgotten, is all that hitherto has stood in human record to attest what manner of men respectively were John Claggart and Billy Budd.

Chapter Thirty

Everything is for a term venerated in navies. Any tangible object associated with some striking incident of the service is converted into a monument. The spar from which the foretopman was suspended was for some few years kept trace of by the bluejackets. Their knowledges followed it from ship to dockyard and again from dockyard to ship, still pursuing it even when at last reduced to a mere dockyard boom. To them a chip of it was as a piece of the Cross. Ignorant though they were of the secret facts of the tragedy, and not thinking but that the penalty was somehow unavoidably inflicted from the naval point of view, for all that, they instinctively felt that Billy was a sort of man as incapable of mutiny as of wilful murder. They recalled the fresh young image of the Handsome Sailor, that face never deformed by a sneer or subtler vile freak of the heart within. This impression of him was doubtless deepened by the fact that he was gone, and in a measure mysteriously gone. On the gun decks of the *Bellipotent* the general estimate of his nature and its unconscious simplicity eventually found rude utterance from another foretopman, one of his own watch, gifted, as some sailors are, with an artless *poetic* temperament. The tarry hand made some lines which, after circulating among the shipboard crews for a while, finally got rudely printed at Portsmouth as a ballad. The title given to it was the sailor's.

BILLY IN THE DARBIES

Good of the chaplain to enter Lone Bay
And down on his marrowbones here and pray
For the likes just o' me, Billy Budd. – But, look:

Through the port comes the moonshine astray!
It tips the guard's cutlass and silvers this nook;
But 'twill die in the dawning of Billy's last day.
A jewel-block they'll make of me tomorrow,
Pendant pearl from the yardarm-end
Like the eardrop I gave to Bristol Molly –
O, 'tis me, not the sentence they'll suspend.
Ay, ay, all is up; and I must up too,
Early in the morning, aloft from alow.
On an empty stomach now never it would do.
They'll give me a nibble – bit o' biscuit ere I go.
Sure, a messmate will reach me the last parting cup;
But, turning heads away from the hoist and the belay,
Heaven knows who will have the running of me up!
No pipe to those halyards. – But aren't it all sham?
A blur's in my eyes; it is dreaming that I am.
A hatchet to my hawser? All adrift to go?
The drum roll to grog, and Billy never know?
But Donald he has promised to stand by the plank
So I'll shake a friendly hand ere I sink.
But – no! It is dead then I'll be, come to think.
I remember Taff the Welshman when he sank.
And his cheek it was like the budding pink.
But me they'll lash in hammock, drop me deep.
Fathoms down, fathoms down, how I'll dream fast asleep
I feel it stealing now. Sentry, are you there?
Just ease these darbies at the wrist,
And roll me over fair!
I am sleepy, and the oozy weeds about me twist.

The Confidence-Man: His Masquerade

by Daniel G. Hoffman

'Strike through the mask!'
—Ahab

I

After *Moby-Dick*, Melville, like Ishmael, managed to survive. Such a survival demanded the Stoic virtues; romantic heroism he had abjured, and the affirmative primitive energies of Eros and Momus were henceforth blighted. In *Moby-Dick* the inner conflicts of the individual and the outer conflicts between the soul and its environment had been magnificently fused. His next two major efforts tried to deal with these problems singly. Emerging from the involuted ambiguities of *Pierre*, Melville turned from that too-personal narrative to one last attempt at a panoramic view of society. Every reader of *The Confidence-Man* as struck by the diminuation of the scale of character and action. The confidence man himself deprecates the mode of the book: 'Irony is so unjust; never could abide irony; something Satanic about irony. God defend me from Irony, and Satire, his bosom friend.' Now there is no mighty hero, no world-mastering whale, no tattooed savages. The great hunters of *Moby-Dick* are replaced, in irony and satire, by these lesser breeds:

Natives of all sorts, and foreigners; men of business and men of pleasure; parlor-men and backwoodsmen; farm-hunters and fame-hunters; heiress-hunters, gold-hunters, buffalo-hunters, bee-hunters, happiness-hunters, truth-hunters, and still keener hunters after all these hunters.

Melville's main interest is in the last-named hunters. The only Ishmael we can find aboard the riverboat *Fidèle* is a frontiersman – a truth-hunter who, despite his truculent independence and strong mind, is nonetheless duped, as are all the other hunters, by the confidence man.

The balanced encompassing of all the antimonies of experience, which saved Ishmael in *Moby-Dick*, had not proved possible for Herman Melville in life. 'Lord, when shall we be done with growing?' Melville had written Hawthorne just after finishing *The Whale*; 'As long as we have anything more to do, we have done nothing. So, now, let us add Moby-Dick to our blessings, and step from that. Leviathan is not the biggest fish; – I have heard of Krakens.' But this ebullience could not last. Hawthorne gives this account of Melville's state of mind five years later, just after writing *The Confidence-Man*:

> Melville, as he always does, began to reason of Providence and futurity, and of everything that lies beyond human ken, and informed me that he had 'pretty much made up his mind to be annihilated'; but still he does not seem to rest in that anticipation; and, I think, will never rest until he gets hold of a definite belief. It is strange how he persists – and has persisted ever since I knew him, and probably long before – in wandering to-and-fro over these deserts, as dismal and monotonous as the sand hills amid which we were sitting. He can neither believe, nor be comfortable in his unbelief; and he is too honest and courageous not to try to do one or the other.

In *The Confidence-Man* Melville wanders to-and-fro over the deserts of an American world in which humane values are impossible and divine laws remain shrouded in mysteries impenetrable to anyone aboard his 'ship of fools.' This is a despairing book, a bitter book, a work of Byzantine ingenuity. It is as though Melville, denied Ishmael's godlike power to grasp the farthest limits of life, tries, and tries, and tries to spin out of the knotted web of severely limited experience the furtive pattern of truth. In *The Confidence-Man* experience *is* severely limited – to the operations of a swindler on a riverboat, playing, it would seem, for low cash stakes. But each of his diddles demands 'full confidence' of his dupe, and each is a 'type' of the Fall of Man.

Despairing though it be, *The Confidence-Man* has a wry gusto that carries the reader over its vertiginous argument. Stylistically it is distinguished, and marks a radical departure from both the high rhetoric and the comic palaver of *Moby-Dick*. This style has a new satiric edge sharpened by images as unexpected as they are apt:

> The miser, a lean old man, whose flesh seemed salted codfish. . . .
> His cheek lay upon and old white moleskin coat, rolled under his
> head like a wizened apple upon a grimy snowbank.

And there is a new rhythm, whose involutions, even in descriptive passages, dramatize the serpentine twistings of reason proposed by the confidence man:

> Goneril was young, in person lithe and straight. . . . Upon the
> whole, aided by the resources of the toilet, her appearance at dis-
> tance was such, that some might have thought her, if anything,
> rather beautiful, though of a style of beauty rather peculiar and
> cactus-like.

What is given is taken away; what is removed, lingers. All is equivocal here.

The literary, philosophical, and cultural materials in this book are fused in so enigmatic a fashion that its interpreters have differed as to what the book is really about. Richard Chase, to whose study of Melville in 1949 we owe the discovery of its importance, called *The Confidence-Man* Melville's 'second-best book.' He sees it as a work of social criticism, drawing on mythical prototypes for satirical intensity. John Schroeder soon rejected Chase's thesis; he reads *The Confidence-Man* as a religious allegory, proving debts to Hawthorne's 'Celestial Railroad' and to *Pilgrim's Progress*. And Elizabeth Foster, uncovering still other sources for her critical edition, finds the book to be a tightly organized satire on optimism in its successive historical forms: the Shaftesbury position, the utilitarians, the Deists' faith in Nature, and transcendentalism. Nor are the critics agreed as to the form of the book, although there seems general opinion that it is fiction, and a novel – whether satirical, allegorical, symbolist, or tractarian.

II

Melville's *Confidence-Man*, like Hawthorne's *Blithedale Romance*, is the attempt of a romancer to deal directly with the surfaces of contemporary life while presenting allegorically an ironic criticism of its depths. As was true of Hawthorne's book, the form of Melville's has a baffling intricacy which results both from the complex purposes of the author and from his attempt to assimilate hitherto unmingled literary methods and materials. To judge *The Confidence-Man* we must first understand it; to understand it we must not only read it with the close attention that its style demands, but also we must follow Melville's furtive hints as to the sources, models, and analogues in his mind as he wrote it. Otherwise we may judge the book by standards inappropriate to its achievements. We are about to deal with the confidence man, and, as he himself tells us the true book says. 'An enemy speaketh sweetly with his lips.' We may easily be misled. (His warning, it appears, is only apocryphal, not Gospel.) We may in fact be taken in by the confidence man.

Although Mr Chase called this work 'a book of folklore' and proposed its central character as a portmanteau figure combining attributes of native heroes (Brother Jonathan, Uncle Sam, the Yankee) with those of the heroes of world-historical myths (Christ, Orpheus, Prometheus), later critics have neither verified nor extended his position. Yet Melville in this book transformed in a radical way several of the dominant themes from folklore and myth which Hawthorne had used before him and which he himself had used in *Moby-Dick*. There is witchcraft in *The Confidence-Man*, and demonology. There are the folklore themes of transformation in an egalitarian society, and the contrasting of regional stereotypes; the dominant tension between characters (as well as ideas) pits images of the East against those of the West. The confidence man is, among other things, an amalgam of America's popular comic figures: the sly, dupe-bilking Yankee and the frontier sharper. Indeed, the riverboat swindler himself was by 1856 a standard addition to the rogues' gallery of American picaresque lore. In this book he embodies these regional characteristics and tries to fleece persons who embody others – not only the shaggy frontiersman but a Yankee peddler who sits for a savage caricature of what Melville took to be Emerson's fatal shortcomings. There are rituals, too, in *The Confidence-Man*. How else can we regard the recapitulations of Orpheus' descent into hell, the parody of Prometheus' fire-bringing in the con man's extinguishing of the Light of the World? For that matter, as the entire action occurs on All Fools' Day, each episode is a ritual of intensification of the theme of the book, as well as a ritual of initiation for each of the dupes, who trades 'full confidence' for the consequences of the Temptation.

What disguises does this confidence man wear in his Masquerade? First (and most ambiguously), a Mute in cream-colors boards the ship, displays mottoes on charity from I Corinthians, begs alms, is abused by some passengers, and goes to sleep. We do not see him again but next observe one Black Guinea, a crippled Negro beggar who lists eight 'ge'mman' who can vouch for his character; a minister sets out to find these, but no matter, when he returns the beggar is gone. As the boat stops at wharves and landings various personages debark or enter. Most of Black Guinea's references do appear in turn: a Man with a Weed; an agent of the Seminole Widow and Orphan Asylum; the President of the Black Rapids Coal Company. The last becomes before our eyes an Herb-Doctor, peddling Omni-Balsamic Reinvigorator below decks and Samaritan Pain Dissuader in the cabin. Again, he is the Happy Bone Setter. He too would seem to step ashore, and is succeeded by a man from the Philosophical Intelligence Office (an agency that hires out boys). As Man with the Weed he had hinted to a businessman passenger of quick profits to be made in Black Rapids stocks; as Herb-Doctor he spreads word that an officer of that company is on the boat; later, he clandestinely sells the shares. These masquerades take up the first half of the book. A variety of dupes accede, sometimes reluctantly, to the confidence man's pleas, and contribute to his begging, his Indian Orphanage, his Universal Easy Chair, his proposal for The World's Charity ('Missions I would quicken with the Wall Street Spirit'). The Naturopath's herbs find customers – misers are especially vulnerable. Sometimes the con man tells stories to his dupes, or they repeat yarns he has told earlier, or they tell tales of their own. We learn of the cruel wife Goneril, of the Happy Soldier in the Tombs, and, later, tales of Colonel Moredock the Indian-hater, of Charlemont the Gentleman-Madman, and of China Aster who was ruined by requesting a loan. These fictitious characters are discussed: was Goneril cruel or justified? can Moredock's character be believed? In every case the con man's views prevail.

In the latter half of the book the confidence man appears in a bizarre get-up made from the national costumes of every country. This Cosmopolitan, 'a true citizen of the world,' is involved with several hard-headed and unappealing characters in close arguments on confidence, money-lending, and friendship. At last he descends into the hold of the boat, cheats the barber, and, blowing out the 'solar lamp' in the cabin, leads a senile old man away into the darkness.

One can see why the reviewer in the *Literary Gazette* complained of 'an uncomfortable sensation of dizziness in the head.' Nor could he accept *The Confidence-Man* as a novel, 'unless a novel means forty-five conversations . . . conducted by personages who might pass for the errata of creation.' We may prepare the way for a better understanding and judgment of this curious book by first determining to which genre of writing it belongs . . .

The form of Melville's story and the rhythms of its development are determined not so much by characters in action as by the dialectical development of ideas. Lacking the dramatic incidents of *Don Quixote*, *The Confidence-Man* yet resembles that work in its intricate shiftings of the points of view from which reality and appearances are investigated. Perhaps the clandestine analogue and probable model for Melville is the Platonic dialogue, in which the search for truth proceeds through query and reply. As is true in Plato, when Melville reaches the limits of rational (or sophistical) discourse he introduces parables. These, like the Platonic myths, dramatize depths of experience beyond the capacity of the rational premises of the argument to define. But the place of truth-loving, steadfast Socrates is taken by the obscurantist, slippery confidence man . . .

III

A further demonstration of Melville's originality is his rendering of the American life with which his devilish con man makes such sport. Melville adapts to his own satiric uses a setting and two types of character long familiar in popular culture, where they inevitably appeared affirmatively in comic stories.

The riverboat setting, while it may have been suggested by Melville's youthful trip to Illinois, would seem to owe much to the fictional sketches of Thomas Bangs Thorpe. At the same time it anticipates Mark Twain's *Life on the Mississippi*; but Melville is doubtless truer to reality in his attention to the unsavory characters aboard – an aspect of 'Old Times on the Mississippi' which rather slipped Mark Twain's nostalgic mind. Even were Melville unfamiliar with Thorpe's 'The Big Bear of Arkansas,' he doubtless read that writer's 'Remembrances of the Mississippi' in *Harper's New Monthly*, to which he subscribed. Thorpe's sketch appeared in December 1885, in the issue following Melville's own story, 'Jimmy Rose,' just before he began *The Confidence-Man*. Here, as in 'The Big Bear,' the passengers are described as a microcosm of the nation's peoples, and the river in terms suggesting Melville's description of 'the Mississippi itself, which, uniting the streams of the most distant and opposite zones, pours them along, helter-skelter, in one cosmopolitan and confident tide.'

The cosmopolitan confidence man is thus an emblem of the national character, but, like the water of the river, he is made up of its parts. The consistent pattern behind both his masquerade and his clashes with his dupes is the interplay of native regional types. During the first half of the book the con man plays the Yankee peddler to perfection. In fact this role allows him to sidle among the throng in the native image most familiar to them, and most like his own nature. As stock peddler and medicine-doctor he wears Sam Slick's mask, but in philanthropic roles the disguise is that of Johnny Appleseed, the Civilizer in homespun.

Yet, as Mr Chase points out, the native image is cunningly intermingled with hints and glints of older heroic figures. Intimations of Christ, Orpheus, and Prometheus appear in such inverted forms as to suggest that the con man is an Antichrist, a mock-Orpheus, a false Prometheus. There are omens of his double-dealing nature in the opening chapter. When the mute in cream-colors appears, 'It was plain that he was, in the extremest sense of the word, a stranger.' Boarding the *Fidèle*, he passes

> a placard nigh the captain's office, offering a reward for the capture of a mysterious imposter, supposed to have recently arrived from the East, quite an original genius in his vocation, as would appear, though wherein his originality consisted was not clearly given; but what purported to be a careful description of his person followed.

The crowd, greedy for the captor's reward, on tiptoe reads the placard, while pickpockets work them over and hawkers sell pennydreadful lives of frontier desperadoes, all dead now; 'which would seem cause for unalloyed gratulation, and is such to all except those who think that in new countries, where the wolves are killed off, the foxes increase.' We are moving into Simon Suggs's territory, whose thought that 'IT IS GOOD TO BE SHIFTY IN A NEW COUNTRY' had appeared a decade earlier.

The mute then traces on his placard the words of St Paul, 'Charity thinketh no evil ... Charity suffereth long and is kind . . .' Accordingly, some readers take this fellow to be a Christ figure; his buffeting by the crowd (who don't object to the barber's sign, 'NO TRUST') indicates the fate of Christ's message in this world. More likely, he *is* the confidence man himself, a mock-Christ, devilishly quoting Scripture to his purpose. What can be on that placard of 'a mysterious imposter . . . from the East' but a description of his own person? In the first of his many masks he walks scot-free through the crowd. He is never what he seems. His parody of Christ's suffering among thieves is a sabotage of Christ's heroism: this 'lamb-like' mute lays him down to sleep. Color symbolism also allies the mute with the confidence man. Here he is white; next he is Black Guinea with a coal sifter. Then he is the Man with a Weed, in gray with a mourning band. Later, as Cosmopolitan, he is a sartorial rainbow, suggesting the 'color-less all-color of atheism from which we shrink' in 'The Whiteness of the Whale.'

The East he arrives from is inferentially not only Bethlehem but the American East, traditional home-base of guile and wile. Like the Yankee peddler, the con man is itinerant, crafty, an inveterate prying busybody and thimblerigger. He never gives up; every man has his fatal weakness – be it his vices of greed or gullibility or cynicism, or, better still, his virtues of philanthropy or idealism. The con man will undo him one way if another won't work, and, like the venal peddler, take a virtuoso's delight in his own mendacity.

Here is one of his more obvious Yankee bargains: A consumptive miser (from whom he has already bilked $100) objects to the price of the Omni-Balsamic Reinvigorator:

> 'Well, if two dollars a box seems too much, take a dozen boxes at twenty dollars, and that will be getting four boxes for nothing; and you need use none but those four, the rest you can retail out at a premium, and so cure your cough, and make money by it . . . Cash down. Can fill an order in a day or two. Here now,' producing a box; 'pure herbs.'

The price is as spurious as the arithmetic (he had just sold three boxes at fifty cents apiece). His line of reasoning is the same as that peddler of brooms whose clean sweep in Providence we observed in Chapter Three.

Melville had often used the traits of Yankee guile, sly trickery, hoaxing, and swift repartee, but never before for satire so disenchanted. Except for Dr Benjamin Franklin in *Israel Potter* (the most extended forerunner of the 'original genius' in this later book), his Yankee tricksters had not been lacking in their 'humanities.' The first such character in Melville's work is Dr Long Ghost in *Omoo*, whose practical jokes are not judged adversely since the narrator, in his beachcomber phase, is not far removed from Long Ghost's attitude towards authority. Ishmael had his trickster side, while Stubb 'diddles' the French whaler of the precious ambergris by a ruse worthy of any Yankee. In fact their sense of humor, displayed in such jolly hoaxes, makes these sometime rascals appealing in our eyes.

Israel Potter himself is, as Chase maintains, closely modelled on the Yankee of popular lore. He is by turns farmer, batteauxman, surveyor in the wilderness, hunter, peddler, sailor, harpooner on a Nantucket whaler, Revolutionary soldier, and prisoner of war. Escaping from a prison ship to the English shore, he must live a masquerade in earnest now and becomes a royal gardener at the very palace of King George. Then as courier for the Continental underground he is dispatched to Paris with messages in the heel of his boot; he delivers these to Franklin and meets both John Paul Jones and Ethan Allen, before the war's end finds him destitute in the London slums. The rest of his 'Fifty Years of Exile' is a testament of sorrows, concluded by his return to his birthplace to find a stranger plowing over 'a little heap of ruinous burnt masonry.' In Israel Potter we see the Yankee character at its best – upright, manly, opposing first a tyrant father, then a tyrant king; outwitting the enemy in the latter's own gardens, besting even Dr Franklin – yet defeated by life in the end.

Israel Potter is clearly transitional between *Moby-Dick* and *The Confidence-Man*, and nowhere is this more evident than in the treatment of Yankee character. For if Israel Potter is manly and resourceful, he is hardly shrewd; Melville separates these two aspects of Yankeeism. Franklin is a 'household Plato' dressed in 'a conjuror's robe,' full of complacent saws and prudent counsel; too prudent to be incorrupt. (This conception of Franklin is Melville's own, for Franklin is barely mentioned in Potter's autobiography which Melville used as his source.) On the other hand, Ethan Allen is a stirring portrait of the idealized American character. Melville takes an unusual view of the half-legendary leader of the Green Mountain Boys of Vermont:

Allen seems to have been a curious combination of a Hercules, a Joe Miller, a Bayard, and a Tom Hyer ... Though born in New England, he exhibited no trace of her character. He was frank, bluff, companionable as a Pagan, convivial, a Roman, hearty as a harvest. His spirit was essentially Western, for the Western spirit is, or will yet be (for no other is, or can be), the true American one.

Ethan Allen seems the fulfillment of that creative promise hinted at in *Moby-Dick* in the mysterious character of Bulkington, 'full six feet in height ... chest like a coffer-dam ... one of those tall mountaineers from the Alleghenian Ridge in Virginia.' Perhaps it is significant that in *Israel Potter* we see Ethan Allen only in chains.

In *The Confidence-Man* the shift of sympathy away from Yankee character toward the Westerner is complete. We see this in the only two characters who claim our sympathies as heroes do: Pitch the frontiersman and Colonel Moredock the Indian-hater. The most savage caricature in the book is of a 'practical poet' of Yankee cuteness – the con man's hardest touch.

But first, the frontiersman. At midpoint in the book the herb-doctor meets 'a rather eccentric person':

sporting a shaggy spencer of the cloth called bearskin; a high-peaked cap of racoon-skin ... raw-hide leggins; grim stubble chin; and to end, a double-barrelled gun in his hand – a Missouri bachelor, a Hoosier gentleman, of Spartan leisure and fortune, and equally Spartan manners and sentiments; and, as the sequel may show, not less acquainted, in a Spartan way of his own, with philosophy and books, than with woodcraft and rifles.

This Ring-Tailed Roarer with the Stoic philosophers under his coonskin cap – a backwoods Ishmael – challenges the con man:

Nature is the grand cure. But who froze to death my teamster on the prairie? And who made an idiot of Peter the Wild Boy?' ...

'Did I hear something about herbs and herb-doctors?' here said a flute-like voice, advancing. . . . 'If I caught your words aright, you would seem to have little confidence in nature; which, really, in my way of thinking, looks like carrying the spirit of distrust pretty far.'

'And who of my sublime species may you be?' turning short around him, clicking his rifle-lock. . . .

'One who has confidence in nature, and confidence in man, with some little modest confidence in himself.'

The double-dealer would seem to have met his match. Typically, the confidence man dismisses the woodsman's knowledge as 'drollery,' and carefully shifts the topic away from his home ground. Seizing a chance remark about the innate bad character of the boys on the bachelor's plantation, the con man asks if he will replace them with a machine, since 'Philanthropic scruples, doubtless, forbid your going as far as New Orleans for slaves?' At this moral cant the Missourian snaps, 'You are an abolitionist, ain't you?'

'As to that, I cannot so readily answer. If, by abolitionist you mean a zealot, I am none; but if you mean a man, who, being a man, feels for all men, slaves included, and by any lawful act, opposed to nobody's interest, and therefore rousing nobody's enmity, would willingly abolish suffering (supposing it, in its degree, to exist), from among mankind, irrespective of color, then am I what you say.'

'Picked and prudent sentiments [replies the Missourian]. You are the moderate man, the invaluable understrapper of the wicked man. You, the moderate man, may be used for wrong, but are useless for right.'

The bachelor has proved a harder nut than the herb-doctor foresaw. The latter retires with condescending remarks about the eccentric influence of the wilderness on human feelings.

At this point the backwoodsman has won the first victory of any passenger over the confidence man. We see him as an Ethan Allen-like image of the West. No longer does Melville envisage 'a most imperial and archangelical image of that unfallen western world,' as in *Moby-Dick*; the Western character now is tested and tempered in adversity, aware of the evil in the world, and on perpetual guard against it.

But the Devil is not so easily vanquished. Soon after the herb-doctor debarks, the Missourian is accosted by another stranger, a grovelling, obsequious agent of the Philosophical Intelligence Office. The talk turns to boys, and the con man now reverses his former position that the bachelor should replace them with a machine. He begs to differ with the conviction that those thirty-five boys, like all boys, were rascals. The bachelor rebuffs him yet again: 'My name is Pitch; I stick to what I say.' But let it not be said that the boy is father to the man; the man *succeeds* the boy as the butterfly the worm. But, Pitch maintains, 'The butterfly is the caterpillar in a gaudy cloak, stripped of which there lies the imposter's long spindle of a body, pretty much worm-shaped as before.' This should draw blood, for the grovelling con man is himself the worm, and in his next recrudescence, as Cosmopolitan in a gaudy cloak, he becomes the butterfly of the analogy. Pitch is already half-aware of what none of the others had suspected – that his interlocutor is a masquerader playing many roles.

Pitch, then, has both the hard-won wisdom of experience and the determination not to be trapped by the confidence man. To maintain this defensive posture he must resemble 'Bruin in a hollow trunk,' abjuring the 'human-feelings of geniality on which the confidence man trades. There is the real danger in Pitch's attitude that, as the herb-doctor said, 'since, for your purpose, you will have neither man nor boy, bond nor free, truly, then, some sort of machine for you is all there is left.' Pitch may go too far in his misanthropy. Perceiving the innate depravity of human character, he claims 'cider-mill, mowing-machine, corn-husker . . .

doing good all their lives long . . . the only practical Christians I
know.' Truth itself, he says, is 'like a threshing-machine.' These
may be said in only half-earnest, yet such remarks portend two
developments. One is the defeat of the frontiersman by the con
man. To withstand him, Pitch would need to give himself completely over to mechanism. But he yet has his humanities, and
these are his undoing. The other is the appearance, in the tale of
Moredock, of a Western character who *has* become machine-like
in his truculent opposition to evil.

Pitch is undone when the con man appeals to his vanity and
his latent kindliness. 'Ah, sir, permit me – when I behold you . . .
thus eccentrically clothed in the skins of wild beasts, I cannot
conclude that the equally grim and unsuitable habit of your mind
is likewise but an eccentric assumption, having no basis in your
genuine soul, no more than in nature herself.' The first sign of 'a
little softening' is all the con man needs to wheedle three dollars
and a pledge of confidence in the boy to be sent, sight unseen,
in two weeks. Then the Intelligence Officer debarks – at a
'grotesque bluff' called the Devil's Joke. At the rail, Pitch ponders
his experience.

He revolves, but cannot comprehend, the operation still less the
operator. Was the man a trickster, it must be more for the love
than the lucre. Two or three dirty dollars the motive to so many
nice wiles?

It is only then that he thinks of the serpent who tempted Eve. At
that moment he is cordially greeted by yet another stranger with
a voice 'sweet as a seraph's.'

The Cosmopolitan, although maintaining that 'Life is a picnic
en costume,' has no success in turning Coonskins into a friend.
Pitch now knows him for what he is: despite genialities, he sees
'Diogenes masquerading as a cosmopolitan.' The latter admon-
ishes him: 'To you, an Ishmael, disguising in sportiveness my

intent, I came ambassador from the human race, charged with the assurance that for your mislike they bore no answering grudge, but sought to conciliate accord between you and them.' Pitch, however, is now confirmed in misanthropy, and Melville leaves him 'to the solitude he held so sapient.' He is indeed an Ishmael, the 'wild man [whose] hand will be against every man and every man's hand against him.' Unlike the Ishmael of Genesis, however, this frontiersman is curiously cast in a reversal of the Westerner's usual role. Possessing ethical vision without power, he is a paradigm of the ironic role of the intellectual humanist in a philistine culture.

Pitch is now succeeded by an unsavory stranger who, far from rebuffing the ambassador from the human race, comes forward to meet him 'with the bluff *abord* of the west.' This is Charles Arnold Noble, with a hint of treachery in his middle name: sly and venal, the Western promise rotted from within, he is soon the con man's pal, seeming to believe in what the Cosmopolitan seems to believe. Together they uphold geniality (while trying to get each other drunk), uplift, progress, and free-and-easies. The Cosmopolitan now calls himself Frank Goodman, and Charlie, having overheard Frank's last exchange with 'Coonskins,' is reminded of the misanthropy of Moredock, the Indian-hater. But Frank finds it unthinkable that anyone should hate Indians. 'I admire Indians . . . finest of primitive races.' Charlie sees that he must explain the 'Metaphysics of Indian-hating' to make Moredock's career comprehensible, and he begins by describing, as though to an Easterner who had never seen one, what a backwoodsman is.

The backwoodsman is a lonely man. He is a thoughtful man. He is a man strong and unsophisticated. Impulsive, he is what some might call unprincipled . . . self-reliance, to the degree of standing by his own judgment, though it stand alone. Not that he deems himself infallible . . . but he thinks that nature destines such sagacity as she has given him, as she destines it to the 'possum . . . As with the 'possum, instincts prevail with the backwoodsman over precepts. Like the 'possum, the backwoodsman presents the spectacle of a creature dwelling exclusively among the works of God, yet these, truth must confess, breed little in him of the godly mind. Small bowing and scraping is his, further than when with bent knee he points his rifle, or picks its flint . . . The sight of smoke ten miles off is provocation to one more remove from man, one step deeper into nature. Is it that he feels that whatever man may be, man is not the universe? . . . Be that how it will, the backwoodsman is not without some fineness to his nature. Hairy Orson as he looks . . . beneath the bristles lurks the fur.

Though held in a sort a barbarian, the backwoodsman would seem to America what Alexander was to Asia – captain in the vanguard of conquering civilization.

This is of course a portrait of Pitch, raised to a higher power of heroic idealization. Yet in Charlie's story there is already an ominous portent as to Moredock's character. In a world where God's works are godless, what is the fate of the captain of civilization's vanguard who follows his natural instincts to become indistinguishable from the beasts of the wilderness? Melville seems to be saying that, though man is damned, he is more damned in isolation from his fellows than when he acknowledges his humanity. Moredock is an ambiguous case. After Indians slaughter his family he becomes the slave of his unquenchable passion for revenge. Yet he 'demonstrates something curious . . . namely, that all Indian-haters have at bottom loving hearts. . . . No cold husband or colder father. . . . He could be very convivial; told a good story . . . with nobody, Indians excepted, otherwise than courteous in a manly fashion; a moccasined gentleman, admired and loved.' No doubt Mr Schroeder is right in presenting the Indians in this tale as devils, as confidence men. Yet Moredock is not, as Schroeder maintains, the ultimate hero of this book. Nor does

the opposite view – Roy Harvey Pearce's – acknowledge sufficiently Moredock's human complexity. 'The Indian-hater,' Mr
Pearce suggests, 'can see nothing but the dark side of life [in
which] he loses sight of his human self. The issue of blind confidence and blind hatred is in the end identical.' But this won't do;
Moredock retains his human self, *except with Indians;* and his
tragedy is that, still strongly feeling his 'humanities,' to follow
instinctual vengeance – even against red devils – requires that he
secede from the human community. He is urged to become the
Governor of Illinois: to civilize the district as its chief of state.
But how could he 'enter into friendly treaties with Indian tribes'?
His monomaniacal passion resembles Ahab's, though his enemy
is more unequivocally the Adversary than was the whale. Com-
mitment to revenge leads Moredock not to Ahab's self-destruction
but into the sterile, mechanical defeat of all his human promise.
What 'The Metaphysics of Indian-Hating' tells us is that the hero
dedicated to extirpating evil must be a lonely isolato. He cannot
be a leader of men.

The con man professes not to get the point. 'If the man of
hate, how could John Moredock be also the man of love?' For
Frank there is no such thing as the conflict between the threat
and the promise of the Western character – between Mike Fink
the retrograde barbarian avenger and Davy Crockett, 'Captain in
the vanguard of conquering civilization.' The confidence man
has a contrary metaphysics of his own. For the unfathomable
complexity of human nature he substitutes his false synthesis of
simplicity; for the true wild rhythms of nature, which Western-
ers well know, he substitutes avowals of regularity and kindliness.
Frank Goodman eulogizes the press as 'defender of the faith in
the final triumph of truth over error . . . machinery over nature,
and the good man over the bad.'

Charlie, telling the tale to show man's complexity to Frank, in
the end agrees that man is simple. He is therefore unprepared
when Frank tests his own avowals of friendship by requesting a

loan of fifty dollars. Charlie indignantly spurns him, as 'Out of old materials sprang a new creature. Cadmus glided into the snake.' In short, Charlie, who has done the devil's office, becomes a human version of the confidence man. But that won't do for Frank, who is a taster, not of devils, but of *man*. With a magic ritual he *enchants* Charlie back to his 'best shape,' laying down a circle of ten coins 'with the air of a necromancer' and 'a solemn murmur of cabalistical words.' Now that Charlie is human again, Frank is about to renew his request for a loan. Already defeated (for the con man has by now tasted him), Charlie pleads a headache, and retires.

There are coils within the coils of logic in this book, as Melville tries to strike through, or peel away, the masks that hide the truth. And he finds, time and again, that the masks conceal yet other masks. Where then does identity ultimately reveal itself? Charlie's place is taken by yet another stranger in whose person 'shrewdness and mythiness' were 'strangely jumbled . . . he seemed a kind of cross between a Yankee peddler and a Tartar priest, though it seemed as if, at a pinch, the first would not in all probability play second fiddle to the last.' Having shown us Western character in Pitch as manly but fallible, in Moredock as heroic but doomed, and in Charlie Noble as corrupt and invidious, Melville now turns to the Westerner's opposite as a final foil for the confidence man. And that opposite is in this book what it was in popular culture: the Yankee peddler.

The description of Mark Winsome as half peddler, half Tartar priest certainly resembles Lowell's set piece on the Yankee character in *The Biglow Papers* – and the same author's double-edged view of Emerson in *A Fable for Critics*. It recalls also a comment of Melville's on the Concord sage – 'this Plato who talks through his nose.' Mark Winsome is his caricature of Emerson, and it would seem that Melville, though spurning orthodoxy himself, was of the same mind as the Reverend Andrews Norton, who, on hearing Emerson's Divinity School Address, had called his transcendental gospel 'the latest form of infidelity.' Perhaps that is why his cosmopolitan devil, upholding the Emersonian idea of the incompatibility of beauty with evil, not only proposes 'confidence in the latent benignity of that beautiful creature, the rattle-snake,' but 'all but seemed the creature he described.' His words echo Milton's when Satan appears before Eve. Expressing this doctrine, the devil reveals his identity. But Winsome is no more concerned to be consistent than is Emerson himself, and rejects the proposal. His mystical air is replaced by 'an expression of keen Yankee cuteness' as he obscurely argues the cosmopolitan into a 'labyrinth.' Winsome, chill and icy in aspect, soon proclaims the spiritual superiority of death to life, and calls in a disciple to take his place and demonstrate his cold philosophy in action.

The disciple Egbert is not so much a smack at Thoreau (as has been maintained) as Melville's caricature of the Emersonian man. Even shrewder-looking than his Master, Egbert is 'a practical poet in the West India trade. . . . if mysticism, as a lesson, ever came his way, he might, with the characteristic knack of a true New Englander, turn even so profitless a thing to some profitable account.' The action he proposes is to debate with Frank Goodman the compatibility of friendship with the lending of money. They take up Frank's discussion where it broke off with Charlie Noble. Now Egbert *assumes the identity* of 'Charlie.' In a savage hit at Emerson's 'Friendship,' Egbert as 'Charlie' tells Frank (who assumes the role of 'Frank') the fable of China Aster, a tart little allegory on the bloodless ethic of Yankee cuteness. For China Aster was ruined by confidence and a friendly loan.

The tale shows us also the fate of the Promethean creative spirit in a world where the confidence man sets the tone of social intercourse. For China Aster, whose name suggests the Star of the Orient and thus hints at Christ, is allegorically presented also as the Promethean spirit in American life. He is 'a young candle-maker . . . whose trade would seem a kind of subordinate branch of that parent craft and mystery of the hosts of heaven, to be the means, effectively or otherwise, of shedding some light through the darkness of a planet benighted. But he made little money by the business.' His friend Orchis, winning money in a lottery, insists on lending him money so that he may 'hold up the pure spermaceti to the world.' The name of Orchis suggests not only the superfluous luxury of the tropical plant (by contrast, the china aster is a common field flower), but also its origin in the Greek word for testicle. Orchis is the confidence man in yet another masquerade. For he is 'a shoemaker; one whose calling it is to defend the understandings of men from naked contact with the substance of things.' He urges the Promethean spirit to abandon the austerities which dedication to his 'mystery' demands, and live in ease and sensuality. China Aster, doomed by his inability to withstand temptation, is ruined in a corrupt world by his virtues too. His honesty is incompatible with success, while confidence is incompatible with his mission of making candles to enlighten a benighted world. And 'the root of all was a friendly loan.'

When Frank persists in asking a loan, Egbert terminates the 'social and intellectual' phase of their acquaintance, for 'If you turn beggar, then, for the honor of noble friendship, I turn stranger.' His Yankee ethic makes friendship an ideal which cannot be sullied by the claims of compassion. Scornfully turning, the cosmopolitan leaves Egbert 'at a loss to determine where exactly the fictitious character had been dropped, and the real one, if any, resumed.' In this practical poet of Yankee cuteness who upholds death over life, mind over heart, the ideal over the possible, and the self over the ties of compassion, the confidence man at last has met his match. For how can the Devil catch a creature who *has no soul?* Who, then, is Egbert, and who Winsome? The philosopher himself had asked Frank, 'What are you? What am I? Nobody knows who anybody is.' And introducing his disciple he had said, 'I wish you, Egbert, to know this brother stranger.' It was the mute who entered 'in the extremest sense of the word, a stranger.' The Mystical Philosopher and his Practical Disciple are 'brother strangers' with the confidence man. Their faith in heartless self-reliance complements his in indiscriminate confidence. His makes no room in the moral universe for evil, theirs leaves none for good. They show that 'defect in the region of the heart' which Melville found so repelling in Emerson's philosophy.

Sophisticated as is the intellectual background of these tortuous arguments, Melville has leavened both sets of confidence men with the common yeast of traditional Yankee character. He found that character seemingly genial, and frigid; ingratiating, and repelling; dealing in abstract ideals, and in shrewd cutpurse bargains. The traditional type of the Yankee peddler gave Melville the master masks in his confidence man's masquerade.

IV

His failure to diddle Egbert does not cast down the Cosmopolitan. A fellow-devil is not his lawful prey; blithely, he goes below decks to finish his work among mankind. The last chapter has occasioned some strange readings of the book. Its final sentence – 'Something further may follow of this Masquerade' – leads many critics to assert either that the book as it stands is unfinished (Melville, the argument runs, was so tired out that he quit in the middle of the book and sent an incomplete manuscript off to the printer), or that a sequel is promised, but never was written. The error of such readings may not be obvious, but wrong indeed they are. The chapter is called 'The Cosmopolitan Increases in Seriousness,' a title which indicates that his masquerade is coming to a close. Let us be serious too; like the old man he meets in the cabin, let us have before us a Bible.

That cabin is curiously described. Many men sleep in berths

ranged on the walls; a 'solar lamp' swings from the center ceiling. Other lamps hang nearby, 'barren planets, which had either gone out from exhaustion, or been extinguished by such occupants of berths as the light annoyed, or who wanted to sleep, not see.' The setting is clearly an emblem of the end of a universe in which man is too tired to grope any longer toward moral choices. All of China Aster's little candles are dark now. The one solar lamp has a

> shade of ground glass . . . all round fancifully variegated, in transparency, with the image of a horned altar, from which flames rose, alternate with the figure of a robed man, his head encircled by a halo.

This iconography is certainly allegorical. But we don't as yet know what to make of it; nor does the old man even notice the fanciful images on the lampshade. He is poring over the Book, with a look of 'hale greenness in winter.' His aspect suggests the beatitude of Simeon beholding the Master of Faith, and one who goes heavenward 'untainted by the world, because ignorant of it.' These and other hints suggest that the old man, the ultimate dupe in this Masquerade, is America grown old in ignorance of evil – a senile Captain Delano. The Cosmopolitan, seeing him read the Bible, genially assures him, 'You *have* good news there, sir – the very best of good news.' From a curtained berth a voice objects, 'Too good to be true.' The Cosmopolitan then professes 'a disturbing doubt' concerning the Book. Despite his good opinion of man, he has been told that it is written, 'Believe not his many words – an enemy speaketh sweetly with his lips . . . With much communication he will tempt thee.' The curtained sleeper interjects, 'Who's that describing the confidence-man?' But the innocent old man sets the con man's doubts at rest; the passage came not from the true book but merely the Apocrypha, so it need not be heeded. 'What's that about the Apocalypse?' cries the voice from the berth – we by now suspect the curtained sleeper to be a voice from the dead, 'seeing visions,' as the Cosmopolitan says. The old man now proposes that 'to distrust the creature, is a kind of distrusting the Creator.' Since the old fellow had 'a countenance like that which imagination ascribes to good Simeon' (who beheld the boy Jesus and acknowledged the Christ), we may take a special interest in the sudden appearance of a young boy at the cabin table. Can this oldster possibly have the spiritual perceptivity of the saint he seems to resemble? Not that the boy is the Christ; he is a peddler, dressed in fluttering red and yellow rags 'like the pointed flames in the robes of a victim in *auto-da-fé*.' From his grimy face sloe-eyes gleamed 'like lustrous sparks from fresh coal.' He offers door-locks and money-belts; despite the old man's trust of his fellow-creatures, the young peddler sells him one of each, throwing in as bonus a Counterfeit Detector. The lad seems in cahoots with the Cosmopolitan, but the old man does not catch his wink, nor suspect anything at all. Now that the oldster has armed himself against untrustworthy fellows, the con man reminds him of his earlier assertion that such distrust 'would imply distrust of the Creator.' The old man is confused; unknowingly he has sold his soul to the young devil. Besides, his new counterfeit detector is untrustworthy too – so complicated are the instructions. Completely bamboozled, when he whimpers for a life preserver he accepts what the con man hands him – a tin chamber pot – and takes his proffered arm.

'Ah, my way now,' cried the old man . . . 'where lies my way to my state-room?'

'I have indifferent eyes, and will show you; but, first, for the good of all lungs, let me extinguish this lamp.'

The next moment, the waning light expired, and with it the waning flames of the horned altar, and the waning halo round the robed man's brow; while in the darkness which ensued, the cosmopolitan kindly led the old man away. Something further may follow of this Masquerade.

The awakened voice who asked about the Apocalypse suggests the locus of unstated meaning in this icon. After the seventh seal was opened, John 'heard a voice from the four horns of the altar which is before God.' This announced the destruction of a third part of mankind by fire, smoke, and brimstone, 'And the rest of the men which were not killed by these plagues yet repented not of the work of their hands, that they should not worship devils' (Rev. 9:13-21). The robed and haloed figure on the lampshade is of course Saint John, who, like the altar of God, wanes into darkness as the confidence man extinguishes the Light. What 'may follow of this Masquerade' is no sequel Herman Melville would write; the consequences of man's traduction aboard the *Fidèle* will be revealed in Hell on Judgment Day.

V

Flawed though it is, *The Confidence-Man* demands comparison with those great picaresque satiric romances whose scope is as ambitious as its own: not only *Gulliver's Travels*, but *Don Quixote*, *Gargantua and Pantagruel*, and *Candide*. Melville in fact goes beyond them, and beyond Hawthorne's experiments, too, in using the romancer's imaginative freedom for intellectual rather than psychological analysis. Although he satirizes many follies his viewpoint is less satiric than ironical. And irony is the uncomforted refuge of perception without power. The great European satires are works of comic imagination based on the affirmation of man's ideals; Melville's, though their equal in indignation, attacks not only human institutions and human folly, but, as they never do, human nature itself.

Melville's life spanned the century in which the community of Christendom was irreparably broken into chaos. His progress from blithe good humor through the extremities of romantic egoism to the despairing ironies of *The Confidence-Man* marked both a personal tragedy and the experience of his culture. It was shared by Hawthorne, in whom increasing confusion destroyed the sources of his creative powers. And it is still more clearly exampled in Mark Twain. He suffered as deeply as Melville but, by suppressing *What is Man?* until after his own death, tried to protect himself from the public consequences of his realization that God had abdicated from the universe. That book and *The Mysterious Stranger* seem the naïve fantasies of a village atheist, compared with Melville's merciless apocalypse published sixty years earlier.

After *The Confidence-Man* Melville seemed to have little choice but to follow the fate of the character in his story 'Bartleby,' and, facing the blank wall, 'prefer not to' write any further stories. Like the Scrivener in the Dead Letter Office, Melville spent most of his remaining thirty-five years as an obscure customs inspector on a New York wharf and took no part in the literary life of his country. His great work had been done, but in the era that Mark Twain called 'The Gilded Age' – and characterized in Colonel Sellers, who is both dupe and confidence man – nobody heeded Herman Melville. That generation sought a literary hero more congenial than moody Melville with his demonic Ahab and sardonic cosmopolitan. In the platform funnyman who regaled audiences with frontier humor and found no fault with President Grant, post-Civil War America thought to behold its avatar. How much his contemporaries overvalued Mark Twain's lesser talents, how little they understood the depths of his genius, our own generation has sufficiently acknowledged. We can see better than they how closely Mark Twain's greatest work draws on traditions similar to Melville's. The imaginations of both are deeply stirred by the lore of omens and witchcraft, and both respond to the bracing tensions of native character and humor. The conflicts between native and stranger, between truth and deception, between reality and appearance, characteristic of the popular imagination, are intensified both in Melville's romances and *Adventures of Huckleberry Finn*. The signal difference in their handlings of these materials is in their conceptions of an 'original character.' Although Twain saw perhaps as clearly as Melville the depravity of 'the damned human race' who line his Mississippi's shores, he made his hero not only moral, and a human being, but triumphant. In doing so he remained true to the ebullient optimism of the folk traditions which contributed to his view of the American world.

OTHER TITLES IN THIS SERIES

The Time Machine
H. G. WELLS

'Great shapes like big machines rose out of the dimness, and cast grotesque black shadows, in which dim spectral Morlocks sheltered from the glare'

A chilling, prophetic take on mankind's possible future, *The Time Machine* sees a Victorian scientist propelled into the year 802,701 AD, where he is delighted to find that suffering has been replaced by beauty and contentment in the form of the Eloi, an elfin species descended from man. But he soon realises that they are simply remnants of a once-great culture – now weak and living in terror of the sinister Morlocks lurking in the deep tunnels, who threaten his very return.

H. G. Wells defined much of modern science fiction with this 1895 tale of time travel, which questions humanity, society and our place on Earth.